Travels of a New Gulliver

Joseph Natoli

Travels of a New Gulliver is a work of fiction. All incidents and dialogue are products of the author's imagination and are not to be construed as real. Any resemblance to persons, living or dead, is entirely coincidental.

Library of Congress Control Number: 2013912845
ISBN-10: 1475111428
ISBN-13: 978-1475111422

DEDICATION

To my father who visited this world warily and supplely,
and to my mother who gave her heart to it all:

Ti amerò per sempre.

Contents

Travels of a New Gulliver

ACKNOWLEDGMENTS

*Perhaps it takes the wisdom of the Houyhnhnms to first acknowledge the material, objective and hi-tech skills that have made this book possible. **Travels of a New Gulliver** would not have been printed if not for the continuing assistance of Einar Nordgaard, an unconquerable Viking, who performed all the tasks that my traditional publishers in the past have done.*

I must also acknowledge that though Swift's genius can only be reborn with the man himself, I early on inherited his suspicion of Pope's assertion that "whatever is, is right," and to it I add my own suspicion of the Millennial tweet that "it is what it is." I've discovered "that it is what loud and repeat messaging tells us it is." I tend also to believe that when a cultural climate reaches a point of absolute absurdity, idiocy and farce, then satire is a good opening response. Beyond that the satirist hopes that such exposure would lead next to indictments and imprisonment, followed then by societal recuperation, and, lastly and most hopefully, survival.

*Chapters of **Travels of a New Gulliver** were published online at **Dandelion Salad**: http://dandelionsalad.wordpress.com/*

All images are from Google Public Domain free images.

Chapter I

In which the Author introduces himself and then sets out

My father left me little but his wandering soul. My mother would avow that my peripatetic father owned a disposition that would not allow him to be happy anywhere yet urged him ever onward in such pursuit. In her opine, a present latitude and longitude would soon grow dark and stormy for my father while some distant horizon would begin to glow. And then he would be off in that direction, my mother and myself following.

I have inherited a belief that it is not happiness to be found in an ever changing latitude and longitude but what can for a time rekindle the fires of interest, reawaken curiousity, and revive the spirit. Such travel can replace the conventional and everyday with a fascination and awe that this planet, this Great Outdoors of wonder, inspires if we just look beyond our own intent.

When my mother grew tired of such wandering, she returned with me to her family's estate in Nottinghamshire and bid adieu to my father who, as was his wont, wandered off.

Upon my mother's sudden death, I found myself in the care of a bachelor uncle who I attended to in his dotage and whose moods and sudden rages were almost at once followed by a mellowness that put forth apologies I could not deny. My Uncle Bruno was oddly wired I suppose from birth or perhaps, like Dickens's Mrs. Havisham, had been jilted. Perhaps he had anticipated a promising career in music but had lost his voice or his hearing. Possibly he had relied on friends and been disappointed. Perhaps all his close friends had died off; or, perhaps the sporadic aches of gout or arthritis or Lyme disease commanded his disposition; or, perhaps a parasite bequeathed to him by one of his cats had lodged in his brain and commanded his disposition. Perhaps the goddess Fortuna had merely spun the wheel against him, or, Odin's thread was wearing thin.

I was never sure of any cause but only quite certain that I spent my boyhood years observing closely the vicissitudes of mind that awaited us all.

My schooling fluctuated with Uncle Bruno's varying moods and so while I began with proper Church of England I did not remain there because the Papist idea that a priest could relieve the mind's anguish took hold of him. As a result, I was removed from Church of England and enrolled in a Jesuitical institution.

One afternoon, upon returning from my classes, my uncle rose up and accused me of believing that his Lord was present in a bit of bread I could then eat? A sudden anti-clerical turn of mind compelled him to now send me to be schooled in an esoteric philosophy that promised to place me in direct communication with the inner workings of all things.

I was at the stage of total bewilderment in regard to this course of study when my uncle, in yet another frenzy, cursed all claptrap which obscured the basic rights of all to share the earth in common without obstructions of private property, money, and any form of buying and selling. My tenure here ended when I suggested to my uncle that it would be best if he gave up all rights to his own estate and divide his property among any and all.

And so I returned to Church of England schooling. Though my schooling was erratic to say the least I have excelled in the study of languages, both classical and modern, history, philosophy, botany, astronomy, rhetoric and debate, and most especially, geography.

What I endured subject to my uncle's dementia caused me to vow to live my life fully before the diminishing of my own faculties. While I had all the capacity and potential of youth, I too would seek what any horizon promised.

In spite of my dedicated purpose to live an adventuresome life, I succeeded after my errant schooling to live a very sedentary life. Outside of the stimulating minds I encountered in the books I read, I became embedded in a way of life that offered only the stupefaction that inevitably inhabits a world of un-inquisitive minds pursuing what is petty and endlessly repeated. My youth began to lose its bloom in the tired dust of paths trod again and again in the selfsame ways.

I became so dazed myself that my former inclinations to escape the tedium of ordinary life gave way to that very tedium. I was on the brink of marriage and on a ladder to a promising career as an Accounts Manager when I contracted a deadly virus that was sweeping the globe and for many weeks lay in a state closer to death than life. My fever went so high as to vanquish all the ordinary barriers our conscious mind erects against the assault of chaotic musings and deeply buried traumatic moments of primordial ancestors that erupt in the present like volcanic outpourings.

I awoke from that nightmarish ride into the depths of my own mind with a certain theory and it was this: If I travelled and so disarranged my life so that the habitual gave way to the unknown, my internal time clock would, of necessity, constantly wind backward.

The more one knows through experience the latitude and longitude of one's surroundings, the more one eats up the future before its arrival. In this fashion each day, each week, each month, each year came more speedily upon the one before. No amount of accidental chance could slow down for long that rapid digestion of time before it was lived.

I called upon my own memories of my childhood. What a summer was to be lay before me then as a great mystery that I attended to second by second as it unfolded. Every part of my childhood world for me was new, *terra incognita*, and my empty slate of mind had no way of instilling the slightest foreshadowing.

We have not the words in childhood to collapse the magnificence of the world into useful packaging, packaging that will eventually enable us to use, command, resist and therefore diminish that world. We learn to talk above the world, or around it and our talk falls into patterns of practicality and efficiency, our talk becomes goal oriented and mission obsessed. We very soon become forgetful of what miraculous majesty resides in the sun, in the ocean, in the flowering of Nature.

Now, with a mind not only filled with all manner of knowledge but of the deadening redundancies of life in one place surrounded by minds equally confined, I was moving more rapidly than I had anticipated to the deterioration and incapacity which I saw in my poor uncle.

Determined then to renew my attentiveness to the world by renewing latitude and longitude, I wrapped up my affairs as they were and prepared myself to leave behind my old life. I quit my promising position of employment, made abject apologies to my beloved and assured her that her future would be brighter without me, made arrangements for the care of my uncle and set off.

What follows here is a very loose account of my voyages, and what I found, often accidentally, often against my own will, and seldom as I hoped.

I took with me only a few presumptions, for as Lao Tzu advises, a good traveler has no fixed plans, and is not intent on arriving. My few presumptions were tied to my intent not to presume at all.

Is there need to say that I was already loaded at my age with all the baggage of immoveable personality? That I already owned my share of prejudices, deeply held beliefs, and absurd irrationalities that we humans inevitably acquire? How resistant or moveable my moral compass was to the challenges encountered in my travels, the Reader must judge. How inflexible or accommodating my political views may seem and to what extent the claims of any society were acknowledged or repudiated, I also leave to the Reader's discernment.

You can see how this fascination to step outside my provincial awareness took hold of me and prompted such a quick departure from my homeland.

Unfortunately, our ship was set astray one dark night by a ferocious storm, broke up upon those angry waves, and next morning I found myself a sole survivor on an unknown shore.

At first the island seemed to me impenetrable jungle reaching almost to the shoreline. Bog grass gave way to bamboo and just as abruptly as if Nature was correcting itself every ten meters, bristly foxtail grass and cocksfoot grass and then to right and left Indian paintbrush, knotweed, and lady's-slipper. I found love-lies-bleeding and moccasin flower as well as monkshood and jack-in-the pulpit. I found profusion and confusion of flora.

After no more than an hour's walk, I came to an open plain of little quaking grass and wood meadow grass and spied a range of hills in the distance. At the base of those hills I saw smoke swirling upward and by noon day could clearly see thatched roofs.

A village! Food and drink. Perhaps the storm had brought me to a propitious beginning of my journey after all for here indeed was the answer to a castaway's prayers. Anxious to tell my tale, I ambled forward, now observing any number of inhabitants moving about.

It was the way some moved about that stopped me in my tracks and caused me to crouch down, desirous now of seeing and not being seen. What I had observed, my dear Reader, was somewhat erratic and therefore disturbing behavior. Hidden as I was, I spied for perhaps an hour, my uneasiness growing.

What I saw of the inhabitants' behavior that disturbed me was this: a walking forward, a sudden stop and then a walking backward, a pause of varying length and then a walking forward but on a slightly different trajectory. While some performed this ritual only once, I observed a woman bent over with age walk only a few steps before stopping, reversing and redirecting. She had a basket over one arm and I presumed she was shopping. She reached no destination during the time I observed her.

Puzzling and even more puzzling for then I saw a young man marching straight into my view and then out of it without ever stopping. So while some seemed to be forwarding and reversing themselves repeatedly, others seemed less inclined and still others seemed not at all affected by this strange disposition I immediately defined for myself as some sort of dementia. I was therefore now hesitant in making myself known but hunger and thirst got the best of my discretion and I once again ambled forward.

Chapter I

I was welcomed graciously and with the sort of compassion one in distress ideally expects of others. By night fall I was settled comfortably in the home of Mr. Parsall, mayor of *Jumpback*, which was the name of this village and I assumed it had the same pertinence as calling a colony of lepers a Leper Colony.

The Parsall brood was large, ranging from diapers to strapping six footers to an elderly granny stationed in a rocker by the fireplace. I ate well for Mrs. Parsall proved to be an excellent cook, and drank liberally of the home brew that was reminiscent of *The Guinness*. I had all the comforts of home but there was an oddness to their talk which paralleled the strangeness I had observed earlier in the manner in which the villagers walked about.

The Mayor, a man about my own age, spoke in stentorian tones but then would pause for what I must say was often an uncomfortable length of time and when resuming would qualify some of what he had previously said. Mrs. Parsall was loquacious but not untouched by this tendency. Only young Ned Parsall, a lad in his early twenties, could carry on in a normal fashion so that normal conversation and exchange could take place. I also noted that he and his younger siblings were the only ones that did not visibly wince now and then as I spoke.

I have been in *Jumpback* for one week and can now, dear Reader, report to you what I have discovered of this unusual village.

The history of the village is extraordinary. In the same manner as Australia and Devil's Island had become the far off lands to send the incorrigibles of the British and French empires respectively, and Siberia had been a land of exile and Guantanamo a place of quarantine and so forth, *Jumpback* had become the godforsaken place to send a variety of miscreants. I note scoffers, deconstructors, nullifidians, disillusionists, skeptics, flip floppers, zetetics, re-examiners, self-grillers, and deep-well probers. What these had evolved into were the present inhabitants of *Jumpback,* a people whose genetic tendency to jump back and re-examine everything they do, say, and hear gradually brought them to a state of aporia, of taking no path, saying no word and hearing nothing they could accept as unquestionably true.

Their end was ignominious: they were shelved in charnel house waiting rooms and gradually wasted away as they could no longer bring themselves to eat or drink, jumping back, if you will, and questioning their own hunger and thirst.

Now you will be fascinated if I tell you that such a tragic state of affairs did not in any way discourage or distress the villagers for they saw the slow incubation of this malady as an augmenting campaign. Against what? I asked. Against illusions, self-deception, chicanery, propaganda, sophistry, disinformation, White Papers, spin, stratagems of market and pol, truisms, product jingles, solid foundations, accompanying statistics, raw facts, numbers that never lie, patent leather credentials, maps and templates, fundamentalist beliefs, and the reliability and transparency of language. All this among a host of other matter and manner upon which I dare say civilization as we know it is built.

I did not hesitate once I had grasped the nature of the *Jumpback* disease – for disease it indeed was – to inform Mayor Parsall that his whole village had inherited a particularly virulent form of paranoia. There were not only talking cures for this but also a whole array of cocktail pharmaceuticals that could be prescribed, to the extent one's purse allowed. My talk did not fail to produce the usual painful winces from the man but I went on regardless and thus laid bare the full extent of my thought on this matter.

He quite surprised me then by asking me why I traveled to which I responded that I sought new lands and new talk, hoping to invigorate the staid reliables of my own homeland. You think then, he asked me, that your talk may be influenced by where you live and when you happen to be living? I said surely that was the case but, glimpsing his strategy, I added that while such variables clearly affected some matters, others were just as clearly unaffected. I thereupon proceeded to catalog beliefs I had apparently picked up along the way. These included my faith in a Celestial Entity and a Spiritual World, the vitals of our human nature, the indisputable recognition of happiness and progress, the marvels of human reason, the blindness of love, the fascinations of Mother Nature, the awesomeness of the beautiful, the great boon of language, the tool-making inventiveness of the human race, and our enviable freedom to choose.

He winced painfully at each of these. In a response that I cannot defend except to say I found his censoriousness deeply offensive, I added to my list.

"Our individual uniqueness has nought to do with when and where," I began. "Our objectivity cannot be diminished regardless of whether we are at the South Pole or the North Pole or whether it is the year 1000 or the year 3000. We strive for justice, condemn the evil actions of evil men, can talk our way into useful compromise, and can ultimately with truthful words drive out falsehood."

"And yet," the good man began, overwhelmed no doubt by the presence of what he could jump back on as many times as he wished without impairing or imperiling the validity of my words, "And yet, you believe that you can journey to different places and hear different talk." I told him that I didn't expect to hear different talk regarding any of what I had just enounced and if I did my sojourn in that land would not be long. He then remarked that if he understood me correctly I maintained that though the purpose of my travel was to encounter different talk I would terminate that encounter in lands where the talk was different than my prior assumptions. He asked me whether I found myself in a paradoxical situation. I could see that his paranoia drove a clever sophistry in debate.

"I am open to all that I see and hear, sir. If upon review I find that any of it violates what I have just declared as universal truths and principles, I dismiss it. That does not prevent me from choosing to adopt what I find to be in accord with those same principles."

"So you are free to choose within the confines of what you call principles?"

"As every right thinking man and woman is, sir," I declared as an obvious challenge to his own unfortunate paranoic state of mind.

"And when you visit a different land," he continued, after his usual stop and go nonsense, "you come prepared to see and hear within the untouchables of your resident beliefs? Are you then open to seeing and hearing what is there? Are you then freely choosing when your choice is already constrained by unquestionable notions?"

"Belief in God is not a notion, sir," I retorted, feeling the heat rising in me, though I am in fact a quite imperturbable man. "Nor is belief in reason and objectivity, justice and mercy, love and happiness, progress and success. Our free mind, sir. These, sir...."

"...are words," the Mayor said in a low voice, eyes cast down. "And phrases. Some resonate gloriously I grant on any occasion and in any land but they are extremely difficult to bring to ground. Most of these ascend to the level of grand illusions. For instance, you say you are a unique individual and yet you repeat the same litany of unassailable Truths as every other visitor to *Jumpback*. If you do jump back and interrogate this matter of uniqueness you discover that there is more sameness than uniqueness among humans, just as it makes greater sense to say that zebras look alike than to base an individual uniqueness on their variant stripe patterns."

"I find the comparison insulting, sir, and not at all consequential."

"Is it consequential then to investigate why this assumption of individual uniqueness, this illusion, is held by so many at a particular time, and I might add, in particular places? May I add that it is more firmly announced in the United States than it is in Europe or Asia."

"Perhaps Americans value individual uniqueness whereas it is valued less elsewhere."

"It may be," the Mayor replied, "that the New World more firmly inscribes this illusion than elsewhere. That would mean that one of your cherished inviolables is actually subject to a cultural mood."

"I protest, sir, because you refuse to acknowledge that individual uniqueness is grounded in freedom of choice which is unarguably an inviolable that you cannot violate with your skepticism."

"I understand as you apparently do not," the Mayor told me, "that my freedom to choose is confined within the boundaries of someone else's choices. I do not feel violated by this but only the need to examine closely those boundaries and the power sources that erect them. I feel violated when I think that my freedom to break out is impeded by my own adoption of the sacred words `free to choose.' The enslaved obstruct their own freedom and allow the inequities and injustices of sheer power to go unruled."

I found all this confounding sophistry to say the least and myself jumped back on the declaration that I for one would not enjoy a life of jumping back and scrutinizing every word someone said and every thought I myself had. This brought a smile and not a wince from my host.

"And yet," I continued, "I admit to a certain curiosity as to your way of thinking."

He replied that perhaps in spite of the axioms that framed my travels I might yet be open to an examination of them and thus make my travels worthwhile.

"Surely," the Mayor said, smiling, "it would be a tragedy for a man who sets out to hear and see something new if he were to be totally guided by what he has already seen and heard."

I burst out with the question as to how this was to be avoided and, still smiling, he said "Jump back on everything."

In the next few weeks I took up in good faith the practice of jumping back, which was most difficult the more firmly attached you were to what required a jumping back. It was rather like going through a large menu to see what you liked best.

I discovered that besides being very firmly attached to my own individual uniqueness and my freedom to choose, I was deeply attached to a "love conquers all" notion, valiantly willing "to die for my country," always ready "to stand up for justice," always in "pursuit of happiness," certain "the truth was out there," and anxious that we all "assumed personal responsibility." I was also devotee of technology making everything 'better, faster, easier," certain "human nature" was unchanging, and quite sure that talk, no matter how muddled at times, would eventually "get the truth out."

If new and startling talk was what I had set out to discover, here in the quaint village of *Jumpback* I had all I could wish for. But I confess that I very soon began to jump back from the Mayor's words which only served to reaffirm my resident beliefs.

I joined the mayor's son, Ned, in each morning's *Jumping Back on Truisms* gatherings. I followed young Ned to the gathering where I found a group of about thirty young villagers and a handful of elders. The seating was circular amphitheatre and Ned and I took seats about half way up. At promptly 9AM a young lady rose from her seat and walked to the center of the stage below us.

"It is what it is," she informed us in a loud voice. "Jump back."

A chap below me stood up and bellowed:

"It is what someone in power says it is," to which someone stood up and bellowed: *"Who speaks the evidence but an observer?"*

At that Ned stood up and said:

"Every observer is positioned somewhere, at some time."

I suddenly found myself provoked to comment and so, dear Reader, I was boldly on my feet before I knew what I was about.

"True observations withstand the test of time. Falsehoods blow in the wind."

I sat down again, feeling flushed but somehow victorious, as if I had delivered the coup de grace of jumping back.

Surely my truism would stand and bring this round to an end. But I must report that it did not for an obese person stood up and said:

"The present moment raids the past to find what supports its own truth stories. It leaves the rest to blow in the wind."

While I was searching for a challenge, an elder took center stage and in a loud voice declared: *"Where there is a will, there is a way."*

This brought on a flurry of jumping back activity that was truly head spinning. And then, suddenly, young Ned jumped up and yelled "Stop! For God's sake, stop!" This outburst produced no challenge but all, including myself, stared bewildered at Ned, who could not manage to say anything else but, holding his arms out as if to hold off any who wished to stop him, rushed down the steps and then out of the building. I went in pursuit.

I did not find him until later that night when I was myself wandering about the darkened streets of the village, jumping back on what I had heard that day and also trying not to do so.

I was about to turn around and go to bed when someone called to me from the bushes. It was young Ned and he had a small pack on his back. I asked him what he was intending and he told me that he had decided to follow in my own footsteps and take to traveling for he was sick of jumping back and greatly feared winding up in a total catatonic state, which was the destiny of all the *Jumpback* villagers.

I then asked him where he was heading and he pointed to the far off hills over which a full moon hung. Beyond those hills was a village his father called *Illusion* but he had heard years before from one of its inhabitants was really named *Trickle Downs*. And he decided he wanted to go there. I at once agreed that it was a proper destination and quite astounded him I think when I said I too would be off if he would wait the short time it would take me to retrieve my own pack and walking stick.

And so less than an hour later and short of midnight we took the road leading into the hills beyond which lay the village of *Trickle Downs*.

Chapter II

In which the Author and his young companion Ned arrive in the village of Trickle Downs and there find that anything is possible, words are never pawns, personal choice matters most, exclamations of "Whatever" replace jumping back, and there are no speed limits.

It has been a fortnight since we left the village of *Jumpback* and arrived in *Trickle Downs* just at daybreak. During our trek young Ned and I had talked much about his hopes and dreams of finding a place in the world where talk was not riddled by doubt and suspicion. He wanted to live and not talk endlessly about the living. He was tired of words and wanted to live in a world of action.

He was perfectly attuned to what befell him as we walked down what we assumed was the main thoroughfare of the village. A sports roadster rushed around a near corner and both Ned and I had to leap aside or be run down. The roadster came to a sudden stop, backed up and a comely lass lowered her sunglasses, surveyed Ned and asked him if he wanted to join her for a spin?

The lad was in the roadster and waving his goodbyes to me in an instant. *Trickle Downs* had just opened its gates for young Ned. Perhaps as the immortal Bard says he was green in judgment, or, perhaps I'm not young enough to know.

Chapter II

And so, I was once again a solitary traveler in an unknown land but I retained a distinct feeling that Ned's path and mine would cross again.

There are three levels of lodging in the *Trickle Downs* village: exquisite five star, faux five star, and hovel. As I had been roughing it somewhat in my digs at *Jumpback,* I decided – and I hope my dear Reader will not hold it against me – to begin my stay at the *Trickle Downs Hilton Resort and Spa.*

You will find in *Proverbs* the opinion that the poor are hated, even by their own neighbors, but the rich have many friends. My own discovery at the *Spa* was that the rich, when they are not talking about themselves and ownership, talk about what obsessions the poor have.

I heard much at the bridge games I enjoyed playing.

For example, Mr. Hugh, who is a well tanned and greased financier who travels with a secretary half his age, told me that as long as fools were busy fighting a war against evil `over there,' he could make a sucker of them over here. A good Christian wages war against the forces of evil. "Do you believe I was told by some self ordained backwater minister that Jesus loves war?"

I remarked that war always seemed to find a way even through the gates of religion.

Mrs Goodheart, a widow who was often my partner, told me that ownership does it. " You can't keep nomads and gypsies and all the assorted ne'er do wells, troublemakers, discontents and such in line but convince them that a piece of property is their destiny and you've got a malleable sort."

Mr. Swearly agreed to a point.

"The beauties of compound interest soothe the savage beast," he told us. "Ownership of stocks will take the piss and vinegar out of any young rebel."

"Ring the fear bell," Mr. Wims said, banging a fist on the table. "It's the lordly Duke who'll protect the lowly serfs from the foreign beast."

"Get any fool to hate that foreign beast," Mr. Hugh told us, "and all the blackness of evil jumps to that beast's back and the homeland has the look of Eden."

"I am always amazed," Mr. Wims said, "how well the race card plays in every one of these damn elections. And how damned cleverly coded these politicians are."

'You think they'll be shooting at the gas pumps?"Mrs. Goodheart said.

"I applaud shootings anyplace," Mr. Swearly said. "I'm certainly not going to be at a gas pump or wherever these miscreants are shooting. Arrest them. Send them to prison by all means. Send them to the prisons I hold stock in. Fill up the empty beds. Can't make a profit with empty beds. Shootings, arrests, prison terms, profits."

"Two no trump," Mrs. Goodheart replied.

I became friendly with Walker, a youngish man who described himself as an adventurous capitalist after I had said I was for the near future no more than a traveler. He seemed to find some link between us and went on about how we had the courage not only to face the unknown but to plunge into it, the greatest adventure being a plunge into risky waters. I admitted that no sign announcing "Here be dragons' would prevent my own journey onward.

I had been invited to Walker's home on a number of occasions but the one I wish to tell you about my dear Reader revealed much to me.

Most of the guests had gone home and I was about to, pausing for a last few moments of warmth by the fire with a brandy in hand, when Walker and his girlfriend, Lyla, a relatively new conquest, began an argument concerning one of Walker's servants.

"She's just stupid is what it is," Walker insisted.

"She's unfortunate," Lyla replied.

"You don't have to tell me she doesn't have a fortune. Why doesn't she? Because she's stupid."

"And that's her fault?"

"My God!" Walker exploded. "Who's fault is it? Mine? Am I supposed to suffer idiots gladly? And pay them exorbitant wages?"

"I'm just saying a little compassion wouldn't hurt."

"Oh, I have to come up with compassion *and* money? Give me a break. Talk sense. You're old enough."

This brought some color to Lyla's face and I could see she was trying to control herself.

"Not everyone has your gifts, Walker," she said. "And you don't even have them all the time, believe me."

He glared at her.

"Whatever I have, you've been enjoying it."

"I think it's time for me to go," Lyla said, getting up.

Walker's mood changed instantly.

"Come on, Lyla," Walker whined. "Where are you going? Jeez, have some compassion." He laughed. "I've had too much to drink. I don't know what I'm saying."

Lyla was deterred. I got up. It was time for me to leave.

Walker turned to a man named Andy who Walker had introduced to me as a fellow adventurer.

"Andy," Walker said, "Give me some help here."

"Lyla," Andy called out. "Give the heartless bastard a break. Stay. We need you."

Lyla sighed, smiled and said she'd stay but she wanted to hear from Walker's own lips when he thought compassion was called for.

"Okay, okay," Walker responded. "Never. No. I'm kidding. But if you mean by compassion that I should hand over my own rewards for what you call my gifts to people too stupid to have any ambition, then I don't have compassion and I don't want to have it. I'm like all those who say they have it. All I have to do is say I have it. But I'm no crooked politician. I'm honest. I don't even say I have it. I don't believe in giveaways. I do believe you let people back themselves into a corner and then see if they're smart enough to work their way out. If they can't do that then what's the sense of asking the winners to support them? They're drowning; why the hell should I go down with them?"

Lyla's face had darkened as Walker spoke.

"My brother Ray's got cancer and no medical insurance," she told us in almost a whisper. "He can't afford it. He can't get the treatment he needs."

"Baby," Walker said, going over to her. "You know I'll help. I'm crazy about you."

She looked up at him.

"Yes, I do know that," she said. "That's why I'm here. It's not compassion. It's not attraction. It's not love. It's something you can understand. It's business."

With that she left us, telling Walker to call her. He looked at me and I think he was surprised to see me still there.

"I'm more than business," he said, angrily. "But I'll be damned if I pull in my teeth because everybody else is toothless. Her brother Ray is a shiftless lazy bastard."

"If some of us didn't have teeth," Andy said, yawning, "there would be no gnashing and if there was no gnashing there'd be no war. And if there was no war..."

"I'll bet Colter made a fortune on this war," Walker said. I had no idea what war he was referring to, not being at all familiar with *Trickle Downs* international relations.

"I'd like to put that bitch in a trench and see how much compassion she'd have."

"If business got really bad here," Andy conjectured, "would we be moving to China?"

"I don't think it's that easy in China to take the money and run,' Walker replied. "I don't love business because it's business. I love the money and when I've got enough, I'm out."

Andy laughed and told Walker he'd never have enough to which Walker responded "Guilty."

He looked at me.

"You've seen cold hearted bastards like us in your travels, Gulliver?" he asked me, smiling.

"I do not judge anyone," I told him. "I believe we all have our difficulties in caring about each other. But I've found my countryman Shakespeare is encouraging: `No beast so fierce but knows some touch of pity.' Of course that's Richard III and Richard did confound Shakespeare's optimism."

I took up golf which I had played and played very well in my own homeland. I was at my locker when one of the foursome I had been part of – Reverend Swot – gave me some advice.

"Here's how you avoid the coming people's revolution, Gullfart. Number one…"

"Excuse me," I said, lacing a shoe. "What revolution is that?"

"You've got the bottom forty percent of the village pretty well beaten up. The middle class is still chasing that rabbit of upper middle class status but that rabbit can no longer be caught. Then you've got the top one percent who are close to owning everything on the board and the next twenty per cent serving them in some professional capacity. 80% hurting; 20% full liquidity. You let the boys play their games until they crash and then you save them because saving them is saving the country. It's a nervy game because at some point -- The Apocalypse. Riots and things fall apart. Revolution."

"So how do you defuse this coming catastrophe, Reverend?"one of our golf mates, Gene Wormers asked. Gene was a corporate attorney.

"I know how," Angelo Rudo shot out. Angelo owned a number of used car outlets. " Shopping, computer games and porn."

"And this defuses the coming revolution you anticipate?" I asked.

"Sure," Angelo told me. "And neat profits are made thereby also, my friend. Technology is sweet and never questioned. Somebody could come up with something to replace the human mind…like a tiny cell phone implant….and people will eat it up. Here, take my mind; give me the digital version."

Angelo laughed.

"You are a very cynical man, Angelo," Reverend Swot told him.

"You don't think people who are hurting can be distracted forever?" I asked Gene.

He shook his head.

"I think disaffection grows into old fashioned discontent which breeds anger, hostility, violence."

"Number two," the Reverend Swot said holding up two fingers. "You need to detour their anger. We do it all the time. The Devil made me do it. The other guy is at fault. Or the system is. Or it's just in the cards. Best of all: people know they need to assume personal responsibility."

"It's the crooked unions is what it is," Angelo said. "I've got seven locations and two hundred and thirty three employees and they think I'm going to let them form a union so they can suck my blood."

"I could say it's the godless," Rev. Swot said. "Or the socialists or the rabid environmentalists or the layabouts who won't work. But at heart it's a joist between those who have a fire in the belly to succeed as well as the brains to know how to do it. And those who don't."

"People lose," Angelo said, nodding. "They want to wake up thinking they can win. Why not?"

"The bigger the piece you cut for yourself," Rev. Swot said, "the less there is for anyone else. Unfortunate. But fortunately, faith is a solace. Our reward is in heaven."

"Giveaways don't help anybody," Angelo said, "My father gave me nothing but tough love and I went out and made it in the real world."

"Moral decline begins," Rev. Swot said, looking at me, "when people forget how to build their own strengths and rely upon themselves and not a government."

" "Is there a moral decline in the village?" I asked the Reverend.

"There's always moral decline in the village," Rev. Swot replied, giving me an indulging smile. "It's Biblical."

When I had a good grasp of this *Spa* talk, which I found to be inspired by somewhat less than the better angels of our nature, I moved to the *Village End,* the scruffiest and most disreputable part of town. I wanted to record on both parameters and in this way anticipate to some extent what the talk in between might be.

I found a room in a boarding house run by Mrs. Bombers, a fiftyish widow, who I discovered had gametic and genetic ties to almost everyone in the house. Had I extended my stay beyond what my conscience would allow I too might be now included on that list.

Chapter II

At first I only had dinner at Mrs. Bombers, my practice being to set out early in the morning and not return until dinner time. I soon found that there was little usable talk on the streets of the *Village End*, most of it encapsulated in a word such as *"whatever"* or *"wanker"* or a phrase such as *"give it here"* or *"roll on it,"* or *"thems me food"* or *"thems me music"* or *"poof off."* But the boarding house table was replete with a good array of boiled potatoes – what Mrs. Bombers called her *"good go to"*—and a good sampling of the sort of conversation that would have had Mayor Parsall wincing non-stop.

The strategy I employed was to throw out to the table an explosive observation as one does a bit of chum in the water to lure trout.

Tonight, for example, I began with this: "I find that heavier taxes on the rich might remedy some of the problems here in the Village End."

To this Mr. Skinley, a pensioner, responded: "Oh, you would, would you? And I suppose Mr. Joe Stalin put you up to that notion?"

"I object, sir," Mr. Rapoort said, pointing at me with his fork, "to agreeing to anything that might turn around and bite me in the arse. Excuse my elocution, ladies."

"Poortie has some idea he's going to be rich any day," Mrs. Bombers said as she laid down a platter of thick brown bread. "That's after he digs himself out of the hole he's in. Of course he got pushed into that hole and didn't dig it himself."

"Mrs. Montrose says I'll be rich and famous because I have the legs and the voice for it," Betty, one of Mrs. Bombers's daughters, remarked as she laid a platter of potatoes on the table. I guessed she was no more than fourteen or fifteen but a quite comely lass, if I may say so.

Mr. Sal, a man in his early thirties I calculated, and who always came to the table with dirty hands told Betty that she could fall back in a pinch on porno work to which Betty responded "Whatever."

"All the child has to do," Mrs. Montrose, a silver haired dowager, proclaimed, "is to want something long and hard enough and it will happen. It's The Secret, dear, and I'm passing it on to you."

"Long and hard," Mr. Sal repeated, winking at Betty.

Betty shrugged and said "Whatever."

Mrs. Bombers remarked that it sounded more like a bowel movement.

"All a man has to do is work hard," a young Mexican named Ramon said, without looking up from his plate. "I think that is the secret."

"Without computer skills you're not going anyplace today," Mrs. Montrose proclaimed.

"Sometimes I wonder," I said, throwing more chum on the waters, if you will, "if it's mostly good or bad luck that brings us to where we are."

"I object, sir," Poortie said, not surprising me, "to being told that all I have made of myself is the result of Fortune's hand at the wheel."

"More like your hand on a fork," Mr. Sal said. "That fork made you fat, no good luck or bad luck about it."

"But if a man's in need of help through no fault of his, shouldn't those who are doing well be taxed to help him get back on his feet?"

I tried to slip this in as harmlessly as I could. No luck.

"We choose all that we get," Mrs. Bombers said, plopping down now at the head of the table, her ample breasts rollicking above her plate. "I chose five husbands. Damn stupid choices all five of them. But I chos'em. We're not machines. We're not programmed. You make lousy choices, you wind up in a lousy spot. Don't look to me to help you out."

"You've got a Red way of thinking, mister," Mr. Skinley told me, squinting at me as if I were difficult to get into view. "Them Reds all got a beef with the successful. Envy is what it is. Them Reds won't rest until they get their hands on another man's property."

"It's not money or property that I think will make me happy," I said, reaching nonchalantly for a hard boiled egg. Mrs. Bombers had told me when I asked what dinners usually consisted of that, in her words, "potatoes, tomatoes, eggs, beer and bread are me foods and that's what you'll be seeing in different arrangements and consortments."

"Right now you're happy with that egg, right?" Mr. Sal wisecracked. I found him most annoying.

"I got what makes you happy, Sal," Mrs. Bombers said, winking at Sal.

"That you have, Mrs. B," Sal replied.

This put Poortie out.

"You want to be happy?" he said, looking at Mrs. Bombers. "Then I say live within your means, don't bring degenerate blood suckers into your life, and tell your children being a porn star is not a noble career choice…"

"They up and took my last credit card over at the Village Emporium," Mr. Skinley interrupted, pulling a bent cigarette out of a crushed pack. "So that brings it down to me and the social security check. Till death do us part."

"Well, make sure I get mine before you go on a binge," Mrs. Bombers advised him.

"It'll run out before you're dead," Sal told Skinley. "Unless you kick off in the next couple of weeks."

At that Ramon made the sign of the cross.

"They say that's a socialist plan," I said to Skinley.

"So now you want to take away my social security check? It ain't a handout. I worked for it. It's me money."

"Better spent on you than on that war," I told him.

"I lost a son in that war," Mrs. Bombers said, "so don't you be saying anything against what he did over there. My son Willy was a patriot. Now I'm not. And I don't know if Betty here is…"

"You would look grand in a uniform, Betty," Sal told her.

"Whatever," Betty retorted

"Well, I'm sure God will comfort you," I told Mrs. Bombers, who was offended by the comment.

"Me and the Lord will have our day in court so you don't need to worry about that. I'll make my case without any help from you, thank you."

"I get my unemployment checks so I guess that makes me a socialist," Sal said.

"It just means you're a lazy son of a bitch, Sal," Mrs. Bombers said. "That's all it means."

"Were you downsized?" I asked.

"Downsized?" Sal repeated, looking down at his groin. "No, I went the old fashioned way. I got excommunicated. One of Ramon's relatives took my job."

"I don't think so," Ramon said in almost a whisper.

"Here's the government's plan," Mr. Skinley announced. "First, you send all the good jobs south of the border. Then you bring up a whole lot of wetbacks to take any jobs white men here in the village might still have."

"I heard someone remark that here in *Trickle Downs* if you don't have a gardener, you are a gardener."

"I used to have a garden," Sal told me, "but it went to pot. Ha ha."

"I mean if you're middle class," I told the table, "you can own a home and have some investments and some medical insurance. You could have some security."

"Who says I ain't middle class?" Mrs. Bombers snapped. "I think you think we're some scum off the street, mister."

"Of course not but doesn't it bother you that the wealthy get everything and you get nothing?'

"I like them that can pay," Mrs. Bombers responded. "And the rich can pay. Who's gonna hire you? Old Poortie there who doesn't have a dime? Or Sal? We need the rich."

"This gentleman," Skinley said, pointing at me, "he prefers them pinko countries where everybody is equally poor and spending their lives cueing up for a loaf of bread."

"First you get the moolah," Sal said, raising one finger in the air, "then you get the muscle. Then you get the babes. That's how it goes."

"What a deplorable life," Poortie said as he reached out and forked another potato.

"You tap potatoes, Poortie," Mrs. Bombers quipped, "like Sal here taps asses."

"If I didn't spend so much time in jail in my younger days," Mrs. Montrose said, "I would have been rich. The rich know how to stay out of jail."

Everyone looked at Mrs. Montrose quite surprised by her confession.

"I ran a boarding house too, dear," she told Mrs. Bombers whose mouth was still hanging open. "Spelled "BAWDING.""

She laughed.

"The government in this village," Ramon said, breaking the silence, "is giving too much handouts to people who don't do no work. It's not right."

"Who needs a government?" Sal said, wiping his mouth with his sleeve. "I don't need anybody telling me what not to do and I damn well don't need anybody taking my money and using it for something I don't need."

"You need the government to send you your unemployment checks, genius," Poortie told him.

"Well, the government better stop killing babies is all I have to say," Mrs. Montrose told us.

"You know I just wonder," I said, "if abortion and gay marriage might be a big issue in the village election."

"Nothing will stop abortion," Mrs. Bombers snapped. "Whether or not it goes back to poor women having it in an alley or rich women at a spa in gay Paree. I'd rather have mine safely and the government pay for it. A gay bloke does my hair. That's the be all and end all of my interest in gays."

"To each his own," Poortie said.

"The gays have gotten to him," Sal said, winking at me.

Betty's cell phone rang then and she turned in her chair with the phone to her ear.

"I don't know about the rest of you," I said, "but I'm getting into a deeper and deeper relationship with all this computer technology."

"Betty does *Faceback* about nine hours a day," Mrs. Bombers said to which Betty, pulling the phone from her ear, said "Whatever."

"There is a game I like called *World of Warcraft*," Sal told us.

"Crap," Mrs. Bombers said.

"Better crap than the crap you watch," Sal told her. "You know they make those soap operas up. Not a bit of truth in there."

"Then how come you remind me, Sal, of one of the guys on *The Loser and His World*?"Mrs. B snapped.

"It is rather difficult to distinguish what's true from what's false these days," I remarked. "And reality seems more like a Hollywood production than what it once was."

"That's just a sign that you need to go to AA," Sal told me with a big infuriating smile on his face.

"Things is what you make of'em," Mrs. Montrose proclaimed.

"Tell me, Mrs. Montrose," I said, "Do you ever doubt yourself?"

"I'm only doubtful of where I might have left my room key," she replied.

"I got it," Sal said, winking at her.

"I just wish we'd do a better job with the environment," I said, sighing deeply.

"You keep the inside all neat and tidy," Mrs. Bombers said, "and the outside will take care of itself. That's what my grand dad taught me."

"I got a nicely furnished room," Mr. Skinley said. "Who needs to go outside? Only socialists go outside. So let them go outside."

"I read about a guy," Sal said, "cares more about mountain gorillas than about his mom. Ain't that something?"

"I sometimes think if someone gave me ten million dollars I'd have a hard time knowing what to do with it?"

That remark made everyone laugh.

"Just pass it on to me, friend and I'll show you," Sal said.

"I mean how much can I spend on myself?" I replied. "I can only sleep in one bed at a time, wear one pair of shoes..."

"Choice is what it is," Sal said, snapping his fingers. "You buy everything you can and then you choose whatever you want when you feel like it. A redhead one day, a blonde the next. Like that."

"I'd want to do something for somebody," I said. "Besides you Sal. I'd want to make things a bit better in this world."

"Let your conscience be your guide, sir," Poortie told me as he speared yet another boiled potato.

"You can hire agents to take care of your conscience," Betty said, now off the phone. "That was a tweet."

"So the agent goes to heaven," Sal said, "and you go where you belong. We're dogs. Face it. We're all dogs and it never turns out good for dogs. We live like dogs; we die like dogs. Dogs don't go to heaven. Why dream about it? It's one run in the park and then it's over. Short run, long run. Everything else is illusion."

The middle class section of *Trickle Downs*, called *Eden Forest,* was marked by chemically treated lawns which were front aprons to cape cods and split level ranch homes. I spied no forests. Here unlike the *Village End* the lanes were quiet and there were few people walking about. I would have a difficult time in getting a sample of the talk but, as luck would have it, there was an Urgency meeting in the community center the very night I arrived.

The urgency had to do with home foreclosures. I attended and sat in the back of the auditorium. After an hour or so, it became clear where the divisions were.

The *Foreclosed* group wanted their homes saved by some community action. A second group that I will call the *Righteous* argued that the foreclosed group were facing the dire consequences of their own actions and should not be asking the village council for a bail out. This group admitted that some prior action by the community could have been taken to exclude those who obviously did not belong.

A third group that I will call the *Scavengers* was willing to purchase all homes in danger of foreclosure at five cents on the dollar. And a fourth group, the *Security Mom* group, were worried about the vacant foreclosed homes becoming crack houses and worse.

Besides these there were a number of randoms protesting a war that *Trickle Downs* had joined in a far off land, the monopoly of the local TV cable company, Moms Against Porn, Vegans Against Animal Testing, Two Hands On The Wheel Advocates, a Save the Aquifer group, a Make Hemp Not War group, an Anti-Aluminum group, Young Mothers for Irish Toe Dancing and Lacrosse group, Converts to Colon Cleansing, Tough Love advocates, Innovation for the Sake of Innovation advocates, More Cereal Choices Group, Fiber and anti-High Fructose groups, a Reckless Leg and Heroin Makes You Sleep group, Tweeting Beyond 140 Characters, and countless others.

Many were evangelically inspired and I, as I tried inconspicuously to position myself where my Dictaphone could do most good, was asked if I had accepted Jesus Christ as my personal savior to which I replied that adhering to the Christian concern for others I had accepted Christ as my personal and societal savior.

On another occasion I was asked if I had any idea how much aluminum was already in my brain, a presence which would ultimately destroy my identity to which I responded that would indeed be a three pipe problem if my own brain ran off with my own identity.

I had a grand opportunity to hear as much middle class talk as I could wish.

I think it best to present what I discovered by contrasting it with the talk at the *Spa* and at *Village End*.

In a capsule preamble this: The *Forest Edenites* do not agree with Sal that they are all "dogs.

I was somewhat surprised to discover that Mrs. Bombers and her boarders were cited more than once as examples of perfidious human behavior and lifestyle.

Slightly different than Sal's view was the *Forest Edenites'* view of the life of man. (You will recall Sal's trajectory: moolah, muscle, babes). Here in *Forest Eden* the trajectory was this: pre-natal Mozart; a mutual beginning of birth, compound interest, and computer literacy; pre-kindergarten violin and/or piano lessons; Judo and karate for five year olds; synchronized swimming and Lacrosse; merit badges and Eagle scout; prep school; State college; dentristy or chiropractic; assortative mating; golf; portfolio; Jesus; mortgage; home in the exclusive (but faux) *Versailles Estate* community; cabin up north; two kids; dog; pre-natal Mozart and around once again.

Other people in the eyes of the *Spas* were either born losers, tax burdens, or lurking thieves, kidnappers and cutthroats. To the *Forest Edenites* other people were either from the neighborhood and therefore safe and familiar or outside the neighborhood and therefore a possible danger to their lawn and their children.

Trickle Downs's government was always a potential enemy to be disarmed in the view of the *Spas*. But the *Forest Edenites* sometimes thought the government did not mean anything in their lives and sometimes thought it was an amoral force with too much intrusion in their lives and sometimes thought it was best run by a CEO.

In regard to happiness, the *Spas* saw it in their stock portfolios while the *Forest Endenites* read coffee table books and watched Oprah announcing the secret of true happiness. They often Googled "happiness."

For the Spas, a review of conscience was a stock portfolio review.

The *Forest Edenites* stood behind family values. If you were a mother, you were always ready to deliver a hot meal, clean sheets, and an aspirin.

At Mrs. Bombers's table, war wasn't over there but started here on the home front as soon as you got out of bed; abortion was a fierce economic necessity; families were mouths to feed and changeable – most often husbands changing wives and wives changing husbands -- by virtue of necessity, and God and heaven and hell were battles too distant to be fought now.

I must report that every boarder at Mrs. Bomber's table was prepared to give the Celestial Entity a piece of their mind. They were ready to be celestially litigious.

In due course my presence became quite well known in every quarter of *Trickle Downs* village and there arose an interest in hearing my traveler's tales. Accordingly I was asked to speak at a community meeting and I gladly accepted, believing that my talk would prove beneficial to the villagers and might contribute in some humble way to an advance in their own talk, and thereby, in their actions.

I stepped up to the podium, glanced at the faces before me, recognizing many, catching a sly wink from Sal, a lascivious one from Mrs. Bombers, a proper nod from several *Forest Edenites* and more than one thumbs up from the *Spas.*

"*Edenites*, if may so refer to them," I began, "believe that what goes around comes around, that God punishes the evil doer, that everyone has the same shot at success, that real rewards are in heaven, and that you can confirm the truth of anyone's words by looking into their eyes or their heart or their soul, and that you make by your choices your own destiny."

I paused, cleared my throat and surveyed my listeners. I could detect nothing. I went on.

"The *Enders,* if I may so refer to them, believe that ill fortune plagues them, that Hell is a real place and they are living in it, that they are destined to a bad end, that if life is a poker game, the deck is stacked against them, that no good deed goes unpunished, that good guys finish last, that bullshit was everyone's stock and trade, and when given the chance, take the money and run."

This produced a low grumble from the audience accented by laughter. I went on.

"The *Spas*, if I may so refer to them, believe that the clever man never gets caught, that life's deck was stacked – by them, that if you look steadily into someone's eyes you could sell them anything, even the truth of what you were saying, and that their own winning destiny was a bricolage they made out of the sweat, tears and blood of lesser men."

Grumbles, laughter and now angry shouts. I wasn't at all sure of this response but went on nevertheless, dear Reader, sure as I was in the truth and validity of my words.

"The *Spas* believe they have a natural gift for living well and enjoying the finer things in life. They hold that spending money is a talent only they do well. Losers, in their view, have debased sensibilities and would in the end corrupt anything fine and squander any fortune that came their way."

At this point I noticed that several fights had broken out among my audience. I went on.

"The *Enders* hold that it's all luck and that their luck can change, that life is a knife fight in a phone booth, that any claims of distinction in anything are elitist claptrap, and that nobody who won anything had done it fairly."

Half of the audience was now fighting with the other half. The noise level had reached tumult levels and I spoke more loudly into my microphone. My words were having an effect, which I saw as the preliminary to recuperative actions.

"The *Edenites* hold a temperate view toward what are called the finer things in life, believe that disciplined shopping is a sign of moral character, and that moderation in dress, language, and thinking is always called for, that the wealthy have problems different than but equal to their own, and that the unfortunate and disaffected were their own worst enemies, their problems easily remedied by a little fiscal discipline, a more developed moral character, an effective lawn trimmer, and regular Sunday service."

Some attempt was now being made to reach me on the stage and the *Trickle Downs* Constabulary were dealing bone crunching blows right and left. With microphone in hand I retreated to the rear of the stage and went on.

"*Spas* laugh at the suggestion of a class divide in *Trickle Downs*. The *Edenites* don't perceive a class difference but only a difference in wealth, and the *Enders* affirm that they have a lot of class but snobs keep them down."

This was the last I managed to intone before hands were on me and I was thrust to the floor, the angry faces of people I knew pushing their fists into my own face. In a matter of seconds, I was conveyed out of the building, tied to a rail, covered with viscous tar upon which chicken feathers were applied and then, the rail being hoisted on the shoulders of the most stalwart, carried a distance from the village where I was dispatched with angry curses into a ditch.

Chapter III

The Author is drawn up to the Floating Island of Babel.

I spent a day and a night in a ditch, alternately shivering in the cold and scorched by the sun, which suddenly was eclipsed by a dark mass a hundred meters directly above my head. A grappling hook was lowered and I, too confused to fathom the event, was drawn up, rail, tar and feathers.

After several days I can report that I was again myself in body but my mind, having gone through a humiliating assault at the hands of the *Trickle Down* barbarians, was not as it had been on the day I had set out on my voyage. But as my own self-esteem was grounded as the blind Bard says on the just and right, I did not allow the injustices and lack of charity of others to abide with me for long.

I did not therefore attribute my present difficulties on this floating island of Babel -- for this is where I was told I was -- to the miseries from which I had been rescued. In brief, I was not able to understand the talk of this island, though everyone spoke the Queen's English, but acknowledgments to whatever was said were askew.

Image, dear reader, a speaker directing his talk one way and a respondent directing his talk the opposite way, as when you move a rudder one way only to go the other. At first believing this was a lack of coincidence apparent only to my much tousled mind, I kept my peace. Upon perceiving that this discord had not abated and was indeed not a projection of my own but a real state in which the inhabitants of this island dwelled, I set myself to bring the matter before his Majesty when I was duly summoned to his chambers.

His Majesty listened to my account with great attentiveness and then, not to my great surprise, proceeded to talk about matters which, I confess, were more than opaque to me. It seemed, however, his Majesty was satisfied with my failure of comprehension for he smiled benevolently upon me as if I were a benign idiot and I was led from his presence.

That evening while I was dining upon a delicious bit of Irish beef though I had asked for mutton shank, I was visited by an Emissary of my own age and of a startling likeness to myself, who, in response to my invitation to join me, readily accepted. I was delighted to be understood and said so. The Emissary attested that his Majesty had assessed that our talk would be compatible. It seems the Emissary and I talked within what he called the same "worlding," that the floating island was filled with a variety of "worldings," and that the inhabitants remained as long as they wished but his Majesty hoped long enough to desire to see what they had not be enabled to see before and long enough to desire to hear what they had not be enabled to hear before.

Not readily comprehending this last comment, I did not despair but merely noted that the "worlding" between the Emissary and I was perhaps not as perfect as his Majesty had hoped. My sense of the whole of what the man had to say was that through the miraculous mobility of his floating island kingdom, his Majesty was rounding up souls, as he had myself, in the hope of gaining their allegiance and loyalty by means of some sort of deep re-cultivation of their senses.

When in due time, and after more than one bottle of good wine, the Emissary invited me to join in a tutorial, my response was prepared. Certainly, I replied and we saluted each other In that spirit of largeness and fellowship that only complete strangers drinking together can display. You may wonder as to why I acquiesced to what I saw as an effort to erase my own perceptions and put in their stead those of his Majesty.

Firstly, though not bound, I saw myself as a prisoner until I could sort out my escape route. We were, please note, floating at least a Rugby field distance from the ground. Secondly, and most pertinently, I am an intrepid explorer into whatever and how many realms of talk I encounter and I will not stand back in fear when challenged by any talk which presumes to dismiss my own.

I may be tarred and feathered and run out of a village on a rail, but my nature is protean: I rise up with renewed vigor.

The next day I was given a children's book to read and make what sense I could of it. It didn't surprise me that any redirection of mind would begin with an imaginary tale directed to the young. What could be the intent here but to rebuild me from the bottom up?

Two days later I joined a group of about a hundred people in a large amphitheatre where our tutorial began. I cannot describe the tutor as he...or she...was non-descript, not so large as to be large, not so small as to be small, not so dark as to be dark, not so light as to be light, with a voice that went in and out, like so and SO in a bad dream. My Emissary informed me that Sydney was Intersex, being neither male nor female. I was working this over in my imagination when Sydney began.

I must say that my attention wandered almost immediately. What I did hear went something like this: we see the world, we use words to describe it. Some alien called "Aunt Beast" doesn't depend on seeing to know the world. And somehow it's important to see the world the way she does, or, recognize other ways of seeing and talking and so on and on.

I woke up as Sydney came to a close and was thanking us for our attendance and walked from the podium. I found myself observing whether she – I mean Sydney – had rather more of a masculine way of walking than a feminine way but could come to no conclusion.

As a result of the comments I submitted after this presentation (which can be summed up as "If my Aunt looked like a beast, I'd shoot her") it was determined that I would be more responsive to a deep tutorial, and so I attended such the very next day.

A man with a great mass of uncombed hair perched atop his head like an orange crown bearing the abstruse credentials of some sort of scientist addressed us in a bold and direct fashion and this was encouraging because I had concluded that my failure to fully apprehend what Sydney had said had much to do with the ambiguity of the speaker. I soon observed that Microft, for such was his name, was wasting his time in a ludicrous pursuit.

"A wise man tells a tale of a mouse," Microft began, "or more precisely, our search for a mouse among old clothes in a closet. The premise is that mice are created out of old clothes lying in dark, hidden corners of our closets"

I was about to mumble something to myself when a sharp and very peculiar voice – I mean peculiar in the enunciation of words as if the speaker were foreign but not of country but planet – cried out: *"Crambe repetita! Crambe repetita!"* My Latin being workable I translated this as an outcry of *"Warmed-over cabbage! Warmed-over cabbage!"*

Microft continued as if he hadn't heard. And then the voice again:

"Frisch auf! the same peculiar voice shot out from somewhere in the rear of the auditorium. I turned to eye the speaker but to no avail. I remarked *sotto voce* to the Emissary that no God fearing man would move on from the *Genesis* view of the world's creation. The Emissary did not respond and I assumed he was an atheist. I held my tongue for The Lord forbid that I would interrupt the insane pursuit of mice in dark closets.

But the heckler in the rear did not desist.

"Moved on from racism! Moved on from specie-ism!"

This time when I turned my head to get a glimpse of who was speaking I targeted a large parrot perched on the back of an empty seat in the very last row. I was quite amazed.

"What we talk about," Microft went on, but my attention was riveted on the parrot.

"Heu prisca fides!" the parrot screeched and this time I had my eye on him. A parrot who quoted Virgil: *"Alas for the ancient faith!"* Remarkable!

Whether Microft was disconcerted by this or not he did at this point bow to us and straightway leave the room. I was up from my seat, stretching my limbs, fully confident that I had not been "un-worlded" or whatever was to occur.

My mood was not good and the Emissary took note of it and before I could announce my desire to leave this confounding floating isle, he asked me to join him at dinner that evening. He promised I would not be disappointed in the conversation. I accepted, not because I wished to go but because I was as yet not sure whether the invitation was a command and indeed whether I was a prisoner or not.

I arrived at the Emissary's home promptly at eight and found that the other guests had already arrived.

I shook hands with Sydney whose hand I report would not have seemed conspicuous at the end of a man's wrist nor a woman's. Sydney's eyes swept over me, top to bottom, and she said, "The Traveller" and then asked me whether I abided by Horace's notion that a traveller oft found a change in clime but seldom experienced a change of mind to which I responded that I hoped my own travels would be an exception, although I was seeking to augment my own awareness rather than replace it for I was not in any way hostile to it. She greeted this with a smile that possessed all the enigma of the Mona Lisa.

Microft was also present and I was tempted to ask him how his search for mice went but refrained. The parrot was also present, perched on the shoulder of an ill dressed man with a black patch over one eye. This pirate gave me a hearty slap on the shoulder and said "Captain Noble." The only other dinner guest of what I would call distinct character dimensions was a huge man wearing a bowling shirt with the name "Walter" in cursive above the shirt pocket. One's expectations would be that such a man would be loud and indeed he was.

We had already dipped spoon into soup when one other guest arrived, a thin, pale man who took the vacant seat to my left, nodding to me and whispering, "They let me out late." I assumed he meant his place of employment but soon discovered that he was a prisoner of the Isle of Babel Correctional Institute and had, among other privileges, dinner privileges at the Emissary's. He introduced himself to me as Brother Frank.

We had not yet finished our soup when the table conversation, which had thus far been restricted to the qualities of the soup itself, Captain Noble announced that though he was seated astern of us all he'd be keelhauled if he didn't avow his extreme pleasure at seeing a seafarer such as myself at table. I said I was obliged to him and acknowledged, somewhat disingenuously, my pleasure at being in their company on this breathtaking floating isle. I was then asked by Sydney what my interest in travel was to which I responded in a manner and substance my dear Reader is already familiar with. The entire table proceeded to mull this over as the fish course was served.

"My interest," Microft said, as he probed his trout's head with a knife, "is in exploring the headwaters of the Nile, by which I mean the magical mindset out of which any sort of unified or competing ways of dealing with things emerge. I am thinking of the dreams we live in. All strategies are hewn from such dreams."

"I'd say we're all in a box-like prison," Brother Frank said, shaking his head, not on the whole surprising me with his imagery. "Dreaming's just what a prisoner's got left. It ain't freedom."

"They fuck you up, your mum and dad," the parrot, who had settled himself on the back of the Captain's chair, shouted.

"Belay that talk, Harry," the Captain ordered.

"I was speaking metaphorically, Brother Frank," Microft went on, quite used to the parrot's manner as did all except myself. "Of the mind. One can be outside a prison cell and yet the mind can be locked up. One can be inside a prison and yet the mind can be free. Witness Martin Luther King or Nelson Mandela or Giordano Bruno or Frank Costello."

"I'm locked up in guilt," Brother Frank replied. "And everybody else looks at me and I know that they're locked up in seeing me guilty."

"Start a business!" the parrot screeched.

"I agree with Brother Frank," Sydney said. "Everyone, from salesman to preacher talks about getting out of their box and at least rebelling against the one they're in. They miss the point. When you're inside you're not also outside."

"Jeez, Sydney," Walter exclaimed, mouth full of bread. "What the hell does that mean?"

"It means Walter that if you're inside a male/female mindset, you're not outside it. You can't be. And I take that personally because that's where I am."

"I did not know that," Walter affirmed, nodding.

"The way we imagine," Microft said after a long silence in which all attention was being paid to extracting fish bones, "and then think within the way we imagine can change. Consider, for example, what enchantments incite the medieval magician to catalog resemblances between animate and inanimate Nature in order to ....turn old clothes into living mice. This is the quest to turn base metals into gold, sullied human nature into deity. Before the rigorous studies of the magicians go on there is this imaginary at work, humans think about the world within this imaginary."

"I'm ready to swear on it!" Captain Noble said, jumping up from his seat so quickly that the parrot fluttered off his shoulder and swooped down the length of the table finally landing on the back of my chair. I was about to make some comment concerning the health issues of this situation when Captain Noble banged the table so hard glasses moved.

"Why sacrifice to the sun?," he shouted.

"Youth must be served!" the parrot announced clear as a bell in my ear.

"Or believe that base metals could be magically turned into gold?"

"And why did peasants believe that kings were divine?"

"King of birds, king of beasts, king or Kaiser, king charles' head."

"Why believe the stars chart our future?

"Why believe looking out for Number One does any of your ship mates any good?

"He's our son of a bitch," the parrot screeched.

"Belay that Harry," the Captain ordered. "Why believe that the purpose of every other species on the planet is to be driven to extinction in the name of plunder?

"Why believe someone else is a threat when you are the one with the weapon ready to board any vessel?

"Any port in a storm."

"Why say corporate business is better than pirating be?"

"Why think that if you surgically move your chin closer to your nose and your hairline closer to your cheeks, you will be loved?

"Sit on your arse for fifty years," the Parrot sang out.

"Belay that talk, Harry. Now mates, none of this talk will stand, mates, without a challenge, but it stands nonetheless and provides the work orders for our chores, our rummaging in sea chests for proof of our convictions."

Captain Noble took his seat again. "I've said my piece. We're all sailing on the same vessel, mates, and heading for the same dark port."

The parrot had his head cocked to one side and one large eye fixed me in a prosecutorial way as if I had failed to answer the Captain's questions correctly.

"Chump change," the parrot told me craning his head close to mine.

"Very true, Captain," Microft said and I was not sure to whom he was responding. "Consider also how Eastern thought is not suffused with an empirical or rational discovery of truth but rather in a reality awareness that frees us from the suffering and bondage tied to false insight. To be released from the bondage of a distorted picture of reality is the goal of enlightenment."

"Talk," Brother Frank said. "All your fancy talk is just saying once we've got our heads up our own arse what we say ain't worth hearing. And we've all got our..."

"Unless," Sydney said in a loud voice, interrupting Brother Frank's version of dinner time chat. "Unless you jump into your time machine and rush forward or backward, arriving at a different locale and a different time, you can't stop talking within the story book of your own day. You know, the one where there's a Prince rescuing a Princess and I can't be found."

That brought silence. But perhaps the silence attended the meat course for a brace of gamecock and a glistening roast pig with an apple in its mouth were brought to the table. Such fare had never been laid out on Mrs. Bombers' table and I must testify, my dear Reader, to my partiality to good Spirits: wine at table and good Irish whiskey at the pub. The Emissary had put before us the good burgundy of Beaune, the fine Barolo of Tuscany, as well as bottles of Pomerol and Pommard, Rioja, Corvo and Rousillon. I do not hold the saying that when the wine is in, the truth is out but hold the view of Mr. Goldsmith that good liquor gives genius a better discerning.

After several minutes and several mouthfuls of the tasty fare and deep inroads into the bottles, everyone was revitalized and the talk resumed.

"You know, Syd," Walter said, pointing his fork at Sydney, "you and I are talking now. We're talking within the Floating Isle talk show of the day. There's no sense wishing for a time machine. We're talking here. We've drawn lines in the sand here. Some talk and walk one way and others talk and walk other ways."

"But I'm saying," Sydney responded, her face flushed, "what if we change the whole choreography so that the whole idea of what walking is and what talking is changes?"

"Let me tell you a story, Syd," Walter replied. "Let's say we go to Iraq. We volunteer."

At that the parrot yelled *"Shut your trap!"* in my ear.

"I believe he's taken a fondness to you," the Captain said to me. "Harry don't take to many."

I wondered why he called him Harry and the Captain told me the parrot named himself and he did it quite habitually.

"What's your name, matey?" the Captain asked the parrot who screamed out "Pidgeon!" and then "Pigtail!" "Napoo!"

"Aye, but what do you want our mate Gulliver to call you?"

The parrot's head went to one side and one frozen eye fixed me.

"Tom, Dick and Harry," the parrot yelled and so I assumed he like the Devil contained legions.

The Captain informed me that Harry sang and did it well and would I like to hear a sea chanty but before I could respond the parrot broke into song:

"What is your twelve O.
Eleven for the eleven who went to heaven,
Ten for a whoop and a holler
Nine for milk in the cocoanut

Eight says Tweed to Till
Different as chalk and cheese
O stinking cod
Five all clothed in green O
Green O free grow the rushes O."

I inquired as to what song was that and the Captain said it was called The Dilly Song but not as any one had ever sung it truth be told.

"*Rara avis*, indeed," I said, quite captivated by the bird's talk, nonsense though it was though amazed as the good Dr. Johnson proclaimed that it was done at all.

"Begging this bird's pardon," Walter said gruffly, "but here's my story. We're soldiers. . ."

I'm afraid I tuned out Walter's story and only revived when I heard the crackling, frightening voice of Brother Frank.

"I found Jesus in a cellblock," Brother Frank said, his head down and his eyes closed. "You may mock that but the Almighty government has a whole mess of power moves but nothing changes the gut feeling that heavenly power alone guides us. And that guidance is true and we all feel it deep down. When folks turn to themselves as judge and jury, that's not just a new way of talking. That is a walking away from Jesus. We don't hear God's voice anymore. It's not God talking but just old Slim or Tex or Bob down the road."

My customary courtesy failed to keep me from asking Brother Frank why he had been sent to jail.

"My soul was bad," Brother Frank mumbled.

"Brother Frank's a suspected terrorist," the Emissary, who had been silent up until now, informed me. "

"There's my point right there," Walter exploded. "You talking with Jesus."

Walter went on until interrupted by Microft.

"Perhaps you would consider," Microft began, looking at Walter, "that power itself, whether supernatural or natural, can bend like the reed to other forces, which are not forces but out of which come all our notions of what power is."

"And that's not a power?" Sydney asked.

"Consider," Microft continued, "how the Zen Buddhist blends consciousness into the material world within a universal, unifying spirit but not in the studied way of magic, rationalism, or empiricism. The foundational figure here is a *basho* – an emptiness – in which world and self are not divided, in which there are no-things and no words are possible or useful. Within this imaginary we move beyond difference between old clothes and mice and unite them within a oneness."

"*Basho!*" Harry yelled out.

"Did you ever think, Microft," Sydney said, somewhat angrily, "that there's no sign of....I mean not one bloody sign of what you're talking about anyplace on this planet. Every goddamn thing is divided. Maybe if we had emptiness, nothing would be divided. But you know what? You also would have nothing. And the world is not nothing and neither is it empty."

I was curious to see that Sydney was angry in the way women rather than men get angry though it would be difficult for me to give evidence as to this. I must say that I found this new combative Sydney quite interesting, a thought I draw back from immediately upon thinking she might be a man.

Meanwhile, Microft was muttering that he himself did not ascribe to the *basho* view but had merely presented it as a counter to Walter's power contesting views. He was, I could see, anxious to regain the table's approbation, especially I think Sydney's, for now he launched yet another "Consider" request.

"Consider, from our perspective, negative imaginaries by which I mean ways of seeing and believing that never arise. Native Americans notoriously fail to imagine the wheel. Once that imaginary begins technology will take us all the way to the SUV and the Hummer2. But it doesn't begin. . ."

He went cataloguing other extraordinary examples until Sydney, red in the face, possibly from wine, interrupted him.

"If you find me in Nature, then I'm okay," Sydney said. "Is that it?"

"My dear, once again. . ." Microft began but Sydney cut him off.

"Well, what I am is not natural to Nature. You have to imagine negatively to come up with me."

"I suggest," I said, hoping to introduce a necessary distinction, "that all that is in Nature is by definition natural, although not all that is in Nature can be explained. That failure, however, does not make the unexplained unnatural."

Those words, however, did not seem to soothe Sydney who seemed for some reason to have lost all patience with me.

"Except in the real world," she told me curtly, "which it seems your own travels have not taken you into, perhaps because you travel within your own ego."

Before I could adjust to that remark Microft said something about the propagation of the species and thus delivered the fatal straw.

"Your precious species," Sydney said, standing up. "I'm a dead end. I do nothing for the continuation of our precious species."

At those words, Harry flew upward and settled on the back of Sydney's chair. He proceeded to do an odd little back and forth dance with his head, hopping from one foot to another and then with his beak almost on Sydney's cheek screeched *"I like your body. I like what it does. I like its bow."*

"Now that's somewhat apropos," I exclaimed, ignoring the tears I now saw in Sydney's eyes.

"Don't take it on yourself, mate," Captain Noble roared out. "We're all just doing a fine job of sinking our ship."

At that moment a servant went up to the Emissary and handed him a note. The Emissary read it and then looked up at me.

"We've taken up a young gentleman by the name of Ned Parsall…"

"Ned!" I shouted, getting up from my chair, surprised when Harry flew to my shoulder.

"He's quartered near you and recognized your name," the Emissary said.

"Can he join us or is…" I was about to say tarred and feathered temporarily and therefore indisposed.

"His anguish is I would say of the mind and not the body," the Emissary replied, a faint smile lurking as if he had apprehended my own thought.

In a matter of minutes I was greeting Ned who was indeed physically sound but had the look about him of one who had met some great tragedy. I introduced him to those at table and when he was seated and had eaten, with a hearty appetite for all his downcast demeanor for a bad turn in youth does not quell the appetite for long.

I queried as to what had befallen him in *Trickle Downs*. That very name made him cringe and I at once suspected that the comely lass who had abducted him had broken his heart. Or, perhaps, his purse.

"All I am prepared to say at this point is," Ned said, clearing his throat, "that what is supposed to stay in *Trickle Downs* cannot possibly stay in *Trickle Downs* because. . . because you take it with you."

Ah! I surmised at once that Ned's genetic predisposition to jump back and review all words and actions had had disturbing effect on his libertine adventures. I counseled him regarding what I consider to be the *sine qua non* of human existence: remaining on good terms with oneself.

Some time later we all adjourned to a very capacious parlor where Brother Frank, Captain Noble and Walter ensconced themselves at a bar at the far end of the room and worked studiously into a bottle of twelve year old Jameson. I noted that the parrot also dipped his beak and thus became quite animated singing one or two ribald songs that I supposed all parrots pick up during their pirate days.

I lingered for a glass or two but was disinclined to go further down that path wherein good whiskey oils the tongue, relieves the watch, and finds a friend behind every pair of eyes. And so thanking the Emissary for his hospitality I departed. Ned was in animated conversation with Sydney when I left and I much admired his ease in doing what I had, in all truth, avoided.

I lay in my bed reading my stalwart Sir Walter Scott as was my bedtime habit and then extinguishing my candle, intent on drifting off into a dream residue of that brilliant novel, found that my stomach was intent on keeping me awake. I have no idea how long it took me to fall asleep or how long I had been asleep when a loud knocking at my door awoke me.

It was Ned. And Sydney. They had come to tell me that whenever I decided to continue my travels they wished to join me. I could detect no liquor on their breaths, but shivering as I was in my night garb and anxious to return myself to Morbius's arms, I promised to carry on the conversation the very next day. Such a response wouldn't do and Ned pushed his way into my chamber, apologizing as he did so, but he definitely – for the sake of his own soul—needed to know how to live in the world without jumping back on everything, letting things go as it were, and yet avoiding the disasters, recently suffered by himself, which attend a letting things go attitude.

I must confess that I in no way believed that Sydney shared his view of me and, bringing the issue into the open, wondered why an egoist such as myself would be considered any sort of reliable or desirable companion? Ned's expression displayed his total bafflement as to my meaning but Sydney at once offered an apology for her prior estimate as to my nature, aware now from what Ned had told her of my very real experiences in *Trickle Downs*. She believed I had been harshly treated for speaking the truth and considered those who spoke truth to power heroic. I told her I found nothing heroic in tar and feathers, being more victim than hero and had I more acutely observed my surroundings, I would have avoided my ignominious treatment. Ned shook his head and told me that he did not believe that was the case, that I was a man who could observe closely but not allow excessive scrutinizing to preempt action. I was also, Ned told me, not prone to launching into action without circumspection.

I, it seems, was a perfect trapeze artist when it came to avoiding the pitfalls of both extremes. I begged to differ, pleading that I had no particular gift in navigating a safe course through the vagaries of human nature and event. I attempted to remind Ned once again of my less than enviable exit from *Trickle Downs* but could not quite dwell on that humiliation standing as I was, albeit in nightshirt, before these youthful admirers.

We would talk now, or, more exact, after I dressed. When I came out of my toilet, Ned and Sydney – Sydney legs crossed on the floor and Ned, long legs stretched out seated on the sofa – informed me that we three would be a veritable *Trois Mousequetaires* of the open road. I saw then that Ned's ease with Sydney was not the result of his having dealt with her gametic ambiguity but quite the opposite. He had identified her as a male, which was not surprising I realized now as he had not been present to hear Sydney's talk. Had she not brought the matter up, a matter that seemed to possess her? My continued interior reference to Sydney as a female was troublesome in a way that I felt no amount of contemplation could remedy.

I brought myself to wonder – purely for Ned's sake -- out loud as to why she – you -- wished to leave the Isle of Babel? Ned blurted out that Sydney had been born on the floating Isle of Babel and had spent his whole life floating above the real world and why then wouldn't he want to leave it and see what it was like to be in the world and not just floating above it? In that desire, he and Sydney were joined. I was about to say something when Sydney announced that she was tired and couldn't we continue this talk next day? I refrained from pointing out that I had expressed that same thought while I was yet in nightshirt and returnable to sleep. But I didn't. When they had gone, I took my pipe and tobacco and went up on deck, hoping that the night air would urge me back to my warm bed.

I found Walter, Brother Frank and Captain Noble on what I called the quarter deck but was in truth a hammock from which one could survey the whole mass of this miraculous hectare of floating earth. They were passing the Jameson and upon seeing me, held it out. Drink is yet another passage to sleep and perhaps the only one left to me so I swigged the bottle and passed it on.

"We're calming the seas with hearty talk is what we're doing," Captain Noble informed me. "And giving Brother Frank here a good launch he'll be remembering until next time."

I noticed at once that Harry the parrot seemed drunk for he was shifting somewhat unsteadily from foot to foot on the railing while singing something so low that I couldn't make it out. I said I thought the parrot was going to fall overboard but Captain Noble looked over at Harry and then shook his head. Harry had stopped his movement and had his head turned and one eye reflecting moonlight fixed on me.

"Don't harsh my mellow," he squawked.

"Dawn," Brother Frank said, dourly, looking up from his cordovans and at me. "I go back at dawn."

"It's a bloody shame is what it is," Captain Noble said. "Every man in his youth's wild and wildness terrorizes the hearts and minds of them that's tame. You can't punish a man his whole life for a wildness that Nature put there. It's like punishing the great whale for being what it is."

Brother Frank then told me that in his youth he had rebelled against the monarchy of the floating Isle, bombs being his particular expression, and would have brought the Isle to ground but for a miracle, which he described as the coming of Jesus into his heart. Of course, he had at first interpreted that divine intercession as the work of an informer but after hearing the words of Preacher Joel had made the right attribution. Preacher Joel, I was told, had been an itinerant evangelist brought up to the Isle in similar circumstances as myself. The Captain winked at me as he said this.

"I accept the condemnation of others," Brother Frank told me. "*Heal me, O Lord, and I shall be healed. Save me, and I shall be saved.* Jeremiah17."

"That he does," Captain Noble said, nodding. "Brother Frank wears it proudly. He's got his privileged prisoner status cause he's a model of a terrorist who's found Jesus."

"Amen, brother," Brother Frank said.

"Dudes," Walter said, swinging the Jameson over his head, "it's all name calling. The way a world we don't know talks to us is through what we call `terrorism.' The way we talk to them is through `war on terror.' Diplomacy has a chance of working if we were in the same boat. But what we have in the `War on Terror' that's being conducted down there is folks in different boats. Why, some ain't even in boats. It's not a matter of boats. Different worlds is what I'm saying. What they see, we don't really know and that's our problem. Then you get a sudden wake up call that elsewhere we are not being imaged as we image ourselves."

"Aye," Captain Noble conceded, accepting the bottle from Walter, "there be strange ways of seeing what's at the end of a spyglass. Some back in the day say there's a god in charge of everything that crawls on land and swims in the sea and it's your task to keep'em all happy. Them ancient folk were throwing bones for guidance or looking to the stars. Back then you were thinking that regardless of what you did your Fate was sealed. Now we think on this here floating isle that that you can be sailing on one sea lane and knowing the others. We can chart'em in. I for one have me doubts. I've been to ports down below where folks think whatever they wish for will come to pass. And places too where the thinking is that peace is blowing bombs, if you'll pardon me, Brother Frank."

"'`Am I not free?'" Brother Frank intoned, "'`Am I not an apostle? Have I not seen Jesus our Lord.'* Corinthians 9."

"Right you are, Brother Frank," Captain Nobel continued. "And then there be some ports where the whole sea locker of this here wide world is no more than`Winners' and `Losers.' Mates, we swim in the powerful seas of our own imaginations where reason is ruled and words fit a ship's heading or they're keelhauled and who puts out the most sail here in other waters stand becalmed."

I must admit that the good Captain's words, like much I had heard on this floating isle appropriately named Babel, floated like albatross on waves before my eyes but try as I might I could not reach out to hold them. When I realized that the Irish had soaked through and I was more asleep than awake., I bid my good nights and returned to my quarters.

I am enjoying the good company of Captain Noble and his feathered companion, Pistol, who sees fit to change his name on every occasion.

Brother Frank seems to ferry back and forth between prison and release, his faith in Jesus never waning if one were to measure by line of Scripture quoted.

Microft continues to beg us to consider his newest thought.

Walter, I have observed, becomes more deeply enmeshed in his multiple realities view the more twelve year old Jameson he drinks.

Ned and Sydney each day are more anxious to begin their travels on solid ground, urging me to announce a day of departure. I fail to do so because, for all my reservations regarding Babel, I yet wonder why I can communicate with so few of its citizens. As much as I have launched my own defense against the madness of this place, I cannot in all honesty and justice dismiss what I find here as inferior in understanding, limited in speech, obsessed by mental chimaeras, or disciplines of discord.

His Majesty, whose counsel I have sought as if the mystery of this floating isle would be more likely to be revealed at the heart of power than elsewhere, points to the blind man who either talks differently in our language about the world than we who see it, or one day is able to see but who yet reports more than what we see. The visitor to our Isle sees what we see but at once transforms it to what he is shaped to see. You have a reason or a cause to see and thus you see, his Majesty tells me.

I have more fascination for this talk than understanding.

I cannot disengage myself from thinking that aberrations and credos, nervous impairments and barbarities do much to explain deviant views of the world. And yet, as I say, excepting for the fact that I cannot communicate with most of these Babel inhabitants, whose words I hear but can make no sense of, I must report that they show no sign of deviance of any kind. Someone's perceptions are impaired here and though I am candid in allowing that the obscuration may lie in reception and not transmission, my critical reason provides no justification for this.

His Majesty has done me the honor of speaking in private conference with me each evening after supper. I find that he is truly the sort of ruler that most rational of Greeks described.

"There is only a mere shadow on the ground below us," his Majesty began solemnly this evening "of the Divine-saturated world before the Reformation in present day embattled `fundamentalism.'"

I nodded, though I was not as yet very acquainted with this notion of "fundamentalism." His Majesty had been pursuing for the past several evenings the subject of how ways of living in this world had wielded authority and then vanished.

"History shows us," his Majesty went on, "from our present vantage point -- many battles – whether Galileo's or Copernicus's science battles, or Luther's and Bruno's religious battles, or Descartes' and Erasmus's philosophical battles – that explain a segue from an `age of belief' to the Enlightenment. However, entrenched belief in a foundational Logos is not a defender behind a wall besieged by `new thought.' Entrenchment means that it is instilled within perception and thought itself. One is reasonable within this regime of reason; one responds to the revolutionary within that same province of reason. And when the sands upon which all of this is built shift, no amount of former `reasoning' seems reasonable. The old island of thought, in short, doesn't get a chance to defend itself. One day Dante's depiction of Hell has a grip on us and the next day it's boring and the day after that it's inconceivable and then, shortly, only a *whatever* matter."

I went away that evening mulling over his Majesty's words, as was my wont, and as usual joined my companions at a favorite pub of Captain Noble. They had all, including Brother Frank, just returned from bowling, a favorite vocation of Walter's.

Walter's query brought me awake, for I had been staring into the creamy whiteness of my pint.

"I asked you whether you figured out why his Majesty can talk to anyone on the Isle," Walter said. I told him I didn't know.

"It's because of power," Brother Frank said. "He's got the power to make his voice understood all over. It's all set up so it fits his understanding. Not ours. *'I have the power to harm you" saith the Lord. Genesis 31:29.'*

"He's a shape changer," Captain Noble said. "Is what he is. His mind adapts."

"Lorenzo!" the parrot screeched.

"He wants you to call him Lorenzo this evening," the Captain told me.

49

"So if God is the ultimate power, Brother Frank," Walter said, "then we're all set up to fit his understanding?"

"Earthly power contaminates," Brother Frank said in a surly tone. "'Behold, the nations are like a drop from a bucket, and are accounted as the dust on the scales; behold, he takes up the isle like fine dust.' Isaiah 40.

At this Brother Frank clenched one fist and shook it as if he were grinding in that fist this isle of Babel into fine dust. I found the look on his face alarming.

I then wondered what linked me to Brother Frank's world? I was a man of faith but my faith did not bury my reason nor did I find need to affirm it on every occasion as Brother Frank did. He was also a man capable of blowing up his fellows in the name of a political cause. I was as far from understanding that state of mind as one could get.

And yet Brother Frank was in my communicative circle. As was Captain Noble who had spent his life steering this Isle along what he called the sea lanes of the open sky. Walter's emotions over ran his reason and were much distant from my own equanimity of temperament and cool deliberation.

I was pondering this when Ned and Sydney joined us. Sydney and Ned had become bosom friends in spite of the fact that Ned continued to assume Sydney was a man. Does anything endure if there is such bedrock misunderstanding?

I have great cause to remember my last talk with his Majesty before that most sagacious of rulers was blown to bits in his own chambers and I was put under arrest by a man, Don Rodrigo, Captain of his Majesty's Guard, who would become the nemesis of my travels.

"No one knows how new islands of seeing and knowing float in and replace the old but they suddenly do," his Majesty began on that fateful evening. "The old sloughs off like the skin of the snake. Perhaps long lasting conflicts, like festering wounds, destroy what is, while nothing is yet there to replace it. Think of the Roman Empire. Or quite by surprise the old order of seeing dries up like a dying leaf and fades away and it is as if it never existed. Or there is a persistent challenge, at first almost unrecognized, which overthrows the resident order. When we look back we can see no bridge from one to the other, from the old to the new. Perhaps we change into whatever technology makes us of. This I think is the saddest state of affairs."

At that moment, Don Rodrigo was ushered in, which was not unusual as he often appeared with some urgent business or other. On this evening he reported that Brother Frank, a privileged prisoner of his Majesty's Correctional Facility, had been apprehended in the garden below. He had been awaiting my departure, as had been pre-arranged. I had no memory of this and realize now that I should have attested to this but I did not for fear of jeopardizing Brother Frank's already limited freedom. I therefore said — and this proved fateful — that Brother Frank and I were to meet and then go on to meet mutual friends. Don Rodrigo, perhaps finely tuned over the years to detecting lies, gave me a puzzled look for if he could tell I was lying, he could not fathom a reason as to why I was lying. As it turned out, they had laid hold of Brother Frank too late for he had already set his bomb. I was in fact seated not too far from it.

"The canopy within which our talk rises," his Majesty went on when Don Rodrigo had left us. "is a nebulous, not quite graspable kind of enclosure, a framing within which we talk or not about things, decide to do or not do things. If we look closely enough we can see that the structure of power is there but it's no more than opportunistic. I am king, my dear Gulliver, but I am under this canopy within which all talk arises. Or not. Here on the floating isle we have sought and found many such canopies and have drawn them up in the hope of establishing a praiseworthy universal communication. I devote my power as King to this cause."

I was awoken first by the sound of the explosion, jumped from my bed and hastily dressed. I had a hand out reaching for the door when there was a loud knocking and then the door was battered open and I was seized by both arms and Don Rodrigo walked into the room. His expression was like none I had ever seen. He slapped me hard across the face and told me that I would pay dearly for what I had done. I professed that I knew not what had been done and he grabbed me with a gloved hand by the throat. "When one kills a king, one kills a world." Before I could respond a halter rope was placed around my neck, squeezed till my eyes popped and I was pulled out of the room.

I counted the days in my dark prison cell by my hunger. A tin plate of unknowable and unspeakable food slid under my cell door when my hunger pangs were at their worst. Every tin plate was a day. After ten days, I was brought out and put on trial. Everything about that courtroom was unbearable: the faces, angry to ferociously angry faces, and the blinding sunlight which I had not seen for days, and the sheer volume of noise that arose when I was led in – all this defeated me, my dear Reader, before my trial had begun.

"Courage sans peur!" a voice I knew screamed out and I saw then Captain Noble and the parrot in a far off row of seats with Ned, Walter, Microft next to them.

I was brought up to the Defense's table where Sydney was standing. I didn't understand.

"I can make them see your innocence," Sydney said. "And, besides, I'm a good barrister."

I listened as the case against me was presented.

I had assisted the prisoner Brother Frank in gaining entrance to his Majesty's quarters where he had planted the deadly bomb. Captain Rodrigo, whose testimony was so detailed and certain that I myself became suspicious of myself, stated that had I not given an alibi for Brother Frank's presence in his Majesty's garden, Brother Frank would have been apprehended and a thorough search ordered of his Majesty's quarters.

"Conjecture and mere speculation," Sydney objected. "The man was on privileged release. He was so because there was no fear that he would be leaving bombs about the place. No bomb search would have been conducted whether the Defendant gave a reason for Brother Franks' presence in the garden or not."

I was encouraged by this counter and hoped it scored well with the jury.

Upon further questioning Don Rodrigo said that had I not sanctioned the bomber's presence, he would have been brought immediately back to prison where he now would be. But Brother

Frank had timed the bomb so that he could make his escape. The assumption was that he had gotten off the floating Isle.

In the closing, Sydney asked the jury to consider why if I were an accomplice had I just gone to bed rather than escaped with Brother Frank? Sydney asked what reasons I could have for regicide when my own history had no connection with the floating Isle of Babel except as one who had arrived by accident, a comment which provoked the Prosecution to afterward point out that I arrived feathered and tied to a rail and so had clearly been punished for some previous crime.

While Sydney was speaking a court attendant brought me a note which I unfolded and read *"He takes up our Isle like fine dust."* Cryptic indeed.

The closing on the other side presented me as one whose words, no need to speak of reasons and actions, were comprehensible to very few on the Isle and therefore it was fruitless to consider motivation. Don Rodrigo had testified that I had on more than one occasion admitted to wanting to leave the Isle but feared expressing that desire. A man who thinks he is a prisoner may strike out at those he feels are imprisoning him, in this case, his Majesty.

The jury went into a deliberation -- a deliberation whose outcome I was never to know -- I was placed in a holding cell in the courtroom and then all the lights went out, the Isle stopped moving, began to shutter and rattle, tremble and convulse, windows shattered, everything went upside down and then like an elevator sprung from its supporting cable, plunged downward. The ceiling of my cell vanished and I found myself flying through the air, along with all manner of worldly goods that so instantaneously become debris in such catastrophes.

The Isle was no more than five meters from the ground when I took flight and had it been any higher my traveling days would have abruptly come to an end. As I lay in a field of high grass, eyes glazed, close to passing out, I saw the Isle above me jerk to a stop and spring upward as if some invisible elasticity had come into play. I then saw the Isle disappear far above and to the west of me. And perhaps, too, it was only my eyelids that had closed and thus I had made the world disappear.

Chapter III

Chapter IV

The Author finds himself in a Dark Wood.

I feared traveling during the day when I could be easily seen from above, from that floating Isle which could, I knew, espy, like a hawk, anything below and swoop down upon it instantly.

I had fallen onto a grassy plain and that night, thankfully moonlit as it was, I made my way to some hills that seemed not far away. I had with me the possessions of a prisoner: just the clothes on my back. I moved through the tall meadow fescue and the next day lay in it and slept.

The next morning, at the edge of the grass I found berries which I recognized as Autumn berry and crouched down I picked and ate like a frenzied creature, nervously looking up at the sky for any movement, nervously looking at the ground for any shadow cast from above.

When I reached the hills I moved through wooded ravines and along creek beds during the day, feasting on flowers, grasshoppers, nuts, berries, newts, frogs, and garter snakes. I vomited up more than I could keep down. Desperate, I made some attempt at creating a fire lighting spark with whatever I could find but I had no success. I tried to deceive my hunger by drinking water until I felt my stomach would burst but I could not work the rabbit's foot for real hunger cannot so easily be distracted and all that I succeeded in doing was, one morning, drinking stagnant and not spring water, with disastrous result.

I will not put you through the agonies of retching, fever, chills, diarrhea, and abdominal pains I suffered sprawled out in that rocky terrain. My fevered mind could not keep from trying to make sense of my cursed experiences on the Isle of Babel, and though some part of my awareness questioned the very sense of this fever sponsored appraisal, I could not stop it. It was as if my mind possessed a Celestial clarity which could not cease from casting its light upon whatever His Exalted High Fever could bring before it.

I should have lived happily on the Floating Island of Babel had its inhabitants but succumbed to the clarity of Reason that our Lord and Savior has gifted us. Unfortunately, this was not so and thus reason and good sense and a correct use of language ensuing from both were treated heretically and most shamefully as mere sock puppets.

Is it not preposterous to hold that humanity can share this same Earth and yet differ drastically as to what is there to be seen, even question that it is our seeing that leads to our knowing, question our own eyes and our own ears?

If I put on a pair of spectacles the lens so ground as to confuse my vision I grant then that there will be dispute as to my talk and those of a man whose vision is clear and unfiltered. Absent such distortion we must all readily acquiesce to the observations and conclusions of reason. Assertions, as those on the Isle of Babel make, that our identities are indebted not to our personal will and choice but to unfathomable conditions unobserved by us is preposterous. Even more preposterous is talk of `worldings,' that are neither commensurable nor conceivable one by the other. All this must necessarily, and my dear Reader must agree, drive a man of good sense to a quick departure.

I concluded that had I not been unjustly and scandalously accused of regicide, had I not by some turn of the wheel of Fate or the detonation of yet another bomb, been miraculously expelled like Jonah from the belly of the whale, my own departure from the Isle was called for and imminent.

Determined as I was that my rejection of all that I had heard was just and appropriate, I yet found myself neither relieved nor refreshed by my mental travels but somewhat downcast. My fevered mind had promised to bring all to clarity, and perhaps it had in some small way, but the feeling that I had failed to see and hear what was there to see and hear, that I had traveled in my own mind no further than where I had begun, would not leave me.

At the apogee of my fever, I brought darkness to perfect transparency but saw that slide, like mud in a pounding storm, into no more than a man tarred in feathers on a rail, and a man in a cell block awaiting execution.

My travels had not begun well.

How long I remained in a state between death and life I do not know but a blessed time came when I felt the sun on my face and I had the strength to stand. I found myself a staff to lean upon and I walked, in a sad state of mind but yet not defeated. After many hours of slow walking and long rests and as the sun sank I was out of the hills on the edge of a dark wood, and finding a path I mustered all the spirit I could and walked into an almost impenetrable darkness.

I realized I had lost my path but where and when? All that came to mind and would not leave me were Dante's lines: *"Midway upon the journey of our life I found myself within a forest dark for the straight forward pathway had been lost."*

For the good part of that day I wandered further in the dark wood until I came to a poster on a tree announcing at the Church of Glad Day the "Spirited Talk of Glad Day! Come and Hear the Reverend Jeremiah Prophet Evoke the Message!"

To my total delight there was a map at the bottom of the poster leading to the congregation site. I followed it with only one or two missteps and by twilight I was entering along with others a steepled church without cross or other emblem of divinity.

I took a seat in a long pew in the rear as a stocky black man in colorful vestments climbed invisible stairs leading to a pulpit. He looked very glad indeed, and I set myself to hear his talk.

"Some call me Prophet Against Empire," the Rev. Jeremiah Prophet began, his voice singing out so joyfully that I found myself, though seated in a back pew, instantly gladdened in spirit.

"I must certainly be on the `no-fly' list in many lands today, but, my friends, I fly but I have no need of airplanes. I must certainly be bound for one free flight to Guantanamo for `interrogation.' Will I be warned in time to escape imprisonment? Will the Angel of the Lord arrange my flight? I must certainly be bound for a night in jail for civil disobedience as our brother Martin went to jail for his civil disobedience."

His enthusiasm for his own plight seemed infectious, judging by the way those around me acted.

"I tell you, brothers and sisters, I am bound some day to pay for my antinomianism. Maybe I am a harmless madman, as free as anonymity and penury can make me. Everyone who opens up a sacred book rewrites it. That's a fact. Satan is the hero of most people's lives. Why do I say this, brothers and sisters? Because their sacred book has been rewritten by them to make it so. Better, they say, to be rich and rule on Earth than wait to reap rewards in a grave that shows us no rewards."

He walked my way.

"When Satan is the hero of your life you reason against your neighbor in a game where you must win and he must lose. Good is what *you* do. Evil is what *he* does. We fire our imaginations to break through the confines of Nature. Brothers and sisters, we need a miraculous jump away from all the so-called truths of our time. We need to spend our lifetime raging against them."

A loud cry went up.

"But –hearken -- most miraculously, we can see through the eye to what this world can be and like Aunt Beast and her kind we can know the world without knowing what `seeing" is."

My sudden alertness at hearing the name "Aunt Beast" caused me to wonder whether I had been fully awake up until then.

Perhaps my fever had not left me. Perhaps I had eaten porridge in the hovel of an Olympian god in disguise? Surely, Rev. Jeremiah Prophet had not said "Aunt Beast." Need I point out that this recognition was not greeted warmly by me. But once again the gladdened face of the speaker urged me to attend further.

"My brothers and sisters, I do not believe this `mortal vale' is providing us with an opportunity to work our way to Heaven.

It's providing the Looters an opportunity to loot our hearts, our minds, our souls, our cash box."

"That's right, Reverend!" the man next to me shouted.

"What is now `that which is' has been imagined by the Looters. We must imagine differently and for all living creatures."

"Who let the dogs out?" the same man screamed. Obviously a lunatic.

"Brothers and sisters, I feel bound to spread the news of the hidden divinity of all living creatures but I know that any talk today can not be liberating but only ensnared within the order of today's Caesar. Whether or not or to what degree cash or fine clothes or jeweled slippers are glorified or challenged, we have to do no less than reach beyond and outside `that which is.`"

Once again, the phrase ..."that which is" sparked a more outcries from the flock, the witnesses to the strange talk of Rev. Jeremiah, a reverend in the Church of Our Own Divinity surely.

"I am fired up today, my brothers and sisters, because I see with a fourfold vision a way out of the dark wood."

My flagging attention rekindled. Finally a way out of dark, depressing talk and the world it creates.

"...a moment of illuminated perception through which we could once again become aware of what we are. The task is not to accept a world created by the Looters but `to cast away the former things' because though the Looters' reason and science say they are real I believe they are not. They are no more than a mask concealing what is real."

"Am I an evangelist then? I am, brothers, like you, a sad bone who once knew eternity."

I saw tears in the eyes of those around me.

"My end will be bad, my brothers and sisters, because my goal is the revolutionary, apocalyptic moment when all the chains tying us to this contrivance of what the world is will fade away. Some see only what is rational as real. I despise the real that a fallen reason imposes upon my free and wandering imagination!"

There were great cries now and I joined in.

"Bring out number, weight & measure in a year of dearth" the Reverend cried and then head down, as if in silent prayer, the

Reverend stood before us for many long minutes. No one stirred or spoke.

I left the church of hether they be the hell to be glad and more than a little disappointed that a promised way out of this dark wood had detoured into an invocation by a madman. The Reverend was also quite clearly an irrationalist and doubtlessly mad in his belief that men were gods and that imagination could somehow transform reality usefully. And I was not at all disposed to make a mentor out of a man who had seen "a world in a grain of sand."

In response to a query as I made my exit as to how I enjoyed the talk, I expressed my persevering dark state of mind. My questioner surprised me by at once urging me to come with him next morning to hear a more orthodox talk, one which he promised would "pick me up by my bootstraps" and refresh my soul. In the meantime I was welcome to share his humble food and board, for a few coins. I accepted, refraining from saying "gladly" as I had now a certain allergy to the word.

The next day I went with my new friend to a huge outdoor emporium in the very center of a large field. As with the Glad Day temple there were no signs of the celestial and our sermonizer was a young man with a crown of curly hair wearing a tight jacket and sun glasses. He had a guitar slung on his back and wore some sort of device which rested on his shoulders and positioned a harp close to his mouth. He mumbled and I strained to hear him. I knew his name was The Bob because those around me were cupping their hands to their mouths and screaming "The Bob! The Bob!"

"You know there's a lot of Bible talk today," The Bob said in a cigarette cracked throaty twang, peering at us over his monumental sunglasses, though very little sun entered these woods, "and a lot of Koran talk and some Book of Mormon talk. Little bit of Gita talk. What about Christian evangelical talk? Yeah, there's always that around here. There's also some Rapture talk. I was born a Jew and I gotta tell you that when I hear this Rapture scheme, well, I'm telling you, it's a hard rain that's going fall in those end days for Jews if you follow the Rapturite book."

Here The Bob swung his guitar around, played and sang and then worked his harmonica to a soulful finish.

"There is a lot of `spirit' talk on TV and the radio," The Bob said, continuing. "If you want to lose weight, I mean really lose weight and not just go on a diet, you need to get in touch with your spiritual side. If you've been downsized, foreclosed on, gone into bankruptcy, lost your healthcare, watched your 401 plan reach the bottom, gotten toxic poisoning on the job, come back from Iraq, can't focus and can't see a doctor, got left on a roof in a flood, botoxed your left eye shut, run out of gas on the Interstate, run out of water, lost your food stamps, stocks went into the toilet, got a boner that lasts more than four hours, or maybe you can't get it up and you can't get your cholesterol down, got a reckless leg, suffering with social anxiety, can't sleep, or you sleep and snore or you got sleep apnea or you can't get Alpha sleep or your wife can't sleep because you snore, can't program your Tivo, got no friends on Facebook, lost your cellphone, had your stomach tied off or your tubes, don't like your nose and need a new one….you need to talk with a spiritual adviser, a new awakening mentor, a stadium preacher, a TV prophet, a genuine Born Again, heaven guaranteed, no money down, Bible quoting son of a gun who talks to God. You need to hear God's talk.

I mean you need to hear somebody talking *for* God."

The Bob once again played guitar, harp and sang.

"You got to admit you got some strange dudes talking for God these days," The Bob now continued. "I kind of like the idea that this world ain't just a `vale of tears' but it's already full of grace. There's no need to separate the City of God from the City of Man. The actions of men and women, mountebanks and cosmic clowns, politicians and economists, dipsomaniacs and hard shelled revivalists, historians and philosophers, low riders and out riders, saints and sinners, losers and winners, saddle bums and brave hearts, addicts and advocates, flat earth folks and cyborgians, folks on hemp, hash and peyote, folks ping ponging between bennies, layabouts and go getters, coke and Dexedrine and heroin, laudanum and Demerol included, all have to own up that 'grace is everywhere.' Once they do that, the spiritual fulfills itself in the world. I kind of like that notion."

Harmonica, crackly voice and guitar and loud applause.

"Some folks got a view that it's God's work when you open up a business, that being a entrepa-nura is a holy vocation. You know some folks think that when you flout some gizmo and advertise it till it occupies brain space and folk'll max out their credit cards to get it, that you're doing what a Divine Creator does. That makes corporations a reflection of a Divine presence and what they're doing in making a whole lot of money for themselves is like giving out sacraments. Now who would have thought corporations help you get to heaven? I had less than any idea of that."

He played a raucous riff of notes on his harp and everyone cheered.

"But you know, the world don't need any middle man, thank you. I mean if everything in the world is all good and all. Of course, a cat burglar could be here or a bad tumor or a wet fart and they're not particularly good. In fact history has a lot of folks who were here who weren't particularly good. Old Joe Stalin was here and he wasn't particularly good. You might say history ain't anything more than a list of names of folks who weren't particularly good."

"You know, if you inherit grandma's stock portfolio and a yacht and ten homes and such you don't need to worry about a whole lot of stuff that plagues the bejeezus out of folks who cut hair and lawns, sling burgers, drive trucks, work on the line, stand on their feet all day, ain't nothing more than a pair of hands doing the same routine all day and just plain work for wages. We got Alphas can't eat enough of the pie to suit them and we also happen to have some folks who want to cut the wealth pie evenly so we all get a piece."

Hurrahs went up.

I had been at first offended both by The Bob's croaking voice and by his piercing harp solos but when he swung the guitar around this time and started to play I realized he was an acquired taste.

"You're a fool if you get your religion from a song and dance man," The Bob told us. "More the fool if you think a song and dance man can cut that pie evenly for you. Or even know how it could be done without resurrecting old Mao and a passel of other history's mad men, just waiting on the right and the left. But I think I can sing us a song where something has religion and politics by the gonads...excuse me for that … has them held real tight and it ain't nothing more than a game of dice that lays a whole lot of people low and inflates with a cocky righteousness and arrogance a very few that take to hiding out or parading their egos as the conditions on the ground change."

"Well, I guess that's all I've got to say."

He drifted once again into some more song, guitar and harp, all of which was enthusiastically greeted by those around me.

I was woken up and realized The Bob had stopped playing. It was all over, sermon and noise, and when asked the anticipated question I responded in a post-nap daze that I wasn't yet sure whether or not I had made Jesus my personal saviour. I was then told that if I thought that was the question I needed to attend this evening's talk. That would settle the matter. I agreed, not at all sure what matter had to be settled. Zombie-like I returned to the field house that evening where we were all addressed by a young bald headed Asian gentleman wearing a monk's robe, who began with these words:

"A man is celebrated and has many disciples because he shows us the Way to improve our lives every day. And what is that Way? Is it The Way for all men? Listen to these words of Chuang Tzu:

`Master Tung-kuo asked Chuang Tzu, `This thing called the Way – where does it exist?'

Chuang Tzu said, `There's no place it doesn't exist.'

'Come,' said Master Tung-kuo, 'you must be more specific!'

`It is in the ant.'

`As low as that?'

`It is in the grass.'

`But that's lower still!'

`It is in the tiles and shards.'

`How can it be so low?'

`It is in the piss and dung.' (sec. 22 Chuang Tzu)

Chuang Tzu tells us that the Way is nowhere that it does not exist. The Way is everywhere. Grace is everywhere. What can we make of this? I am a curious man and I am curious to understand this.

If The Christ found grace in the human heart what need then to redeem it? I see then that The Christ did not find grace in the human heart and therefore it is not to be relied on but rather chastened. There's a burden of sin in a fallen world that cannot of itself save itself.

For some then what The Christ's way to salvation means and how it is to be achieved cannot be realized through the fallen world or by what one feels in one's heart. Here in this fallen world the Way is not everywhere; Grace is not everywhere."

Here the Monk paused and remained silent with bowed head, waiting for us to absorb, apparently, his last words.

"Piss and dung in the world and in the human heart are not Grace and are not the Way. Is Chuang Tzu wrong then? But who is to tell us who is wrong and who is right? Chuang Tzu says

`Right is not right; so is not so. If right were really right, it would differ so clearly from not right that there would be no need for argument. If so were really so, it would differ so clearly from not so that there would be no need for argument. Forget the years; forget distinctions. Leap into the boundless and make it your home!'

I am a Taoist and it is not my burden to settle an argument among Christians nor is it my place to advise you to do what your culture can make no sense of.

But you Christians rule the world I live in and you now have attached yourself to a spiritual thought that condones your extravagant materialism. You eat up all of this planet and now honor yourselves that such acts are the Way. This I will stand opposed to, though I may break."

Dear reader, I was spellbound, fascinated by the quiet nobility of this monk's words and now as he stood before us silent, ready to accept whatever abuse we would throw at him – and we did not for everyone around me was transfixed in the gaze of this young man – I felt my own despair, like an invisible hand on my shoulder, lift.

"The Way," the monk continued, "is not self-designed. It has no will nor does it adapt to anyone's will. It is not personal. It is not a relationship with Divine Authority. Your worldly success is not impervious to the Way nor is it the Way itself or a sign of the Way.

I have heard of a way which makes personal and private the Christian God/Man relationship, and it goes beyond the prophet Luther, for here a spiritual relationship can be self-designed, like a career, a stock portfolio, an addition to the home, a network of friends on a website, a wardrobe, a look, a politics. This is talk which excludes everyone but You and God. It's *Mysoul.com*."

A silent pause. You could hear the proverbial pin drop, and it didn't.

"What about other people, those neighbors The Christ wants you to love as deeply as you love yourself?

"I have heard these words: *You have to take responsibility and learn to keep yourself happy."* I think if The Christ had said these words there is no Christian belief now.

The Christ took all mankind's sins into himself and died. Everyone dumped their woes on him and he did not refuse them. I say this as a Taoist and I ask your pardon.

Christians say the Way is a path to personal salvation. Now there is re-writing personal salvation to be only what you will it to be. It is a smiley face emoticon because once you choose to have that relationship it can only be good because, once again, `grace is everywhere.' This is all very appealing to the Western mind, especially Americans, who have launched yet another nostrum of self-design, *The Secret*, to great success. `Happiness does not depend on your circumstances...It's a choice that you make.'

The Way is not a choice. The Way exists without choice. I apologize for this, for the opaqueness of this. Words are welcomed in the Western world which cannot go beyond the personal and the choosing that confirms the personal.

If you have allowed the causes which have acted without your choosing to make a poor man of you, without employment, without money for a doctor, without a mind to understand the complexities of modern life, if some tragic loss fills you with sadness, if you have been falsely accused and convicted and are now imprisoned, if you are ill because the illness resides in your genes, some darkness that fills your soul and you cannot see beyond ... if this affects your happiness, you need to make better choices.

If you have self-designed your earthly life to ruin, you have also done so for eternity. If not only the world but eternity is yours to will and choose then every rich man is doubly blessed and every poor man doubly cursed."

A silent pause, long enough for me to realize that I had slipped into the arms of Morphius and then out again.

"When the Way is no more than a man's will, there is no Way. `The Great Way is not named.' Chuan Tzu, 39. I say if men name it, it is not the Great Way. If men choose it, it is not the Great Way.

This is also a moment in which everyone in the most powerful country in the world is advised to avoid `the negative' for the sake of one's well being.

What is more negative than `fire and brimstone'? No one will burn in Hell if they choose not to. What is more negative than images of genocide and starvation in Africa? No one will be a victim of genocide if they choose not to.

No one will starve if they choose not to. If you look at the people of China and India, only look into the faces of those fortune has blessed. Do not look into the faces of the suffering.

If The Christ gave no privileged place to the rich and powerful, we do now.

Jesus is not the First Socialist calling upon you to work for the good of others and renounce worldly goods. The Jesus I see now in the West wants you to be a Winner and to feel good about it. `He created you to live abundantly.' 95 Americans who are 4% of the world's population and consume 40% of its resources do this – live abundantly.

You can wish everything and take everything.

This is not the Tao.

Salvation and eating up the whole world are not the same thing. You now can not only will and the world will reward you but you can choose to see 'grace everywhere' and reward yourself with salvation.

This talk is most harmful. I apologize for saying this in this way."

The young Monk now went on his knees, head bowed. The sight of him made me feel very guilty indeed.

"It is not so easy to put the whole world aside and live only in your own personal choosing. What do you say then of those lives broken on the world's wheel?

I do not think the sick, the poor, the handicapped, the depressed, the grieving, the war torn, the victims, the exploited....all these and more have failed to choose to Win, to be happy, to be smiley faced.

What does a man do who thinks here the Way is corrupted?

He speaks here.

Plato, Marcus Aurelius, Jesus, Buddha, Mohammed, Lao Tsu, Chuang Tzu --- all of Western and Eastern talk on moral knowing -- none said that conscience comes into play when 'you do something that is not beneficial or something that will get you into trouble.'

Here the Way is infected. You feel it in those words that retell in a terrible way the story of moral conscience. In this talk the blind way of profit joins with the blindness of personal choice as the Way. Because this is now talk of what is happiness and what is holy, I am for silence.

I end with Chuang Tzu and humbly beg your pardon for where my curiousity and fascination have taken me.

'When the yin and yang go awry, then heaven and earth see astounding sights. Then we hear the crash and roll of thunder, and fire comes in the midst of rain and burns up the great pagoda tree. Delight and sorrow are there to trap man on either side so that he has no escape. Fearful and trembling, he can reach no completion. His mind is as though trussed and suspended between heaven and earth, bewildered and lost in delusion. Profit and loss rub against each other and light the countless fires that burn up the inner harmony of the mass of men. The moon cannot put out the fire, so that in time all is consumed and the Way comes to an end.' 132

Need I say that when this monk left the podium, he left us all in a profound silence. My mind indeed was suspended between bewilderment and delusion but I was not at all prepared to leave off my belief that a Celestial Entity can only speak to us through our own human reason and that any talk of relaying or interpreting Celestial talk was no more than chicanery. Therefore, it was not my practice to heed evangelicals, whether they be the hell and brimstone variety or the happy face variety.

I am bewildered by the Monk's talk of a mystical way that rational discourse can not reveal. As I listened, I was moved but it is difficult for me to believe that the meaning of all things is inexpressible, that paradox is what the world puts before us, and that impenetrable obfuscation waits for us at the end of the road of human understanding.

I suggest that if the unreachable Way the Monk speaks of comes to a dire end as he warns, its inscrutable distance from human reason may be a cause. Perhaps Aunt Beast would find the Way intelligible but that makes little difference to me as I find Aunt Beast equally inscrutable.

Unfortunately, my travels thus far into strange, inhospitable, perverse and irrational realms of talk, such as talk of the Way, had so assailed my reason that uncertainty now shadowed my mind. I am mindful of Montaigne's warning that we can not venture too far from our native notions of truth and reason and so inevitably judge whatever differences we encounter as irrational and false. If I believed this was the case, I would spare myself the vicissitudes of travel and remain in my own bed.

I spent yet another night in this strange dark wood community and then guided by a map, I made my way out the next morning, intent on traveling to more real and rational domains of talk.

Chapter V

The Author's dangerous voyages into strange worlds of talk.

Once outside the dark woods I followed an every widening stream till it poured into a huge body of water where I took passage the very next morning on an outgoing vessel and thus remained at sea until we reached the last port of call, some three weeks at sea and ample time for me to replenish my natural reserves of pluck and determination. But it was good to get back on land. I then took to the rails, not as a Jack London but as a respectable passenger.

I was at the train station surveying times and destinations when I overhead talk of a murder trial that was beginning that very week in a town close by.

My curiosity was piqued for what affords us more fascinating talk than murder trials where the accused, whether in actuality guilty or innocent, must allow the talk of his advocate to seal his fate?

The prosecution must drive its own talk toward absolute conviction on the part of a jury that everything said by the defense is spurious, concocted only to make a small hole in that wall of certainty the prosecution's words have built. Selected observations are woven into facts which are woven into a tale of evidence and that evidence is further woven into a tale of innocence or guilt. It is nothing but talk and the Accused's life hangs on a rope of words.

I duly bought a train ticket and arrived that afternoon in a town called *Clearview*.

Chapter V

I was seated next morning several rows behind the Defense and, given my first opportunity to examine the Accused, discovered to my utter amazement that it was Sal, Mrs. Bombers' Boarding House Sal, who was the accused murderer. At the same time that I made this discovery, Betty Bombers had discovered my presence in the courtroom and now had both arms wrapped around my neck as if I were a long lost uncle. Over her shoulder I saw Sal turn slightly and give me that sly smile and wink as if he and I were complicit in some private understanding of the universe or more particularly his crime.

I followed Betty out of the courtroom, noting that she had, rear wise, put on some weight. When we were seated out in the hallway I noted that Betty bulged a trifle up front. She saw my look and told me she was pregnant. Tears flowed more steadily now and I found myself quite uncomfortable to say the least. I was quite amazed at her transformation from someone who had responded to life with a "whatever" attitude to this pregnant, fully devoted to her man, fully engaged young woman.

In the next five minutes Betty told me how she had run off with Sal and what grandiose plans they had in some far off fantasy land. But raw reality had intruded when they arrived in *Clearview* and Sal was arrested almost immediately.

The Prosecution accused Sal of being the multiple murderer, the serial killer who had been sought for three and a half years although there had been no direct witnesses to any of the murders, nor was there, remarkably, any physical evidence, including DNA. The Prosecution was making its case solely on a precise match between Sal and the protagonist in a lurid German novel.

I kid you not.

A behavioral analysis team had put together a profile of the murderer before they discovered a well-worn copy of the novel in the possession of a suspect. They had examined it and found the murderer in that novel was the murderer they were seeking. The real world serial killer had not merely adopted the methods of the fictional murderer but had become him in every way. The suspect had then been arrested and was now, as the Accused – Sal --

standing trial for murder. The Prosecution had connected events in Sal's life with those of the fictional murderer.

I kid you not.

Betty said she hadn't read the novel. She didn't read what she referred to as "off-line" but she knew in her heart that there was nothing about Sal that was fictional. I had to concur, silently, to this as Sal indeed was the very essence of raw reality.

Betty begged me to step forward as a character witness, an eventuality I found frightening. I protested that while I did not believe that similarities between Sal and a serial murderer would lead to Sal's conviction and that surely a jury of *Clearview* citizens would see the absurdity of the Prosecution's case, I did not feel that I could offer any deep analysis of Sal's character or in any way attach it to an incorruptible goodness.

None of this meant anything to Betty who continued to implore me and, my dear Reader, I finally acquiesced, hoping that as the trial proceeded I would find the tenor of my testimony.

The first person the Prosecution, a M. Dent, a fat faced man wearing a tiny powdered wig atop his head, called to the stand was the State Profiler, M. Armand, who would examine closely the life of the fictional hero, thereby setting up a subsequent correspondence with the Accused. I was, as they say, all ears. M. Armand testified that the peculiar psychopathology of the accused had been textbook described and also given its most exact delineation in several works of fiction. He went on making this case as the Prosecutor questioned him

"Does a man such as this," the Prosecutor asked, not looking at the State Profiler but at Sal who was looking at the fingernails of his right hand, "possess the appetites you describe in the manner of a normal man, a man of social conscience, a man who can feel guilt?"

"Not in my professional opinion. What give significance to the Accused's world are only objects that arouse his sexual passions, and women are no more than objects. As `justice, conscience, God, joy, responsibility, humility, gratitude, etc.' have no qualities that appeal to his gross sensuality, he does not know them.   He has no urge to acknowledge what has no existence for him. He is, however, keen on defining and classifying what he considers the conquests of his genius."

"And so he is something of a collector of conquests who are, in short, his victims?"

"Yes, most certainly."

"I object," Sal's barrister roared. "Pure conjecture and supposition. This is a unique case. There is no precedent. . ."

"Overruled," the judge said, banging his gavel. "The witness may answer."

"Collectors require full possession," M. Armand told us. "I think M. Nozar found it necessary to kill in order to take full possession of his victim. It was a fulfillment of his orgasm."

"Who's M. Nozar?" I whispered to Betty.

Sal's barrister, M. Piombino, pursued an interesting line of questioning of the State Profiler.

"Would you say, M. Armand, that your assumption that the villain of a novel reveals the psychology of my client, a real man on trial for his life, is less than scientific, is in fact outrageously nonsensical and unprofessional?"

"It would if I had based my conclusions solely on that work. But a thorough psychological profiling of the accused has confirmed what the novel revealed."

"Your honor I would like to read from M. Armand's conclusions. `The serial nature as well as the heinous desecration of the bodies points to the terrorist nature of these crimes and defines the perpetrator as a perpetrator of terrorism first and murderer second.' Why, M. Armand were you making this effort to introduce the words "terrorism" and "terrorist" in your report? Could it be that you were tailoring your report to my client's name – Saladin Nozar – and the fact that he is Iraqi by birth?"

"I object, your honor," the Prosecutor bellowed. "The Defense is attempting to introduce an unsubstantiated prejudice."

"Sustained. The jury will ignore this line of questioning. M. Piombino you will restrict yourself to the facts at hand."

"Let me then question your comparison of the Accused to a shark," M. Piombino said to M. Armand. "

"M. Nozar's extreme deviance has created a psychopathology in which diabolical acts produce no affective response. Like a shark he collects whatever he is drawn to and like a shark there is no remorse because there is no conscience. M. Nozar is a veritable monster."

That drew every eye in the courtroom to Sal who, fair to say, had the blase demeanor of a man unimpressed by M. Armand's depiction of him as a monster. If body language told me anything it told me that Sal was bored.

The court was adjourned until 10 AM next morning. When the courtroom had cleared Betty introduced me to Sal's barrister, M. Piombino, and told him that I would be a character witness who could clearly show the jury that Sal's heart was in the right place. At this, I must have revealed more than a little of my own consternation for M. Piombino requested a private talk with me.

We went off to the Merchant Inn and Pub where Betty was staying and M. Piombino, who asked me to call him Bino, and I went to the bar while Betty went up to her room to collect herself, as the saying goes.

I had not started on my second pint but had already told Bino the complete history of my acquaintance with Sal.

He admitted that it didn't amount to much. He concluded that I had concluded that Sal was a man who was more led by his penis than his brain. I told him that I believed Sal had been a paramour of Betty's mother, Mrs. Bombers, as well as a Mrs. Montrose, a self-declared whorehouse madam. I had not observed any particular viciousness in Sal and wondered if his single minded devotion to amatory conquest indicated a lover not a murderer?

Bino wiped some beer foam from his mustache and told me that the fact that Sal was very much like a fictional murderer who had at that moment captured the fearful fascination of many in *Clearview*, including, unfortunately, all members of the jury made any rational defense very difficult.

The next day I was called to the stand and after answering Bino's questions as to my own assessment of Sal's character, I faced M. Dent, whose tiny wig was askew and therefore my sole focus.

What M. Dent extracted from me was that Sal was healthy and young but on the dole, had a penchant for the ladies, had sexual relations with a mother and a daughter, and expressed a philosophical belief that all humans were no more than dogs, and had a fondness for referring to his genitalia when speaking to women.

As I stepped down I could see Betty biting her lower lip and the tears streaming down her cheeks. I prayed to our Celestial Entity that she could at that moment regain her `whatever' attitude and return to self-concern. I find self-absorption more healthful than absorption in one such as Sal.

And then the Prosecution made its closing argument.

"He is his own reign of terror," M. Dent told the jury, "as he murders without conscience merely to fulfill his dream of self-realization: to bring into his own mad world the lives of those who can only give themselves to him completely by being murdered by him."

For his part, Bino ended very cleverly, casting doubt once again on a case that would have no legs in a world that was not deceived by fictional fantasies.

"My client has sex with living women and goes on from one living woman to another. He has not murdered his young wife, Betty Nozar, but has impregnated her and both of them would now be looking forward blissfully to the birth of their child had not my client been arrested and put on trial for acts that nothing in his own personal history would lead us to believe he is capable of."

Dramatic pause.

"Unless....unless we fill our heads with a fantastical description of a fictional monster we have convinced ourselves is not only our murderer but that murderer is indeed my client. I beg the jury to regain their senses and allow my client to return to his life, a normal life like yours and mine."

That night the barristers of my own mind ran their deliberations before me: Sal would surely be found innocent – instantly amended as exonerated – in the absence of any hard evidence. The evidence wasn't even circumstantial but only analogous and the analogy itself was grounded in fiction. No one could understand the monstrous nature of the murders, so beyond and outside normal conceivability. The retreat then to fiction where a type and a psychology that could be made to fit are found. Enter Sal. He can be made to fit; he is a stranger. He can be made to fit the profile of the type they are now seeking. It's all rather like forcing a few puzzle pieces into places they don't belong. After awhile, the fact that they don't fit becomes obvious. Thus, after some deliberation, the jury will see they are being asked to fit Sal into something where he doesn't fit.

My opposing barrister doomed Sal for the simple reason that everyone in *Clearview* imagined the crimes in a certain way, the murderer in a certain way, and imagined Sal as that murderer. For them to discard all this, they would have to discard their seeing and their thinking, their capacity to understand and to act. They would have to doubt themselves on a very scary level. And they wouldn't do that. They wouldn't leave themselves skeptics of their own minds.

I did not remain in *Clearview* very long after Sal's execution, only long enough to arrange for Betty's return to Mrs. Bombers.

The talk of the fictional villain had most assuredly sealed the fate of poor Sal, a man who had indeed declared that we all lived like dogs, and I suppose, he died like a dog, crouched below the guillotine. I was certain only that the people of *Clearview* did not have a clear view of anything. Whether or not others elsewhere did, I might soon discover. Or not.

Some poor fools were not the captains of their ships nor could they chart the seas upon which they sailed. The fault lay in their senses which had drifted so far from normalcy that their reason was askew. And yet it seemed it mattered little how accurate your charts were or how well you kept your course if the heavens tilted against you or you found yourself adrift in an imagination not your own.

I spoke with Sal just two days before his execution and though I dreaded this Death Row meeting, fearing that Sal would fall apart and I would just sit there incapable of any solace, I found the same Sal that I had known at Mrs. Bombers' boarding house.

Chapter V

He hadn't done the murders, he said. Not in his line. He liked the ladies lively, not dead. And he had no fear of meeting his Maker but assured me he'd stick up for some part of the life he had lived, though he'd bend a knee and ask for pardon for the other part.

The thought I had when I left him was that I had misjudged him, that he was not simply an incorrigible ne'er do well who lived in the hope of getting by with as little effort as possible, at least his own effort.

It was only when I saw Betty at the prison gates, eyes still full of tears, and she asked me if Sal was worried about her that I realized Sal hadn't mentioned her. I told her that Sal made me promise that I would pay for her return home and that I would see to it that she received proper care during her pregnancy.

I made all of this up because I was crushed by the utter injustice of Sal's trial and execution and I suppose I needed some spark of goodness to redress and counter all of it. In this fashion I did a good deed as much for myself as for Betty, which may inevitably always be the case.

That very day I bought a train ticket that would take me to the furthest outpost of this land where I hoped to escape what I had witnessed in *Clearview*.

Do you know how it is when you are so intently set in one direction and hoping to avoid any detour or any return to what you are running from that you invariably run into your Nemesis, namely, you are forced to face and listen to what you despise?

Well, on that train I had the misfortune, after some hours alone in my compartment, of looking up and seeing my former headmaster, Rev. Base, whom we all called Rev. Starbase because of his devotion to Other Worlds, what I remember the Reverend calling "worlds not made by our Creator."

After a jubilant greeting, forged on my part, the Reverend proceeded to question me on the last twenty years of my life, which I was loathe to do but succeeded in abstracting to about three minutes of talk, omitting of course tar, feathers, rail, regicide, and criminal pursuit.

The Reverend was not satisfied and after peering closely into my eyes demanded to know what troubled me. God only knows why I decanted like an old wine the full volume of my recent perturbations.

Upon conclusion, the Reverend begged for a few minutes introspection, closed his eyes and after awhile began to snore. When he awoke he told me that my only hope was to go deeper into my illness. Our talk now, the Reverend told me, his aged, watery eyes blinking, is held within the Devil's fist and the Devil wants war and gold and gain and domination and torture and great fear and deceit and trembling and an injustice and predation across the land and enslavement and selfish indifference.

He paused in this litany to blow his nose and he resumed by asking me where he was. Selfish indifference I said.

I suggested we should all perhaps go to another planet and start over again. He responded as if I had pronounced the Abracadabra of the inner life of things. He told me that he was on his way to a remote Shangri-la that he had reason to believe had been founded by an alien race of beings. Would I join him in his quest? I at once agreed, though I surely did not look forward to the companionship of the Rev. Starbase.

The Reverend then proceeded to tell me what he knew of the place to which we were going.

We shall most certainly find this region very hot and humid, the Reverend told me. The name we humans give to it is *Thermal* although the aliens living here have never experienced any thing other than this heat and humidity and therefore call their domain simply *Uma*. There is no seasonal dualism, no Winter/Summer and thus without the notion of Fall or Winter cold, the *Umates* have no sense of summer heat. Climate is unicameral, unidimensional – summer and its heat are not considered in reference to other seasons but only self-referentially.

I interrupted the Rev. Starbase and told him there was no need to belabor the point. He nodded.

"Not just seasons are conflated in this village," he told me, like someone about to pull a rabbit from his sleeve. "The people you will find here are both male and female. They are androgynous until they go into a sexual phase in which they then for a brief period become either male or female."

He let that sink in, confident now that he wasn't boring me.

"There is a return to the androgynous state and the cycle continues. These may be descendants of the original aliens or they may be a hybridized alien/human mix. I won't know until I have an opportunity to examine them."

At that he closed his eyes and was soon snoring.

It has been a month since I arrived in *Thermal*, a furnace hot place so humid that you could swipe a cup across the air in front of you, drop a tea bag in and tea is served. I am about to depart on the morrow.

The Reverend Starbase is no longer with me as he, upon arrival, immediately set out into thick jungle to uncover the legendary starship which supposedly brought the aliens to this spot.

I have not, however, been without comrades as I have found both Ned Parsall and Sydney Noble in *Thermal.* Sydney has come to find what she calls her origin, convinced that her own intersex being is somehow connected with interplanetary space travelers. Ned has followed her here out of loyalty to his friend, though he readily admits that he has remained stunned by Sydney's revelation that she is neither a "he" or a "she" but both at once.

Since arriving in Thermal, Sydney has copied the cyclical sexuality of the locals and has therefore given up a rather ambiguous appearance and now, depending on the time of month, adopts a decidedly male or female persona. The day Ned brought me to see her she was a very alluring young lady and I could see that Ned was both bewildered and in awe. I suspect he chose to remain in *Thermal* and in this perplexing state because of the utter fascination with which it filled him.

As I did myself. I had not realized that Sydney was the offspring of the good Captain Noble but Sydney had grown to believe that she was an orphan Captain Noble had taken up, perhaps in this very region.

I was curious as to what transpired on the floating Isle after my ignoble and sudden departure. It was believed that I was dead, having fallen to my death, but Don Rodrigo had sworn to turn me up, either dead or alive. Brother Frank, my supposed accomplice, had disappeared but there was a huge reward on his head as well as my own. Both Sydney and Ned affirmed their faith in my absolute innocence and for this I was extremely grateful, yet fully aware now that actual innocence or guilt had to await the temper of the times and the disposition of a presiding jury as well as the popularity of pulp fiction.

I do not mean to imply that the relationship between Ned and Sydney was in any way smooth sailing. There was much to deal with and very little instruction. For instance, Ned was in a continuous state of male sexual readiness, which he found unremarkable, as this was a given among the human race. Sydney, on the other hand, could only meet Ned's readiness when she had cycled into a female. Adopting the ways of the local *Umates*, Sydney put herself totally into whatever was her sex at that moment. When she shifted out of her female self and into her male self she became totally male. There was therefore no time in which she was intersex. She was now always one or the other. You can easily discern, dear Reader, what problems this created for a classic boy meets girl love affair. When Sydney was fully male, he had a penchant for bar wenches, especially one who was quite obviously taken with Ned. When the female rose in Sydney, she was enraptured by Ned and jealous of any rivals, especially the bar wench she had, the month before, pursued.

I was discovering that a very simple swerve in "that-which-is" can create monumental changes. And just as I cannot help feeling drained by the heat of this place though the natives do not comprehend and therefore do not feel what heat is, I cannot, for the life of me, extend to Sydney the reality of his/her own ambisexuality. Division and dualism permeate my world and affect all basic aspects of the "that-which-is" of this infernal *Thermal*.

But I have after a long month here come to understand much, although my very understanding is under attack.

First of all, *Thermal* is not a world of "either/or" but "both/and." And this difference, which we would perhaps initially confine to romance and breeding, confounds my capacity to interpret and understand. It is so great a shift into a mindset I cannot enter that I find myself acting continuously against my own best interest. On more than one occasion my failure to know and respond to this alien world I am in has led to great confusion. Let me explain.

I am talking past the natives here although we share the same language and the same geography. What matters is not *where* we are which is obviously the same place at the same time but *how* we are here. Certainly there is a difference regarding the native response to the heat and my response. Or their response to their sexual shifting and my response. I certainly have difficulty with all this. But *Thermal* is in no way presenting what I shall call, "objective conditions" that affect us all equally. The way Ned and I are here in *Thermal* is from within the heartland of our own world where hot is understood as hot and very hot is understood as very hot, where male is understood as male and female is understood as female.

I do not mean to become frenzied but the question – and it is an astoundingly vital question -- is whether or not Ned or I can do anything more than display and repeat the absolute inappropriateness, call it incommensurability, of our own way of being who we are and seeing what there is to be seen. We are here but we can never be here.

Ned is admittedly in a much tougher spot than myself because his task is to present his love for Sydney in such a way that she, constituted differently, can understand. At the same time, he has to love what he cannot understand and indeed love what does much to corrupt his notion of what love is. His talk has to bridge the Grand Canyon between his identity and her difference. And for this, Ned in my view seems unprepared, unsuited, incapable. How do I know this? Because I remain unprepared, unsuited and incapable.

For her part, Sydney is convinced she has discovered a secret tactic by which people in one world can communicate with people in another world. I find this mystical at best, rather like the notion of Ch'i in Chinese thought, and clearly absurd, rather like the Star Wars notion of "The Force." Of course were there some tactics by which we could bridge differences, by which our understanding could mesh with the understanding of others and therefore our talk would serve some purpose, I would be a devout follower.

But if such a tactic existed, brought to this planet by visitors from another planet, I failed utterly to find it and could not recognize its existence in others. I did not reject anything I found in Thermal as a rational choice but rather I couldn't do anything but reject what lay outside my rational reckoning.

Do I make myself clear? How Sydney came to comprehend within a *Thermal* way of comprehension, I cannot say. Perhaps she was a descendant of the ancient aliens who had dropped from the sky. Perhaps, too, she had found here what she had come to find: a way to be what she was. What is clear to me is that without some mystical transformation I will remain unknowing and unaware of what this place called *Thermal* is in itself.

I don't know if this will be Ned's plight or whether he will both re-define what love is and find that love with Sydney. I remain convinced that dealing with someone who could at different times be a different sex would indeed confound a normal human relationship, although I am discovering in my travels that that notion is itself confounding.

I ran into Reverend Starbase at the rail head. He had failed to find the proto-starship, had contracted a bit of malaria, and had run out of Church funds. He was thus on his way home. I told him that I had also given up and had decided such was the wise course.

He disputed this vehemently and proceeded to go into a long lecture reminiscent of my prep school days. Over the next hour, he wandered off down a variety of pathways, none of which I could make much sense of, except to note that while he seemed to think other realities were not freakish and rare but were there to be found if we went in search, especially in the realms of imagination, and that there was some merit in doing so, something akin to Christian salvation, I, he affirmed, seemed to have little capacity to entertain much beyond my own resident beliefs and reasons.

I told him I was guilty and that he had me dead to rights, and then pulling a flask of good Irish whiskey out of my pocket I tempted the good Reverend to join me in a toast to the beauties of unknown worlds and the tragedies of the known.

I can report truly that I made my adieu to the good Reverend Starbase more honestly than I had made my greetings. But the world and its talk called to me and I had not given up my quest to find places where my understanding would benefit and not, as thus far, be assailed as confined within the worst proclivities of my own time and country. I was not so much troubled by my failure to recognize what lay outside my own rational order as I was by the absolute confounding of my natural instincts, civilized sensibilities and sensible valuation of whatever crossed my path.

I was, in short, not at all prepared to turn my world upside down and unravel my own image, convinced as I was that it was an image that reflected, though humbly, the rationality of Celestial Being. I also concluded that our human susceptibility to absurd and outrageous fantasies, to the illogic of our own imaginations, led to results I had so recently observed in the trial and execution of poor Sal.

I went on until the rail terminus and there, after two days' seeking, signed aboard a ship bound across the Sargasso Sea to the West Indies. But as I am destined -- and I do not believe in destiny -- to tragedy, my ship ran into foul weather, I was thrown overboard and when rescued, found myself in hospital with a concussion, faint memory, and nervous collapse.

Chapter VI

The Author makes a miraculous recovery and sets out to find less talk.

How I was able to recollect who I was and where I was from given my fevered state of mind, I cannot say, but I did eventually find myself in my own bed, until such time as my doctor thought it best that I be sent to an Asylum for the care and treatment that could not be afforded me at home.

I was at once placed on a drug regimen and monitored daily for my reactions.

The first drug trial sent me into a deep melancholia, the next made me so giddy and ecstatic I could not sleep, the next produced the opposite effect and I became catatonic, the next brought down a curtain of suspicion that extended to the food and water I was given, the next brought on sudden eruptions of nonsense talk and wild profanity, and finally after many weeks I found that pharmaceutical that allowed me to be my old self but without any enthusiasm for talk.

I, however, retained my nomadic wanderlust and, taking a good supply of my drug with me, decided to seek out those places in the world where talk had been given up, or at least, distrusted and deflated to a degree that allowed an enjoyment of the world without blather.

I took passage on the first ship out of my home port and was instantaneously invigorated by the salt air which I took above deck at every opportunity in calm seas and when the noise below deck grew offensive.

I did not seek talk but yet it found me one day as I leaned at the port side, gazing into the moving face of the waters. "*The dragon-green, the luminous, the dark, the serpent-haunted sea*" were lines that came to mind as I gazed out. The mind cannot but project its mood upon the waters.

A gypsy woman named Maleva spoke to me. When we docked, I followed her to the nearest village called *Yarbles.*It was an impoverished and tawdry village that we traveled to by foot, arriving late at night. But we did not tarry in the village but kept on. How Maleva could find her way on a moonless night I had no idea but surmised that somehow she either knew the path ahead the way she had known my mind or she had an owl's vision.

I saw a faint light ahead and soon heard soft sounds of human voices. She called out before entering the encampment and then a whistle summoned us ahead. It was a small enclosure formed by three wagons and though I could see no horses I could smell them. There was a fire and we were welcomed with food and drink. The gypsy woman spoke to her confreres in their own language and judging by the glances in my direction I was the subject of the conversation.

I didn't much like the attention and truthfully I didn't much like the looks of this group and thought I'd take my leave at dawn. I was given a blanket and directed to the underneath of a wagon where I stretched out and, being fatigued by our long walk, fell asleep before I could properly question myself as to what I was doing there.

When I woke in the morning I was alone with no wagon above my head, no wagons to be seen, and no gypsies either. I got to my feet and realized at once that my wallet was gone. Cursing my own stupidity, I set off in what I thought was the direction of the village we had passed through the night before.

It was noon by the time I found my way to that village and I entered what I took to be the only inn. I was both hungry and thirsty and after explaining my plight to the publican received only a curt shake of his head. "Thems that pays, eats and drinks," he told me. I promised a two fold payment once I could connect with my bank but he remained unmoved.

I turned to leave when a young man who had the look of an able bodied seaman touched my arm and with a noticeable stutter invited me to join him. I accepted most gratefully. His name was Billy. I reiterated my promise to repay but Billy waved that off. He was in his words repaying kindnesses he had been treated to in his life. I nodded and inwardly dear Reader thanked the Heavens for Billy's presence at that moment in my travels.

I related my adventures with the gypsy woman, remarking that had I lost my faith in people at the same time as I had lost my faith in their talk, I would not have been so easily tricked. But my new friend protested had he lost faith in people we would not be enjoying ourselves so sociably at that moment. I heartily agreed and we clicked glasses yet again.

It was then that a thin man wearing a tweed jacket sized for a man with shorter arms who had been lurking on the edge of our conviviality, neither smiling as one who sees himself apart yet part, nor unsmiling as if in some manner of reproof, came forward and introduced himself as Chick Wagstaff, a salesman of sundry goods traveling through.

He had overheard what I had said about my loss of faith in talk and announced to us that any and all assaults on anything piqued his curiousity. If I wished to launch a double barreled assault on conversation he was up for it. If I wanted to go further and storm the Bastille of bullshit, he was a ready volunteer. If I wanted to line every lying salesman, politician, lawyer and journalist against a wall and shoot'em down like dogs, Chick would be at my side.

Billy managed to say that he didn't think such extremes were called for and that a little moderation would go a long way. Chick promptly bought us a round of beers on that sentiment. I told them I saw no reason why I shouldn't hear some more talk in preparation for my total abstinence from the same. Before you give up drinking, Chick told us, you always have a drink to mark the occasion. I acquiesced and we adjourned to a cozy spot near a hard coal fire in the corner of the pub.

"A man does lose faith listening to human palaver," Chick began, in a very breezy style. "The religious fundamentalist turns to The Good Book where the Word of God is a Green Zone liars can't reach and in time corrupt. But who has `The' Good Book and who ain't got it, whose Word and whose God trumps, is a sharp spur to some nasty talk in the world."

"No…nothing is settled," Billy stuttered, "when you quote *your* Word. It merely incites *their* Wo…wo…word."

"And bingo!" Chick said, slapping his hands, "you get the Thirty Year War. But wait, that's history. More to come, boys, more to come."

At that moment our conversational turn caught the attention of some young chaps who had come into the pub a short time before and were drinking pints. They were oddly dressed and the tallest who had one eye encircled with a tattooed star and who wore a derby hat and was carrying a parasol approached and introduced himself as Alec and pointed to his companions whom he called his "drooogs: Rick, Ollie and Finn. Alec was a big fan of Harpo Marx. We invited Alec and his Drooogs to join us.

"Take a good dose of rapid fire, zany playfulness with the old Queen's English," Alec told us, as soon as he had sat down. "Like this: `*You're an abject figure, Chicolini.'* `*I abject,'*, fester in some satirical barbs of the satirical sort, add some massive hemorrhaging of your overstuffed pomposity sort, with a coup de grace of manic irreverence of the manic and irreverent sort that don't spare the sacred more than your profane and you get the weightless free fall of your Marx Brothers' movie."

"Shagged and fagged and fashed," Finn told us but I had no idea of what he had just told us.

This garble was picked up by Rick, almost as outlandishly dressed as Alec.

"My dear citizen Babbitt," Alec said, looking at Chick, "A lot of ultrasonic violence is what it is. Everything is so rapidly and with unseemly outrage dismantled that nothing is left of the burgher world –and let burghers go to burghers ad infinitum and amen, lads -- no life preserver, to hold onto. Any response to the question what was it about—which is the first question a burgher asks -- would automatically neglect the non-stop hilarious shambles the brothers have made of this holy Roman empire. And who goes there to stumble on the absence of meaning? Stand and identify yourself!"

Alec stood up and shouted across the room and some at the bar turned.

"In brief," a quieter Alec now said, "you could be too uptight to acknowledge a genius in the absence of sense. Your sweat glands could be tied to your laugh chords and on up to your brain where the Burgher God rules. To take the Marx Brothers seriously, if that word can be used, would make you immediately an easy mark for devilish assault. The Marx Brothers were out further than anyone wanted to go. Further, Father."

"The old in and out of the gulliver," Finn told me, pointing to his drink which he called diet plus.

"Ultimate ultrasonic violence against sense," Alex added.

Billy had opened his mouth to say something when Alec and his Drooogs jumped up and holding their pints high chanted:

"Hail! Hail! Freedonia!"

Alec sat down, pulled out a deck of cards which he showed Chick:

"Never mind that. Take a card."

"It's not all nonsense, kid," Chick said taking a card. "I mean you show that kind of irreverence only after you think there's nothing worth respecting."

I agreed with this.

"Or si...si...silence," Billy said, nodding.

"Hello, I must be going," Alec quipped.

"We need to drink more," Chick said, motioning to the uncharitable publican for another round.

"When one stops believing in a Celestial Entity," I pointed out, my thinking here facilitated by the drink, "one does not go out and celebrate or harangue the minister with witticisms."

Alec stared at me.

"Listening to you hurts the old gulliver," he told me, "And that may be why your name's Gulliver."

Rick, Ollie and Finn had gone out to get some air, which is what they said, and when they returned they had a slim girl from the circus with them – the Flying Molly Furkey– a trapeze artist.

She seemed very amused by Alec and his Drooogs.

"Do you catch what they're saying?" she asked me after awhile.

"I believe they create their own patois," I told her. "And also, perhaps, a world in which to use it."

Alec held out a gloved hand – he wore but one glove – to Molly.

"As soon as I viddied you it flashed in my gulliver to have you straight way on the floor with a bit of the old in and out."

"I don't touch ground much," Flying Molly told him. "Too much trash on the ground."

"Ground to *Yarbles*," Alec told her. "Shows what a shambles government can make of individual life. Me Drooogs and I have only a night time release of our pent up energies, mostly violent, angry, and cruel. Oh, the laughs and lashings of the old ultrasonic violent!"

"Cockles and mussels alive alive O!" his Drooog companions sang out.

Flying Molly couldn't help but laugh and I must confess I found these odd companions quite amusing, though somewhat frightening.

"I don't understand a word you say," Flying Molly told Alec, who immediately sat back and put a very sober look on his face.

"Queen's English," he announced. "Harken closely."

"One supposes that after Magot Hatchet noodigates society for the zillionith time to Western Trivialization, Drooogs like us are free to drop pathology for EntrapManureship. We can drop our own linguash franks and learn corporate sleak. Goobye ye old random mayhem that takes a bloke to the Chateau Deaf, we can direct our protoplasm toward `glowing a biznest' without any fear of the Bobbiesox. But the Guzzlemint wants to get hold of us and with some slick neo-anderole modifidefactuation teckaniks run the old Ass Salt right out of the ole brain pan and then, using the same niks, return us to bloody`ultrasonicviolence.'"

"In a "free" world," I said, and there was a pause in all conversation in our little nook and all eyes were one me, "In a free world, talk will naturally possess a moral dimension. There will be no need to condition someone like Alec out of `ultrasonic violence' into normal behavior. There is then no need not to talk because talk itself is an expression of free will in a free society. In a free society people freely talk. I've only withheld my faith in talk because I have thus far in my travels failed to find such a liberating society."

"Me and me Drooogs freely choose ultrasonic violence," Alec retorted angrily. "And we choose our own talk. You can get that in your gulliver, right Gulliver?"

I am not easily intimidated but I could tell by the way Alec twirled his parasol that he used it as a weapon. Billy felt no fear but had his say.

"If ….if…Alec and his dro..Drooogs talk a talk that doesn't talk to us, it's not their choice to do so. For them to be reclaimed the whole society has to be re- re -….."

"Refrigerated," Ollie said.

Exactly," I said, mustering some courage to speak. "Individual free choice appears to be free but is actually dependent upon the prior existence of a free choice society. And, obviously *Yarbles* here produces a teenage subculture of `ultrasonicviolence' with a `private language' which is no more than an uncommunicative language. Before vandals are created, free talk itself must be vandalized by all manner of irrationalities and perversions of our naturally endowed moral sense."

Billy nodded in wide eyed homage. Chick was still amused by me. Alec and his Drooogs had mean looks on their faces. And Flying Molly Furkey sipped quietly on her pint.

"You know vat?" Alec told me. "What you yarble is a real monster's howl and you should noodle twice about saying it."

"My dear young rebel," I told Alec, "I have no idea what oppresses you here in *Yarbles* and perhaps it is something so old fashioned as governmental regulatory uniformity. But if you have given up their talk in order to create your own, I understand you. I have thus far in my own travels not found the talk I would wish to call my own."

"I harken that," Alec said.

"Well, when you've been in sales as long as I have," Chick said, "Nobody talks... off script."

We then fell into a long period of private conversing with long hard pulls on endless pints paid for by Chick who said it was all part of his expense account.

I saw only darkness outside the windows and had I a place to stay would have already made my farewell to this group but as I did not have a place to go to, this pub and this little corner of the pub were my home.

About midnight when most of the place had cleared out except for our group, a man entered and went straight to the bar. He wore a thin, threadbare, ink stained jacket and his face was clearly visible: chalk white and eyes of a blind man.

We were no longer holding ten different private conversations but were back to one subject and all attending to the one person speaking at that time.

"All endings will be voiceless," the ink stained man said, not moving from the bar. We heard him because, as I say, the pub was silent except for our own voices.

He came toward us, drink in hand.

"I've taken the name Bartleby," the man told us. "My psychiatrist tells me it was a mistake. Perhaps a fatal mistake. We shall see. I believe I can re-attach myself to my fellow man."

I was about to strike a similar note when Billy whose face had been moving toward speech, suddenly said:

"Billy Budd, in sudden shocked rec rec...recognition of the na...nature of a gratuitous evil Cla cla...claggart has launched at him, falls into speech...spee...chlessness: *'Speak, man!' said Captain Vere to the transfixed one, struck by his aspect even more than by Claggart's. 'Speak! Defend yourself!' Which appeal caused but a strange dumb gesturing and gurgling in Billy.'"*

"Nothing can be made clear, friends," Chick told us. "if the Almighty himself don't make it clear. I for one never heard a bit of heavenly sense out of a bloke's mouth and I don't expect to. Talk ain't a defense against the ...what did you call it? Gratuitous evil I've seen. "

"Then you all will not be surpised," Bartleby told us, "if I have a deep inclination not to talk to you?"

"Nothing personal, I'm sure," Chick said, winking at Flying Molly.

"I'd like to know more," I said to Bartleby, "as to why you have given up on the world."

"It's a quiet giving up," Bartleby said, sipping his pint. "The mystique of Bartleby's quiet refusal to engage the world around him seems to me an understandable response to our human absurdity. I mean we are absurd in our own nature and in what we do and have done. What's to hold on to? It's...I mean we have gone on long enough."

"Yes, but Melville creates because he has hope. His greatness lies not only in disclosing what could only have been latent then but in seizing upon this deep anomie as if it were a new virus of human nature. We could possibly resist it if we could identify it."

"You think he has such hope?" Bartleby asked me and the manner in which his dead eyes peered into mine made me feel that he had read the bleak despair of my own soul. I could not answer.

Whether I had already traveled too much and seen too much or whether I had as yet not traveled enough or seen enough, I cannot say, but I could not then find the words by which I could pull this self-inflicted Bartleby from his own disenchantment.

"No one gets a chance with Bartleby for he prefers not to talk," Bartleby told me. "He prefers not to answer our questions or fulfill our requests or comply with what one expects of a scrivener on Wall Street.

"Let me remind you," Chick said, "that there ain't any more scriveners. Do you really think a Bartleby could exist in our own day? He does some work then prefers not to do some work and then prefers not to do anything and then hangs around haunting us. That won't go in business today I can tell you."

"Perhaps our information society has succeeded in eliminating an incurable malcontent," I volunteered, "part of the `creative destruction' of our market genius. We live in a world in which the Bartlebys get attention only if they make the tabloids, only if they give up their passive resistance and do something sensationalistic. But that wouldn't be our Bartleby then."

Our Bartleby shook his head.

"Do you think *Yarbles*, this village today could accommodate me and somebody here could get any further than the Lawyer in getting me to talk? Would they be able to dig deeper and find out the underlying cause of this deep malaise, this slow dance to catatonia and then a return to the womb in death? Do you know what my psychiatrist prescribes? He offers me a pill. See something I don't like? Take this pill. Hear something I don't like? Take this pill. Deep psychopharmacology, turn me into a new and improved Bartleby, a Bartleby who would do everything we asked him. Bartleby would talk to us then but consider that we would be talking to Bartleby on some mind altering drug."

I was at that moment fingering my own bottle of pills in my pocket and I resolved at that moment to rid myself of them.

"The flesh is gorgeously made, oh brother!" Alec shouted out, slapping Bartleby on the back. "Let the wonders of chemicals sharpen your gulliver and get you ready for a bit of the old ultrasonic-violence."

"Or," Flying Molly said, smiling, "you could do a flying act above all that Bartleby nonsense. He ain't you, now is he? Come on, love, what is your real name?"

"It's sales, kid," Chick said, "You have no opportunity to prefer not to; what we prefer and do not prefer is now set up differently. There's nobody on *You Tube* saying `I prefer not to.' Everybody prefers to be something or have something. It's called multi-tasking. I bet if your Bartleby was multi-tasking he'd have a whole better view of himself."

"And everybody wants to talk," Flying Molly said. "I go up very high so I don't have to hear it."

Bartleby stood up.

"I prefer not to," he said, nodded to us and walked out of the pub.

"Strange sort," Chick remarked and we began to talk about strange people we had known.

Flying Molly told us about a trapeze artist who was only at ease when he was aloft with his bar to hold onto, and Chick Wagstaff told us of a man he called the Hunger Artist who he managed for a brief period. This Hunger Artist had made a daily rejection of eating his only way of living in our world, a suicidal way. The Hunger Artist believed if he could eat he would be able to give up his solitary campaign of self-starvation, would perhaps mingle in, get a real job, meet someone, have a family, take a vacation, maybe become quite a talker.

"He never did," Chick told us. "The way I see it, and this is maybe because I'm a salesman and talking is my game, talking is a bond with people in the world. Abused children freeze up and don't talk; the begrieved give up talking to anyone for a time as if now that a deep bond is broken, talk is at an end."

"I'm thinking bedways right now," Alec said, getting up, followed in this by Finn, Ollie and Rick. "A night of no small expenditure, as the author says. But worth gallons."

At that Alec went to the door, opened it and looked out.

"Country dark out there," he said and went out. The Drooogs nodded to us and followed him.

That darkness outdoors seemed though to enter into our minds just then.

"Maybe the whole world has gone bad," Flying Molly said, "And some people are like canaries taken into the bowels of the mine to alert us when the air goes bad or is actually gone. Like the trapeze artist I was telling you about. He was alright when he was far above it all but he had to come down sometimes. And he couldn't last down here."

"We do the best we can," Chick said. "Lord knows it ain't a picnic."

"Lo...lord knows," Billy repeated.

"I take to the high trapeze," Flying Molly said, toasting us with her pint. I enjoyed Flying Molly's company. She was indeed strange, to employ Chick Wagstaff's judgment, but to me she seemed ... very alive."

"You know," Chick said, looking down into his beer, his voice sad, "sometimes I think we talked ourselves into a ruined world and ruined ourselves. For what? For a few widgets and gadgets."

"There will be a trial, I think," Flying Molly told us. "Down there where we have ruined the world. And this is the crime for which we are all on trial."

I thought of Sal's utterly lunatic trial and I shivered.

"There is a mys ...mystique to this world," Billy said, in his quiet but impressive manner. "It troubles me. You know we only pass through brie...briefly and we can't understand. And what we say re..re..reveals nothing b..b.but our bl..bli..blindness."

"Lots of histrionics there," Chick said, providing his usual summation. "Let's drink up."

We drank with a vengeance and as I went deep into reflection, I failed to notice what my companions were already responding to as they stood by a window: a strange light in the night sky coming toward us.

It was only when I heard the familiar whirr of the floating Isle's engines did fear grasp me like the claw of a giant predatory bird. I ran toward the door just as it smashed open and his Majesty's Royal Guard pushed into the room with muskets sweeping to right and left. I saw Don Rodrigo, pistol in hand, but I was already rushing toward a rear door. Someone fired a pistol. I heard someone scream. As I grasped the door, I saw that Don Rodrigo's pistol was smoking and Billy was on the floor, blood spreading into his white shirt.

Billy had gotten between me and that fateful bullet. I was outside now, caught in the false light of the Isle but running nevertheless, already feeling bullets fired into my back.

But then not one but four motorcycles were careening around me and one threw up dirt as it blocked my path.

"Garbles and yarbles in *Yarbles*!" Alec screamed, reaching out an arm which I took and swung to the seat behind him. We went roaring off, each Drooog in a different direction and within minutes we were riding in a darkness that I welcomed.

Chapter VII

Revised, The Author sets out for the country of Fauxville and then climbs to the Mountain Monastery of Mock.

I owed my life to Billy, a young man I hardly knew, who had courageously taken a bullet meant for me. And, as I watched Alec and his Drooogs roar off into the night on their Harleys, leaving me at a freight relay, I knew that Billy's sacrifice would have gone for naught had these rebel strangers whose very language was a mystery to me, also not rescued me. Language is the house of being and I knew not them. And yet that didn't matter.

I hopped a freight whose destiny was unknown to me and sat in that dank, odorous darkness, no longer believing the words of my dear Plautus that every man was a wolf to man.

I had long heard of the country of *Fauxville* but had judged it mythical so it was to my great surprise to discover that such a country existed near the Phoenix Islands just south of the Equator. It took me two months of hard though uneventful travel before I reached Rotterdam.

I signed on as crew aboard a fine yacht just out of the Rotterdam shipyards and owned by Mr. Mark Spark, an American hedge fund manager –of enormous wealth who was strange to say a sharp critic of the system that had brought him such wealth.

His own disposition in private life was to share what he had with others although he was bound by that very system not to extend that magnanimity to his business affairs. He told me he was bound to respect the Mother of All Moral Hazards which was this: undeserved award or reward would destroy the will to compete and win and therefore initiate a moral decline leading to a loss of one's immortal soul.

Mr. Spark, however, drew a firm line between business and his personal life and therefore the MOAMH rule did not apply on his yacht. It was not unusual, therefore, to find any number of the crew dining with Mr. Spark and his trophy – in the parlance of our day –wife, Mrs. Spark, whom the crew privately referred to as "Hot" Spark.

Because my duties had me up before dawn, working right up until Mr. Spark appeared for his breakfast, I was called to join him one morning, and, as he found my talk entertaining that invitation was extended to several mornings thereafter.

Mr. Spark was a corpulent man, somewhere in his fifties I believe, who sat and ate more breakfast than an Irishman, and though I do not totally believe the words of the Frenchman Brillat-Savarin, who was obviously prejudiced, one can learn much of a man by observing what he eats. Mr. Spark ate tranche de boeuf, loblolly, kippers, coquillage, sinkers, gooseliver, cotelette, macaroons, spuds, salad nicoise, aspic, Charlotte Russe, bismarcks, and ample Brie all in one sitting.

Besides his breakfast, Mr. Spark was especially interested in my quest to explore the worlds of talk as, it turned out, he paid little attention to talk in his business life and always asked for the numbers. There was, he affirmed, no hidden meaning in numbers but only truth, though talk did its best to confound this.

I asked him why then he showed interest in my own talk and my own quest, a question which elicited roaring laughter and a slap on my back. This is my private life he told me. This was private talk. In his private life he looked upon every man as his brother in arms, devoted to a solidarity which could stand strong and speak truth to power.

Talk is community, he would often say, his eyes always blazing, and words are the bridge to each other's life, and when we look deeply into the lives of our brothers and sisters and we see ourselves and in that partake of a spirit of oneness, why then a whole world of injustice can be turned on its head.

He was fond of quoting Mr. Donne on no man being an island and the equal peril of clod or promontory being washed to sea. He joined M. Robespierre in advocating the rule of a general will in society which trumped the personal self-interest advocated by Mrs. Thatcher. Like M. Bentham he believed that legislation and morals are grounded on the greatest happiness of the greatest number and so greatly deplored the current passion for putting all the wealth in the fewest possible hands. He believed with Mr. Burke that society was indeed a contract between all who are living but also all who have died and all who have yet to be born. The task of the individual, as Goethe had so clearly shown us, was to work through the self to society. Mr. Spark was a perfect Marxist, in his private life, in the matter of requiring from each according to his abilities and giving to each according to his needs. "We must love one another or die," he told me one morning as he applied a deft knife and fork to a soufflé. His dream was to start up a small anarchist community on some far off island he would one day purchase.

Mr. Spark was a highly spirited *sans culotte,* an egalitarian of the noblest order, a radical revolutionary ready to stand and fight for freedom and justice at the barricades. Mr. Spark truly believed that all men have the right to revolt. In his private life.

I learned in the course of the next few weeks that in his private life Mr. Spark was the most astute critic of what Mr. Hobbes called 'war of all against all' talk. The goal of that talk was to divide each and every individual into an isolation of self-concern where all judgments begin and end with personal will and choice. Lost in such self-absorption and self-obsession, no one is fit to see the plight of his comrades, fellow human beings who are reduced to opposition, antagonists, competitors in a game where only you must win.

"When you win in this competitive game, all the profits are yours," Mr. Spark told me this morning, as he speared another kipper, "because the game from start to finish has nothing to do with anyone but you and your talents which you owe to no one but yourself. When you lose, you assume personal responsibility for the same reasons."

This thought would invariably put Mr. Spark into a fine rage, his face turning beet red, and I must confess that I too was angered by this terrible violation of human solidarity. Were we not all joined hand in hand heading to a mutual end? Did not in the end the king and the pawn go into the same box? My blood was up. At the conclusion of the meal every morning we sang the *Internationale*:

"Arise ye workers from your slumbers
Arise ye prisoners of want
For reason in revolt now thunders
And at last ends the age of cant."

I thanked Mr. Spark many times for his insightful talk and he always responded by saying "Oh, in my private life, I can talk with the best of them!"

On one occasion, when we were at dinner:

"Do you believe in the uniqueness of your Youness, Gullwog?" Mr. Spark asked me, a bit of éclair on his chin.

We humans I said are deeply connected to our own uniqueness so any talk referring to our talent to self-design, self-therapy, self-improve `makes sense.' I saw no harm in this. This produced an explosion in Mr. Spark, who dropped the drumstick of the self-confessed hen and glared at me.

"The harm is this: you can will yourself better than what you are and there is nothing preventing you except `Your Youness.' How can the downtrodden revolt against their oppressors if they believe they're the cause of their own oppression? And worst than that they believe they can privately through their own will vanquish tyranny."

"There's a good bit of truth in the truism `you are your own worst enemy.'" I informed my host, not at all intimidated by his manner. "So often we are the cause of our own failures."

Mr. Spark eyed me narrowly and then focused on a soft shelled crab.

"I'd like to remind you once again, Gullquiver," he told me, "that we are talking privately and what I have to say is not for distribution."

I told him I understood perfectly.

"Then you'll allow me to remind you that the degree to which an individual is responsible for what befalls them greatly depends upon the circumstances they're `thrown into' and that some of those circumstances, say, gravity and no wings, the need for water, air and food, are real constraints."

I nodded in agreement.

"I'm referring to birth, as well as the circumstances that prevail during the course of an individual's life. Personal responsibility remains to be assessed. And, Gullford, it's variable from person to person. I could say I'm totally responsible for my success. But any honest assessment would modify that."

"If men are thrown overboard," Mr. Spark continued, "why, that was by their own choice. I'm telling you this, Gullfever. Don't believe it. Keep your eye on the hurricane, the one caused by men of power, such as myself."

He pointed a greasy finger at something in the calm waters we were at that moment sailing in.

"What to do to escape it? Tame it? Prevent it? Stop it? And learn the causes. I tell you, Gallagher, it will take the Devil himself in the coming years' riot and revolt to continue preaching the nonsense of self-will and self-creation and a totally deaf and dumb man to swallow it."

Mr. Spark once again cast his gaze on the waters and not his plate. In the distance we could see the port of *Fauxville*. I was anxious to visit but Mr. Spark would not set foot on shore. He despised the place.

"It's a 24/7 spin cycle in *Fauxville*," he told me, shaking his head. "The greedy and rapacious use their power to soak the citizenry in endless delusions and deceptions. It's like being in the water with a shark gnawing at your leg but you're listening to someone the shark has hired to tell you that you're gnawing on your own leg. Preposterous."

Not, I think, as preposterous as the conceit. Had Mr. Spark noted the similarity between "spark" and "shark"? An interesting case of self-loathing. Or, self-deception.

"The poor will eventually grow distant from this kind of talk," Mr. Spark went on.

He punched one fist into another.

"Oh, wouldn't I like to be around when that happens! You'll see that the unfortunate may be less amused by a celebrity leisure class. They may wonder why one man cruises on a yacht around the world while they scrape to get by."

I said I had some sympathy for this leisure, equestrian class if they also believed that a mere assertion of will would bring them happiness.

"You must be joking," Mr. Spark rejoined. "Why on earth would you have any sympathy for the shark?"

I said that the equestrian class was in a customized bind: they have the means to possess what the poor cannot but their happiness remains an unfinished project. Always. They must assume that it is a failure of personal will but more insidiously a failure of yearning. If they could yearn beyond what they can possess, they could assert the will to fulfill that yearning. Their unhappiness lies in not being able to `close the deal' here. They can yearn for no more than what they already possess and happiness is not forthcoming. For as it is said all seek joy but it is not found on earth.

"Nonsense!" Mr. Spark sparked. "Look about you, man. The sharks have it all. The best of everything. The best food. Have you seen what I've eaten? The best drink. Have you seen what I've drunk? The grandest yachts. Have you seen this yacht? The most lovely companions. Have you seen my trophy wife? Whatever they wish is theirs. Don't waste your tears on them. Look to yourself, man."

Here Mr. Spark paused and poured himself another glass of Madeira, which he drank liberally day or night.

I was not blind to his torment nor to the fact that he was seeking to convince himself that he was content.

I saw the quandary of having the means to fulfill whatever you yearned for while becoming increasingly aware that your yearning is inadequate and not to be trusted.

If what you already possess does not make you happy and you lack the capacity to yearn differently, why then, I believe you are in precisely the place where Mr. Spark was. He had had his fill of the finest food and had become fat, the finest wines and become an alcoholic, and I daresay none of this positioned him to have his fill of Mrs. Hot Spark. He may have yearned but yearning couldn't complete the task.

I had not sought the lady's attention but she had grown interested in me.

I did not flatter myself that she was interested in me as a lover, for I believe an able bodied seamen filled that role, but only as an informer as to her husband's thoughts, as he had long since given up conversing with her. She admitted to me that her husband had twice tried to take his own life, for reasons she could not fathom. I promised her that I would delve into the matter, feeling perhaps that if I could in some way staunch his suicidal tendencies, I would be, in effect, saving his life. And as my life had been saved, I felt that I should some day be a savior myself.

"It was my public self," Mr. Spark told me late one evening when the Madeira had more than loosened his tongue. `My private self is too concerned with the poor plight of others to dwell in any serious way on the moods of a billionaire."

And yet, I thought, those moods had brought him to self-slaughter. I kept this to myself.

"What do you think," he asked me then, "whether or not a man who needs a doctor and cannot afford one is more tragic than a man who finds sailing around the world in a grand new yacht tiresome and can only find some distraction in talk with his crew?"

"Each has his own need," I said.

"No," he answered himself decisively," "my private self has no time for the ennui of the decadent. "

My thought at that moment was that perhaps Mr. Spark's private self would one day succeed in doing away with him—the final revolt which is death -- and that his public self would not be able to talk him out of it. It was, after all, his private self who was mounting a strong prosecutorial case against his public self, a self whose defense was not words but numbers that were mute, though they added up to billions of dollars. I do not hold the certainty of compound interest to be equal to the power of thought.

I was anxious to go ashore but as yet only mess crew buying supplies had been given permission. When I wasn't on duty, I spent my time writing and watching TV.

Mrs. Spark and I had a mutual fondness for Martha Service who administered everyday self-help, a sort of conquest of stuff, endless crafting toward perfect hominess kind of talk, which I found, I must admit, comforting in light of the less than pleasant adventures my travels had so far placed before me.

I allowed that Ms. Service knew a lot about a lot of stuff.

"She's a sort of down home materialist," I said.

"She's an evangelist," Hot Spark told me. "Of stuff."

"The beatitudes of stuff," I said and she laughed and told me she found me different than Karl. Karl was the able bodied seaman. I don't believe he spoke English, at least I had never heard him speak English.

"Say something else," she told me, suddenly finding me amusing. "I love your Oxonian accent."

"Well, I'm a little nervous about talk of stuff because the planet has been pillaged for this stuff. I've always minded Mr. Thoreau's advice to simplify."

I asked her if she thought Ms. Service could turn Thoreau's shack on Walden Pond into "something really nice and cozy?" Mrs. Spark told me she didn't know about that but people did go into homes and "redo" stuff into something "amazing." Kitchens and bathrooms are remodeled to the nth degree. Fast food deliveries and microwaves require nth degree kitchens I said. And no man likes an indoor outhouse that doesn't have a boudoir décor.

I kept on like this because it amused her and the more amused she became with me, the closer we got until she had both arms around my neck and I got up the nerve to call her Hot. That made her laugh and then kiss me. I pushed onward, waxing witty for a purpose.

"One wonders," I said, "what people did before Ms. Service came out of jail to show them how to crack an egg or dig a hole in the garden."

"One wonders," she said, biting on my ear.

"For the planet's sake we must stop making stuff," I said, suddenly realizing that I was taking greater liberties with my hands than propriety would allow, "stop projecting desires onto stuff . . . stop swooning over stuff, stop fetishizing stuff. . . stop listening to talk about the stuff you should have or the stuff you can take with you on your trip."

The word "stop" had little effect on Mrs. Spark and I soon found that her amorous intent had overwhelmed all the ambages I could summon. In short, dear Reader, I succumbed, my own lust proving irresistible, persuaded -- yet still believing in the reasonableness of my own moral nature – in the maxim of La Rochefoucauld that we are only able to resist our passions when they are weak. Mine, I confess, at that moment, were not. I was a pawn to the lady's majesty and am quite sure if Ms. Service had been there, she would have attempted to be instructive.

Realizing that it was a severe breech in etiquette, not to mention a severe besmirching of my own immortal soul, to remain on the Sparks' yacht, I awaited an opportunity as well as an excuse for jumping ship.

I need not have worried for able bodied Karl facilitated my exit by informing Mr. Spark that I had been "sparking" his wife. In this manner I discovered that Karl could speak English and that Mr. Mark Spark and I had not, over the course of weeks of daily conversations, developed any sort of relationship for he had Karl and three other able bodied seaman cast me -- "Throw Gobbler over the side! -- head first overboard.

Mr. Spark had been speaking to himself and not to my lowly self. I only became real when I threatened his "stuff," that is, Mrs. Spark.

I was not sorry to leave the company of Mr. Spark even in so ignoble a fashion for it was clear that his antinomian private self was a sop to his own conscience, a dupe worked by a public self who waged a war of all against all as strenuously as the private self talked of `Sticking it to the Man!' And in the end, actions mattered and his private talk didn't.

I regretted having been so exploited by Mr. Spark in his wicked game of retaining a conscionable view of himself. He had used me like a sock puppet but as I swam the last distance to shore and then in the shallows stood up, bone tired, and walked onto the gravely beach, I felt strangely exhilarated as if finally I had come to a place where my fortune would change. As I headed down the pier toward the bright lights of the town, my optimism returned as I looked forward to what *Fauxville* would offer.

I have been mute for the past several days because immediately upon arriving in *Fauxville* I was accosted by a person calling herself a "Producer" who informed me that new arrivals to this country had to be interviewed in order to see what Reality program they would become part of.

I protested my strong wish not to be so included as my traveler status obliged me to remain an observer rather than a participant. Further, I saw no need to enlist into reality as such imbrication occurred naturally.

I was told that every citizen of this country – whom they referred to as "contestants" – had to be on one Reality program or another. Visitors were not exempted and so I went through an audition and became a "housemate" on a travesty of reality called "*Cruel Shoes*."

As a "housemate" I was denied any communication with the outside world, a somewhat unnecessary abjuration because, as I subsequently discovered there is no "outside" world in this country, and it is only because I was "voted out" of this faux Reality that I have been able to retain my sanity.

Upon my eviction I was sent to a half-way house where I joined with other evictees to ponder I suppose my sins, in the fashion of a review of the soul one supposedly makes in Purgatory.

Cyril was a self confessed scoffer, skeptic and cynic who had accidentally landed in *Fauxville* and cashiered into *Cruel Shoes*.

Prince Krokov, self-described, had been robbed of his fiefdom by what he called Modernity.

Guy Beecher had been cleverly maneuvered into making a pact with the Devil, in his own words.

Emily spoke angrily of that confederacy of bitches who had conspired against her.

Carla was intent on returning to the game through some secret stratagem.

Tout court, dear Reader, my new half way house mates were indeed as the Bible says made a trifle lower than the angels.

I was intent on escape but as there was no area in the half way house not surveillanced by cameras and as the one door to the outside only led to an enclosed outside, I soon resigned myself to living through this imprisonment.

Several times a day we were summoned by a faceless voice to the lounge area where we sat in front of a large flat screen TV and were forced to watch the continuing "reality" of *Cruel Shoes*.

Afterward, we were addressed by our TV hostess who reminded us that everything we did and said while in the half way house was a live feed 24/7 webcast that everyone in *Fauxville* had access to.

The style of living in this half way house was to do whatever suited you, confirming Goethe's observations that we all believe doing what suits us is always the right thing to do. There was always a quantity of unhealthy microwavable food and each of us went about, like hamsters, feeding whenever it suited us. We were not communal in any way, conversing only when we happened to be sharing the same space, and that talk I must say neither instructive nor refreshing nor memorable and most often ending with the words "bitch," "whatever" or "for sure."

One evening as I sat reading in what was called "the library," the Prince entered and asked what book I had before me. He was not impressed and informed me that good breeding was not to be found in words but in ancestry. His supercilious and disdainful manner irked me.

"These....housemates," he whispered as he sat across from me. "How do you find them?"

"I have read my illustrious ancestor Jonathan's account of Yahoos," I told him, "and so I am able to recognize the type of creature my "housemates" are, although their babble, ferocity, and vanity far exceed that earlier description."

The Prince took the trouble of setting his monocle to get a better look at me.

"You seem to me a man of good breeding, sir," he informed me.

"I'm afraid," I replied, "that my actions of late are those of a bounder and not a man of good breeding."

"Our worth is in our manners, sir," the Prince told me. "And in that regard I find the residents of *Fauxville* worthless."

Just then Cyril entered the room, some sort of food wrap in hand. Cyril was a native of *Fauxville* and in his thirty odd years had been a contestant and a housemate and a survivor and a dance partner and a *Fauxville* idol and a swap and a mock defendant and so many other simulations that he could only recall in bad dreams.

He plopped down on the far side of the sofa upon which I was seated. The Prince glared at him and Cyril smiled back.

"What's up, Krokov?"

"Prince Krokov, if you please."

"Oh, yeah, well we're not on a Reality show right now so you can drop the Prince bullshite. What did they call you in the real world? Krock?"

"Worthless," the Prince said, getting up and marching out of the room.

I was curious as to why a cynic like Cyril had spent his whole life going from one faux reality to another. Surely, I asked, his deconstructing disposition would have compelled him long ago to leave the country of his birth? He shook his head, still smiling, and told me I didn't understand what addiction was.

You watch any of these mock ups for a month," he told me, "and you'll be addicted. Take *Cruel Shoes*. I know here..." and here he pointed to his temple... "that it's a load of crap. But someplace else, you're hooked. You won't want to talk about it just like a recovering drug addict doesn't want to talk about drugs but you'll be thinking about those people all the time and waiting to see what they're going to do next even though you know they're going to do something stupid, something you'd never do. But then you keep thinking `what would I do in their place?' You'll go on the twenty four hour webcast just to see what they're doing. You'll stop living your own life after awhile just to see what these idiots are doing. You get to really hate some people and you probably will fall in love with one of them and you'll dream about her and if you were there what you would do."

He was talking faster and faster now and his eyes were popped, his lips dry, his hands gesturing wildly.

"Then all you want to do is get into that reality," he told me. "You know why? Because in spite of what your brain tells you, you now know that that's where reality is. With those idiots. Your housemates. You belong in that stupid place. Then when you finally get in there, you're screaming happiness like you went to heaven. You start playing the game of playing other people so they won't know you're playing them and at the same time you can't believe anybody because they're probably playing you. After all, everybody wants that half a mil. Maybe you think if you don't talk to anyone no one can figure you out. They'll think you're harmless. You're too dumb to be a threat but then you'll wake up in the middle of the night thinking harsh thoughts about idiots thinking you're the idiot and you yell out 'We'll see who wins the $500,000!' And it gets even worse until your girlfriend, your real girlfriend, disappears from your brain pan. It's like she never existed and all you're interested in is one of these housemates who just lounges around half naked in front of you all day and all night, her belly baby fat hanging out."

Cyril was now standing up and bending over me as he spoke.

I asked him when his skepticism kicked in.

"Sure," he replied, nodding and catching his breath. "Like skepticism is a cure for addiction. You tell yourself you have to go cold turkey on this show. You've got to get out. You can't even watch it any more. Every time you think about it, you have to draw the curtain and think of something else. You have to detox and it takes a long time because believe it or not this crap gets deep into your soul. This talk goes deep. You tell the whole world to get lost and leave you alone so you can return in peace to this phony, bullshit world."

"So getting ejected from *Cruel Shoes* was a victory then?" I asked. "I mean one would conclude that your skepticism did win the day. I mean you're here. Half way out of it."

"Yeah," he mumbled, "but I'm half way in it, too."

107

I felt quite sympathetic to the young man at that moment and heartily wished that his innate skepticism would one day extricate him from his addiction to faux realities. I thought of advising him to visit the village of *Jumpback*, as a sort of detox sojourn. His advice to me was to be wary of Guy Beecher whom Cyril said was "certifiable."

Guy Beecher, I subsequently discovered, lived in a world certified as real by none other than his own mind.

Perhaps this is true of all of us, but I flatter myself, as I am sure you do, that such things as travel, the talk of others, Chance, the Celestial Word, and our own reason detour us from living in total fantasies.

Beecher had no such controls. His was a very twisted mind indeed. He frequented faux realities the way an evangelist preacher frequented houses of ill repute. And, like that preacher, he was as drawn to indulge as to convert.

His critical views of the spin worlds of *Fauxville* possessed a degree of lucidity that only the maniacally focused mind can achieve. I found myself more and more in his company, as did Emily, whom Beecher was intermittently converting and seducing. His acerbic assessment of our former housemates appealed, I quickly saw, to her conviction that some cabal of treachery had led to her rejection and ejection.

I've neglected to mention that Beecher was an Englishman, about my own age, and like myself, had come down from Balliol. His speech had that crispness of Empire that only the finest public school could impart.

"If all the chatter you currently hear on the telly were in a time capsule," Guy now told us, a glass of port in one hand, "and that time capsule floated through endless ether to a habitable planet in a distant galaxy . . ."

He sipped his port. Emily, in her usual near naked lounging attire, lounged on the sofa by his side. She was spellbound by his locution.

"Well, I'll tell you this, my dear Gullible, even philosophers cannot provide the hermeneutics leading to understanding in such a situation."

"What are her man's utics?" Emily asked. Guy ignored her.

"Our show," Guy went on, "the show we were so unceremoniously ejected from, is exemplary telly of the moment and I mean exemplary not in praise but merely as representative of what attracts us. What is revealed by the many hidden cameras and microphones? And one must of course keep in mind that all the `houseguests' here are aware they are being filmed and recorded every second."

"Greed and vanity?" I suggested.

"What is revealed, old chap," Guy revealed in thunderous tones, "is a sort of bottom muck of the psyche that once upon a time could only be dredged up with much resistance and guardianship by Freudian defense mechanisms."

"I would have thought a moral compass would be your protection from the evils of human nature."

I said this with a marked edge as I found Beecher's patronizing intolerable.

"All that blows in the wind now, old chap," he replied, breezily, old chapping me yet again. "Conscience, sin, redemption, virtue. They blow in the wind. Here in *Fauxville* everyone seems to blather freely as if talking into their own navel, other people being no more than a button on their belly. Other people are their camera lens, their microphones."

At this point Emily began to talk and giggle to her navel, which was, as always, exposed.

Guy turned to observe this.

"I find the real world much more amusing," he said.

"I suppose some watch to be amused," I said. "And to be entertained by the houseguests. Perhaps it's all no more than a passing distraction, momentary relief from the `real world.' I'm sure they found you amusing, Guy."

"If they did, my dear Gullivere," Guy rejoined, "I'm sure I would still be a houseguest. Dumb people doing dumb things is just funny. Clowns and fools have always amused their betters. I am neither dumb nor a clown nor a fool."

"But you were there," I insisted.

"Like you, I am a prisoner. Unlike you, I believe I can liberate these people from a false consciousness."

He looked at me but ran one hand down Emily's thigh.

"What about you, Emily," I asked. "Do you think everyone in *Fauxville* is imprisoned in mindless fabrications?"

"Isn't what's in your mind," Emily said, pushing herself from a lounging position to a sitting up one, "what you put there? And then you believe in it because it's, like, you? And then you realize there's, like, nothing you can't be and If you really believe in yourself you can win a half million dollars and then you'll have your fans, just like you're somebody else's fan now."

"And I take it your Guy's fan now?"

She nodded enthusiastically and squeezed Guy's arm.

"He's going to get inside their heads and re-arrange the furniture."

"I'd love to hear that plan, Guy," I said, noting that Carla had come into the room and was listening.

"Yeah, if you know how to win the half million," Carla said. "I'm all ears, Guy."

"I'm not interested in the money, Carla. I have all the money I need. My interest is in bringing minds out of a darkness."

"Into what?" I asked. "The brilliance of your own mind?"

Guy ignored me.

"Tell me what's dark about *Fauxville?*" Carla asked, also ignoring me.

"Observe our former housemates," Guy said. "The revelation of consciousness that we receive is smooth and flat, like the brain of a perfect idiot or the ass of a newborn. No interruptive self-reflexivity – veneer thin – no interruption from the past or awareness of it – morally blank – nothing occasions a review of conscience --- solipsistic – a community that has no room for others – simulated   in both talk and action -- and atavistic. No recognition or appreciation or respect for the ingrained hierarchy of the world: superstitious, demotic, brutish, nasty, despicable, degraded, corrigible, passable, acceptable, good, better, best."

Guy held up a finger for each of these.

I assumed he himself represented the *summum bonus* that went unrecognized.

"What we see on *Cruel Shoes* or any of these mock reality shows is the naked barbarity and doltishness of our nature's own dark abyss. There is no civilized presence to counter this."

Once again, I assumed Guy was that civilized presence we dolts had failed to recognize.

"You're still not telling me how I can win," Carla demanded, lighting a cigarette and in doing so clearly breaking the rules of the half-way house. She seemed not to care. "If everybody that is still out there competing for a half million are dolts and barbarians and you're the brainiac in the loser house here that's got it all figured out, then how come one of those idiots is going to get a half million and you're maybe going to get inside Emily's pants?"

"Hey," Emily shouted. "Easy, Bitch!"

"I'm not into winning," Guy said smiling. "I'm into converting."

"I believe Guy has his own religion," I told Carla, "and I believe he's The new Jesus. Guy BeJeezus."

"You know what I think?" Carla said, ignoring me and pointing to Guy. "Your little stratagem was as obvious as your girlfriend's ass to those dolts and barbarians. They saw through you like a clear window. That's how clever you are."

"What did you say about my ass?" Emily said, getting off the sofa.

"I admit to being a real threat to my fellow man," Guy said, putting out an arm to restrain Emily. "And you? You're unlikable, my dear. Despicable. You can't help it. You haven't an ingratiating fiber in your whole being. You were thrown off because no one could bear having you around."

What followed is a terrible scene I will spare you an account of. Suffice it to say that Carla attacked Guy but was brought to ground by Emily before she could do more than get her hands on his throat.

I woke up in the middle of the night and crouched slowly out into the garden, immediately ducking behind a shrub. It was a moonless night, pitch dark, and I had hopes of scaling the garden wall unseen by the surveillance cameras or at least hopefully over the wall before any action by my captors could be taken.

I was about to move forward when I heard a rustling behind me. I turned and saw Carla. She was beckoning me. I wasn't going back. I was going to that wall. Then here she was, her face close to mine.

"I'm coming," she whispered. I hesitated. She grabbed my face and pulled it close to hers.

"We both go or nobody goes."

I nodded. I had thought of pulling a lounge chair close to the wall and climbing on that but I wound up hoisting Carla up and watching her disappear over the wall. I went for the chair, climbed up and to my amazement had both my hands grabbed by Carla and thus I made me way over the wall and outside that damnable half way house.

I had heard of a mountaintop retreat built by an order of Eastern Orthodox monks in the middle ages and I decided to make that my destination.

Carla wanted to travel with me at least until she was a safe distance from *Fauxville*. And so we began our long trek, foraging for what we could, stealing when we could, doing chores for meals, dumpster diving, queuing up for free lunches, accumulating what gear we needed to eat and sleep under the stars.

It was more than two weeks on the road before Carla spoke of what had driven her and now drove her to escape.

"Everything in our high and mighty nation of *Fauxville*," she told me as we both stared into our small fire. "It's all a soma pill. You're either on one of these shows or you're watching them. Day after day. You can't think away from them. If your life is in the crapper because you lost your job or your kids are sick and you can't take them to the doctor. All that shite. Soon as you get pissed off enough to say `I've had enough!' you got some kind of soma to calm you down. And all your buddies. They're in the crapper too but they get their soma. I get to care more about these pissants on these Reality TV shows than I do about my own life. That, just that, keeps the system going. God bless *Fauxville*. Let's sing the national athem."

I didn't say anything but merely poked the coals of the fire.

"And then," she said after a long while, "I get to thinking, why shouldn't I take their money and run? I'll go on one of their shows like I don't know what a brainwash it is. I'll pretend I'm just some midriff with her head up her ass. And I'll play them all into thinking what I want them to think. You know how that turned out."

"They smelled the wood burning," I said and she smiled.

"Yeah. There's being simple and then there's playing simple. And anyway, that asshole Guy was right. I hated all of them. I couldn't stand their airhead, nasty, backstabbing, self centered chatter. And I guess they smelled that too. Like wood burning."

We both laughed. I hadn't laughed in awhile and I suspect that might have been true for Carla also.

"Then when I got kicked off and sent to the half way house I figured I'd rethink and make a comeback. Somewhere. That's all *Fauxville* is now but spin fests. You get a chance to compete like a vicious bitch for the limelight or for the dollars. And then.. ."

"And then you decided to run."

She laughed.

"I'm running from what all that has made me. You heard Guy."

"Unfortunately," I said. "Travelers like myself too often travel to talk they prefer not to have heard."

"They threw you off first," she said. "After you made that speech. I know you wanted to be thrown off but I think right then what you said changed me."

I was tremendously gratified by her words. The horrific simulations of Fauxville will turn you into a vegen, perhaps a misanthrope, perhaps a zombie, perhaps a suicide . . . but we had escaped.

As unsatisfactory as my brief sojourn in *Fauxville* had been, I was delighted that it had ended with an innocent escape over a wall, and also delighted to be with a companion I was becoming attached to -- a decidedly better exit than had been my lot thus far.

It was an arduous climb to the mountain Monastery of Mock where I had been told the hyperreality of *Fauxville* was cleansed by the devout practices of the Monks of Mock.

The Monks of Mock accepted Carla and myself most graciously as acolytes and we were soon shown our quarters – Carla with the female acolytes and myself with the male – and acquainted with the daily regimen of an acolyte.

We rose at dawn, ate sparingly, listened to the Monks, read the ancient texts, meditated, ate lunch, walked along the mountain top, one on one with a mentoring Monk, engaged the enemy, meditated, robust games, dinner, music, meditation and then bed

We learned the sacred tenet that much nonsense talk could be treated homeopathically, by which it was meant with an equal amount or more of nonsense. The more anything seemed sensible, the more power was invested in it, an equal amount of power had to be invested in the insensible. As both Carla and myself soon found the daily regimen pulled us apart when it seems we both had a growing desire to be together, we decided to leave the sacred Monastery. I was also not inclined to be submerged in a similar sort of irrationalism that I had discovered in the village of *Jumpback*. There, a constant re-examination of every assertion had led to a fatal undecidability. Here, at the Monastery, it was assumed at the outset that nothing made sense and twas best to jump headfirst and happily into such insanity. *Jumpin* was a fit name for this sacred Monastery of Mock. And so we took our leave.

We were on the road again. At our first evening camp, she asked me whether I thought our long arduous climb up the mountain had been worth it? I asked her whether she had not found the High Monk's talk somewhat interesting?

"The High Monk is a man," she said, "and he talks like one. Plus I think he's got a pretty good life here as the top guy. I mean, if somebody's pushing a lid on your head, you don't mock the dude. You fight back. His Highness doesn't need to fight back so he doesn't have a clue. If he ever met someone mad, bad and dangerous to know he'd need to do more than mock."

I told her that I found myself disengaged from talk that denied the existence of firm, universal foundations. Without them we spun in all directions at once until we collapsed, or, we charged madly into such a mad world in hope of accomplishing something. I knew not what. Feed nonsense to nonsense till it is all transformed into sense? There was no sign of the Celestial in any of this.

She gave me a rather amused look.

"For all your travel," she told me, "you seem a little wet behind the ears."

I did not find this amusing and promptly made a defense of my observational skills and the variety of my travels.

"You know what I liked about The Monastery?" Carla said, lighting up a cigarette. "Some particular bits. Like, oh, they call this a sacred Monastery but they're all atheists."

I objected to that. "The High Monk..."

"Of Mock," Carla said, interrupting me. She blew some smoke circles. "You said it yourself: a mocking god creates a mocking world? I liked that bit about people's personalities being machined. I mean when everybody thinks they're living in this great big free choice circus. That they're all bloody unique. Types are what we've got. And not many either. You've seen them. Zombies, airheads, egoists, tramps, moguls, and assorted trash."

She smiled at me.

"And a few walking blind."

"I like the way The High Monk de-personalizes what's going on in the world so you don't think if you could just run down the Evil Guy everything will be alright."

"And who should we be running down?" I asked, rather annoyed by her reference to me as the walking blind.

"Oh, I'm not opposed to running a whole lot of sons of bitches down," she replied, laughing. "I'd just like to get into the running gears of this world and make some adjustments. You know, twist the gonads and make them holler."

She made a quick twist with one hand and laughed. Carla Lope was intimidating and I was not at all surprised she had failed to ingratiate herself on *Cruel Shoes*. I don't think she was likeable enough to win. While I do not pretend to be an expert on women, I do know that bold women are not very popular with men.

"I don't think there's an evil conspiracy going on in the world," Carla went on. "I believe that human nature is bent. And it's bent toward having everything. And when you have everything you have the power to make what's best for you seem natural. What did the High Monk call it?"

"Axiomatic," I said.

She nodded.

"It's just the part of human nature that wins. The bent part. But the world's bent and if it isn't bent in your direction, you don't respond with the better angels of your nature. If it is bent your way, it's all good. You're a saint or a hero or a philanthropist. But they're not special. Nobody has a special, different human nature. We're all bent. The world just brings it out differently."

She lit up another cigarette and crossed her legs. She had nice legs. It wasn't the first time I had noticed them. She was maybe early thirties, long, straggly brown hair, dark eyes, olive complexion. She had a wide mouth that gave her, when she smiled, her own special mocking look. I had not paid any special attention to her before, even on our long trek here, on all those nights we had camped under the stars. She had, as Guy Beecher had said, the sort of bold personality that I found did not suit women though it was an asset to men. At any rate, I had early on dismissed her from any further attention but now I found myself intrigued.

"I like that," she was saying. "Axiomatic."

"Yes," I replied.

The word "axioms" had reminded me of my Euclidean geometry course and how one proceeded to solve a problem was guided by such axioms which were infallible truths of geometry. To me it was as if once human greed was set in motion and allowed a free hand it would be guided by internal commands or principles – axioms – which no amount of talk could repel. As there was no real opposition to an axiom but only a kind of carping around the edges, which best described a Liberal position in the U.S, what was needed was a frontal assault on Euclid himself, a non-Euclidean assault, but what that would look like I had no idea.

"A mocking parody," I said out loud, "which needs no ideological frame from which to launch its attack, could serve until we could talk our way beyond false axioms to true ones."

Carla gave me another one of those looks that suggested I was still talking like a blind man. As I went on, she listened to me with eyes half closed, her face behind a cloud of cigarette smoke. Perhaps she was a fervent Euclidian.

I fell in love! And I am astounded to say that love was returned, and though, Ovid was not wrong in describing love as a kind of warfare I was indeed the most happy of warriors!

I was fired up for anything and everything. On her part, Carla was enthralled by the idea of the "axiomatic." She was ready for a full frontal attack on the "axiomatic."

In this high state of enthusiasm we both set out for that wild, uncharted realm that I had long feared entering: I would now voyage to the political frontier and I would do it in the company of my beloved. We were both ready – or so we thought.

Chapter VIII

The Political Frontier and what the Author finds there.

You may think that the Political Frontier is easily reached but it is not for the simple reason that the borders of that frontier are continuously changing and the reasons behind that have much to do with the volatility of political climate.

Volatility is a euphemism. Havoc and misrule, lynch law, mobocracy, chaos were what we found. Paradise indeed lost as Milton described it with ruin upon ruin, rout on rout, confusion worse confounded.

I lost my gullible foolishness there. I was blind and then I was made to see.

I lost Carla Lope there.

But here I must begin where things are always at their best as Pascal wisely saw.

What I learned on that Frontier is that you cannot rely on what you hear from any one source, cannot expect that talking to anyone will make you wiser, and cannot expect that your reason will stand above all the talk and see you through. You cannot expect that speaking in your own defense will defend you. You cannot expect that talk will save your life or the life of the person you love. You cannot expect that a simple, declarative sentence will not be taken up as its direct opposite. You cannot expect your reason to be universal or even to travel further than your own arm's length.

It took us three weeks traveling across waters, over dried arid land, over endless mountains to finally reach the real Frontier. I say "real" because we had come upon any number of *faux* frontiers which invariably referred to themselves as "The New" Frontier or the "Millennial" Frontier but we kept on, persistent as Carly and I were in the belief that political talk, as Aristotle had affirmed, engaged and activated all other talk.

Carla and I spent many a night sitting by our campfire and talking about everything from what had crossed our path that day to what we could make out of our life experiences thus far. I supposed it's the way lovers talk, everything from the trivial to the majestic ennobled by the speaker, whom we loved.

There was a debate at the Last Chance Saloon and Carla and I arrived early so that we could secure seats. The room was jam packed with colorfully named characters. The moderator of the debate was Wild Bill Buckaroo, a tall, rangy, leathery man with a lot of whiskers and wearing greasy looking buckskins. He carried a rifle and when he got behind the bar he leaned it down alongside him within easy reach.

Wild Bill babbled on for awhile and I began to nod off until Carla poked me and I caught the summation.

"Well, to summate what I'm saying here folks. It's hard to figure the thought processes going on here on the Frontier. And the darn Media ain't helping. There ain't no talk about how foreign business is mixed up with Frontier business and vicey versy. Now them boys have a power we didn't elect but sure as hell is running our lives. I ain't ever had a vote in any corporate doings."

At this point Wild Bill raised his rifle and shot a round into the ceiling.

"I got myself all riled up and ready to ask these candidates a whole passel of questions. Here we go. If you're running for office and got somewhat to say, line up over there by the bar."

A man in creased jeans and a button down shirt explained that the only way the Frontier could expand was by what he called "new start-ups" which would employ folks and everyone would prosper. The danger was in giving some of those profits to those who didn't own businesses or weren't employed.

Moochers. Now, giving away money to people who didn't deserve it was done through taxes and taxes were collected by the government. That same government put all sorts of obstacles in the way of making money for all sorts of zany reasons but mostly because regulating folks' personal freedom is what government does. A vote for him would put him in the catbird seat and he'd make sure government got out of the way of folks making money. He would also do everything he could to let businesses grease the wheels of progress and get the government drag off those wheels. Enough profit could be made that the whole Frontier would be feeling the good times. There was no way in a democratic Frontier that a whole lot of wealth that businesses created wouldn't make for a prosperity for all. And the beauty of it all was that folks could get in there, compete and choose to be as prosperous as they wanted. And if that prosperity wasn't siphoned off to the freeloaders, to those among us always looking for a free ride, the trajectory of prosperity for all would not be confounded.

We listened to several more speakers who talked in the same way and then there were several speakers who talked differently. Their talk opposed and rejected everything the others had been saying. A lot of folks just couldn't start a business so they depended on wages and right now on the Frontier the wages were going down and the owners' profits were going up. The workers' share had to be increased and both unions and the government could do the job. Some folks also fell on bad times through no fault of their own and we could just let them rot or we could do something through government assistance. If we did nothing more than say "You're on your own and go start a business," the Frontier would never become a civilized society. Back in the cave man days, folks just let other folks drown in their misfortunes. Some folks might just be lazy moochers and just wait around for the government to take care of them but it would sure be hard to separate that bunch from the herd. Some wanted to treat all the "Losers" as layabouts and some wanted to treat them all as just savaged by circumstances beyond their control. It came down to a vote for whether everybody who wasn't as rich as you was just a mean, shiftless dog or whether some were like yourself, a mixed bag of goodness and shite that we called being human.

It reached a point when both Carla and I were supersatured with this code duelo talk. I took Carla's hand and we moved to the back door of the saloon. Violence it seemed to me was imminent. There we saw a camera crew.

"Kate Whack, Travelling Press," a woman holding a microphone shouted at me. She told us this here was a cock fight. Or we could think it was a salesman pitch battle. Who gets sold on their product. Whether you've got a jingle in your head or you like the looks of the lady who's holding the product.

"It's sales," she told us, pointing her cell phone at Wild Bill. "And it's crude and rude and mindless but it's the way we do things here on the Frontier."

"You're looking for good theatre?" Carla said, sarcastically.

Whack nodded, smiling.

"The media sets up the contest, pushing all folk in the direction we want them to go. If the Kid doesn't get into that Apache knife fight, then Sassy here, Johnny's hired gun, knows what kind of prod works with every gun toting Frontiersman."

I shook my head, amazed. The Frontier was not turning out to be what I had expected. I looked over at some of the characters Whack had mentioned. The one called the Kid was in a face off with a wildcat called Sassy.

"Nobody's taken an oath to give up red meat just because the Kid turned Vegan," Sassy yelled out. "Elect me and you can buy any light bulb you want. And where in The Constitution does it say the feds should regulate potatoes in school lunches?"

Gunfire and riot. I could not discern any sense in what Sassy had shouted but it seemed effective.

Wild Bill fired some shots into the ceiling and the Kid went on until Sassy fired a shot at his boots

"I just don't think the Kid thinks the way we do here on the Frontier," Sassy said, smiling. "He ain't born here. We don't back down from a fight. We don't cut and run. And Lord only knows that we think a marriage is between a man and a woman. And if there's a baby, we don't ask the government to kill it before it's born. We don't wait around for the government to do what we can do ourselves. You just don't know our ways, Kid, being that you're kinda half an unknown whatever and all."

"He's an Injun!" somebody yelled.

"Terrorist!"

"Lynch'em up!" came the cry and before I knew it a cowboy on a pony burst through the batwings and he was swinging a rope. He let it fly and it looped around the Kid. A couple of brawny Regulators pulled the cowboy off his horse and started to thrash him. Shots were fired and this time both Carla and I ran for the back door and made the proverbial hasty exit.

The next day we returned to the saloon to hear more speakers. We were only half inclined to do so but we had come far to find the Political Frontier.

"Amigos," the first speaker that day began, "we didn't read in the papers this morning that money and power will do all it can to trash anyone who makes a connection between money and power.Like Pancho and me.We didn't get an editorial whether it's okay for us to let `the invisible hand of the market' rule our Frontier.We didn't ever get notice of the re-writing the Preamble to the Constitution to read: *We, the People of the United Corporation of Americas, including corporations as people and money as speech, in Order to maximize profits to shareholders, increase the bottom line, privatize health insurance, hand over the Social Security treasure chest to Wall Street brokers, and secure the privacy of the wealth class, promote Work not Welfare, and secure the blessings of property to ourselves and our Posterity, do ordain and establish this Constitution of the United States.*"

"I don't recall that re-write every being published but it's bible and the Cash Barons here on the Frontier are hard-shelled believers."

"We object to these scurrilous attacks in the mouth of a man who hates the Frontier!"

"We object to this socialist harangue!" a group referred to as Cash Barons jumped up and shouted.

"I ain't going to sit here any longer listening to a bunch of Commies," a cowboy shouted, his voice like a frog croak.

We recognized the next speaker, the one who wanted to grease the wheels of progress.

"I too object to the profanation of our Frontier Constitution made by my opponent. What our Constitution urges us to do is become all we can be. To do that, we need to grow this economy so it can be all it can be. And to do that we need to get behind businesses who make profits, pay salaries and keep us alive. You know, after we exhausted our own resources with giveaways to people who need incentive not welfare checks, we are now borrowing money from foreigners. I will not borrow from foreigners to keep people who should be working on the dole. You know, partners, it's a simple fact that if we don't' remain strong on the Frontier, marauders will sweep over us and take away our Constitutional rights. They'll be able to do that because while we were putting roadblocks up preventing our best and brightest from getting in there and winning, they were betting on their Winners and advising the Losers to wake up and make something of themselves. Folks, if we don't forge ahead, we go backward. And if the world was the nice, sweet, reasonable place that my opponents see, we could enjoy that sort of politics. But that ain't the world we know here on The Frontier. We're not into illusions and delusions. We see reality and we know what to do with it!"

This produced pandemonium followed by mayhem but I was slow in seeing that progression.

So absorbed was I in what I was hearing that I lost track of Carla until it was too late. I don't know what the argument was and how it had started but it quickly turned into a brawl. When I rushed to the back of the saloon to where I had heard angry shouts I saw, to my utter amazement Carla jump forward, grab a young woman I didn't recognize by the neck. The action propelled both of them to the bar where the young woman went down, her head hitting the brass foot railing and knocking her out. Doc Holliday went over and raised her head, felt her pulse and then put a small mirror to her nose. He looked up.

"She's made her last phone call," he pronounced.

I had no time to grab hold of Carla and get her out of there. Two Regulators stood on either side of her, guns drawn. Whack's cameras were now directed on the scene. Before I could say anything a young boy slammed through the batwings and yelled:

"There's a run on the bank!"

The saloon cleared out in no time and Carla and I once again made a rear door exit. People were all running in one direction, toward the Bank I assumed, so Carla and I headed in the opposite direction.

I must, for my own sake, encapsulate what occurred in the next few days.

It seems a number of Frontier Cash Barons had colluded with foreign Cash Barons to loot the Frontier Banks. The Cash Barons that could be apprehended were immediately lynched and their bodies left hanging from trees. All of the big ranches couldn't meet payroll and angry and broke cowhands roamed the Frontier. Most of the Whalemarket brand was rustled and Mrs. Whalemarket fled to Paris for safety. Mr. Skinley, who showed up suddenly, tried to rob the bank even though there was no money in the safe. He was quoted as saying he was getting what was owed him. Martial law was declared by Judge Strickland and the Regulators were empowered to shoot on sight anyone on the street after 10 PM. The Regulators kept a close eye on the livery stables to see who might be making a run for it. Everyone leaving by stage had to pass a close security check.

Carla and I would have taken our chances by foot, the way we had come into the Frontier, but I didn't know if Strickland had issued a warrant for her arrest. And I didn't know if we'd be shot on sight by Backshooter Cal Rover who apparently felt that in this free fall environment he had an opportunity to wipe out whomever he considered to be offenders on the Frontier.

Several candidates had gone into deep hiding or had escaped to hard scrabble Frontier brush country. A vigilante group with an eye out for anyone who had a sizeable amount of cash to spend had been formed.

So Carla and I remained frozen in our room at the Frontier Hotel for days. Long days and long nights. And then more than a week went by. We seldom left our room and had our meals brought up to us.

One morning the waiter came in and told us there was a warrant out for Carla's arrest for murder.

We had to leave. We didn't succeed. Carla was arrested and put on trial. She was found guilty. I pleaded for her life but my words fell on deaf ears. No one had time for anything, certainly not for rational arguments. The temper of the moment was to lynch and lynched she was.

Suffering, Wordsworth reminds us, is permanent, obscure and dark and shares the nature of infinity.

It is where I went.

I did not see Carla die because at hearing the verdict "Guilty" I had jumped up, a gun in hand, a gun I don't know where I had gotten, intent on doing I know not what, but stopped before I could do anything. I heard the shot, felt deep, sudden pain on the side of my head, my eyes blur and I fell. I see Carla. I hear her scream my name and the sound of her voice is like a long, slow drinking of my soul.

And then I see and hear no more.

Chapter IX

The Author attends a war, is fire bombed and escapes.

The bullet had only grazed me but for some days I lay in a concussed stage at the Frontier Hotel. Carla had already been buried. I stood and wept by that grave, blaming myself for having brought her to this hell. I stood there by that grave now knowing what grief was. Her presence was palatable, so near yet so far as Tennyson had written.

I went back to our room...my room at the hotel and quietly pulled my few possessions together and made my way to the street where I headed for the wharf, intent to barge down the canal and get as far from this wild Frontier as I could.

I found my bargeman willing to depart at once and for a few gold coins my passage was made.

There were other passengers huddled on the deck – I had been told the cabin was full – but it was too dark to make out their faces. Quiet indeed it was, only the sound of the bargeman's walk up to the box and then the soft sound of his pole moving in the waters. I was grateful for the peace and quiet, bearing within me now a love that was not buried there in that graveyard but in my heart. Soon my head fell forward onto my chest and I was asleep.

I was woken by a strange noise and loud cries of I knew not what. Fear? Joy? Anger?

I had in the darkness of the night before couched myself in between some barrels anchored by sturdy ropes to both sides of the barge. Now I rose, clasping a barrel side and a rope and in the first light of dawn saw my fellow passengers aligned on the port side all gazing down into the water.

In the midst of them was the barge man holding the end of what looked like a double branched pole. I recognized him by his hat, a broad brimmed fedora. I was curious as to what activity they were engaged in and so, after performing two or three mandatory stretches of the lower limbs and upper appendages, I approached the nearest fellow and after bidding him a good morning I enquired as to what had everyone's interest.

After giving me a surveying up and down look, head to toe, he told me that the Dredge Man was bottom dredging for scallywags and scamps as he did every morning and that was that and that's what every God fearing citizen of the Frontier knew. He then gave me another scrutiny with a look on his face as if I had just been dredged up. I therefore nodded and made a quick removal from his presence.

I did not succeed and before I knew it a case, barely literate, was made against me as a "bottom dredge," whatever that might be, and my Oxonian inflections mounted as evidence in support, I was summarily thrown overboard.

I swam to shore slowly, my clothes and shoes weighing heavy, and upon arrival I crawled upward like some primordial amphibian until I was in dry grass and there I lay, eyes closed, cursing my fate. But the immersion in that water proved to be a kind of baptism out of a numbing grief and back into life. I stopped cursing my fate. My fate was to travel, to go on, not to forget, but to go on.

I don't know how long I remained in this state but it was my empty stomach growling for sustenance that caused me to rise and go in search of humanity.

I had not gone very far before I came upon a small village and in the distance on a hill what looked like a medieval castle for there was a moat. Indeed, the whole affair –village and castle and moat – seemed quite feudal to me but I put my curiosity to the side and walked toward what was clearly a market.

I was no more than partially dry but the sun's rays were becoming stronger and more direct by the minute and soon my appearance would mark me as more human than rat. I bought some bread and cheese and a bottle of cider and finding a fountain encircled by steps I sat down and ate with great relish.

I did not know whether I was as yet on the Frontier or in some new region but I had long before Carla's death come to the conclusion that this Frontier was too wild for me, all talk here fueled as it were by directly opposing axiomatic forces, neither of which could dispel by talk the force of the other.

History shows us that when clash went beyond the threshold of anyone's summary comprehension and entered a place where all dissenting talk was dismissed, there would be blood. It came to me then as I sat on the steps of that fountain in the middle of the village piazza that there was so much blood spilled on this wild Frontier for very simple reasons: a large mass of people were not angry at the Whalemarts and Cash Barons. Their anger, strange to say, was ignited by whatever and whomever pricked their own illusions, and so their blood was up and they struck out against those who vexed by unwanted intrusion.

I had already heard the talk that drives a man to look at his own navel and not up and into the face of the world. I had already been to realms of talk where one is enchanted not by the Sirens, like Odysseus, but by one's own reflection, like Narcissus. The self-enchanted were not positioned to be anything but indifferent to the lives of others and yet others drove them to angry response.

I had wandered into a field, and finding a shading spot beneath a beech, I lay down and began to reflect.

Violence and blood are a way of life on the Frontier as the benumbed but angry majority stands like a tormented bull in the ring not knowing where the hurt is coming from but nevertheless driven to attack. The tormentors cannot, for their own self preservation, draw back from continuous contention, division, battle, war, violence and blood for, strangely, in that melee their iniquities mount and go unnoticed.

Chapter IX

Thusly, I concluded my thoughts and was laying my journal in the grass, my eyes half closed, drifting into sleep when I saw . . . I cannot truly say what I was dreaming. But I heard a far away echo ask me if I knew I was in His Lordship's Domain of Tug?

And then daylight eclipsed and I felt something like rough cloth over my mouth and eyes. . .

I woke to find myself recumbent bound hand and foot, a state of affairs I immediately discovered upon opening my eyes, though the morning sun was so piercingly bright that I could but feel my bondage and not clearly see, so blinded was I and so distorted my vision that I thought I saw a man no bigger than my hand standing on my chest and peering into my face. He was surely there because upon seeing my eyes flutter, he began to squeak, I mean speak to me, informing me that I could consider myself a prisoner of his Majesty Smashmouth in the Kingdom of Tug.

I had the honor of being addressed by Prince Sabbagio who would escort me to his Imperial Majesty. I asked that I be untied, but whether it was because my voice was too loud and deep to be heard, Prince Sabbagio did not respond.

I was thereupon raised up by countless miniature arms and set on some wheeled contraption and in this manner was rolled, not without severe discomfort, as far as I think was possible and there I was left unattended and in time fell asleep.

I was awakened to find a tribunal of small creatures on my chest, one of whom, most ceremoniously dressed, informed me that I would now be interrogated.

I answered all their questions forthrightly and briefly, making every effort to appear exactly as I was: a humble traveler, whose heart had been recently broken but who honored that love by not allowing time and chance to break me but rather urge me beyond despair to hope.

After about an hour of this, the tribunal whispered among themselves, not without occasional high spirited theatrics which I could clearly see though I could not hear what was being said. The decision was finally made to unbind me and after being given the opportunity to relieve myself behind a bush, I followed, treading very carefully between my tiny acquaintances until we reached an open field where the King's court had been assembled for the occasion.

A loud alarum sounded and a multitude of equally tiny men on tiny horses rode into the field, or, more precisely and most extraordinarily, rode within a large, rolling bubble into the field!

Their arrival caused great consternation among his Highness and his cohorts who, to my astonishment, rolled out a similar transparent bubble into which they hurriedly secured themselves.

"Burst their bubbles and make Tuggian Christians of them!"

Ah, a religious war, I surmised. A new crusade.

The clamor and din rose to an unbearable degree and I was sorely tempted to raise a boot and crush one and then the other but I refrained, not because I no longer believed that out of such mental derangement, some understanding would emerge. I refrained because I would not bloody my soul.

Someone cried: "Cry havoc and let loose the dogs of war!"

Havoc indeed I thought as some mud slapped against my right thigh. Behind the dogs were several hunters firing their shotguns to the right and left at what I couldn't make out but succeed they did in peppering each other and so only one reached the bottom of the hill unharmed.

The din rose up like an infernal noise. What saved me I know was the fact that my ears were so high above their little voices that I was spared the full impact, but were I leveled among these creatures, I surely would have lost my mind.

An emissary then made his way toward me and walking into the palm of my hand I elevated him to my ear.

I asked him then if he could explain what the cause of disagreement might be between the bubbles on my right and on my left.

He explained to me that the Leftist Scum -- who were morally degenerate, cowardly in the face of foreign attack, indolent as workers, and rebellious as subjects --lived in a bubble which included only an East Coast and West Coast understanding, and that that understanding was far removed from that of the vast majority of Tugtians, such were they called, who lived in the vast regions in between.

In these mid-regions, southern and far west Tugtians had not given up their faith in a personal relationship with Jesus, in the sanctity of the family, in gun possession, in hard work and personal responsibility, in red meat, in truth and honesty, in the love of their country and their willingness to die for it, in good old common sense, in unbridled Capitalism, in Christian moderation, in armored vehicles, in a fair and flat tax system and freedom from government intrusion in their personal lives, in the exceptionalism of the Kingdom of Tug, in the beauties of global warming, in the Tugtian language and not foreign languages, in criminals not being coddled but punished, in work not welfare, in the criminality of abortion, in an eye for an eye, in marriage being meant for a man and a woman, in the sanctity of the missionary position, in compound interests as the best means to achieve happiness and success, in Nature and her creatures as food, in the capacity of the Tugtian military to keep the kingdom secure and to bring swift justice to those who threatened the Tugtian freedoms.

He catalogued all this with lips that barely moved, only a quick, explosive side of the mouth action, as if words were bird shot. He told me he could say more but what it all came down to was that the Leftist scum in their bubble felt that there was no intelligence to be found outside their coastal urban strongholds and that they thought that while their secular, libertine values had no negative impact, God-fearing and patriotic values did.

He provided me with this list in as succinct and efficient a manner as one could conceive and I was at once enlightened, so very much so that as I leaned down to return him to his bubble I cast an unfriendly look at the bubble of barbarian, Leftist scum.

My conversation as well as my unfriendly look had been noted by some in that bubble and I was not surprised to see one of them come out and wave me toward him.

I transported him on my palm close to my face, committed as a traveler to hear him out but not disposed to accepting anything he would say, although my dear Reader is well aware of my impartiality.

He had a florid face and an engaging smile and I saw a half-eaten cheeseburger peeking out of his pocket. He asked me to call him Mr. President and that he would be honored to have me included as one of his friends.

Mr. President looked up at me and told me that there were some stuck up folks who didn't appreciate ordinary folks in both bubbles, that he was a God fearing man but he didn't hold with putting anyone's faith into the Big House, which is what they called the house The Decider lived in, that he upheld family values, let women decide what they wanted to do with their bodies and didn't think only a man and a woman could experience love. He didn't like Big Government or taxes but sometimes you needed both, you see, because we were all in something like a Monopoly game that put all the winnings in one pocket, which wasn't really good for the few winners or for the many losers, and history had made that clear and government and taxes sort of re-levelled the board so democracy could go on without being ruled by the moneyed class. He was for work and not welfare but thought that a man looked for welfare when he couldn't find work and that telling him to go to work wasn't any kind of help at all.

I put him down gently and watched as he walked toward his bubble. He would have reached his destination but a tidal whitewater wave coming out of nowhere swept over him.

I was wondering out loud how such a debate would end when a series of tugs on the cuff of my pantaloons caused me to look down and I spied a tiny figure seated on the toe of my right boot.

He had heard me and responded in this fashion: It was in his view easier for the wealthy to talk about giving than it was for the poor to talk about giving. The wealthy could afford Jesus's Beatitudes though they were aware that the Beatitudes were not the road to wealth.

Most of the people of Tug would prefer to keep their own money than have it go in taxes for ventures they would not privately support. The goals of every loyal Tug subject were freedom, personal liberties, to make their own choices while shopping, voting, going to a doctor, to maximize their comfort without being pestered about carbon footprints, African starvation and genocide, species extinction, nuclear waste, and global warming, not to be taxed on behalf of anybody, not expect anyone to do anything for them, and to answer all intrusions on their private property with the wrath of Jesus whipping the moneylenders out of the temple.

Those who had a superfluity of capital and had worn out the urge to shop might possibly think about other people, the environment and the multitude of other creatures who share this planet with us, and whether or not there just might be a judgment after death. He put his money, though, on there not being an end to an urge to shop and luxuriate in stuff.

I admit to being quite struck by the little chap's cynical outlook and queried whether it was possible through talk to reach the higher angels of the Tug humanity?

He gave me a flat "No." It was he said impossible to talk about redressing the pain and suffering of others to those who were themselves in pain and suffering. People in poor economic shape still want a great deal but what they want doesn't include assisting others in similar shape. People want someone to show THEM the money. Unfortunately once the money gathers in the pockets of the few, there is less to show others and less incentive all round to do anything but adopt an "I've got mine; you get yours" attitude.

I asked him whether there was any hope of charting a course around these difficulties. La Guillotine, he said flatly. And then after a pause, "Some say Cyberville."

"And not faith?" I asked him. "A Celestial Entity?"

I supposed I was the one trying to hold on to something. The tiny man whose name I never knew gave me nothing.

But Rousseau: "Everything is good when it leaves the Creator's hands; everything degenerates in the hands of man."

I was still deep into the grandiloquent musings of my friend Mr. President and the commanding peppershot of Under Decider Dick and now, truth to say, somewhat shattered by the sober reflections of the little cynic on my boot but thought 'ever onward!' and thus I would travel to Cyberville no matter how far away it was.

Instantaneously, as the destination was set in my mind, I discovered that I myself was now the subject of a fire bomb drive by which had, before I was aware of it, set my pantaloons on fire.

A flashy multi-colored banner adorned the bubble that had firebombed me. The banner read "Timber!"

I threw myself on the ground and rolled about like a lunatic. Then, without further ado, I raced smoldering as I was across the field toward the canal and plunged in head first.

I welcomed the comforting silence of those waters and would not have sought to re-emerge had I not seen a hand I knew wavering above me.

I swam toward it and upward.

Chapter IX

Chapter X

The Author's arrival in Cyberville and what he found there.

I shall not relate the many untoward incidents, unwanted adventures and unappreciated sights which befell me as I made my way to the little town of Cyberville, a town which I had been led to believe had overcome the noisy partisanship and senseless warfare I had witnessed in the Kingdom of Tug.

I do not blame you for believing that the hazards and havoc of the wild Frontier should have prepared me for the abyss of the Kingdom of Tug and that any ounce of interest in my fellow man or in the possibility of lucid interrelationship should by now have been drained out of me. I do not blame you for questioning my sanity in traveling to Cyberville in the perpetual hope of finding the worst of our human nature transcended.

In my own defense I can but say that I believe the wild Frontier and the Kingdom of Tug cannot be all that we humans are capable of creating. I believe the people of Tug were tiny because their souls and hearts were tiny and that their reason and their faith were also too tiny to redeem them. And I will not end my travels in that tiny place. I will not end my travels in a place that Carla would not want me to end.

There is but one road to Cyberville, deeply rutted and pot holed, and it winds its way through aged forests whose trees lay or lean where they fall. There are few automobiles, most quite old, more horse traffic, and a scant amount of foot traffic, mostly foraging and not on a *Wanderjahre* like my own.

The impression one receives when one first spies Cyberville, which is built in a clearing in the woods and surrounds a large lake, is abandonment, as if the appearance and well-being of the village had been relinquished, as when one caught in the fever of some pursuit neglects all but one's passion.

Shingles had fallen from roofs, houses were sagging on their foundations, streets were flooded with sewage, yards were overgrown with weeds, sidewalks were fissured so badly that one was constantly detouring, though I saw very few people in the streets.

The people here in Cyberville – called not Cybervillians but *Digerati* -- are of normal size though many have bloated bellies and their eyesight is not good. These conditions are due to their sedentary lifestyle which amounts to many hours sitting in front of a screen of rapidly changing images. The Digerati's vision is good up to about three feet and thereafter deteriorates rapidly, not as disastrous a problem as one might think as the villagers seldom look away from their image screens. Their heads lean to one side at about a 45 degree angle owing to the fact that they almost always have a small device held to one ear. One arm therefore is constantly in a bent position and has, except for the purpose of holding this device to the ear, become almost vestigial. Some display a miniscule apparatus in one ear and are able to keep both hands free. The other ear is connected by wire to a small device worn on the belt which delivers directly into the brain any of several thousand songs representing the personal musical tastes of the owner.

Many more Digerati walk about observing the palm of their left hand quite intently. Upon closer observation I discovered a tiny device with a tiny screen of images that could be altered by quick and dexterous fingering. In order to get the attention of any of the Digerati it is necessary to phone – "cell" is the word the Digerati use -- them, even if you stand at that moment before them.

Most of the Digerati's time is spent on-screen, jacked into a cyberspace connection through which they create a buffer zone of themselves and the outside world. As soon as they waken, they enter this buffer state which possesses a certain comforting womb-like quality as it is self-designed to exclude the unfamiliar, the worrisome and the simply annoying, the bewildering and potentially mortifying. No one chooses to look at what annoys or troubles them and because they hold their personal choosing as sacred, they dwell in what they call friendly social spaces.

Outside this rookery, the Digerati communicate by what they call texting and tweeting on a variety of hand-held devices which I have observed they treat most fondly, as a mother with a babe in a cradle, and like a mother tending her babe, the Digerati are anxious to make frequent, reassuring visual contact with a device out of, I believe, some psychological necessity.

I observe that the need to transmit and receive messages is a very great need among the Digerati and one would expect a high level of human interaction and societal advance resulting from such steady interrelationship. But, alas, as I have intimated, such is not the case for the Digerati are exceedingly self-enclosed, confining as they do their contact with others to a select few of friends, and that contact further confined by its virtualized nature.

Caged within their own desires and preferences and blocking out all else, the Digerati ironically believe that they are far reaching communicatively and therefore display a grandiloquent human nature. What I have thus far seen, however, reveals a high degree of enervation in all aspects of social interest, interaction and justice as well as that pity for the afflicted the Bible asks of us.

The language the Digerati use in their texting is called "Emoticon" and is hieroglyphic and iconographic, more in the manner of primitive cave drawings than Egyptian. I conclude that the primitiveness of Emoticon, by which I mean its severe limitations in transmitting complexity beyond "I'm on the bus" and "Cool, with sunglasses," is owing to the nine second attention span of the Digerati, making a reading of anything beyond a "Tony has a pony" depth a cognitive impossibility. There is also a limit as to how many characters can be employed in the most widely used form of communication, the "tweet." So popular is this form of expression, that Goggle scholars are going back and translating ancient texts into "tweet." So far they have a "Tweet on the Mount," The "Tweet" Dialogues, the tweet version of *Hamlet,* The Tweet Manifesto, and and a *Prolegomena to any Future Tweet.*

It did not take me long to realize that the absence of these devices creates suspicion in the Digerati and so I purchased a full complement and took every opportunity to bring them to my ear, stare at the palm of my hand, talk loudly as if someone was there, and show continued caring concern for their well being. I thus blended unnoticeably into Digerati society.

I had been in Cyberville about a week when I by chance took a counter seat at a diner and found myself sitting next to Walter, dressed in his customary red and gold bowling shirt.

He greeted me with great enthusiasm, quite surprised to find that I had survived the bombing that fateful day. I was anxious to find out how Captain Noble fared.

Walter told me that the Captain had given up piloting the Isle of Babel after the King's death and was now running virtual voyages at www.webepirates.com. right here in Cyberville.

Raggee, the name the parrot now called himself, and the Captain would be damned surprised to see me. They were living, along with Microft, in a small hotel in the *centre ville*, The Raifort Arms, the architectural equivalent of a strumpet in her decline or an octogenarian in full senility. But as my purse was thinning, the Raifort was a good price.

I asked about the fate of Brother Frank. Walter cursed the scoundrel and said as far as he knew Don Rodrigo was hot on his trail. I did not mention my run in with Don Rodrigo and my narrow escape. I asked if the Floating Isle made stops in Cyberville and Walter shook his head. He hadn't seen the Isle since the day I got blown off it.

The parrot had ceased shouting phrases in Latin and Greek and was now interjecting words in English that could, with some effort on the listener's part, be viewed as well placed in whatever conversation was on going. Upon seeing me he shouted *"Cabron, with God all things are possible."* I wondered out loud whether the parrot was a Christian as he now quoted Matthew.

The Captain put a finger to his lips and leaned forward. We were in the sitting room of the Raifort passing the Captain's flask of good Irish whiskey back and forth.

"There be two holier than holy individuals right here in this hotel, matey," the Captain said. "And it won't do to say old Raggee there..." he pointed to the parrot... "is a Christian, as they be saying he's the Devil's work."

I nodded and looked over at the parrot. *"Let copulation thrive,"* the parrot screamed and the Captain told him to belay that talk and shut his trap.

We were soon joined by Walter who said he had finished work for the day. When I asked him what that work might be he simply said he was a recruiter for a good cause. It sounded mysterious but I didn't press.

In the course of a long evening I recounted my adventures, ending as you would imagine with tears in my eyes as I told Carla's tragic tale.

When Microft walked in I was at the end of my tear flow.

Microft looked worn out and deeply troubled and I discovered that he was in an exhausting legal battle with a company that had turned his scientific work to what he called dehumanizing use. He spent most of his time with his lawyer, Bino, in court, or with his psychiatrist, Dr. Maleva.

Upon hearing both those names I cried out, "Why, I know Bino! He defended poor Sal who was executed for a crime he didn't commit." Microft didn't like the sound of that and so I did not pursue a possible link between his psychiatrist, Dr. Maleva, and Maleva the gypsy woman who had fleeced me and left me for dead.

I began to talk, under the influence of Mr. Jamison, of my travels, remarking on how much of an inferno I thought the political Frontier was and how the Kingdom of Tug deserved nothing more than a total disembowelment.

This talk amused all three of my old companions and I queried as to why they were smiling. Walter then told me that however stressful I had found the Kingdom of Tug I would yearn for that stress after spending not too much time in this village.

"Here," Microft said, "there is nothing social but all is an atomized privacy."

I pondered that peculiar phrase and asked what he might mean by it.

Walter, the Captain and Microft then proceeded contrapuntally and orchestrally to explain to me what was meant.

Had I noted any face to face exchange? Had I heard any talk not cell talk? Everyone in Cyberville dwelled not in the village but in their own privately designed electronic village, dwelled in a personal space in which personal interests could be pursued day and night without any accommodation, recognition or confrontation with other Digerati or any presentation of Mother Nature.

I found this quite startling, to say the least. I asked whether war and the enmity of opposing political views were anywhere to be found. I was told one could play at a countless number of war, slaughter and mayhem simulated games but the game of adversarial politics was not a favorite. Most preferred armed robbery, breaking and entering, rape and pillage, insider trading, extortion, kidnapping, downsizing, foreclosures, drive bys and wilding, Texas Hold'em and Execut'em, Working Welfare Queens, Rap Ho's, backyard cluster bombing, Ethnic Cleansing, and prison survival games. *We Be Pirates!* was also a very popular cybergame as was *Fifteen Seconds in the Limelight* and *My Other Life*, a Digerati favorite. Participants could invent a false virtual identity and compete in a virtual game with other false virtual identities, and spend real money.

I asked whether the Captain had become wealthy with his popular virtual game but he said he was no more than the picture on the box, the costume at the conventions, at the photo ops, and in the adverts. He was no more than a promo of a seafaring man. They had made a sort of Ronald McDonald pirate out of him.

He took a hard pull on the bottle which had long since replaced the flask.

"It's all masquerade," the Captain said, glumly.

"Qu'ils mangent de la brioche!" the parrot screamed but nobody paid him any attention. I was thinking my own thoughts and could not be distracted.

"And when they marry?" I queried, wondering when the physical would apply.

Captain Noble had just gotten a finger to his lips when someone behind me said:

"Most prefer the on-line marriage of virtual identities to real marriage."

I turned and saw yet another man I knew: Rev. Swot, my golf associate from the Trickle Downs Spa.

He came into the room, holding his hand out. I got up, somewhat shakily, and shook his hand.

"You know a simulated self avoids the troublesome aspects of real marriage," Rev. Swot said, taking a seat. "Good evening to you, Brothers."

Walter, the Captain and Microft nodded and I could see the Rev. Swot was not a favorite with them.

"Sexually transmitted diseases," Rev. Swot said, "not to mention divorce, abortion, and the need for marriage counseling. Better virtualized than real."

Walter grumbled something, Microft had his eyes closed, whether he was asleep or pretending I cannot say, and the Captain was making some sort of head gestures to the parrot.

Rev. Swot went on, oblivious to the state of his audience.

"Sexual congress as biblically approved love between real people," Rev. Swot told us, "has been atomized into a solely private act of orgasmic release most often facilitated by cyberporn. Cyberporn recognizes our deep, private lives, our self-absorption, and our greater ability to love ourselves more than others. What does Goethe say? `The man who masters himself is delivered from the force that binds all creatures.'"

This talk disgusted me and I at once told the man that Goethe had not been referring to self abuse and if Rev. Swot, as a man of God, had ever asked himself what progeny would emerge from such solipsistic lives? How could this village persevere if there were no real births?

To this Rev. Swot responded that the young arrived from elsewhere and soon became totally absorbed in life as it was lived in the village of Cyberville.

Had I not felt the paralyzing magnetism of Cyberville? I said that I had not and he replied that some Analogues were resistant but my very presence in Cyberville indicated I had been magnetically drawn

I told him quite indignantly that I was a traveler, a voyager to remote realms, and as such I kept my head up and my eye sharp and my ears open for what was new and remarkable that I might see and hear. A traveler does not cast his eyes into his own navel and make of himself a self-enclosed planet.

"I do not travel within circles of my own mind, sir," I told him defiantly, to which he responded he was sure I didn't and then got up and wished us all a good evening.

"Mother of all moral hazards!" the parrot screeched. *"Autant!"*

And indeed we were, with the good Rev. Swot's departure, as we were. Captain Noble passed me the Jamison. When I had taken a pull and felt my anger subside I asked my companions what sort of preacher was this Rev. Swot?

"He's one of those the Almighty will make you rich preachers," Walter told me.

"He's making money hand over fist, he is," the Captain said. "He's Mrs. Montrose's silent partner in www.nudeangels.com., a porno site."

"What?" I sputtered. "Who did you say?"

"Mrs. Montrose," Walter said. "She lives here. Swot's here to keep an eye on her or she's here to keep an eye on him. Anyway, both of them are here."

"Aye, mates," the Captain said. "They don't live large being sort of on the dodge."

I asked why they were on the dodge. The Captain said that was beyond his compass but Walter volunteered that like all maestro hypocrites Rev. Swot had turned totally bi-polar.

"When he lives here," Walter said, "he's wearing his hairshirt and living a St Francis of Assisi life. Probably doesn't know what the Porno Preacher is doing during the day, which is dragging the ville for young and innocent angels who will be happy to strip naked as long as they get seen by the thousands who are cruising cyberspace."

"We're in the eye of the storm here, matey," Captain Noble told me, shaking his head. "I would go back to sea but I'm too old to get a ship."

"You cannot fight the future," Microft said, opening his eyes. "And this place is the future and the future is a place everyone likes better than the past."

I conceded that the village seemed to be an exceedingly popular place. Countless immigrants arriving each day, Walter told me.

"I doubt if you'll stay long, matey," the Captain said. "It's all a mystery to a man who may be in rough waters but can read the stars."

"The Digerati will not mourn your going," Microft told me, "for the Digerati believe they are an advance form of humanity and have left behind the snares and superstitions of physicality."

I then told him that I didn't think either Nature, which in the wisdom of Francis Bacon must be obeyed before commanded, nor our own human nature, which as Blake observed is ripe with cruelty, jealousy, terror, and secrecy, were illusions and that gravity and greed would eventually bring the highest flights of fancy to ground.

As I said this Walter nodded and observed me closely.

"Maybe," he said, "you'd like to join a little bowling team of ours? Interesting talk between frames."

Walter winked at me and when I looked at the Captain and at Microft they both nodded.

"Fire up!!" the parrot screeched.

There was a pub, *The Langooty*, a couple of doors down from the *Raifort* and all the Luddites, or cyber rebels which was what Microft called Walter's associates, congregated there at all hours.

I found that if I went in before noon, I'd find one or two Luddites. At lunch time the place was packed with cyber rebels. And in the evenings, the place was packed and noisy with people anxious to go "face to face," people who were going "screen free" or "off-line" as they called it.

There was live music in the evening and tonight a rockabilly band called *Travelling Press* was playing. The lead singer was, of course, someone I already knew: Kate Whack.

Immediately upon recognizing her – she was singing a Bonnie Raitt song and not at all badly – I looked around for the cameras but there were none. Could it be that Ms. Whack had given up her journalistic career to be a rock star?

After her set, she came over to me at the bar. The parrot was on my shoulder as he had apparently attached to me in the Captain's absences, which seemed now to be often.

"Groupie?" Kate said, as she came up to me, hand held out.

"This is …"I began but then said I was afraid I didn't know what the parrot was calling himself that day.

"*Canard!*" the parrot screeched and Kate laughed.

"So you're doing some sort of undercover expose?" I asked.

"Nope," she said, motioning to the bartender and pointing to my drink and then to me and then to herself. "I'm out of that racket."

We clicked glasses and she drank off half her whiskey. We were both silent long enough to realize it. I then started to say something but she interrupted me.

"I gave it up after what happened back there on the Frontier. To…your…friend."

We soon needed another round and this time I did the buying. She told me her story since I had last seen her and I told her mine. The band was touring and Cyberville was on the tour, though this place, the *Langooty*, paid the lowest in town. She told me that she had a legendary bass player, Dickie Flatts, whose name I might remember from the Frontier. I did and told her I thought he was mythical. Ray, her guitar player, was hoping to make enough money to pay for his chemo treatments. He had testicular cancer. Only somebody so close to crossing over, Kate told me, could play the way Ray played. I was going to tell her that I believe I knew Ray's sister but I was not at all anxious to have this confirmed.

The drummer was young and autistic and her name was Hester. Her consciousness came at the world through music and numbers. Kate was lead vocals, played the flute and did most of the song writing.

Kate left me at the bar when it was time for the second set. I stood there drinking and listening and thinking. I assumed Bino and Microft were working on his case and I knew the Captain was at another board meeting but I wondered where Walter, who was always here by now, might be.

I should have expected another face from the past to emerge in their place but I wasn't prepared for Guy Beecher, who came in, with Emily wrapped around him like a boa, saw me and, eyebrows raised in disbelief, came over to me.

"My soul," he exclaimed, "it's old Gullible. You remember Emily? It's like a *Cruel Shoes* reunion."

"What are you doing in Cyberville, Beecher?"

"My dear Gullible, I'm entrepreneurial..."

"Chump change!" the parrot squawked, perched now on the bar close to my right elbow. Emily seemed to have just seen him though the parrot was immense and luridly colored. She put out a finger to pet his head and the parrot pecked her hard enough for her to cry out.

"You've found the elevated talk you were searching for, I see," Beecher said.

"They fucked you up, your mom and dad," the parrot screeched, hopping from one foot to another.

"Malice is of low stature," Beecher said, instantly enemies with the bird, "in the words of Lord Halifax."

"How is Carly?" Emily asked.

"She's dead," I said, flatly, taking my glass and walking away.

I noted out of the corner of my eye that a young man who looked like a very familiar sailor was talking to a very amused Emily while Beecher was parlaying with Rev. Swot who had come in unobserved by me.

"What kind of world are these jackasses living in?" I said, angrily, as our waitress came over with another round.

"I'm alright, Jack!" the parrot squawked.

If you take a Fool poll, Gully," Beecher was saying loudly so that everyone in the place could hear, " and I don't say you should, you'll find very little interest in politics. Why? Well, I'll examine the reasons but they don't because what they're not personally interested in isn't worth examining. The self-absorbed Fool spends all his time checking his own navel. He sort of curves inward and back into himself. When that happens to a potted plant it eventually dries up and dies. Our talk here is going to incite riots in Cyberville with every Fool jumping forward to tell us how `connected' they are to everything."

I suddenly became aware that Hester, the autistic drummer, was standing there, looking at us. I hadn't been aware of the music stopping either.

"Hello," Hester said to Beecher and myself.

"Hello," I replied, standing and holding out my hand, which she stared at.

I introduced myself and Beecher, who nodded but said nothing. As she said nothing but remained standing there, I asked her to join us, which she did. I beckoned to the waitress who came over and Hester, in response to the waitress's order request, simply said yes. I pointed to my Jamison and said she might like this and she said yes. I told her I thought she was a fine drummer, in the pocket I believe was the expression but she ignored me and was staring at the parrot who was perched on the back of my chair with his head under a wing.

"Who's that?" she asked, as Kate Whack came over to our table and sat down.

"Follow the hounds!," the parrot squawked.

"I was wondering where you were," she said to Hester, who didn't respond.

"I believe he's calling himself Mario this evening," I told Hester.

"Start a business!" the parrot screeched.

"Does he know what's happened?" Hester asked, not looking at anyone. I noted that she established presence that was indeed somewhat spellbinding owing to her eyes, the way she spoke, her movements, the way she pointed at the bird, the ways her eyes never met yours.

"What has happened?" Beecher asked in almost a whisper, not at all like Beecher. I could see that Hester's presence had broken through his own thoughts.

"Hester has a phenomenal memory," Whack said. "She'd make a great journalist. We've just gotten into this burg and she already knows a lot about it. She attaches phrases from the newspapers to numbers and when you say a number she repeats the phrase."

"Five," Beecher said, in the same quiet voice.

"It's late December right now," Hester said, almost at once, her eyes on the sleeping parrot, "for a whole world of people. They won't last much longer. The page will turn on them as if they've never been. The world won't go back for them. They have to go. We know that. We're not stupid."

I was wondering what those sentences might mean when the parrot pulled his head up and shouted: *"Water is best!"*

"Not tonight," I told the parrot, picking up my Jamison.

"She sort of makes sense if you search for it," she said. "Third set. Hang around."

I had been glancing over at the bar where sailor Karl and Emily were now joined by Rev. Swot. She looked more buoyant than usual and it seemed by the look of it than Swot and Karl were trying to persuade Emily of something. Beecher followed my gaze, shoved his gadget in his breast pocket and mumbling something, got up and went to the bar to rescue his nubile possession

I took my leave shortly after, the parrot on my shoulder.

Kate Whack eventually told me what had brought her to Cyberville.

Kate had learned that really big, clever hack jobs were Cyberville contracts. And so she was here undercover to investigate.

A few days before I had arranged to leave Cyberville, Kate told me she had tracked down the hacker and wanted to know if I'd accompany her on what she called an "exploratory." All her leads had brought her to a part of town called Blogosphere and the person she was looking for ran a site called www.relentlesswinning.com.

Kate had gotten an appointment to see the CEO, Ms. Sheherazade Skamble, by saying that I was running for mayor in my hometown, Kate was my campaign strategist, and we wished to hire Ms. Skamble's company to run the polling data and analysis and any and all relevant stats.

Kate gave me this bit of news on our way to the Blogosphere. I protested that I was absolutely without a clue as to what I would say as I had no knowledge of or interest in any political appointment. Kate reassured me that she would do all the talking. I was not reassured.

If the space one chooses to live parallels the physiognomy of one's personality, then my immediate impression of Ms. Skamble was that she was an octopus. Her being was multitudinous and as such carried on multifarious connections contemporaneously.

The office was not one but fragmented into a number of different sites, smaller desks orbiting Ms. Skamble's own L-shaped desk, her assistants – I counted four – at these desks like satellites or moons, their faces hidden behind computer screens.

Ms. Skamble waved us in with the hand that held what I recognized as some sort of very intelligent phone, a web portal and I had been told so much more. She held a cell phone to her ear with the other hand. There was a Sony Vaio laptop in front of her and a desktop PC to her right. All of these would have been unrecognizable to me just weeks before.

Ms. Skamble terminated her cell phone conversation and rested the phone directly in front of her. She held her BlackBerry throughout her visit and she glanced frequently at the laptop, the cell phone and the BlackBerry. Each time her phone rang she begged our indulgence and answered it. The calls were very brief but frequent. She informed us she was following second by second some very important people on Twitter.

There were two TVs in the room, one tuned to a 24/7 news channel and the other to a 24/7 business report. The volume was muted on both and text appeared at the bottom of both screens. Ms. Skamble's gaze periodically went over our heads to both screens. I was also aware that she was closely monitoring the activity of her assistants.

After listening to Kate's bogus story, she told us that she could strategize my campaign without leaving Cyberville and would relentlessly pursue my victory, by whatever means necessary. I was curious as to how she could strategize, as she called it, without ever visiting Clabberton, the small town Kate had invented.

I put this question to her and saw at once the look Kate gave me for I had promised to remain silent.

Ms. Skamble was not taken back by the question. She spoke in the manner of a gifted collegiate debater—quick jolts of very decisive thoughts -- and when her free hand was not tapping a key here and there on the lap top, she was deftly twirling a pen between thumb and index finger.

"So I go there," she said, "and I see Mr. Farmer and his chickens and Mrs. Country Club and Ms. Cheerleader and Rev. Saintly and so on and so on. And I do some blah blah yadda yadda with them. I go to a pig roast, Sunday service, the meeting of the Moose lodge, the Mothers Against War and so on and on. Yadda Yadda. Or, I stay here, throw a net on every statistic available on every person, every bit of history, every belief, every credit card, every school, business, leisure activity. I create a cyber profile. What do I have? Something much more useful than Yadda Yadda."

It took her all of three seconds to say this while at the same time tapping at the laptop and glancing at her phone.

"I want to be totally understood here," Kate said. "I live in Clabberton. Poverty, unemployment, fixed retirement incomes, school drop out rate of 50%, credit cards maxed, houses in foreclosure or close to it. . ."

"On Friday night," Ms. Skamble said, interrupting her, and at the same time fingering her BlackBerry, "bowling, bars, and the hospital emergency get the most business. Every so often a BMOC rapes a cheerleader or a desperate housewife takes a nude swim with the plumber."

"Every night the ER gets business," Kate added. "One out of five hundred has any medical insurance."

Ms. Skamble smiled.

"And? What did you want me to understand? So far from what you tell me this is a very winnable election."

"If I thought so," Kate replied, smiling also, "I wouldn't be here. Mr. Gulliver's platform is not populist."

"Have you ever heard of Rapacious Walker?" Ms. Skamble replied. "He ran against a populist in a place suffering even worse than Clabberton. His financial backing came from bloodsuckers who had crushed any assistance to the people whose blood they were sucking. Pardon."

She answered her cell phone. I looked at Kate. Would we get anyplace with the formidable Ms. Skamble?

"Okay," Ms. Skamble said, snapping her phone shut, "the bloodsuckers won. They got their victims to vote `keep on sucking my blood.' I can do the same thing in Clabberton. You've got racists? We run on a slave ticket. Cultural Elite? We NASCAR our opponent? Gay bashers? We quote the Bible. The poor? A tax rebate. No health insurance? Promise them one. Education? We'll reform it. Gun control? Our man will pack a gun and shoot a moose from a copter. Abortion? You kill a baby, you go to jail. You say the word fetus, you go to jail. And Yadda Yadda. No problemo."

"Mr. Gulliver here is a monarchist," Kate said, after a longish pause, determined to break Skamble's composure. "He's running on a return of royalty ticket. You can't spin the Clabbertonians into supporting that."

Ms. Skamble's eyes focused on me for the first time. I must say I was astounded by what Kate had said.

Ms. Skamble's free hand drifted to the PC and she did some tapping and mouse work and then looked at Kate.

"Is it a Christian monarchy?"

Kate shook her head.

"Hedonist. All the drink, food, gold and women for him and his dukes kind of king."

"Apres moi le deluge," I added.

"Does he have any celebrity status?" Ms. Skamble now asked, still tapping at her PC.

"He's known as a pig," Kate said, looking at me. "He's popular with other pigs. Inherited wealth. He treats his staff like scum. He treats women like whores. Has run out of expensive distractions and now feels it would be nice to be the king. He wants to make torture and child abuse Reality TV shows. He wants to re-introduce slavery."

Ms. Skamble now seemed to be using every digital device around her, all at once, as she searched for a winning strategy.

Kate now played her card.

"I came to you because I've heard that you know how to make the computer help us win."

This did not get any notable reaction from Ms. Skamble.

"Militarist?" she asked me and I said "Pardon?"

"Been in the military? Captured? Tortured? Silver medal? Bronze stars? Yadda Yadda."

I shook my head for each one.

"Fear," Ms Skamble said. "Feareo is our strategio. We could say Arab terrorists are about to launch another 9/11 with Clabberton as a target. Bombs go off. Black helicopters. Masked men on camels. Yadda Yadda. Or there could be a crime wave. Pensioners get robbed and mugged in their own homeos. Women get fondled running in the park. Kids get kidnapped on the way home from schooleo. Epidemic of identity theft. Yadda Yadda."

She pointed at me.

"Goldfinger here stops a bank robbery or car jacking. Rescues a hired damsel in distress. Defuses a bomb in a mall. He takes his private army into the toughest part of town where the punks are and he tells them he'll make their dayeo all Dirty Harry like. The ticket is this: order is what's needed and a monarchy can restore an order . . .When heads need to roll, who does it better than a king?"

"Where everyone knows his place," I said, nodding, fascinated by the way Ms. Skamble's mind worked.

"No," she told me decisively. "You can restore an order where the worst elements are imprisoned, the undeserving and the lazy and degenerate are kept in their place. This might be the whole population but everyone thinks it's not them but the other person who needs to be kept in line. Everyone believes their problems are someone else's fault and if that someone could just be restrained and go to church or read the Bible or mow their lawneo. Yadda Yadda."

Kate shook her head. I believed, my dear Reader, that Ms. Skamble, who seemed to have nothing but ridicule to launch at everyone and everything in the world, had checkmated us but Kate was a determined journalist out to get her story.

"No one will ever look to Gulliver here as a superhero. That's number one. Number two is that Clabbertonians are used to violence. They've already got all the Yadda Yadda crime you mention. They don't wait for someone to throw a punch for them. They throw it themselves."

"I won't be waiting for things to happen," Ms. Skamble told us, "we pay for the dramatic events we need. It's not chance. It's all computer driven."

"So you're saying we just commit the crimes ourselves?"

"I don't commit crimes, Ms. Whack," Ms. Skamble said, still smiling. "But I can see to it that a whole barrageo of crime . . ."

"Pardon me," Kate said, "but I find that very annoying."

"What's that?" the Skamble said. "Something I saideo?"

"Just that," Kate said, "Saideo and barrageo and crimeo. What is that computer talk?"

"Grand delete," the Skamble said, running a finger across air, "so we can have crimes reported day in and day out. We might also be lucky enough to get some cell phone video we run on *YouTube*. There will be no crime and there will be no victims because we will pay for both the criminals and the victims. But we will have the video. Appearance is reality."

"We have limited funds," Kate said, not willing to concede.

"No crown jewels and kingly coffers?"

Kate shook her head.

"Spent it all, or most of it. What we need is just a representation of the vote that makes Gulliver here the winner."

"Tampering with votes is a felony," Ms. Skamble said. "I do not commit crimes. However, I can see to it that no fraud transpires to your candidate's disadvantage. Pardon."

She spoke not more than fifteen seconds on her cell and then looked at us.

"That's agreeable," Kate told her. "Cost?"

The Skamble fingered her BlackBerry and then held it out for Kate to see.

Not ready to give up quite yet, Kate turned as we were leaving and addressed Skamble who was poking at her palm device.

"And you can spin the slavery away?"

Skamble looked up and smiled.

"Workeo and not welfare. Tough loveo. What greater love can you show to a welfare moocher than give him workeo? Steady employment. Only the layabouts call it slavery."

Kate sighed and gave up and we walked out of the indomitable Skamble's office.

An hour later Kate and I were at the bar at the *Langooty.* Kate, earplug in, was listening to what she had secretly recorded in Ms. Skamble's office. I wasn't quite sure the clever Skamble had incriminated herself and so Kate and I listened to her fraud response several times.

"She doesn't say she's going to fix the return," I said, "but merely see to it that no one else does."

"She's asking for a quarter of a million dollars," Kate told me. "That sum means she's giving us more than a computer protection system. She's not going to allow any voter return except a winning one for us."

I reminded Kate that there was no "us" as I was not running for mayor on a royalist ticket and there was no Clabberton and she wasn't my campaign manager as there was no campaign. Kate advised me not to be so sure.

"When she goes to the campaign website," Kate said, smiling, "she'll find everything you said doesn't exist. Great shots of you by the way wearing a crown. Remember, she said she didn't need to go to Clabberton. On that website there is indeed a Clabberton. With a lot of history too."

"So she's promised to falsify the cyberspace returns of an election in a town that only exists in cyberspace?"

"And I'll get a real story out of it," Kate told me, winking, "and she'll do some real time in jail."

I ordered a double Jamison and that night checked the rail schedules for my departure from Cyberville was long overdue.

Chapter XI

In which the Author runs into yet more old acquaintances, witnesses a murder, and then finally leaves Cyberville.

I was rather surprised the next day when I received an invitation from Mr. and Mrs. Mark Spark to join a luncheon aboard their yacht which was moored on the other side of the lake.

There was a brief note attached: "Please allow me the opportunity to make amends for the unfair and ungentlemanly manner in which you were treated when last on the yacht. I have since discovered my wife's perfidy. Mark."

When a man has you thrown overboard because he believes you have had congress with his wife, and you have, and then writes to say he was wrong and that some other party did the congressing, do you accept the invitation and inform him that he was correct in believing that you did indeed had congress with his wife and would be correct also in believing others had also enjoyed his wife's favors and that therefore no apology to you was necessary?

The matter was sordid and besmirched my love for Carla. I therefore tore up the invitation and thought no more of it until that evening at the *Langooty* when a quite crestfallen Captain Noble confessed to us that unless he got his hands on a considerable amount of money very soon, he would be off to jail.

Bino told him that crime and punishment were no more than a link made with sentences in the mouth of a barrister. This did not cheer up the good Captain nor, truth to say, myself either, having before me the innocent but executed face of Mr. Sal.

It seems that Captain Noble had given the impression that he held a controlling interest in webpirates.com in order to leverage loans from several on-line banks. He told us he wanted his own ship and he saw a chance of getting it and as his days were running out, he had jumped at the chance. Like a pirate. As none of the loans had actually gone through the only charges he faced were being made by webpirates.com.

"And the man who owns that bit of ballast," the Captain said, "is anchored right here on the lake. A Mr. Mark Spark. I'm of a mind to row out there and make my plea, one seafaring man to another."

I told the Captain that whatever Mark Spark was, he wasn't a fellow seafaring man. I then recounted my brief tenure aboard the Spark yacht, ending with the invitation I had received that morning. As you can imagine, I was barraged with pleas to attend the luncheon, speak to Mark Spark, and save the good Captain Noble from prison.

I of course acquiesced and the next day at noon I was in a launch heading across the lake to the Spark yacht.

Mr. Spark greeted me like an old friend, clasping my hand in both of his and telling me *sotto voce* that my being here was more than he deserved and would I hold him forgiven?

Before I could reply I saw Mrs. Spark coming toward us. Mr. Spark saw my surprise and whispered that he had not yet confronted his wife with her adultery. She said something to me about how nice it was to renew old acquaintances and I mumbled my agreement.

Mark – what he now insisted I call him – was more anxious to introduce me to his festal board than his guests. Arm in arm we toured the eatables, Mark reminding me that nine tenths of the global population would never see, no less eat all that was before us, from the *potage a la tortue* and bouillabaisse to the *poitrine de veau, crevette* and *homard*. His eyes lit up as he pointed to the patisserie and to a magnificent Sicilian cassata. I noticed how his avid gaze went from the patisseries to where his wife was standing talking to Guy Beecher, whom I was surprised and not surprised to see there. Mark's gaze took her in like she was another digestible, but one that was no longer agreeable, although I am nothing if not honest and I must admit, that Mrs. Hot Spark looked very alimental indeed.

Besides Guy Beecher and Emily, I also knew among the guests Rev. Swot and Mrs. Montrose, for indeed that traveling baggage was present. She greeted me as if we had never met and I took this to mean that our days together at Mrs. Bombers' boarding house for ne'er do wells was not a suitable recollection on the present occasion nor would it suit her present image.

Mark introduced her to me as a Digerati entrepreneur who ran several very successful websites in which he was considering investing. She was not my biggest surprise. Maleva, the gypsy fortune teller who had robbed me, stood before me, a big smile on her dark face. Dr. Maleva, psychotherapist. She showed no sign of recognizing me. Mark told me that Dr. Maleva was his wife's therapist.

After we had all circumnavigated the luncheon groaning board countless times and had imbibed large quantities of champagne, we took to chat clustering and I found myself in a deck chair at the stern surrounded by Mark, Swot, Mrs. Montrose, Dr. Maleva, and several gentlemen whose type I had recognized on the Frontier and were there called Cash Barons.

We were all listening to Mark Spark hold forth on the logistics of seizing new markets. I saw at once this was the 'war of all against all' Mark Sparks and I sat back waiting for the `share the wealth' Mark Sparks to come forward.

"And it is there," Mark was saying, stabbing the surrounding air with a Cuban cigar, "we must go if we wish to follow the money for it is axiomatic ..."

Axiomatic. Ah, the word conjured memories both sweet and sad. It had been dear Carla's goal to find what was axiomatic and reduce it to rubble.

"...for it is axiomatic," I hear Mark say, "in the pursuit of profits to open new frontiers of profit wherever and whenever they materialize. The second axiom involves the seizing of all opportunities technology affords so as to create those frontiers. And the third and final axiom here is to establish in the consumer a connection between the unique design of identity and technology, in this case the infinitude of websites offered in cyberspace. Any proliferation of consumption opportunities means a proliferation of profit."

"There is deep psychic matter here," Dr. Maleva said, sounding exactly as she had sounded when she asked me if I wanted my palm read. "Those who like to talk about being citizens or God's servants, or Winners or rebels or artists or football heroes or deer hunters and so on don't really think of themselves as 'consumers' and don't want to be called such. Shopping is like washing your clothes. It's not significant enough to define you."

"Shopping is just a thing we do," Rev. Swot said, "when we feel like it and it's not really consequential. We can be 'totally whatever' about it. It's innocent. It's casual. Surfing the Web is a 'free to choose' matter that is individually designed and not corporate driven. We need to find out about something or we need a bit of fun. Digital speech. Vast number of choices. Kid in a well stocked candy shop."

I could not refrain from asking the Porno Reverend whether these same kids roamed his nude angels website? The good Reverend went red in the face and protested any connection with nude angels. Mrs. Montrose seem unperturbed and told us all that she was proud of her nude angels website for it had reduced STD's in *Cyberville* by forty three percent and unwanted pregnancies by fifty-nine per cent.

"I don't buy the whole malarkey about the innocence of this whole cyberspace attachment," Mark Spark boomed out, the socialist Mark Spark. "They're finding the stuff they're putting in their heads. And what's already in their heads – and that's a horror --- is doing the looking. This is nothing more than high speed enslavement. And damn it. I won't stand for it!"

I wasn't the only one unaffected by Mark's sudden explosion for my companions made no attempt to take up Mark's challenge.

"Most *Digerati*," Dr. Maleva said, "believe that they are finding every part of what they are, from public self to private self, incorporated within a myriad of websites. Your `surfing' terrain parallels the physiognomy of yourself, from the personal – love, grief, ambition, anger, depression, dreams, health, travel – to the public – politics, business, community, education. The deeper and wider you go in cyberspace, the deeper and wider you become. There are no limits."

"Sounds like Eden," I said and then burped.

"Damn it to hell," Mark shouted, going south of Eden, "money makes limits. Money is made and power compounds like interest. There's no equitable distribution of power in cyberspace. You make money convincing people to go along with what makes you money. Cyberspace is no more than an accelerated form of brain ownership. Products and services. Not justice and compassion. It makes me sick."

Mark got up shakily and made his way to the patisserie, coming back with a cream puff in one hand and an éclair in the other. Thusly is the anger of Zeus assuaged.

"I do not think Cyberspace is ungodly," Rev. Swot said. "The path to Enlightenment and to human self-development is self-designed but self-design is best fulfilled through cyberspace. Only here can individual uniqueness be found."

"For a minute there, Reverend," I said, "I thought you were going to quote the Bible where it says through cyberspace find salvation."

"Look, friends," Mark said, waving an éclair at us, "you're not creating yourself out of that web. It's all prefab. An already constructed space that you're not choosing. It's leasing you."

"Look, Gullman," Mark addressed me, "there's always a kind of profit that results. I'm speaking of the profit made from linking a sense of individual freedom and personal development to a web search and thus opening up a new market frontier. So, the walls of a private self which weren't reachable before are now scaled. We could never reach everybody. Now in this digital world people are carrying our products and services' transmitters on them. You don't have to hire Madison Avenue. People are selling themselves. It's a businessman's wet dream."

"Do not neglect the fact," Dr. Maleva added, "that there is also the profit made directly by your purchases, goods or services, of what you need to be YOU."

"And the Almighty also helps you to be you," the Rev. Swot told us.

"Let me tell you how the private self expands to the public self," Mrs. Montrose said, ignoring her partner, Swot. "What you do next is publicize your web-created self onto the web so that every part of your private and personal soul can be broadcast to the world. Without this public offering of yourself, you cannot properly own your private, unique self. It must become available for all to see, and to `visit,' perhaps visiting YOU in order to harvest a bit more of what will become eventually their own uniqueness."

One of the Cash Barons pontificated on the beauties of free choice in a free market enhanced by the infinite number of web sites in cyberspace to freely choose from and thereby expand the domain of choice we freely roam within. Yadda yadda as Sheherazade would say.

"If you follow the money," Spark said, as jelly oozed from the Bismarck in his hand, "it goes from your interminable pursuit of yourself through cyberspace transactions to the pockets of shareholders."

He bit into the Bismarck on one side as the jelly spurted from the other side onto the deck.

Although I should have taken the first launch back to *Cyberville*, I decided to find a secluded place and sleep off my inebriation. My intent was to rise up sober and confront Mark about the Captain Noble matter. As I knew the yacht well, I knew where my private womb was to be found

I don't know how long I was sacked there but it was quite dark when I awoke and several seconds before I realized that sounds nearby had woken me.

I heard enough to know that some lovers had sought privacy also. I recognized Emily's giggle and I recognized her lover because she used his name. Karl. After what I thought was too long a while and I was about to stand up and reveal myself I heard

Karl ask her if she was ready to be a nude angel to which she giggled and said she was ready.

I wondered how my compatriot Guy Beecher would take this news. My musing along these lines was abruptly interrupted by two gun shots and a scream. I peered out and saw a man in the shadows holding a gun. He and the screaming Emily seem to spend long minutes looking at each other and then the man turned and disappeared into the darkness.

Emily was crouched down now over Karl's body and I took the opportunity to make my escape. I knew whoever was still on board would have heard those shots and I decided quickly to be one among the curious.

Hours later I was staring at Chief Inspector Louis Picon who was conducting the murder investigation. Guy Beecher, Mrs. Montrose and myself were the only guests yet on board and we joined Mark and his wife and the entire crew in the main salon as Picon had ordered. Emily's hysteria had not abated and she had been given a sedative.

It was after three AM when the police launch took us back to *Cyberville.* In answering Picon's questions I did not reveal that I had been an unwilling spectator of the lovers' assignation or the murder. I felt that I needed to talk to Bino first.

" You think you're paying attention to things in this here world if you're clicking your mouse real fast?"Walter was saying, as I entered the *Langooty.*

"Aye, matey, we're not changing," Captain Noble said, two topsails to the wind and it was only a bit passed the noon hour. The good Captain had been drinking hard of late.

"We're finished," he said, soaking a biscuit in his rum and holding it up so the parrot could nibble at it. "We're caught in the mud of what is so five seconds ago, what is old school, what is old, over and adios. That's what they say when they see these white whiskers."

"Call me a poor soul because I don't even carry a cell phone so that I can be reached by the outside world day or night," Walter said, "but, excuse me, I don't have any face friends. I've

163

got real friends in the flesh standing here at the bar. Drinking here."

"You are pitiable though," Kate Whack said, a shot of Irish and a pint in front of her. "You can only talk one dimensionally. You're like the man with a buggy whip in his hand cursing a Model T. You know what you're full of? Fear. Fear of the future because it's not like what you know. And you won't be in it. The same shit gets repeated over and over in history. It's tiresome is what it is. Why, you can't even multi-task."

"I'll give it a try," Captain Noble cried out, "if you tell me how to do it."

"Well," Walter told him, "you need to think about your own self. All the time. That's the first task. If you're talking to someone else, say, me, then that's multi-tasking."

Kate turned to me.

"You're not multi-tasking," she said. "You're obviously just thinking of you."

I was indeed distracted, anxious for Bino to walk in so I could consult with him about a matter than was looming more ominously in my mind every hour.

It wasn't Bino who then walked in but Guy Beecher. I asked him how Emily was doing and he said that she was blessed with short term memory loss plus attention deficit disorder plus her brains were fried on diet pills and seemed today as giddy as a paramecium.

"Of course, that bloody inspector Picon has some foolish idea I killed that sailor in a fit of jealousy. But he does not have an ounce of evidence. I am not worried. Real events, like a murder, do not absorb the *Digerati* half as much as a virtual murder. The *Digerati* mind cannot stay fixed for long on a real world event."

He ordered a port, leaned back against the bar and surveyed my companions with a raised eyebrow. But Walter had heard the last words.

"Fly wheel minds," he said, nodding. "Jumping frog minds. Everything going in and out, back and forth, over and under. As long as it's moving."

Beecher looked at the huge bulk of Walter, taking his time surveying him from Wellingtons to chartreuse bowling shirt to shaggy red beard.

"I must point out, old chap," Beecher said in that condescending manner he had honed to a fine edge, "without everything going in and out of fashion in the average rustic's mind and in their bumpkin world, the *Digerati* economy would go bust. Say, you're spinning cloth and happy doing it. A perfect boor. Why, you're holding back progress. I mean if you are not looking for change every eighteen seconds or eighteen months, you are obstructive, a retardant in the new technoculture world. Do you not realize, sir, that *Digerati* entrepreneurs need to speed up the rate of consumption in order to `grow' their returns? Why, man, you wouldn't want to stand dumb and unyielding like a beast in the road?"

"Who you calling a beast in the road?" Walter roared, putting his pint down.

"Ass kickers!" the parrot, slightly tipsy, sang out.

"It seems like you're very comfortable here in *Cyberville*," Walter said to Beecher.

"And why not?" Beecher responded. "Cyberspace. Now there's a highway for infinite acceleration. It makes product and labor portable alongside capital. It speeds up change to digital levels. And you know it eventually gives you the kind of awareness that admires and needs both that acceleration and that change. It's a perfect Frankenstein creator. We are at the very cusp of a robotic future where we will learn to despise our own humanity."

Walter looked at me. I shrugged. How could I explain Beecher's bitter irony? Beecher bought a round for all of us. I was beginning to see that he wasn't as calm as he pretended, that indeed Picon had made it clear that he was his number one suspect. Beecher ordered a whiskey and soda for himself.

"Now of course," he went on, "this isn't the kind of change that history records. It wasn't just marketing stimulation back in the day that changed things. Or didn't. It was ideas and actions, power and chance, will and belief. They stepped up strong so that if you were in business you had to find a place to sell your wares inside or around all that. Now change itself, the faster the better, is The idea and no other idea impedes it's progress. How glorious for humankind!"

The parrot began to sing the *Internationale*. This was very eerie to say the least. We all stopped drinking and listened to him.

"Did you teach him that?" I asked the Captain who shook his head and told me the parrot picked up all sorts of things.

"I agree," Whack said, but I had no idea what she was agreeing to. "I'm sick and tired of chasing tomorrow's story. Being bored with today's because I already know it. And yesterday's? It's nothing. Like it never was. We're mayflies. Nothing holds us for long."

It wasn't even early afternoon and my companions had already primed their pumps. I knew why I was drinking. I had seen the face of the man who shot Karl. And Kate Whack? She was here for something besides playing in a band and that something was whacking the hell out of her.

She now had decided to let the rum take its course.

"Talk in this town isn't directed to understanding the conundrums and complexities surrounding us," she told us. "No. Understanding is not where your multi-tasking is leading. You know why? Because if you were set on understanding you'd be shortly losing your delusions."

The parrot seized the pause to sing a bit more of the *Internationale.*

"No, " Kate said, with all the firmness of a judge, "what Cyberspace offers is endless `information,' mostly about products or services or celebrities or sports or pop culture trivia. Going after this `information' in Cyberspace is a kind of quest without an end."

"One must work for one's delusions," Beecher said, finishing his whiskey and pointing to the empty glass.

"Nothing in this town is a threat to your delusions," Kate said angrily. "The longer you stay on-line being `entertained' or `informed' the more useless you are to this real world we're living in. You're in the worst possible place to understand the interrelationship of all things. I sound like Walter. I don't want to sound like an old bitch. I'm young. I love my phone."

"Ah," Beecher exclaimed. "the interrelationship of all things. It is never so clear as when one is intoxicated. It is a wonderfully clear sentence."

"Well, Lord Fauntleroy," Kate said, pointing to Beecher, "You can run a real election in the real world and get a real vote. Or, some *Digerati* can let you have a virtual vote and then, God only knows, whose got the best cyberhacker. And then it's all goddamn not true. And we'll never get back to digging out the truth. Jesus, we'll elect the wrong man and when has that ever happened?"

She knocked back her drink and marched out of the *Langooty*.

The parrot sang a bit more of the *Internationale*.

My mind was racing. I had understood and not understood what Kate had said.

"Of course," Beecher said, "I agree that the interrelationship of all things is quite different than being caught in a 'world wide web.' I've never been partial to verbs...I mean webs. I pull'em down."

His smile immediately vanished when Picon accompanied by several uniform police came into the pub. Picon marched up to us. I could see Beecher's face go bloodless.

"Monsier Guy Beecher," Picon said. "I arrest you for the murder of Karl Mensur."

Bino didn't show up until later in the evening. Kate Whack had returned with Hester and the guitar player, Ray. We were at a table in a far corner. The discussion was money, or those who had a lot of it.

"Whether we choose to 'grow' the wealth of .01% of the world's population," Kate said, not yet quite sober, "or whether we choose to 'grow' a healthier and safer environment, something other than a huge wealth divide, or individual happiness. . ."

She paused.

"Excuse me, what was I saying?"

"You were saying," Bino told her, "that what they have here in *Cyberville* does nothing more than liberate us from the world and circle us back up our own anus."

Kate nodded.

"You cannot self-design your own Youniverse," she said. "Only Deluded Fools believe that. And at the very moment you believe you are doing your self-designing thing, `you' have already been wound up to go down that Fool's path."

"Rich people want to keep things going their way," Ray said, bitterly, his eyes bloodshot. "If they got to fill your head with shit, they will. But it's just as easy to let you rot in ignorance and poverty and drugs and let you kill yourself. Or, just make sure they don't pay for your medical bills."

Ray didn't look good, dark rings under his eyes, his clothes seem to hang on his lank frame, his matted hair hung down to his gaunt shoulders.

"You know," he said, his eyes widening, "this place here sucks up all the energy of what we used to have. I'm talking about the cranks, aliens, outlaws, junkies, musicians, poets, rebels... "

"All masterless men and women," Kate said, nodding.

"They'd break things up," Ray said. "Tear them down. The bloodsucking rich got no peace. But now they're all on the one big soma pill. Cyberspace."

"The *Digerati* don't agree," Bino told Ray. "They feel they have a voice in cyberspace."

"Sure," Ray shot back. "Everybody's got a voice on that web. But you know what? Whatever I say? What I'm saying here? It's like an empty can of Coke floating in outer space."

"I think Hester wants to say something," Kate said and indeed she did.

"We are now a village which is implanting `freedom' elsewhere," Hester said, as if reciting, "hoping to force a change that will bring others into the logic of progress is growth, growth is an economic measurement, change serves economic growth, Cyberspace accelerates change. Once bound by this logic, others will be as `free to choose' as we here in Cyberspace are."

"I smash that logic!" Ray said, banging the table.

"She was just quoting from memory something she read or heard," Kate told him.

"Well, somebody should tell her it's stupid shit," Ray said.

"She's a unique young lady," Bino said, studying Hester.

"I watched Ms. Oh's TV show," I said, "and she said we are all as unique as snowflakes and I could see that the audience held this to be an infallible Truth. But I thought: snowflakes are all doing the same thing. They are all falling. But the *Digerati* don't seem to be able to see that they've all fallen into the black hole of Cyberspace and I, for one, and I am a mere traveler traveling through, cannot see how they can get out."

Bino slapped me on the back.

"I thought you were leaving the old order behind and journeying to the new?"

I shook my head. No, I told him, I had traveled much and seen much but I had not made the journey he spoke of. I saw the new in old ways but I had no allegiance, nevertheless to the old. I then quoted Lord Tennyson in full support of my fear that one good custom could corrupt the world.

In due time I managed to get Bino alone and related to him all that had happened on Mark Spark's yacht. The murderer I had seen was Mark Spark and not Guy Beecher. I had not yet testified to this because I was hoping against hope that some way could be found to both persuade Spark to bail Captain Noble out of his difficulties and to also prove Beecher's innocence.

"So you'd be willing to see Mark Spark get away with murder?" Bino asked me.

"I don't want to see the Captain go to jail," I said, twinging a bit as I recognized the murkiness of my moral calculations.

"And you're hoping I can get Beecher off?" Bino said. "Without you testifying."

"There were no witnesses to testify he did shoot Karl," I said. "They haven't even found the gun."

Bino nodded.

"Did you ever wonder why Spark would even care who Karl was romancing, as long as it wasn't his wife?"

Bino sat there, saying nothing for a long while and then told me that he needed to do a bit of detective work and I was not to go to either Spark or the police until I heard from him. He left me immediately and I sat there wondering whether the *Digerati* might be wise to ignore the travails of the real world and escape to their cyberwomb.

The next day my own perturbations were trumped by those of Microft who had failed in his attempt to obtain an injunction against the further use of his work, work I cannot describe for you in any detail except to say that it had been shanghaied by a dot.com cabal and corrupted.

Microft had not gotten out of his bed that morning and when I, along with Captain Noble, parrot perched on his shoulder, and Walter, paid our visit at cocktail hour, about five, he was still in bed, and more agitated than ever. He held a jug of wine by him as he lay there, head propped up by pillows.

Upon seeing us he at once warned us of the creation of what he called a *humachine.*

"I am not an enthusiast of the creation of a new hybrid human and cyber being," he announced. "I am not talking about the old Frankenstein creature stitched together from organic parts retrieved from the newly dead. I am talking about a *humachine* that becomes part of the cyberflow, which no one owns and no one can command."

He held up his jug to us but as we had our own flask of Irish, we declined.

"Human nature can change," Microft said, "but what it will change into no one can be sure but there are signs all around us in this wretched place. I believe it will be a monster."

"There be monsters in all waters," Captain Noble said, nodding. "Not just in these waters here."

This comment did not go down well with Microft at all.

"Have you ever seen an *Invasion of the Body Snatchers* pod in its formative stage?" he asked us. "That's what you observe in this *Cyberville*. The *humachine* seems harmlessly self-obsessed but it's gestating. What will it become?"

"Everyone has his reasons," the parrot cried out.

"You can find it in the chat rooms," Microft whispered to us, " hear it on webcasts, read it in text messages, follow it on

Facebook or *Myspace* or *You Tube*, hear it in cell phone talk, experience it on the blogs and on podcasts and webcasts and live feeds. Every search engine shows you what we will become."

"I agree," Walter said, speaking up for the three of us who had become speechless before Microft's prophecy. "What you find all around you here is an elevated egoism, like an elevated blood pressure."

"And it grows steadily worse," Microft burst out, "the more fools believe the world shapes itself to their likes and dislikes. It's a false dominance contrived for the sake of profit. They've bent my work to the will of profit. Made it another deceit for fools to purchase."

I suggested that the new humachine, as Microft called it, was no more than crude *amour propre* amplified to dehumanized proportions and accelerated at frightening speed.

"Narcissism has never been fed so richly and so continuously as among these *Digerati*," I declared.

I felt somewhat pompous in my pronouncement and was not altogether free, dear Reader, of a desire to placate what I feared was a certain paranoia on the part of my friend Microft.

Microft's eyes had closed and we took the opportunity to tip toe out of the room. We had reached the door when Microft awakened.

"I leave you with these frightening words," he told us in a strange croak, "these people are stitching together a human nature devoid of any social awareness and a clear threat to the survival of the human race. It's alive!"

I spent the whole of next day wandering about *Cyberville* hoping to abate my impression as to how deeply rooted into everyday life was the technophilia of these villagers.

I considered as I ate a hearty breakfast that someone had cooked this porridge, fried these eggs, toasted this butter, brewed this coffee. The young and comely waitress who had served it and had a cheering smile and welcoming words and had walked to the table, handed me the plates, poured the juice and coffee was in the world. And the world was not named *Cyberville* nor was it encompassed by cyberspace.

We are in the world regardless of our desires to retreat or our opportunities to do so. A country peasant stands head down toiling in the field. Is this a communion with Nature? A villager here in *Cyberville* surfs through cyberspace. Is this destructive of Nature? Someone plays chess before an open fire with an old friend; someone plays a virtual game with a virtual opponent. Is there a loss of human interaction, understanding, empathy? True, there is no public square in this village, no public phones, no Speakers' corner as in Hyde Park, no bowling in teams. Two people facing each other are most often not speaking to each other but engaged with some hand held electronic device.

This was not a matter to be answered fully in the present and that though I and my companions were refuseniks and luddites we had not the prophetic rectitude of a Jeremiah.

I was anxious to depart *Cyberville* but much weighed on my conscience, including the life of Guy Beecher and the fate of Captain Noble. I was also painfully aware that the issues facing me were consequential and my actions would be writ large on my immortal soul. What also troubled my conscience was my dismissal of a way of life to which the *Digerati* so avidly and devotedly gave themselves.

A devilish aspect of this Cyberville is the notion that somehow cyberspace not only improves the quality of our talk by simple magnifying the quantity of it but the more we talk the freer we are. The Digerati have the notion that we are all situated equally on some grand cyberspace talkfest, that all talk bears equal weight. If that's an enchantment that has little power over us, we can always fall back on our bedrock enchantment: my talk in the end is all that matters because it's my talk. It's not Ourspace.com. No one is working our computer mouse but us. We are guiding our way through cyberspace, stopping to talk not because other talk matters but because we need other people to mark our uniqueness, our freedom, our self-designed being-in-the-world.

An intriguing part of the *Digerati*'s self-absorption, an outcropping, is their need to competitively self-assert. In cyberspace they can publicly expose the wondrous design of their own selves. They can cast into the shadows lesser beings, less admired, less talked to souls.

The *Digerati* commitment to talk then is not to secure their freedom but to talk others into the aura of their own self-absorption. And they are talking to others equally committed to drawing them into their uniqueness. *Cyberville* is dark because of what we can call our self-deceptions. But we are aided in our illusions. Profit is made on self-absorption as well as on individual paths to self-revelation, self-empowerment, self-fulfillment, self-realization, and spiritual awakening.

This review of my reasons did not relieve my conscience for I had recalled the thought the parrot had fractured: everyone has his reasons...and this is the one terrible thing in this world.

I did soon depart. Nothing turned out well. I must qualify that: I was not arrested for the murder of Karl the sailor, but for Bino's advocacy, I would have been.

This is how it all transpired:

Bino finished his investigations a couple of days after I visited Microft.

It was late and I was about to put my book up and turn the light out when Bino arrived. I made us some tea after he protested anything stronger saying he needed to keep his head clear. He went right into it as if he were making a summation to a jury.

"Firstly," he said, holding up one finger, "Mark Spark was surprised it was Emily and not his wife with Karl. He shot Karl in the back. Karl fell and revealed Emily beneath him. To Spark's surprise. The police went after Beecher so Spark didn't have to put into play his plan. Which was this: you were going to take the rap. Where was the gun? He was going to plant it on you. Why would you have murdered Karl? You had been Mrs. Spark's lover. Karl had exposed you and you had been thrown off the yacht. Revenge. Why did Spark give you that invite after what you had done? He was setting you up. If you go to Inspector Picon and tell him you saw Spark shoot Karl, you'll force Spark into going through with framing you. I don't know what that frame might be but we don't want to test it. And Mrs. Spark will testify her husband was with her at the time of the shooting."

The more he talked the more I was convinced that my travels would end with my imprisonment. I told him that Emily had surely seen Spark and would support my testimony.

"She's bought off," Bino said. "Forget about her. She hasn't stepped forward to clear her own boyfriend so she's not about to step forward on your behalf."

I was pacing the room and Bino was watching me.

"You could keep your mouth shut," he told me, "and let Beecher take the rap. He could use some time in jail in my opinion. Suck some of the cockiness out of him."

I didn't respond.

"You could go to Spark and make a deal," Bino said. "You keep your mouth shut in return for him keeping Noble out of jail."

"That would work?"

"Can't be sure but I think he'd see that as easier than having you eye witness that he shot the sailor. You know, I could make him not want to go to trial with me defending you. Yeah, he'd bail Noble out."

"And Beecher? He's innocent."

"If I defended him, he wouldn't fry. He'd probably get at least twenty years though. Jealous rage. I'd get the jury to empathize."

When I finally told Bino that I would have to turn Spark in and take my chances, he nodded, got up and began to look around my room.

"You figure one thing Spark has to do to frame you. That's to plant the murder weapon on you. Or in your room. What say we give it a search? If you see it, don't touch it. Repeat that."

We found the gun and Bino had it re-planted on Spark's yacht. Mrs. Spark performed the deed, entirely willing after Bino explained to her that she would be either of two things in the future: either the ex-Mrs. Spark or dead. She needed to put her husband away before he put her away.

Mark Spark was arrested, Beecher was freed, Captain Noble went on trial and then to jail for a year, Microft disappeared and

Walter went after him, Kate Whack left me a note saying she was going on with her rock tour. And I...I left the next day before daybreak, the parrot, placed in my care by the Captain, on my shoulder.

Chapter XII

The Author retreats to a Magical Garden, witnesses a psychic battle, makes his exit and meets the Sales Team.

The quickest way out of Cyberville was by air so the parrot, who now called himself Frit and rode my shoulder with his head under his wing, and I boarded a hot-air balloon and thus made our way over mountains that rivaled the Himalayas. Upon alighting in a lush green valley I proceeded to walk, stopping only for food and water in local villages, intent as I was to put as much distance as possible between myself and Cyberville.

Nature is surely recuperative and I found such to be the case once again. And as Mr. Addison says, I here quote from memory: Nature is full of wonders, every atom is a standing miracle, and endowed with such qualities, as could not be impressed on it by a power and wisdom less than infinite.

After several days, however, the verdant surround gave way and we found ourselves barraged one night by the most frightful noise. It sounded to me as if all of Nature was being excavated and rebuilt. I imagined construction rising up where previously only hills and streams, flowers and grass, rock and trees had been, though it was too dark to confirm my fantasy.

In daylight I discovered that much of the arid plain ahead of me was indeed a construction site.

I made my way as best I could, finding a small bistro into which I retreated for the sake of sustenance as much as for the sake of my hearing.

Chapter XII

At the counter as I plied into my bacon and eggs, providing Frit with bits of toast as I had seen the Captain do, I was accosted by several salesmen hawking a variety of wares and services, none of which did I need or desire. My demurral however had little impact on these importunate souls and I was nearing an explosive moment when the parrot flew up, screaming: *"Laissez-nous faire!"* and circled the heads of the importunate hawkers, who scattered in all directions.

"So you found a friend you could talk to," someone nearby said and when I turned I saw Chick Wagstaff.

Chick was in *New Babylon,* for such was the name of this noisy construction site, on business, for *New Babylon* was a salesman's paradise. Anything could be sold and everything would be bought.

I told him that mere chance had brought me here, hoping to find more amenable surroundings than what I had found on the Frontier and in *Cyberville.*

Chick shook his head sadly at the mention of *Cyberville* informing me that he was the last of his breed, the door to door, product in hand salesman. He didn't have a website nor did any of the manufacturers he represented have websites, believing as they did in the old fashioned adage that if you gave a good salesman fifteen seconds of the old "face to face," he would make a sale.

"It's the opening gambit," Chick told me. "You've got seconds to scope the target and seconds to decide on the approach. The goal? Make them feel like you're the kind of guy they can have a beer with. Trust. You could be selling a mop that plays tunes or a pair of plastic shoes or a youth elixir. If you're in sync with how they see things, you can sell anything."

I couldn't help noticing that Chick looked somewhat shoddy with brown and white shoes that were well polished but down at heel and leather worn, a frayed shirt collar, a stained neck tie, a checkered suit jacket that I'm sure was too tight to be buttoned. His hair was clumped.

I believe he saw the concern in my eyes for what was clearly his fallen state but he assured me with a sharp slap on my back that something was seconds away from turning up for him. And it was big. Very big. He would be mingling, as he phrased it, with millionaires.

Then suddenly, looking at his watch, he finished his coffee and told me he had a sale's appointment and had to run. He hung out in a pub called the *Shakedown*.Easy to find him there.

He started for the door and then paused and asked me if the parrot could be taught to say some things, like a sales pitch? I said I didn't know and that I had not trained him but was caretaking him for awhile. Chick pondered that, then waved and was off.

I soon retreated once again into the *New Babylon*. In the distance I could see long queues of people and much gaudy signage surrounding them.

The sky was full of missile-like packages with crisscrossing trajectories arching above a rush of vehicles headed in every direction. I saw hunters and sportsmen and footballers and product placements and contingency lawyers and oilmen and brokers of all kinds and nail emporiums and urgent entrepreneurs and litigious lawyers and the homeless and naked survivors and desperate housewives and botox treatment centers and old people with reckless leg and erectile dysfunction and rapid hearts and abandoned stem cells and apprentices and arthritic thumbs and high school dropouts and tough love advocates and branding gurus and abortionists and the terminal and the terminally greedy and Jesus Warriors and Ponzi schemers and Cash Barons and logo merchandisers and gold buyers and gladiators and evil doers and saints and church music and fortune tellers and the foreclosed and the investment counselors and insomniacs and rapists and peaceniks and militarists and the agents of change and the agents of agents and brokers to the stars and the stars themselves and the downsized and silicone celebrities and soccer moms and their precocious prize and poor moms and haunted deadbeat dads and bitter sons and abused daughters and the compassionate conservatives and the private security and recidivists and dot.com billionaires and whiskey priests and wounded vets and social anxiety therapists.

I saw signs that read "Chamorro spoken here," and "Limbu spoken here," and "Servers Speak Mongolic" and "Uzbek/English lessons" and "Nootka/Ibo lessons" and "Cadoan only spoken here" and "Turko-Tartar Public Bath," and "Cherokee Strip Club" and "Karankawa Home Market" and "Urdu Fish Fry," "Invisible Hand Investment Services." And many, many more.

It was then, in a state not far from collapse being so assailed, that I made my way to a walled citadel beyond which I could hear no deafening commotion and to me, at that moment, it was as if I were at the gates of Eden.

I found a door and as I banged on it the parrot screamed *"Start a business!"* but our clamor was nullified by the surround dissonance. When I turned and looked back at the way we had come, I saw a phalanx of vendors and entrepreneurs bearing down on us. I despaired. Frit, however, did not and took to flight. I followed him until he disappeared over the wall.

Seconds before the vendors reached me the parrot came flying back and was on my shoulder just as the door opened. I entered and I was immediately asked whether I was the one who commanded the parrot?

I was about to say something to the effect that I was not the owner and so on when the parrot yelled out *"Observe the opportunity!"*

I heeded him and simply nodded. The door was shut behind us and we were led into the interior of a vast garden, surprisingly quiet except for the sound of birds and insects. I had no idea how the cacophony of the *New Babylon* was kept out. I read the words inscribed on a fountain: *"The Lord God planted a garden eastward in Eden."*

The parrot and I drank from the fountain and then were brought into the shade. I stretched out and closed my eyes and soon fell asleep. I was indeed in a magical place.

When I awoke I was told I would be brought before the Sorcerer who was the administrator of the Garden. I admit that my expectation was that here would be a man who either looked like a long white haired Merlin or an acrobatic Houdini. I thought also of Zvengali as played by John Barrymore.

It would have been more realistic of me to expect this person to be someone I knew. And indeed it was: Dr. Maleva, who informed me at once that she was not a doctor and certainly not a Dr. Maleva, although she might have been a Dr. Maleva in some other lifetime, and neither was she the Sorcerer but simply a sorcerer's apprentice. She was to take me to the Sorcerer.

I followed obediently wondering what Maleva's racket was. She seemed to reincarnate across the path of my travels.

She held the door to the Sorcerer's study open for me and as I passed through she whispered in my ear "The parrot," and then she closed the door behind her.

I saw a scattering of papers and bottles of ink on the desk the Sorcerer rose from as I entered. The room was full of shadows as it was only lit by candles. In the light where he stood now, hand held out, the Sorcerer looked like a young man with a fresh, hopeful face,but when he led me to a corner with chairs and a sofa, I saw an old man's face in the shadows, a face dark in itself as you note in a face full of rage or spite or envy or jealousy. And, as eerie as it may sound, as he spoke, his countenance, indeed his entire body, seemed to flow in and out of an ebullient bloom to a tragic forlornness.

Over tea, we talked of places to which I had traveled, what I had seen outside the Garden, and what sort of refuge the Garden was and what manner of magic he administered.

He told me that everyone now living in the Garden had once lived outside but as the *New Babylon* grew into a giant behemoth ruled by rude instincts and avaricious appetites, more and more of its inhabitants had sought a safe haven in the Garden.

I asked him how the Garden had come into being and he said simply "magic." Out of necessity, the Garden had been imagined and then made real for did I not hold it true that whatever could be imagined could be made real? I deflected my response by querying how particularly the baseness of our human natures, catalogued since the Epic of Gilgamesh, displayed itself in the *New Babylon*?

He said he was not able to express what it was but only what it had seemed to be. You look at the stars, he told me, and you make constellations of them. Aquarius, the Water Bearer, Musca, the Fly, Virgo, the Virgin. But they are stars in some alignment that we make familiar to ourselves. As a constellation, the *New Babylon* would be more like Canes Venatici, the Hunting Dogs, or

Capricorn, the Horned Goat, or Lupus, the Wolf, or Vulpecula, the Little Fox.

It cast an aura over the *New Babylon* and slowly it became a place where men would sell their souls for an ounce of ease, where the first commandment was I've Got Mine, You Get Yours, the second Thou Shall Show Tough Love, where millions should suffer while a few lived well . .

And then the Sorcerer stopped, apparently upset by his own words. He apologized to me and said that everyone in the Garden suffered with a deep sense of loss.

I asked him what had been lost and he said one word, "Magic." What had created the Garden was in danger, was being drained by the growing fanaticism of what lay beyond the wall. Every effort to regain this, he told me, was countered by what he called a dark logic that turned the uplifting breezes of inspiration to nothing more than hot air.

"Every effort to lift ourselves from the mire of our own self-destructiveness is countered by the dark logicians among us." I asked how they were tolerated in the Garden to which he merely replied, "How can we not? They are us."

I was somewhat startled to see a figure in black suddenly appear at the Sorcerer's side.

Frit joined me in that surprise for he took to wing, circling the room and when he alighted again on my shoulder screeched loudly:

"Son of a bitch!"

The Shadow was identical in size to the Sorcerer and from what I could see of a face shadowed by a hood, he was the Sorcerer's twin. The Sorcerer showed no sign of recognition and seemed not to be aware of his shadow presence. I noted that the Sorcerer's face was completely young and fresh and no longer haunted. I immediately concluded that in some fashion that reason could not follow, the Sorcerer's shadow self had gained its freedom.

I found all this quite strange and not at all comforting for this Garden, like the biblical garden, clearly had its serpent and whether or not the Sorcerer's own mind had imagined and therefore brought into being its own present difficulties I could not say but my preference at that moment was not to linger.

I began to talk my way to a graceful exit, believing now that I could more easily face the tumult of the New Babylon where I would face the horrid but fathomable than I could what apparently was here in the Garden, the amicable but creepy. I believe Frit shared my mood because he continually flapped his wings in my ear.

The Sorcerer however had some questions about Frit and I soon saw that he believed Frit and I possessed some magical powers which I suppose he thought would be useful in the Garden. I attempted to correct this view by telling him that I had no idea what Frit would say nor did I believe what he did say was in any way a response to what he heard. In fact, I pointed out, Frit didn't really "say" anything. He mimicked sounds he had heard.

I could see the Sorcerer was not convinced. He had decided that Frit could help him best with, as he called it, his Shadow self, whose existence he was painfully aware. He had been for a long while holding off the challenges of the Shadow but he knew he had grown weaker while the Shadow had grown stronger. The Shadow had recently been able to detach himself from the Sorcerer and oppose him on what had become an equal footing. Unless the Sorcerer squelched the Shadow's challenge, the Garden would quickly be absorbed into the New Babylon. Every day, the Sorcerer told me, the magical veil which kept out the New Bablyon was growing weaker and soon the noise of that pollution would deluge the peaceful silence of the Garden.

For a quick exit, I promised to return the next evening.

I was intent on not doing so but the next evening, Frit and I returned to the Sorcerer's study where the Sorcerer and his Shadow awaited us. I had been magically drawn back.

As soon as I entered the room the Shadow approached me. He was darkly hooded and I could not see his face. The parrot took to wing and perched on a high shelf of books.

"Rollins," he said, extending his hand which I shook and identified myself. "Good friend of Zechariah."

Zechariah shook his head and sighed deeply.

Chapter XII

"All talk is lost when uninspired by the imagination. The world outside our Garden is detained and detoured by `business,' a business of profit mounted on a self-interest that imagines only within its self-decreed world."

"Ah, but brother," Rollins boomed in a voice filled with confidence and command, "look how richly clothed each man and woman's life is today compared to your poet's time. The simplicity of a bucolic yokel is now replaced by symbolic analysts, innovative entrepreneurs, venture capitalists. Consciousness itself has become broadband and globalized. We are free lance and multi-tasking in an information age of high technocapitalism where each day we build pleasure domes not of fancy but of real stone and brick."

This speech, delivered in a quite supercilious, off-hand manner, had an instantaneous effect on Zechariah and it appeared to me as if each of Rollins's words were like arrows piercing his heart.

It was impossible for me to retain any rational apprehension of this drama before me. I believe that legerdemain can pull a coin from behind an ear but I do not believe a man can project part of himself as a real physical presence. Nor do I believe that we have within us such disputatious and hostile contrary selves.

"I forbid you to call me brother," Zechariah stuttered, his face flushed, his hands trembling. His facial features now displayed the careworn ravages of age while Rollins's face, which was now visible, looked positively cherubic.

"I wonder, brother," Rollins said, pulling a cigarette out of the air and lighting it, "I wonder, brother, who's carrying his load in the real world? The man who imagines or the man who acts? The man who accepts the bitter pill of our own confused humanity, takes it into account and inches forward. Or, the man who imagines an ideal that never will be and does nothing."

"*I serve!*" Frit screamed, pulling his head from beneath his wing.

This brought a smile to Rollins's face but caused Zechariah to shake his head repeatedly.

"We serve each other differently," he cried out. "But look at the *New Babylon*. What do you see? Everyone serving himself.

Nothing can conceal a sort of rapacious cannibalism that infects everything."

Rollins laughed.

"Brother, you've seen those *Matrix* films too many times. I know you have. Don't deny it. I was with you don't forget. We watched a whole host of sci-fi films where aliens camouflaged as human are inhabiting us. *Invasion of the Body Snatchers.* I was there watching them with you. Difference was, brother, that I was momentarily entertained – although Keanu Reeves is a dreadfully wooden actor – while your imagination ran away with you."

"They're here!" Frit screamed.

"The world has become sophisticated by virtue of our own technology, brother, and we each command that sophistication but you, unfortunately, believe that it commands us."

"It does!" Zechariah shouted. "We are deeply seduced and distracted while our very minds and souls are fettered by profiteers. Don't you see that nothing in the *New Babylon* is for anything good and decent but only for profit to an infinitesimal few? There is no invisible hand extending from greed to charity."

"My brother the moralist," Rollins said to me, blowing a series of perfect smoke rings. I could see that Frit was impressed with this. "I, for one, or at least half of one, am sick and tired of vacuous declarations of the Good. They all come down to childish plots concocted by marginalized men. A few, an infinitesimal few, dear brother, have moved the mass of men out of the mud, despite the lethargy and hypocrisy of those same masses. If those same infinitesimal few make themselves rich in the bargain what else would one expect?"

"My childish plot, as you call it," Zechariah retorted, waving away smoke, "can be found in the Christian Bible. The complexity I see in my fellow man can be found in Shakespeare. But your cynical and simplistic view of human nature and human history serve the ends of power and rapaciousness."

"Pardon me, brother, if I can't provide you with the proliferating ins and outs and what have you of a Hamlet. Quite frankly I can't see what all the fuss is about. My plot is from Disney not Shakespeare. I believe that choosing a product off a shelf can be as deeply an ontological matter as anything else.

185

We're all as deep as the moment requires, though you, dear brother, replace the moment with dream stuff."

"And you do all that you can to crush dreams!" Zechariah shouted.

"It's fun," Rollins quipped. "Follow your desires, not dreams of Xanadus built on air or fatuous bombast about what noble creatures we are. We're dogs, brother, and I make my apologies to the dogs for that comparison."

This wasn't the first time in my travels that I had heard someone declare that we humans were dogs and lived like dogs. I was quite amazed as to how deeply divided Zechariah and Rollins were. By what magic had this psychopathology, this bi-polarity become embodied in two distinct, discrete individuals? I mean to say, whose power – Zechariah's or Rollins's – was behind what I was now seeing and hearing?

"You believe that we can will the world to meet our desires."

"A few can," Rollins replied. "Most obviously can not."

"And those few fulfill their desires without any concern for the fate of others?"

"Nobody's stopping anybody from doing anything," Rollins said. "Have at it and may the best man win. Oh, you can pretend that's not the case and the pretense is a good front. We can't win elections by screaming "Dog Eat Dog!" But it's dangerous, my dear brother, to get sucked into believing that given the chance and enough power the other guy won't swallow us whole."

And then I saw something ...I don't know quite what I saw except Zechariah's glance at Frit with a look of desperation and despair and yet something more, as if he were imploring the parrot but at the same time giving...something.

"The paths of glory lead but to the grave," Frit screeched, as Zechariah's eyes closed.

The poet Gray. Not unusual for Frit to quote but only in fragments. Not unusual for Frit's mimicry to weirdly seem apropos at the time. But this was different.

Rollins's glance went from Zechariah who had now collapsed in a chair and seemed to be asleep to the parrot and then to me.

"We believe that the signs of winning in life are unambiguous and we demand, as in a Superbowl game, for the winning to be full, someone has to lose."

That comment was directed at me. I said nothing. I had scant idea of what was going on.

"Of course, it's what happens in a game," Rollins said, in his usual cavalier style, "that can be fun. We don't only play to win. We play to play."

Silence. Rollins looked over at Zechariah.

"It seems I've put my brother to sleep," he said. "Game over. I win."

"Is...is he dead?" I fearfully asked.

"Think of it more like his having been `creatively destroyed.' What my brother stood for has become extinct. Something new and better will arise. Me."

I stood up.

"I'm afraid I don't know what any of this means."

"My dear sir," Rollins told me, as he walked about the study picking up and examining this and that, "each individual is the final arbiter as to what talk is to mean. Suit yourself. That's all that counts in the end. You're where the buck stops, believe it or not."

"I much admired your brother's respect for the imagination," I said, wanting to make my exit but also wanting to put a hole in Rollins's confounded arrogance. "I sought refuge here in the Garden. I found the *New Babylon* to be rather like one of the circles in Dante's Inferno."

"All hope abandon, ye who enter here!" Frit squawked.

"I see my brother has conveyed some of his nonsense into the bird. As for your own failure to enjoy the *New Babylon* and your escape to this Never Never land my brother has conjured up and which I will annex to the *New Babylon* in short order . . ."

"Drill, baby, drill!" Frit shouted.

"We certainly shall, thank you," Rollins said, pointing to the parrot. "Your malady, sir . . ." He now looked at me. "would be beyond my grasp as I don't know you at all. But if you are the pilgrim seeking in his travels some enlightenment, I may be of some assistance. What you see in the *New Babylon* is the future and it works. You see there technology and capitalism making real what my foolish brother was content to only imagine."

I told him I saw only the commotion of buying and selling, and, on the faces of all, the predatory look of the gluttonous, the grasping, the greedy.

"Innovation and entrepreneurship is what it's called," Rollins told me. "People who have their eye on the future always look alarming to people such as yourself and my brother who have their eye on what never was and never will be."

"I believe, sir," I retorted quite fed up with his insolent manner, "we must strive to bring out the better angels of our nature rather than wallow in what there is of the beast in us."

"Oh, if you're going to float moral vapors like my brother...Better angels of our nature? Every man, sir, is split between seeing what's there to be seen and acting accordingly, and, seeing what some balderdash story in their heads says should be there. My brother went as far as he could with his nonsense and then I had to step forward and save us both."

"A moral sense is not nonsense, sir," I replied. "It compels a moral review and without that we are nothing more than a threat to each other."

"Eats first, morals after," Frit yelled.

"Precisely," Rollins affirmed.

I was wondering which side Frit was on and whether the poor bird had lost his mind. And then I realized that thought indicated it was my own mind in jeopardy.

"I find, sir," I said in my most stern voice, "that you are no more than the amoral sociopathic abyss your brother had, up to this moment, suppressed."

"For sure," Frit squawked.

"I see it as useless talking to you as to my brother," Rollins replied. "You can't accept talk that recognizes our post-Truth, post-Fordist, globalized techno-inventiveness and the elegance of competitive entrepreneurship. No, sir, you find it useful I suspect to talk of how many angels on the head of a pin or whether Christ carried a purse or whether the lion will lie down with the lamb and whether you'll take your body with you to heaven and other such twiddle-twaddle. But take this on your travels: Action is useful, friend. Talk is just talk."

I told him that I thought I had a greater facility with talking differently than he because whereas he was entrapped with what he called the elegance of this or that, I relied upon imagination to conceive something entirely other.

He responded by saying that hi-tech would make everything conceivable possible. I told him that I had recently been to *Cyberville* and had seen how cyberspace did not liberate but only facilitated a constant circling within our own resident beliefs. It was just vastly easier to find what confirmed those beliefs and strengthen one's allegiance to one's own choices.

"So, in your travels," Rollins said, smiling that enraging smile, "you just find everyone talking the same? I've found that everyone talks differently. That's what makes communication the tough nut that it is. It's a real marketing challenge is what it is."

Rollins's arrogant manner seemed then to me unassailable and I felt as if all the energy I needed to continue talking was now gone.

"The many, sir," I stuttered, "fulfill the agenda of predators."

Rollins laughed.

"So what is this Garden of my brother's? A refuge? An escape?"

"I believe Zechariah wants to create a place where the imagination can be revived and offer a possibility of living differently than as they do in the *New Babylon*."

"Senor Gullivero," Rollins said, lighting up another cigarette, "We've imagined ourselves out of human sacrifice, the Divine Right of Kings, horses and buggies, pen and ink, and leeches as a cure all. And a whole lot more. That's entrepreneurial ambition and technological know how."

"Restored to life!" Frit yelled and at that very moment Zechariah regained consciousness. I wasted no time in making my exit, unwilling and unable to witness Zechariah's battle with his own divided self.

I awoke the next morning to the sound of walls crashing and crumbling, screams and howls, barking and weeping and gnashing of teeth...I exaggerate but, in truth, I found myself no longer within the Garden's silent and peaceful Eden but once again in the *New Babylon*.

The parrot, who had told me as soon as I opened my eyes that he was now to be called Tim, and I made our way through the rubble and once again were assailed by the clamor of construction as the *New Babylon* raised its towers of brokerage and global finance, its emporium of vendibles, its enchantments of luxury and ease. And the ceaseless chatter of auction, sales pitch, vending, hard sell and soft sell, of huckstering and bargaining and bidding, of Robocalls, tweets, skypes and Robo instructions of all sorts.

I remembered the name of the pub Chick Wagstaff had said he frequented, the *Shakedown,* not a name, I thought, to instill confidence but, after stopping now and then for directions – and the inevitable sales pitch – I found the place.

It was about noon time and the place was jammed. I spotted Chick at the bar. He had the same outfit on but it was now even more disheveled than the last time I had seen him. Clumps of hair shot up out of his head as if they had been electrified.

Chick introduced me to his "sales team," one of whom, to my great surprise, was the snobbish aristocrat Prince Krokov, way down on his luck by the look of him. The Prince peered at me through his monocle, clicked his heels and said "Monsieur Gullifoy" The other member of the sales team, Stringer, was called Statman because he handled the statistics.

The sales team expressed an interest in the parrot.

"Polly wants a cracker," Chick asked him.

"Wanker!" Tim yelled and they all laughed.

"Start a business!"

They hadn't fared too well since arriving in the New Babylon about a week before but it wasn't their fault as Chick described it. I had bought a round of drinks and Chick was now huddled over his beer and shot.

"Credit is tight," Chick almost whispered to me, "tight as an oyster that won't shuck. Bottom's dropped out. Total...and I mean...total loss of confidence. Global melt down. Don't repeat it. Recession. Depression. Petrol dollars. That's it. Can't sell short.

Bundling. Swops. Hedge funds. Deriviatives. Underwater. Subprime moment. One hundred and fifty years. Gone. No bail out."

I nodded as Chick revealed the causes for his sales team's hard times. I asked Chick what the team was selling and he replied with a wink: trust and confidence and the will to win.

"That spirit, like our own personal Will to Win," Chick declared, standing tall at the bar now, "bangs a triumphant gavel at the end of each day's trading on Wall Street. The tides of our *New Babylon* may be rising due to polar icecap melting but our talk remains triumphant. Does the tide come in? Do women launch ships? Do young men party? Does piss trickle down the leg of the rich man? Why?"

I said I didn't know but Chick asked me to play along because this was part of the new script to instill trust. First, Chick told me, you run down the negatives. If you want the buyer to trust you, you can't hide what they already know. But, if you tell them what they already know...you build trust.

"First, we run through some depressing blah blah," Chick said. "Okay, we now have the depressed buyer thinking we're depressed too. We're not like those guys who threw everyone a line of crapola, took the money and ran. We tell it like it is. But then we challenge our negatives. We give the guy some hope. Statman, run down the positives."

Statman took some index cards out of his pocket and read them in the same monotone:

Number one: there's a lot of money to be made with the greening of the polar icecaps.

Number two: no war is useless when it protects us from another 9/11.

Number three: globalized free market was a far sight better than medieval village penury.

 Number four: genetic engineering will improve the lot of every species.

Number four: Big Government needs a corporate CEO to make it profitable.

Number five: the poor will always be with us so don't mess with the Bible.

Number six: the digital generation is far better informed and more able to join together in the name of progress than any previous generation."

Statman put the index cards back in his pocket and went back to the sheets on the bar.

"Now," Chick said, his eyes wide, "we hit them with the talk of triumphalism. We are at a triumphant moment for cybernetic technology; we are at a triumphant moment for global market capitalism; we are at a triumphant moment for self-absorption."

"Amen to all that," Tim squawked.

"Self-absorption is good?" I asked Chick.

"Sure it is," Chick said. "For sales. Everybody has a hungry heart and we don't want them to starve it. How does that happen? Tell him, Crapoff. He's our behavior...what is it Crapoff?"

"My name is Krokov not Crapoff" Krokov said. "Prince Krokov. Behavioral analyst. I analyze with my eyes. It's in my blood. I can smell peasant roots the way some men can smell feet."

"Blood sport!" Tim yelled and I couldn't help smiling.

"The Prince here is worth his weight in coke," Chick told me. "He can tell what a guy's heart is hungry for faster than that bird can molt a feather."

"Quite a gift," I said, nodding to the Prince, who was dressed in shabby elegance and wore some sort of egg stained crest on his jacket pocket.

"You are skeptical," the Prince told me.

I explained that I simply did not think that it was an easy matter to sell people, as Chick referred to it, even though you knew what they desired.

"Do you know why the aristocracy held a privileged place for so long?" the Prince asked me. "Because the human heart is first hungry for a ruler. God answers the call. But that is the Heavens. Here on earth. The Prince. They want to bend to my will. It's in their nature. Just as it is in my nature to stand above them. It is the task of the Prince to keep them diverted and amused. They are like children who tell me `Stimulate and seduce me into a world of personally chosen distractions and I promise not to look at who is sucking my blood.'"

"Anybody who suspects they're being cheated," Chick said, "we say they're paranoiac."

"Once the peasants have their toys," the Prince said, "the power of the Prince is not even noticed. Gladly will the ruled be oblivious to the newest tragedy in Africa, to the smirking strut of the worst little Napoleon a madhouse could concoct who stands as a leader, to the hundreds of thousands dead or wounded in Iraq and Afghanistan as the Dow Jones breaks 12, 000 or plunges to nothing in the hands of thieves, whose god, Compound Interest, swells the portfolios of those who expound but do not fight, those whose short term investment interests manipulate patriotism, morality, and fear."

"Quite a speech," I told the Prince.

"Too much venom," Chick said, "I've told you Crapoff, we don't want to turn our marks into rebels."

"I told you Mr. Chick," the Prince said, "Only the Losers hate the Winners and no one wants to think of themselves as Losers so no one hates the Winners."

In the course of the next few hours, Chick told me about their present campaign, as he referred to it, which involved eating up, as he referred to it, a number of foreclosed properties in the Bluestocking development, a re-gentrification project that had lost its credit line following the recent vicious economic crisis, and then selling them back, at a hefty profit, to the former inhabitants.

Statman had run the numbers and they were a very sweet deal indeed. As the banks were no longer lending, Chick had gone to a group of private lenders.

"These guys," Chick told me, very amused by what he was telling me, "these guys are in a club, a Topiary Fund, the Resurrection Club over in the Tenderloin, that you need millions to join. I don't say they break anybody's laws but they don't run your deal through the Boy Scout handbook. You know, more risky behavior than the regulators will allow. Not that it isn't open season and good old frontier justice here in New Bab."

"Whopee!" the parrot screeched.

"Bird's enjoying himself," Chick said.

I, however, wasn't, my head suddenly aching, perhaps from hearing the world "frontier." I left Chick and his sales team, and the parrot and I returned to the *pensione* where we were staying, a *pensione* run by a Mrs. Angeloni.

Chapter XIII

The Author's discoveries, acquaintances and sudden loss in the New Babylon.

A strange mood had come over me which eluded my examination. Much of my enthusiasm for travel was gone and I now took Seneca's words to heart "to be everywhere is to be nowhere."

I had selected Mrs. Angeloni's *pensione* for the immediate reason that she allowed the parrot occupancy but my deeper reason was this: I wanted and I believe needed not to be identified as a traveler but as someone who belongs someplace. At least long enough for me to see and feel the routine everydayness that a traveler misses. I needed some old fashioned down home hominess.

I would not have selected the *New Babylon* for this nesting but I had no choice for I had no inclination to travel further and I desperately needed to deal with my grieving for Carla, my disappointments in my fellow man, my loss of faith in my own reasoning faculties and my feeling that a sense of the absurd had replaced my faith in a Celestial Entity.

I suspected I was in the world and had traveled through much of it but did not know it. I remained trapped in the portmanteau of my own mind.

Mrs. Angeloni's was perfect for me because I became not just another boarder as in Mrs. Bomber's but part of her extended family who lived and dined in the same rambling wood framed house in the Bluestocking district. There were many equally old and rambling houses in the area with foreclosed signs on the lawn. This was the neighborhood destined for destruction and reborn as part of the *New Babylon.* Unfortunately, credit for this and other huge resurrectional schemes had dried up.

I have not ventured out of this neighborhood for weeks and indeed I seldom leave the house, doing so only for the parrot's sake who seemed not to be in as great a need for inertia as myself.

Because there was no building going on here and because there was no money here and therefore no salesmen prowled, I enjoyed a silence almost as notable as that of the Garden. Only Mrs. Angeloni's grand children would occasionally break the silence but after a time I grew not to look upon their sounds as noise.

Unlike Mrs. Bomber's boarders who stayed year after year, Mrs. Angeloni's guests were usually for brief periods, often just overnight. Some were salesmen whose commissions weren't great enough for them to stay in the better part of town. They adopted a haughty air here. Some were attending business conferences the way jackals attend a carcass, some were job hunting and had to keep moving about in the fashion of primitive hunter gatherers. Some had lost their homes nearby and couldn't quite leave the neighborhood just yet. These had a haunted look as if they were attending their own funerals. Some had just returned from a war front and were thinking about going back home but could not bring themselves to do it as so much blood had been spilled in the name of home. Some were vagabonds, like myself, seeking the closeness of their fellow man the way a drowning man reaches for a life preserver.

We were at lunch the day one of Chick's sales team, Statman, came by.

Mrs. Angeloni had twin sons: Carmine and Mario. They were long haul truck drivers who had owned their own tractor cab but had been unable to keep up payments and the tractor had been repossessed. Now they drove for other haulers but those jobs had become infrequent. Mario wasn't married but Carmine had a wife, Rita, and two adolescent sons, Carmine, Jr. and Michael, who were fascinated by the parrot who had taken to calling himself Tom. Mrs. Angeloni's own father, Pino, was close to a hundred and always sat at the head of the table where he seemed to follow every discussion very closely but said nothing. Mrs. Angeloni's husband was a traveling salesman who had been compelled to take longer and longer trips as nearby consumption dropped to arid levels.

The day Statman rang the doorbell there was a quiet young veteran from the Iraq war at the table as well as a young couple who had been evicted from their condo. An elderly black man, formerly retired, had just gotten a position in the kitchen at the Resurrection Club. He was temporarily staying at Mrs. Angeloni's until he could find his own place and send for his wife who lived some hundred miles south of the *New Babylon*. There was also an itinerant inspirational speaker at the table whose message was Cold Cash, Consumption, Comfort, Cadillacs, and Credit.

I had gotten into the mnemonic habit of calling the day guests by a distinguishing feature and so the Vet was simply the Vet, the evicted were Mr and Mrs. Condo, the kitchen retiree was Cook, the inspirational speaker was Comfort. I am not unaware that such a reduction of an individual to a shorthand feature was no more and no less than a sign of my alienation from all proper human feeling.

As was my habit, I was trying to incite a conversational riot.

"The price we will ultimately pay for our comfort and ease," I said, addressing myself to Comfort, "may be paid by future generations. And is certainly being paid by others right now."

"Are we not free, my good friend," Comfort boomed, "to pursue our own comfort? Our own ease? Do we stop consuming because others cannot? Should I give up my Cadillac because others ride bikes? Should I stop priming the pump of prosperity by failing to consume? Should I stop consuming because others think credit is a bad word? No, sir. Freedom allows you to do what you want. Period."

"Joy, Oh, Joy!" Tom sang out but no one paid him heed.

"You ain't got a Cadillac," Carmine, Jr. growled, head down over his chop. "You got a bike."

"I was speaking inspirationally," Comfort replied.

197

"They did what they wanted," Mr. Condo said angrily. "They threw us out of our condo."

"Was that an illegal act, my good friend," Comfort asked. "Or do you assume some personal responsibility."

Mrs. Condo glared at Comfort.

"I just think some people have got all the freedom and others don't."

"Lessen thy meals!" Tom screeched.

"The *New Babylon* is a radically divided class society," I said, cutting into my chop, "in which opportunities to become qualified are radically unequal."

"Jobs ain't good either," Cook said, nodding.

"Friends," Comfort said, looking up and down the long table, "One must become qualified within this new 21st century technoculture. What is our rallying cry 'To the best qualified goes the spot!' That rules in Heaven as well as here. I'm referring to the order of the Angels. Remember: No one is prevented from becoming a Winner here in the *New Babylon*. Obstacles vary but the more obstacles the more challenge the more perfect the Winning."

"One of you is lying!" Tom screeched.

"Don't talk about winning," the Vet snapped. "What does a soft slob like you know what it takes to win?"

"What was that?" Comfort said, his face flushed.

"Hey, buddy," Mario said to Vet, "my mother likes it peaceful at the table."

I could see the Vet's jaw tighten and his eyes narrow. He looked like he was ready to snap into action.

"Me and Mario did a couple of tours in Iraq," Carmine said in a very calm voice. "Winning was getting my bro' and my buddies back safe. Everything else was some politician back home running at the mouth."

The Vet seemed to be still agitated but he returned his attention to his plate. I observed that the sudden outburst had taken the wind out of Comfort's sails.

We all plied knife and fork in silence and then Carmine said:

"What did that guy who wanted us to drive for him tell us, Mario?"

"Wait," Mario said. "I wrote it down."

He proceeded to take a folded bit of paper out of his shirt pocket. He read:

"Lack of initiative and the Will to Win nurtured by governmental dependency will burn away a fighting competitive spirit."

"Yeah, that was it. We think we're over there trying to kill the enemy and the enemy is trying to kill us and let's call it war and whoever don't get killed, wins and if you do get killed, you lose. But this guy thinks it's all about some bullshit competitive spirit, like our product can kick the shite out of your product. Pardon the expression, Ma."

"Eat."

" And the government? We're not fighting to preserve it. No, this guy thinks that if you're patriotic and willing to give up your life for your government, you're becoming dependent and you can't fight. Mario won some shrapnel and I won a severed arm tendon. If we would have won anymore we'd be dead. So, yeah, soldier, we don't let anybody talk about winning at this table."

The Vet's lower lip was shaking.

"You go home," Mrs. Angeloni told him in a very soothing voice. "You go back home."

The Vet shook his head.

"I'm sorry, Ma'am. I...I don't know what home is anymore," he said. "It doesn't hold up. They're in their homes...you know...our bullets found them. Bombs don't know homes from rat holes."

He dropped the knife he was holding in his hand, got up and left the room.

Statman soured the mood in the Angeloni home even further when he showed up and announced that Wagstaff and Associates held title to the property and the Angeloni family were being evicted.

This news put the whole household into an uproar. While Mrs. Angeloni screamed that her mortgage was with the *New Babylon* First National, Carmine read the paper work that Statman handed him, Mario put his jacket on and went outside, a very hard look in his eyes, Pino still sat at the luncheon table with a bottle of wine in front of him, and Rita told the boys to go to their room.

Mrs. Angeloni told Statman he was not the bank, her bank, and he should take his piece of paper and get out of her house. Carmine, looking up from his close reading, told her that what the paper showed was that after their mortgage rate had gone up, they had fallen behind on their payments.

"I remember that," Mrs. Angeloni said, "and so we took from grandpa's pension what was owed."

"Yeah, that's what I thought," Carmine said, looking over at his grandfather who was staring at his glass of wine.

"Property is theft!" Tom yelled and I made a snapping sound near his beak to shut him up. I couldn't help searching the one dark eye he focused on me for some small clue that he knew what he had just said.

"Your grandfather took a loan from Wagstaff and Associates and in return signed over title of the property to us. Until such time as the loan is repaid. Unfortunately, due to the recent credit crisis, we must re-sell the property in order to keep ourselves solvent. I can show you the stats."

"Show us his signature on a title to you is what I want to see," Carmine replied and Statman immediately obliged after shuffling through his briefcase. Carmine studied it closely. Mario had come back inside the house.

"Well, you can't sell it," Carmine said, giving the paper back to Statman.

"I'm afraid we must," Statman replied.

"The old man is close to a hundred," Carmine said. "His signature ain't any good."

"It's his name on the original title," Statman said. "No other signature appears. He has the right unless, of course, you have power of attorney for your grandfather. We have a witness to his signature verifying both his agreement to the conditions of the loan and his competence to sign."

"You guys think of everything," Mario said, "I mean when you're suckering old guys. I mean did you think at all how you're going to get out of this house at this moment in time?"

"Kick ass!" Tom squawked and I quickly apologized for his language and behavior. No one paid us any attention.

Mario smiled and shuffled his eyebrows up and down. Like his brother, he looked fit and dangerous. Whether he was also mad and bad, as Lady Caroline Lamb said of Lord Byron, I truly cannot say, but I could see that Statman was calculating his chances of a safe departure.

"Be quiet, Mario," Mrs. Angeloni said, turning to Statman. "We can buy the house. We'll pay the mortgage."

Statman shook his head.

"You won't find a bank that will go along with you," he said. "The stats are against you. We've got to sell to people who can get the credit. If you can do so, fine. Here's the number we're dealing with."

He wrote a number down in his pad, ripped off the sheet and handed it to Mrs. Angeloni.

At that, he made a quick exit, Mario moving away from the door as a wave of Mrs. Angeloni's hand directed him.

The days after Statman's visit were not good days at Mrs. Angeloni and even the quality of her cooking dropped off dramatically.

Anxiety that goes before something dreaded awaiting us in the future had replaced the cheerful and peaceful ambiance of the Angeloni household. With mortality of course comes dread of what awaits us in the future but that seems neither to have the urgency nor the impact of what so suddenly and clearly lies ahead.

While we Christians could transform an afterlife into a stunning opportunity, it is difficult for those same Christians to face eviction from their home. Life after eviction had not the cloudy nebulousness of life after death.

Mrs. Angeloni would lay a platter on the table, announce mournfully that the dish had been her mother's but would have to be left behind. There was no room on the street for serving platters. There would be no serving on the street because she would no longer have guests because she would no longer have her *pensione.* And so in this fashion her life went on.

For me, it was all a terribly drastic change for I had come very close to anchoring myself to one spot and had begun to feel the contentment that domesticity can offer.

I had become, in short, part of the Angeloni household and I had experienced no inclination to move on. But now in a matter of no more than a week, the Angeloni's dislocation and discomposure had become my own. I believe the parrot was similarly depressed because he said little at table now and spent a good deal of time with his head under his wing.

I decided to do something about the Angelonis' plight and in doing so regain the harmony of my own soul. I was, of course, looking forward to the reclamation of Mrs. Angeloni's cooking which would follow swiftly on the reclamation of her home.

The parrot and I therefore set out late one night for the *Shakedown* where I hoped to find Chick Wagstaff, seize the chance to talk to him of the straits Mrs. Angeloni was in and hope that he would afford her some relief. If this indeed was the future prospect that Chick had indicated to me he was waiting for, it seemed very ugly indeed.

I did not find Chick when I arrived but the band that was playing was familiar to me. It was Kate Whack's group and I concluded that some investigative journalism had brought Kate to the *New Babylon*.

I was not mistaken as I soon discovered. She and Hester joined me during their break. Ms. Skamble had proven to be too slippery a fish and had gotten away. But only momentarily, Kate told me and then slugged on a bottle of beer.

"Some topiary fund group called Resurrection is paying her big money," Kate said. "To do what, I don't know. But I know there's a story. A big story."

I told her what I had learned from Chick Wagstaff about Resurrection funding his real estate scheme which had oddly enough touched the boarding house where I was living. I had shown up tonight hoping to find Chick.

This seemed to amuse Kate.

"So you've become a knight errant?"

"I don't think so," I said, rather annoyed. I explained to her that the Angeloni convulsion had bollixed my own respite, one that had till that moment allowed me to see and hear what my travels had denied me.

"Oh, I'm sure your self-interest is operative. But perhaps this time it lags your benevolence a trifle."

"The French call it "fraternity," said Hester, who had sat there quietly not seeming to be listening, "but I think a concern for other people brings with it a concern for social justice and right behind that emerges a social conscience."

"Is she quoting someone?" I asked and Kate shrugged.

"An awareness of the plight of others extends the moral sense," Hester went on. "Not hugely distanced in the way we live, in the economic circumstances of our lives, we are able to look upon each other and see ourselves. We can walk in each other's shoes. We can sympathize with the unfortunate because we can imaginatively project into their lives."

I didn't think that fit me.

"I share nothing with the Angeloni family," I said, strangely defensive. "I don't see them as unfortunate but there is a huge distance between us. I have no idea how Mario, for instance, or Pino walk about and make sense of things."

"And yet you're here to make some effort to help them," Kate said, smiling.

"I've told you. I'm at home there. It's as simple and as inscrutable as that. And I damn well don't look forward to being evicted!"

"He hath eaten me out of house and home!" the parrot, who now called himself, Sod, yelled.

"Besides," I said, trying to get Hester to look at me, "what you've just described has never existed in any society. It's all easily refuted if you take a close look at human nature, if observed without rose colored glasses. I have not in my travels observed a moral compass that directed anyone beyond their own interests."

"I would say, Gull old boy," Kate said, poking a finger into my arm, "that you sympathize with these people because you know somewhat how they live because you're now living under similar conditions. You've become part of a small familial society. And that's something travelers like to be on the outside of."

"The word `society' is not abstract to us," Hester told us in the same computer like voice which I found most annoying. "Society has flesh and blood, a face. We know something of what we are as individuals because of our observation and empathy with those around us. When all this collapses in a vicious war of all against all, a zero sum game in which the Winners cannot enjoy their successes unless someone else loses, then we stand, as we do now, as yet another failed society in a history of failed societies."

"Hate to interrupt and reject," a man dressed like a Columbian drug dealer and standing behind Hester said. "Society is an abstraction. A myth. The most profitable way to think of it is as a business. Period."

He looked at me.

"Gulliman, isn't it? Walker. You remember Andy?"

Gulliver, I said, correcting him. Yes, I did. Members of the *Trickle Down Spa*. I shook hands with both of them, noting that Andy also seemed to be in costume as something but what I couldn't really say. He had on a small straw fedora with the brim up, a lot of jewelry and tattoos, and his vest and pants were black leather.

"Rock star," Kate said, nodding at Andy.

"I've heard you," Andy said. "You're the rock star."

"And this lady is dynamite on drums," Walker said to Hester, leaning over and putting his hand on her shoulder. She immediately jumped up as if she had suddenly gone aflame and before Walker could say anything she had rushed off.

"She's different isn't she?" Walker mumbled.

He sat down without asking and Andy followed suit.

"You're the one they call Rapacious Walker, aren't you?" Kate said.

"Cause I like to walk fast," Walker said and Andy laughed.

"I heard it was because . ."

"Hey, there's Lyla," Walker said and then yelled out "Lyla!"

I remembered Lyla also.

"We're here tonight because of Lyla," Walker said as Lyla joined us. She didn't remember me but I think she did. The evening she had met me had been one she surely wished to forget. I was jettisoned.

"Ray was with me," Lyla said. "Where did he go?"

"You're a Resurrection Club member, aren't you?" Kate asked Walker in a voice that I can only describe as flirtatious.

"Every chance I get," Walker said, putting an arm around her chair.

"Thanks for coming, Sis," Ray said, coming up to the table, and giving Lyla a kiss.

Ray pulled up a chair and sat down next to his sister. Sod took the opportunity to cock his head and direct one large luminous eye into Ray's face.

"You're called Rapacious because you probably don't let any chance go by," Kate said to Walker.

"We all want to get it all before the curtain falls," Walker replied, lighting a cigarette."

"For sure," Sod squawked in Ray's ear.

"Hey, what's with this bird?"

"How come this bird makes some kind of sense almost," Andy asked.

"He's like you Andy," Walker told him. "He listens to his betters and mimics them. Not a real thought in his head."

Andy gave us a sick sort of smile.

"You are correct, sir," he said. "I am a mere minion."

"I've observed that it's technology that's a minion here in the *New Babylon*," I said, clearing my throat. "Rather like a Myrmidon of transnational capitalism."

My comment was greeted by silence until Ray remarked that science could cure a lot of diseases but there was more profit to be made with a sick man than a healthy one.

Ray was pasty faced and I suspected he wasn't getting the cancer treatments he needed.

"That's your problem, Ray," Walker said, "you're too cynical."

"No, my problem, Walker," Ray snapped back, "is dying."

"The good die first," Sod sang out.

"We all gotta die, Ray," Walker said, not to Ray but to the parrot. "It's built into the genes."

Walker had a wide smile on his face, what you would call more of a nasty smirk than a smile.

"Why the hell do you stay with this guy, sis?" Ray said to Lyla.

"Don't," Lyla said, shaking her head nervously. "Just don't."

"Your sister wanted to hear you play," Walker said, as if someone had asked him why he was here. "So here we are."

I must say I was feeling quite uncomfortable and would have made my exit but I held on to the notion that I might be able to do the Angeloni family some good by talking to Walker.

"We back a lot of medical research," Andy said in an attempt to revive the conversation.

"Is that what you're doing in New Bab?" Kate asked.

Andy looked at Walker who said they were trolling the waters of New Bab just to see what they could hook.

Kate laughed and said she never heard of a shark trolling for sharks.

"We let the blind force of Chance run the show," Walker said, in his mocking style that was very reminiscent of poor Zechariah's shadow.

"So if investors like you run the world," Kate said, "and just dumb luck runs you then you could say everything going on here in New Bab is here because of dumb luck?"

"*Buona fortuna*!" Sod yelled.

Walker studied the parrot closely.

"Do you want to sell him?" he asked me and I told him the bird wasn't mine. He got a chuckle out of this and told me that it's money that makes people do things. He then turned his attention to Kate.

"Why don't you come over to the Club and I'll show you how we get luck to go our way."

He took a card out of his wallet and handed it to her.

"Call me and I'll have a car pick you up."

Kate took the card.

"Gotta play," she said, getting up.

"Don't we all," Walker said as Kate and Ray walked over to start their next set.

"She's smart," he said.

"It's always easier when they're dumb," Andy said.

"What is it, Andy?" Lyla said, wiping some tears from her eyes. "Am I dumb and easy or smart and hard?"

"No offense intended, Ms. Lyla," Andy said. "You are …"

"All quiet on that front, genius boy," Walker said, holding a hand up.

Lyla told us she was going home and she left us abruptly. Walker looked up at me for I had stood up.

"Why are you upper class Brits so polite?" he said to me.

"Hundreds of years of good breeding," Andy said. "Like dogs. You keep mixing and matching until you get somebody who stands up when a lady leaves the room."

"Come vuole la carne?" Sod screeched.

"What did he say?" Walker asked me.

"He said `how do you like your meat?'"

"You teach him that?"

I shook my head and said I hadn't taught him a word nor had his owner Captain Noble. I said that I was staying at a *pensione* in which Italian was often spoken and I suspected the parrot had picked up a few phrases. I didn't remember Mrs. Angeloni ever asking me that question but perhaps she had.

Walker ran a finger along his pasted Columbian drug dealer mustache and then pointed a finger at me.

"Why don't you come along with the rock star," he said. "And bring the bird. I'd like some of our friends to see him."

I thanked him for the invitation.

"He hath joined the great majority," Sod announced to all as we walked away.

I was waiting at Kate's hotel a couple of days later when the car came to pick us up and take us to the Tenderloin district where the Resurrection Club was.

It was a surprisingly old brownstone and the foyer we entered had the look of a museum entrance, dark with even darker paintings and tapestries covering the walls.

We were led into what I can only describe as a medieval mead hall. The walls were huge quarried stone and were draped with tapestries that looked authentic to me. There was a fireplace that one could walk into without bending and a fire whose blaze lit the immediate surround, the remainder of the hall being lit by candles and therefore deeply shadowed.

Two Irish wolfhounds, of typical size, lay by the fire. Upon seeing the hounds, the parrot squawked and hopped from my right shoulder to my left and took to trying to hide behind my ear. There were a number of people, perhaps a dozen, sitting and standing about, drinks in hand.

Walker, now dressed rather less like a Columbian drug dealer and more like a fop in his digs, greeted us with a quizzical look on his face. When he saw the parrot, he snapped his fingers.

"The guest of honor has arrived," he announced to his guests. "What's his name?"

I was about to say Sod when the parrot screeched *"Tranquillo."*

"Tranquillo," Walker said. "And this is a rock star friend of mine..."

"Kate."

"Kate and this is an old friend, Lord Golliman."

"Start a business!" the parrot shrieked.

"More correctly known as Mr. Gulliver," Guy Beecher said, coming over to greet me. "Spark is on death row and not me. Thanks to you, old chap."

I was also greeted by some other *Trickle Down Spa* members: Mr. Hugh, Mr. Swearly, Mr. Wims and Mrs. Goodheart.

I wasn't surprised to see them but I was surprised to see Rollins and flatly told him so to which he laughed and said he was sick and tired of the insipid peace and quiet of the Garden and now, having come into his own as it were -- and here he winked at me – he had made the New Bab his home. He was to go through some Club review for acceptance that very evening

Besides Kate and myself there were three other guests that evening: Chick Wagstaff and his sales team: Prince Krokov and Statman.

After Kate and I had drinks in our hands and had greeted all of the Club's members Walker asked me how to prime the parrot to talk.

"What sets him off is what I mean," Walker said.

I told him I had no idea, that the parrot exercised a free will to speak when he wished. He was not programmed.

"That's hot," Mr. Swearly says. "My man here says that a bird has a free will. A bird. We can produce and program human beings like products but this bird brain here isn't owned by anybody. That's hot."

This comment produced a great deal of laughter.

"There's a good time coming!" Tranquillo shouted out.

That produced uproarious laughter. The hounds had gotten up and were now installed in front of my chair, eyes glued to the parrot. I prayed he didn't wing off for that would surely get the hounds after him.

"How do you do it?" Walker said, looking at the parrot and then at me. "How are you cuing him to speak? Andy, get some video of this."

I once again declared my innocence in the matter and was as mystified as anyone else at the parrot's delivery. Walker looked at me as if I were up to some sort of chicanery, a trickster who was having fun at his expense. I could see his eyes narrow and his whole face darken.

"Magic," Rollins then said, loudly, getting up from a sofa and walking over to the fireplace. "In a magic trick the first gesture is called the pledge where the magician reveals a state of affairs and promises to disrupt it and imperil it. The second gesture is the turn where the magician actually accomplishes and fulfills the pledge to our amazement. The third and final gesture is the prestige where the magician returns us to a pre-disrupted state of affairs though now we are astounded, entranced and full of wonderment as to how all this could have been accomplished."

Rollins had a mesmerizing way of speaking and indeed every eye was on him and every ear was attentive to his words.

"Some trick has been performed," Rollins went on, "there is a secret withheld that if we knew would dispel the magic aura and return to us our sense that we know the world and we know how to know it."

"Well, I for one," Chick Wagstaff said, after a long pause in which the parrot said nothing nor did anyone else. "I don't feel astounded by hearing that bird. I'm not amazed. To me, it's just another voice. A bird voice so I don't look for anything in it."

"I would agree," Prince Krokov said. "The bird is not the only low life speaking gibberish I have encountered in my life. He's to be eaten, not conversed with."

"Perhaps, gentlemen," Rollins said, smiling, "I can explain your disinterest in this way. The world we are creating in *New Bablyon* is unmagical and subverts and reverses all of this. In an unmagical world nothing can really disrupt or imperil the individual. Nothing can be fulfilled that has not been initiated by the individual. There is no ensuing amazement nor wonderment because the individual is prepared to assume responsibility for what he himself has chosen."

"That's the world I live in," Andy told us.

"Pledge and prestige," Rollins went on, "are in this outer world simply personal choice. Whatever disrupts this can be countered by a dispelling or ignoring of that disruption. Choices are not magical but maximized by what entrepreneurial and investment choices are made by your Resurrection Club."

"You are correct, sir," Andy said.

"Keep it to yourself, Andy," Walker said, "and keep the camera on the bird. If Gullpin here isn't running the parrot and I know I'm not and I know none of you are. So it's magic."

"I would opt for some form of technology," Mr. Hugh said. "Perhaps a microchip in the bird's brain."

"It's art," Kate said, winking at me. "You know, like drama. A theatrical performance. They've rehearsed."

I was curious as to what Rollins thought had brought about such a high degree of self regard in humans that their own activities rendered uninteresting everything outside themselves.

"Self-absorption is the rule here in the *New Babylon*," Rollins replied, "wouldn't you say? The more you pursue your own self-interest, that is your own self-absorption, the more you aggrandize in *New Babylon*. You find here a place where you can make a god of You and this place finds in you a sacrifice it can feed upon."

We all seem mystified by Rollins' words, including myself, for I knew what Rollins was: a magical embodiment of Zechariah's tortured being.

"Look, Rollins," Walker said, running out of patience, "you want to join the Resurrection Club you'll have to keep it short and clear. Now is there some magic going on with this bird we can't appreciate but you can clue us in on?"

"Oh, the bird is magical for sure," Rollins said. "It's just the New Bab which is unmagical. And it empowers you by creating in you a great disdain for anything that is not you. What the Unmagical pledges to you is that it will not in any way disrupt or subvert your personal narcissistic order of things. You will be entertained without any lasting consequences. So I suggest dismissing the parrot as in any way consequential. A little amusement perhaps."

"Maybe you're right," Walker said, glancing at the parrot.

"La vie est vaine," the parrot sang out.

"Let's get to the business at hand," Walker said. "Board room."

We all followed him out of the mead hall, down a long passageway with ancient knightly armor as sentinels along the entire route and many castle deep doorways of monumental size.

Walker stopped and cast open the doors leading into what he had called the Board room. The members went at once to what I assumed were their regular places and Andy motioned seats for Wagstaff and his sales teams, Rollins, and Kate and I. Walker sat at the head in a chair more like a throne.

For the next forty five minutes we sat there listening to Mr. Swearly run through investment figures, gains and losses, interest rates, outstanding and past due, liabilities, foreign and domestic assets, debentures, bonds, negotiable instruments, bills of exchange, commercial paper, Series E bonds, general obligation bonds, trustee mortgage bonds, unsecured bonds, street certificates, flotations, Irish dividends, swings and declines, warrants off and on, thin and shoestring margins, flash prices, call prices, scrip dividends, price quotations, watered stock, stock splits, inactive stock, callable securities, ten-share unit stock, cyclical stock, glamour issues and high fliers and very much more.

Occasionally one of the Club members would ask a question which Mr. Swearly would answer by providing more figures.

I must confess that I had no understanding of these numbers but I did have some notion of whether all these numbers bode well or ill for the Club by simply looking at Andy's face, a face which instantaneously registered comedy, by which I mean joy, or tragedy. Walker's face, on the other hand, remained a blank.

When Mr. Swearly's report was over he announced the blessed event and we all sat there digesting I suppose. Only the parrot spoke up.

"Some are Movers and Shakers. Some get moved."

"He threw his voice!" Andy yelled out, pointing to me. "I saw him. Goldfarb is a ventriloquist!"

I had indeed been applying a handkerchief to my upper lip at the time the parrot spoke.

"Amusing," Rollins said.

"Theatre," Kate said.

"Who's ready to give up any little bit of technology," the parrot screamed out. *"Raise your hands."*

"Inform the parrot that he's a guest here," Walker said, looking at me. "Okay, Wagstaff, let's hear your report on the Bluestocking properties."

Chick stood up and cleared his throat and then proceeded to describe how the Bluestocking neighborhood had been in the midst of a re-gentrification effort when the credit market had collapsed and Chick Wagstaff and Associates, funded by the Resurrection Club, had bought up foreclosures as well as secured title to devalued mortgage properties whose adjustable mortgage rate had gone sky high.

Statman then stood up and went through the figures.

"We can sell all our holdings at considerable profit right now," Mrs. Goodheart said. "as Resurrection has obtained complete ownership of the Garden property."

"Which means," Mr Hugh added, "Garden residents will be in the market for homes."

"What's the plan for the Garden, if I might ask?" Chick said.

"Eden theme park," Walker said, "or maybe a gambling Monaco. We could also do high end condos. First thing is to get those Buddhists or whatever they are out of there."

"I've heard it's a capital offense to chop down a tree," Andy said. "Or shoot and gut any critter."

"What's the matter, Andy?" Kate said, "Don't you like Mother Nature?"

"He's not used to it," Walker said. "No one living here in New Bab is. That's why this property is priceless. We could just turn it all into a open air museum for Nature starved souls to walk through. At a price. Trees, birds, animals, rocks, brooks, flowers, insects, dirt. The whole nine yards."

There was then a bit of chatter about the weirdness of those who had chosen to live in the Garden and not New Bab, no one speaking up for life therein.

Andy asked Rollins whether or not the Garden hadn't been his birthplace to which Rollins replied that it was and that his half brother still lived there. Mrs. Goodheart was curious as to why his half brother had chosen to remain there.

"I can't comprehend the thinking," she said. "Unless of course there was ownership involved. And accompanying income."

Rollins shook his head. His brother was the spiritual leader but like all the residents had no income but each shared work and the fruits of their work.

"Your half brother absolutely requires his other half," Mrs. Goodheart remarked.

The Club found this amusing but I could see Rollins was not amused. Perhaps if he had been dormant within Zechariah's psyche, Zechariah might now be dormant in his? And as Rollins had awakened, perhaps Zechariah was now awakening?

I must say I was fascinated as I was now observing the astounding, the truly magical. A traveler into the human psyche. Rollins did not disappoint, or, should I say, Zechariah?

"It may be, Madam," Rollins began, "that your appreciation for both the natural and the spiritual has atrophied."

Mrs. Goodheart head jerked backward and her head trembled as her mouth opened to respond but Rollins rolled over her.

"To become a pure product of capitalism, a *homo economicus*, a *homo consumerus*, first before all else – as is the case in New Bab and among your Club -- is to put aside those human faculties and capacities that would enable you to comprehend the heart and soul of a man such as my brother Zechariah. My brother contests the inordinate power of a club of speculators such as this. For him to leave the Garden and enter the world of The Cash Nexus would be like entering a Monopoly game where Park Place and Broadwalk are already owned and all the wealth is sequestered in the hands of a venturesome club of the wealthy. But in this game you are not moving your shoe or hat, your Monopoly piece. You are that piece being moved by the privileged few for their own profit."

"You said all that crap like you share your brother's views," Walker snapped. "What is he? Half brother? Whole brother? Your Nature brother."

"I know my brother's script," Rollins replied.

"Well, if you want to get into this club," Walker told him sharply, "I want to hear you challenge that script."

"Show me the money!" the parrot screamed.

 Rollins stood up.

"I'm just giving you the reasons why my brother chooses to live the way he does."

"We're evicting him," Andy said but Rollins went on, ignoring the comment.

"Many are daily immersed within awesome and magical transformations of our self designed spaces but are seldom themselves astounded and transformed. It is not that the world has ceased to be magical, that all creatures great and small, all things solid and airy, all thought and all flesh, all leaf and all rock, all flowers and worms, all oceans and all skies, all stars and planets have ceased to be magical. It is simply that outside my brother's Garden, here in New Babylon, here in this club, none can witness wide-eyed their magic. Nature, like a magician, accomplishes right before our eyes an overturning of our narrow worlds but I dare say no one sitting here can see it."

Loud protestations and angry retorts rose up like a cacophony chorus behind Rollins whose voice rose loudly above it all.

"For the reasons I've given and more, Zechariah and others have escaped into the Garden where they seek to regain the magic of their imaginations, imaginations not dedicated to an entrepreneurial innovation which has already exceeded the bounds of humanity and planet. Unfortunately they live within a deep sense of having lost those magical powers and like the poet mourn for what was once possessed."

"Just Do It!" the parrot sang out.

Walker, his anger showing, threw something, perhaps a pen, at the parrot, missing him wide, and then screamed at me.

"Take that damn bird and get the hell out of here!"

I wasted no time in making my exit.

I had an overwhelming desire to fill the commonplace with the fantastical. I had had enough of "raw reality." The hypothesis of magic is that the world is all of one piece but not glued in any rational way nor accessible in any rational way. It is accessible in every outlandish way that the imagination can conceive, and, that imagination is not man's alone but shared like an underground river feeding the face of the earth. I had not enough desire to accept that hypothesis.

The parrot and myself went back to the Garden where we found Zechariah once again in possession of his darker self, Rollins, and in control of it.

There was no need for me to tell him what had transpired at the Resurrection Club for he had been present, though not recognized by any but myself. He seemed not to be anxious about the Club's plans to evict and build, saying to me that were the magic and imagination of the Garden in full bloom, the tyranny and invasion of lesser men would be like the sting of a mosquito on the back of the elephant.

I did a bold thing and invited Zechariah to dine with me at Mrs. Angeloni's in the hope that his words might give them some comfort. I was painfully aware that I had utterly failed in being of any help to them with the Resurrection Club.

The evening Zechariah joined us, there were some new guests at table, including my old acquaintance from Mrs. Bomber's Mr. Rapoort whom we called Poortie.

Poortie had come to New Bab at the invitation of an old friend's lawyer who had written to say that the old friend had died and it would be to Poortie's benefit to attend the reading of the will. So Poortie was filled with great expectations, which, I observed, seemed to have expanded his appetites even further than usual.

The Angelonis' now lived as if they were wilderness folk anticipating an attack at any moment. Carmine and Mario had already had an encounter with a public official who had tried to place an eviction sign on their door. He had not succeeded in that act but had promised to return with ample forces. So the Angeloni boys sat there calmly eating but I'm sure their weaponry was not far away.

Mrs. Angeloni had heard of Zechariah and was honored to have him at her table but she seemed slightly disconcerted and her customary forthrightness was decidedly chilled. He was indeed I believe an alien presence.

We all ate in silence which was quite unusual at Mrs. Angeloni's table.

One of the overnight guests remarked that he had heard there was a 44% return on anything you went into in New Bab. His broad, red face glowed with the thought of this.

I found it incomprehensible. I asked him how it was possible to go into something and return so reduced in size?

"A good one!" he told me, jabbing his fork in my direction.

A young woman, another overnight guest, informed us that hundreds of her on-line friends had told her what a wonderful back in the day, old school, off-line place this neighborhood was so here she was. It was like going back in time.

Mrs. Angeloni remarked in very serious, measured tones that she was going to be severely disappointed because most everyone had been evicted.

"It's a sad city," Mrs. Angeloni said to the young lady, whose face had blanched, "except for the wealthy. Probably your hundreds of on-line friends are wealthy. Here, off-line, we are being scrunched."

The young lady told us she didn't know, having never really, like, flesh and blood seen them but they all texted their lives were magical in New Bab.

The word brought Zechariah's ears up, so to speak.

"I'm afraid, my dear," he said in his newly empowered voice, "Most of the people in the *New Babylon* live in a highly unmagical moment. The magical transformation of the world achieved by our imaginations and displayed in our art is rarely found, seldom pursued, hardly valued."

"Talk history, sir," Poortie gurgled, bits of food shooting out of his mouth. "Life for so long in past ages was short. Solitary and brutish. So poor that most starved for want of a good meal. And I've read it was intolerably nasty. Did I say short? Survival instincts were honed by the many and intermittent doses of bread and circuses provided momentary escape. There's some fancy at work I suppose in escape but mostly, sir, it's bread. And circuses. But mostly bread. I could not live on bread alone."

"Eats first, morals after," the parrot yelled.

Zechariah studied Poortie closely and then said,

"Yes, in unmagical times we resort to whatever palliatives we can find. Or, as is the case here in the *New Babylon*, that are found for us. The soma tablets of escapes have varied over time as has the necessity of so tranquillizing the masses."

"Nobody tranquillizes us," Mario said very calmly and almost inaudibly.

"Bourgeosie self-policing works," Zechariah responded, "until it is strained to the breaking point."

"Until we're evicted from our own home," Mrs. Angeloni said angrily to which Carmine promised her that wouldn't happen.

"Economic ruin," Zechariah said, "destroys the ethos of restraint, control, discipline, from your children's behavior in public to the edges of your lawn."

Chapter XIII

On-Line, for such is the name I gave the young lady at our table, disagreed with Zechariah's portrait of the people of New Bab as leading dismal lives and referred once again to the enthusiastic testimonials of her on-line friends.

Zechariah responded by saying that perhaps her friends spent more of their time on-line than in the real New Bab? They were themselves, he politely suggested, perhaps too distracted to recognize their plight and the plight of those around them?

I could see this made On-Line furious and she accused Zechariah of perhaps being too old and analogue to comprehend the optimism of her on-line friends, a suggestion Zechariah readily accepted.

"It is perhaps true," he said, "that my age and remoteness from the world your own friends accept so heartedly influences me greatly. But I believe that regardless of one's age or philosophy what can be observed in the *New Babylon* is wealth that is amassed by few is not making the lives of the many better. Problems of control of the disaffected arise."

"That's not what I heard about the New Bab," 44% said. "I heard there's no regulations holding you back here. It's totally free wheeling and go-go."

"They've got prisons here in New Bab, don't they?" On-Line said.

"Whoever controls the human mind, controls destiny," Zechariah told them in his usual no drama style.

As I had recently experienced what Zechariah was talking about I spoke up at that point, explaining that when I had traveled through *Cyberville* I had found that microchips and algorithms were the new instrumentation of the human imagination. Product and services innovation defined imagination.

"What's your problem with software that can go faster than you can?" Ms. On-Line asked me. "And come up with more results than you can find in a book? Like, hey, it's the software of the imagination."

"That's the problem," Zechariah said. "The human imagination has no program nor can it be replaced by any manmade software. It is, in short, not profit driven."

"I'm thinking we're fighting for our house," Carmine said, "and not the human imagination."

"When you live in a society," Zechariah said, "where only profit and loss can be imagined you can expect all manner of inhumanity."

"You know," Mario said, "when that all manner of inhumanity shows up here, we mak'em human."

I was pleased to see both Carmine and Mario laughing but I was quite sure that their humanizing efforts would place them in prison.

"I'd like to know, Mr. Zechariah," Mrs. Angeloni said, "why it's so different in your garden?"

"It isn't so different." Zechariah said sadly, "We've failed."

"Didn't you see it in the papers, mom?" Carmine said to Mrs. Angeloni. "They're evicting all of them out of the Garden. Going to build an industrial park or something."

"We did once imagine, however," Zechariah said, "that in the Garden rapaciousness could be reduced to the place bartering had in human affairs and personal ambition modulated by a concern for the well being of others. We, for a time, could imagine the ruling passions of the *New Babylon* as only consequential on a small corner of the human stage. We were wrong."

"I disagree with you most adamantly, sir," 44% said. "Nothing should get in the way of personal ambition. One man's will can change the world. I presume to advise you to buck up and assert your will to win. A 44% return awaits you, my friend."

"I agree," Ms. On-Line said, shaking her head at Zechariah. "You can choose to be anything you want to be. It's all up to you to make the world entertaining to you or, like, you know, give up and expect other people to do it for you."

"The more the *New Babylon* is entertained the more unmagical it becomes," Zechariah said, "and the more unmagical the world around you becomes, the more you can find no way out."

Ms.On-Line mumbled something about now knowing why old people had to die off.

"The time has come to talk of many things," the parrot yelled then put his head under his wing and went to sleep.

I returned with Zechariah to the Garden. When I woke the next morning, the parrot's cage was empty. I searched throughout the Garden but he was no where to be found. I think now if I had remained at Mrs. Angeloni's which was so well guarded by Carmine and Mario, the parrot would not have been stolen.

I cannot tell you how agitated I became over Captain Noble's parrot and this depth of distress exceeded what I was prepared for.

On some level of awareness unknown to me the bird had become my companion and I had begun to see into a nature that I had wholly misconceived. Now I felt his absence in a manner that almost rivaled, nay seemed to exceed, any loss in my life that I had previously suffered.

I recalled Walker's bid to purchase the bird and I rushed to the Club but was denied entrance. I was very soon apprehended by the police for the disturbance and threats I had made.

Upon my release the next morning I went to the *Shakedown* where I found Chick who was drowning his own sorrows in whiskey.

What sense I could make of Chick's words, interspersed with great, shocking oaths, was that Walker had absconded with all of what Chick called `his liquidity' and left Chick facing criminal charges.

I had to finally grab Chick by the shoulders and shake him to get any response from him as to where Walker had gone and whether he had my parrot with him.

"Brigands' Stronghold," Chick said. "I don't know about the bird but I know he wanted it and Rapacious Walker gets what he wants the Devil take his soul."

I had heard in my travels of the *Brigands' Stronghold* where money talked so loudly that nothing else could be heard.

I set out at once to find Brad, for such was the name the parrot had last called himself.

Chapter XIV

The Author arrives at the Brigands' Stronghold, is captured, rescued, and gradually learns how money talks.

This is what is said about the *Brigands' Stronghold*: it is neither on a flat open plain or nestled in a valley nor is it high on a mountain or ensconced by sea or river. It is not Xanadu. It is not a hi-tech re-issue of what Ozymandias had built nor a luxurious retreat for global billionaires. It is not Francis Bacon's New Atlantis or Eden or Arcadia or Shangri-la or Dr. Johnson's Happy Valley where we are told 'all the diversities of the world were brought together, the blessings of nature were collected, and its evils extracted and excluded.'

The *Brigands' Stronghold* was no Happy Valley. It is more like Satan's Pandemonium as the blind Milton saw it.

The dark mythology that surrounded this place referred to it as a vast honeycomb below ground, a warren, a funk hole where brigands of all types keep their stash secure, an unholy sanctuary, a hellish bolt-hole, in short. It was said that the most respected and admired people in the world used the Stronghold as a home base, as did the most vile desperadoes, re-emerging periodically with new identities. It was indeed a place like Hell but a place that nonetheless attracted many who settled here, the way pigs can comfortably settle in shite and mud.

Chapter XIV

What I found to be the real *Brigands' Stronghold* was, in appearance, nothing as the mythology had foretold, although I soon discovered that the myth described the unseen heart of the place.

As soon as I stepped off the train at the *Stronghold Station*, I was arrested, for what I do not know, and taken to jail, which was indeed a bolt-hole!

I don't know how many days I was kept in my darkened warren with the only ray of light entering when my food and drink were slid through a small shuttle. I imagine now that this was to soften me for interrogation which began when my beard was long enough for me to pull.

My interrogators varied but were consistent in one regard: they didn't question their own premise that I was a spy of what they disdainfully called The Government sent to somehow terrorize them.

Of course I dismissed this as arrant nonsense and paranoia but as they were prepared only to hear the specifics of my terrorist plot – which was what I was accused of advancing -- no protestations on my part could reach them.

Faced yet again in my travels with water boarding, I quickly developed a strategy in which I would reveal my machinations in return for civilized treatment such as clean, well-lit accommodations, decent food and some time in the sunlight. The better I was treated the more I would reveal, including the identities of other terrorists at that moment in the Stronghold.

I had nothing in mind beyond this relief and hoped only after improved treatment to be more able to conjure an escape plan. But truly I had no plan of escape and could not but think that my travels would end here.

The Goddess Fortuna had other plans for me and one morning as I was making a tour of a walled garden, the prison facility was attacked. Rockets whistled over head and struck the ground with deafening explosive force. The garden wall was breached and in the pandemonium, I managed to forge through and with head lowered and dark fumes engulfing me I raced forward, heading not toward but away from. Out of the smoke, horses appeared and suddenly a face bent toward me and a hand was held out. "Come Prisoner. This is your day to escape!" I took the hand and swung up behind the horseman.

And so I made my escape, or so I thought, for indeed I had escaped one Brigand band only to find in my rescuers another.

"Money is the second global means of absolute control," a cheery faced Brigand told me on my first day.

I asked what was first and he informed me that he was quoting sacred text. Nuclear war was first, cyber-communication was third. Money, he said, would never be shared equally but in the end it was better to be poor than dead. The rich wouldn't let nuclear war happen because it was indiscriminate in its destruction. A "limited" war in which the rich could avoid risking their own lives proved profitable and not dangerous to them.

I was left to wander about this brigand camp, which called itself Brand Camp, on my own after a very brief conversation with what was called the Brigand Board. I explained to them how I had been arrested upon my arrival at the Stronghold and how disastrous that experience had been. I thanked them profusely for rescuing me and was told that was a residual of their transaction. Every band in the Stronghold made raids upon the other. It was a way of life. In this manner they could assume all the assets and personnel with one fell swoop. Here in the *Brigands' Stronghold* a fierce competitiveness found its logical culmination in fierce and bloody raids.

Often they gathered up young, fertile minds whose imaginations could be detoured from day dreams to entrepreneurship.

"We get them around the third and fourth grade," a Board member told me.

Another goal of the raid was to round up the reckless who they defined as those who had allowed their fancies to run away with them and believed that they were either prophets, rebel leaders, healers, rock stars, super heroes, idols, gurus, or messiahs.

For my edification I was informed that cyber technology had greatly magnified the sacred activities of Branding which were, in short, a means by which one could reach deeply into the very furnace of Being and implant there Foundational Needs and Basic Desires.

I queried as to what these might be and was told in an off-hand fashion "No matter. Safer, bigger, faster, easier, leaner, younger, richer, stronger, happier, hotter, sweeter. Kind of a variation on the Seven Deadly Sins. That sells best. But it could be faith, hope, charity, justice, equality, temperance, industry, fellowship. No matter. The link to the Brand is what's important."

I was about to question further when the Board adjourned. I was urged to "innovate a new product or service" or "start up a business." And then I was out of the room and in an elevator looking at a plaque with the words **"Wealth Maketh Many Friends."**

The Reader knows by now my proclivity for life in boarding houses. The hostelry is the traveler's homey respite, whether it be a fleabag or flophouse, whether there is a tavern on the ground floor or on the first, whether the groaning board of nightly fare is an arena of battling forks or not, this is the habitation of the perennially dislodged, whether the life to be found there is more of a menagerie than a society.

I refer to the professional traveler such as myself. We are self-exiled from our own birthplace, mislaid creatures who have never found the hearth around which our fellows gather. We haunt the roads and sea lanes, truants out in all weather, on French leave forever, fleeing what others cling to, off-center, off-balance and always in the view of the sedentary no more than aimless ramblers and sorry gadabouts.

But I have found that if all observing is situational, the traveler expands the lens but does so most dramatically when his preferred transient abode is the boardinghouse. Here is the hive of varying activity and talk where the traveler, like a far-ranging Ancient Mariner, a knight of the road, an inveterate landloper, a homeless waif, finds that recuperation which being among one's own kind, however briefly, does provide. What is more kindly, my beloved Aeschylus tells us, than the feelings between host and guest?

I found a room in a *pensione* called the *Cloister* which provided breakfast and dinner with other boarders. I found these boarders, like all boarders I had encountered in my travels, to be quite interesting.

The place was run by Mr. and Mrs. Clotter and was more like Mrs. Bomber's than Mrs. Angeloni's in that the guests here were mostly permanent boarders, which in very practical traveler's terms means that the playing field – and here I refer to a well-laden table – is not equal.

Mrs. Clotter was very anxious about The Government's intrusion into her toilette, which was how she referred to her private life. Her cooking was anti-governmental which was how she described it to me when I asked about meals. I had no idea what she meant but soon learned that she bought all her perishables at a market whose merchandize was guaranteed to be "Governmentally Un-inspected and Un-regulated."

Mr. Clotter, a robust man of perhaps fifty, was what he called an anti-unionist and told me that not a nail in the house nor a lick of paint nor a copper pipe nor a bit of brick or tile had been put there by a Socialist. Every man jack of them who worked for Mr. Clotter accepted his terms or walked on. He called it an "At Will" arrangement and the will was his. He also told me in strict confidence, revealing two pistols under his jacket, that he had enough guns on hand in case the Socialists attacked the boardinghouse, which he expected to occur at any moment now that The Government had gone Red. I told him I was much relieved by the news.

The boarders were much engaged with various phone calls on their own handheld computer devices at breakfast, hardly noting what they were eating. At dinner they were deflated like hot air balloons and now quite fizzled out. It was at dinner that I could at least hope to gain their attention and pursue my double purpose of first, finding the parrot, and second, interrogating the human heart, being anxious to find there recuperation from past travels.

A boarder named Peter Cuff had a peculiar habit of prefacing all that he said with the phrase "*from a marketing point of view.*" If the topic was that day's weather, Cuff would say, "From a marketing point of view, today's rain has minimum agricultural impact, considering we are at harvest, but commercial aquifers will see a bottling increase."

Chelsea Bonze was a Provocateur of Alternative Life-Style Choices who said she made a living packaging Resistance into a cool and edgy "X-treme" product. She showed me a "Refusenik" robot about ten inches high and said it was programmed to shout back when certain liberal and leftist words were used within a twenty foot radius. She placed it on the table near the salad bowl and told us to just continue talking.

Mr. Gideon Pinch, a stern looking man who said little but growled a good deal, was, I was told, an Angel of Privatization, a particularly ill-suiting title in this instance I thought but did not say.

Pressed by me, Mr. Pinch growled "Anything supported by taxes can be privatized for a profit." Such as? "Such as," Mr. Pinch picked up his plate of meat loaf. "Lunch. And breakfast and dinner. Such as words. Prisoners. School kids. Soldiers. Libraries. Bread lines. Government Cheese. If it's free, it's not appreciated."

At the word "free," Chelsea's robot shouted out *"This land is my land."* I was at once reminded of the parrot. Mr. Pinch growled. "If there's no money to be made, it's parasitic."

I could not refrain from asking whether the government of a country such as the United States of America was parasitic, in his view?

"Depends," he growled. "When it's corporate, the parasitic turns to private gain. That country is not going to see another FDR."

"Private gain" prompted a shout of *"Down with the Public good!"*

Ashley Free, a name she had given herself, a twentysomething sitting to my right, then told me that personal life-style choices were private choices and had become totally detached from public concerns. "We're social within a privately chosen space," she said, smiling at me.

"Of course," the gentleman to my left who was nicknamed Short Sales then remarked, "back in history, societies could interfere with a guy's private life and start wars but then sales and marketing weren't what they are now. You know society isn't a lifestyle. Only you can make your own lifestyle. Your own wealth."

At the world "wealth" the robot shouted *"Down with the Commonwealth!"*

I found such conversation quite dismaying and could not refrain from mentioning poverty and sickness and war and education and the well being of our fellow creatures and of Nature itself as societal as well as personal matters.

That was greeted by a rebuff from retired Major General Chuck Shroom, called behind his back by the other boards as "Magic Shroom," who insisted that wars were never societal affairs. The personal feuds of gentlemen swelled to wars. The personal lust of one gentleman brought the Greeks to Troy. The mania of psychopaths swelled to wars. The personal greed of gentlemen swelled to wars. The personal religious beliefs of gentlemen swelled to wars. And the present war the Americans were fighting in Iraq was no more than the son of a gentleman seeking revenge for an insult to his father. It was all bloody personal.

"Not to mention," Mr. Pinch growled, "my own personal fortune and that of my gentlemen friends made on this war."

At the word "fortune" the robot shouted *"Get Yours!"* I was, dear Reader, put off my meals by such talk and much aggrieved to see how any counter-talk out of the mouth of a toy did no more than make us laugh.

Short Sales sold "Coolness" which once may have been thought of as a free commodity, rare but free, elusive but within one's purchase —but not financial purchase.

"Now," Short told me as we strolled in the garden after dinner, "you can buy Cool. It's been taken off the Mystique shelf where no one knows how to buy it and no one knows where to buy it. Now you can see it in the lifestyle of that celebrity, that model, that person famous for being famous. It's in Angelina Goali's's lips. So you get some collagen. Or it's a nose. So you get Hannah Banana's nose. Or a chin. So you get George Baloney's chin. Or breasts. So you Pamela Mammela's breasts. Or Jennifer Lopo's ass. Coolness is in your ride, your shoes, your purse, your haircut. Coolness isn't just private and it isn't just public. It's that hard to get at something that's still hard to get at but nevertheless you can buy it. Or try to buy it. That's the thing. You never stop trying, searching for the new cool."

He gave me a head to toe scrutinizing look. "I suppose you could be cool in some world. But not here." He then laughed. "I could put you into a whole new look for less than a grand."

It was hard to keep Short Sales off of sales but I managed to bring up the parrot and asked him if he knew anyone who had a talking bird? He didn't and he didn't think it was cool to have a bird at the present coolness moment. He recommended I acquire a coral snake. I asked him if he knew a man called Rapacious Walker and he shook his head.

Another boarder -- Ralph Revelation was what he called himself but we all called him Baby Face -- was a far better salesman than Short. He was called that and I never learned his real name but as he had the face of a cherub I thought his sobriquet quite appropriate. He was a Special Adviser to the People's Congregation who were dedicated to making everything more spiritual, including government, schools, businesses, entertainment, plastics, communication, class, war, football, race, language, mixed drinks, poverty, cooking, child rearing, atheism, working, sex, Bridge, gender, sports, shopping, lounging, coitus, traveling, sales, and dying.

Coolness he told me involved mystique but a worldly mystique and as such `you could be called out on it' as Baby Face put it. Spirituality, on the other hand, was all myth and mystic as it had no real worldly presence. It was what wasn't here, what would never be here, what had never been here and therefore it was perfect. He was free to say that it was doubtlessly behind what was here.

"So how do you pitch that?" he asked me. I had no idea. "You can sell Bibles and crucifixes. Send around the collection plate. And mass cards and religious education. In the middle ages they sold indulgences. How do you privatize spirituality?" His baby face creased into a broad smile. "Mammon talks, God walks. God talks, Mammon walks. Either or."

I thought about it and then told him I didn't think you could capitalize on spirituality. He then asked me why Ms. Oh could take time out for what she called "Spirit" on her TV shows. Why did the American presidential candidates have to line up and vow their belief in the Bible? Why did George W. Wabushwa say he talked to God?

He believed that even though spirituality was as much an invisible product and service as Coolness, if you linked with either one, your product and service would sell. Baby Face Ralph explained to me that spirituality is made to talk money.

When I asked him about the parrot, he questioned my interest in a parrot which he felt was associated with pirates, profanity and lasciviousness. I would be wiser to be in the market for a dove or a sparrow as they had a Spiritual brand to them.

I went around with a disheartened look and it was Ashley Free who called me to an accounting. I explained to her that while my travels had been deeply disheartening and tragic I would not dwell upon them. Free was frankly puzzled by my reliance on the talk and actions of others to settle what she felt was a purely personal matter: being happy. As far as the past tragedy in my life was concerned, Free took the view that the past was dead and finished, that memory was like the pictures on a *Facebook* page: only today's page mattered.

She advised me to virtualize not only myself but my community. She told me with a smile – and I could see she was quite amused by my predicament – that what was once called human self-development was now called branding. The trick was to enwrap yourself totally within a brand which then becomes your identity. When that branding wears thin then a new brand is adopted. The time honored search for identity was now no more than the search for a brand.

When I questioned Free about the parrot she advised me to go on *Easebe* and get a new one.

I continued to feel that one or more of the *Cloister* boarders knew of the Resurrection Club or had heard of Rapacious Walker, whom I was now certain had taken the parrot. I read the *Brigands' Times* each morning in the hope of some chat column referring to a very remarkable parrot, for indeed I thought his talk would cause a stir here sooner or later.

My next conversation was with Peter Cuff who invited me to his rooms which were, in his words, decorated "from a marketing point of view." What I noticed around me as I sat down on a small, worn sofa was the digs of a rather impecunious pensioner. Cuff had heard from Free that I had lost a talking bird and I told him I had and asked him if he might know of its whereabouts. He, not surprisingly, took a marketing point of view in regard to birds: The Government shouldn't raise them or regulate them and that Asian Bird Flu was a result of Communist control.

"I see you're against the marketing point of view?" he said to me, sitting there in a faded wool sweater with patches on the sleeves and threadbare carpet slippers on his feet. His face was patchily shaved, grey bristles here and there. He peered at me over half lens reading glasses whose both arms were taped.

He had made us some tea and as he handed me a cup he said,

"I say a market point of view ended feudal dukes and fat kings and disease and poverty and ignorance and bad plumbing and rotted food and holes in the roof and holes in your shoes. There's nothing wrong in being led by profit and loss and a whole lot wrong by being led by governments who play God."

I was about to say that it didn't appear to me a marketing point of view had done much for him but I only suggested that a globalized market point of view had so far sequestered wealth in very few corners and that no political regime had ever before succeeded in such grand scale looting.

Mr. Cuff squinted at me from above his Franklin reading spectacles. There was a scarce amount of long, white hair on his head, all of which had been combed over his baldness. Through the thinning hair I could see brownish age spots.

"You're a wasteful user of words, sir," he told me. "From a marketing point of view. Many words is like a brick wall being built to keep out the truth. I'll ask you to just give me a yes or a no on questions my friends and myself have composed from a marketing point of view."

I nodded and he got up from his rocker and went into the next room, returning shortly with a small, tattered notebook. He sat down again and opening the book, finding his page, began his interrogation.

He questioned me regarding competition, free enterprise, justice, an equal playing field, wealth redistribution, moral hazard, layabouts on the dole, talking money, personal responsibility, entitlements, public restrooms, pensions, and cats.

Mr. Cuff spent some time tabulating my responses then looking at me declared that from a marketing point of view I was either an Idiot, a Communist, a Terrorist, an Ironist, or a stand-up Comedian.

As I was about to leave, Mr. Cuff asked me whether I'd be disposed to looking at some of his hobby handiwork? I said I'd be honored and he once again left the room and this time returned with a large hatbox which he laid on a coffee table. I noticed among the papers he pushed aside to make room for his box several *Cloister* Boardinghouse bills stamped "Past Due."

Out of the box, Mr. Cuff proceeded to carefully remove small, delicate figures that had been carved in soap or wood.

"This was my great grandfather," he said, holding up a figure no more than five inches high. "He was at Bull Run."

He handed it me and I examined it, being very careful not to injure it for it was indeed a remarkably detailed piece of work with the smallest features – eyes, mouth, nose, fingers – done so masterfully, and the whole painted so deftly, that I could not put express my sincere admiration for this artistry. He showed me piece after piece, finally picking up one with such great care that I was not surprised when he told me this was the late Mrs. Cuff, as she had been when he first married her some forty eight years ago.

What can I say? She had all the loveliness that long devotion and cherished memories can give.

"From...from a...a market," he began and then said no more but re-wrapped each figure and returned it to the hatbox.

"Each is beyond price," I said.

He looked up at me and I could see his eyes were moist.

"Would...would you be a purchaser of any of these?" he said and I at once realized that Mr. Cuff was, from a market point of view, in desperate financial straits, so desperate that he would be willing to part with these figures that clearly represented what was most dear in his life.

I therefore told him that I would not purchase any he had in that box but would pay him well to carve me my parrot. I had a number of pictures he could copy from. Before he could respond I took out my wallet and handed him an amount sufficient to pay his board at the *Cloister* for the next six months. He protested the large sum but I told him business was business and that from a market point of view whatever he carved now would one day be worth ten times what I paid him. He agreed that it made sense from a marketing point of view.

My daily regimen did not alter: I spent the morning wandering around the town, going in pubs, cafes, bakeries and butchers, greengrocers and haberdashers, searching through markets and parks, questioning strollers, proprietors, officers of the law. I asked all I met as to whether they had seen or heard of a fine talking parrot. I took my lunch in pubs and then in the afternoon returned to the boardinghouse where I napped, read and wrote, and then before dinner I was once set out in search of the parrot. After dinner I frequented pubs, a different one each night and then returning to the boarding house read before falling into deep and rewarding slumber.

Clearly I was arming myself in my reading and thinking for our dinner time conversations which had gone from the desultory to the avid. We now launched into a storm of debate with the fewest of words.

This evening, Cuff held forth from a marketing point of view on the condition of autism, which was and always would be the sort of enigma that would support a very thriving medical practice, provided of course the parents were wealthy.

I remained quite surprised by Cuff's continued advocacy of a creed that in no way valued what he had clearly shown me he valued most in the world: memory, love, and art, none of which can be assessed in any satisfactory way from a market point of view.

I now asked what would be the consequences, from a market point of view, if the parents were impoverished?

To which he replied that in the case of impoverished autism, it would, from a market point of view, be best to keep the private health insurance bar quite high. At the same time, he felt that the subtleties of autism would not be observed and would remain statistically non-existent, as much having to do with the impoverished remained from a market point of view non-existent.

"I dread socialized medicine," Mrs. Clotter said, visibly shivering. "I will not de-robe before a bureaucrat. I insist that my body remain privatized."

She sat on one end of the groaning board and Mr Clotter sat on the opposite end.

Bonzo Bonze, who was called Bonzo I suppose because of her insistence that one should push one's lifestyle to the extreme edge where the strange and the new replaced the redundant and ritual, now announced that her company was very close to making what she called "Species Enhancement" a lifestyle choice among the rich and famous for being rich.

The phrase "rich and famous" incited a bout of talk regarding what was called "the Brigands Dream." I was not surprised when the consensus opinion was that the Brigand's Dream was money and more money.

Bonzo told us that the famous for being famous would be a difficult niche to crack in her view as their inexplicable fame precluded any need for any sort of enhancement. They would not risk changing the fortuitous and arbitrary conditions that had made them famous for being famous. Had they some particular gift or talent that had rendered them famous then it was of course possible to convince them that Species Enhancement would maximize that gift and therefore make them more famous. But, alas, the famous for being famous had nothing to enhance and all to lose.

Short Sales, ever alert for a new market frontier, inquired as to what this Species Enhancement entailed.

"Say, you're a *homo sapien sapien*," Bonzo replied, motioning with a bit of potato on the end of her fork, "and you wanted to be more feline and thus more graceful."

Cuff interrupted and said that from a market point of view feline agility would give one an edge in a dance competition such as "Dancing With The Stars."

Pinch remarked that genetic engineering was safe as long as it remained in corporate hands and kept The Government out of it who were liable to make sheep of wolves and mice of men.

I must say I dropped the peas balanced on the back of my fork and looked up in amazement at Pinch. Someone long ago I believe had tampered with his brain.

"It's costly to raise *Humals*," Pinch informed us in his bear like growl, directed at myself. "Profit must be made. Stuff a pig with enough human genes and you'll have all the vital organs to harvest and sell. A rich man could afford all the organs he wants and so easily move toward eternal life."

Mr. Clotter barked out like a platoon sergeant and told us that with enough renewable organs and enough ammunition a rich man could hold off an army of Socialists.

I was pondering that confrontation when Short Sales commented that surely the *Humal* industry was an industry the government would regulate. For the good of all.

"All for one!" Mr. Clotter shouted. "We're all in this for one!"

Gen. "Magic" Shroom would have none of this regulation and insisted that just as an individual was self-regulated or not worth his salt on the battle field, industry had to be self-regulated.

I could not help observing that surely an army operated as a unit, as the proverbial well oiled machine, and therefore abided by all the requirements of interrelationships that are key in societies. Indeed, I offered as tactfully as I could to the General who stared at me with huge bulging red eyes that did not blink atop cheeks and nose that displayed the ravages of whiskey neat, were there not manuals of regulations in the military? And was not boot camp devoted to diminishing the impulses of self-regulating individualism?

Magic Shroom then announced to the table that I had clearly never served my country, whatever and wherever it might be.

Free, leaning toward me and whispering in my ear, asked what species I would like to add to my DNA.

Before I could think of what to say, Baby Face Ralph told us, with a straight face, that the DNA of angels, specifically Thrones and Dominations, had been discovered by chance in the DNA of a boy in Kashmir.

Cuff said that from a marketing point of view the DNA of angels would be worth more than the DNA of the lower orders, provided it wasn't contaminated with idolatries such as Russolatry and sociolatry.

Free laughed and told us that it was not possible to identify the DNA of celestial bodies, first ,because angels didn't exist and, second, if they did there was no record of their DNA, if they even had DNA.

Pinch said that if it was profitable for them to exist then we should consider them existing.

Mr. Clotter worried that Angels might not be able to handle a gun.

Mrs. Clotter wondered if Angels had a government or were just free ranging like wolves.

Short Sales remarked that the Angel brand was too delineated not to be real and he proceeded to refer to Principalities, Seraphim, Cherubim, Thrones, Dominations, Virtues, Powers, Archangels, Angels of Death, the Deuce, Old Harry, Old Scratch, Elvira, Zacherley…"

I interrupted him to say that I believe he had confused angels with evil spirits and TV ghouls to which Sales replied that there was no morality to brands.

"I have a bit of the angel in me," Baby Face Ralph told us to which Free replied that it didn't seem to do him much good as he was more rapacious than a rat.

"I suppose," Pinch mused, "that if one had a bit of Angel in him, one could fly but who would be making a profit on that?"

Cuff had the penultimate word on this fantastical subject: "From a market point of view, there's much to be gained by replacing human DNA with biochips. If we become more like animals, we might do ourselves in. There'd be more union organizers right off. Not to mention bleeding heart Bambis. On the reverse side, if we were to go robotic we could just shut troublemakers down and save on the cost of prisons."

Mr. Clotter didn't like the idea of robots.

"I'm against anything a bullet can't stop," he told us then asked for the peas to be passed.

Chapter XV

The Author hears more talk at the Brigand and Stronghold hotels, rescues the Parrot, attends the Church of the Trademark, and, preferring the talk of the Parrot, manages to once again make his escape.

I had the good fortune to be invited to lunch with a Mr. Harrison Borko, a man in his early thirties who was considering developing several hundred acres of refuge for abused tigers.

I say good fortune because Mr. Borko was a member of the Resurrection Club, a fact revealed to me by Baby Face Ralph who was Mr. Borko's spiritual broker.

A spiritual and moral broker, according to Baby Face, was a go-between between the natural world and the spiritual world whose job it was to assess the other worldly worth of everyday activities. A quarterly report to Mr. Borko might reveal that he had accumulated an equivalent of fifty thousand dollars in spiritual asset. Two and a half per cent of a real fifty thousand dollars would be Baby Face's fee. I found the situation preposterous but after some thought concluded that if this sort of moral brokering brought some peace of mind or solace of conscience to Mr. Borko, I suppose it was money well spent.

However, what I discovered in Mr. Borko was a man of smirk and smugness, confident in the privilege his wealth granted him and not at all urged to review his conscience regarding any of his actions, as that whole business was in the hands of his spiritual broker.

I had been recommended as someone who had traveled widely and could alert him to where he best might locate said refuge. He identified himself as an investor in defense, prisons, and luxury items, and as a person who identified closely with the large, predator cats. He was investing some twenty million dollars in providing a sanctuary.

I met Mr. Borko at *The Brigand*, the finest hotel in the Stronghold. The dining room had high ceilings, dark drapes, and oak burnished floors. Mr. Borko was dressed like a lion tamer, or so I thought.

"What I like about vagabonds like yourself, Mr. Groveller," he said, as soon as we had shaken hands, and sat down. "is your free-lance independence, devil may care, go where you want, a freeman of the world. Non-partisan and tolerant because you don't want to get stuck in the mire of the sedentary. But you have a will of your own and do as you please. Travel breaks all shackles and frees the mind."

I corrected him as to my name and also his estimate of my own estimate of my travels. I told him that thus far my travels had contributed greatly to my mental discomposure as I had experienced much that alarmed me and much that remained unintelligible to me. In point of fact, I confessed, my travels had left me to the judgment that all men are dogs fighting for a bone, and as such a plague to women and all sentient creatures.

"Precisely!" Borko shouted just as a waiter came to the table and put down a bottle of good Irish whiskey. "They're shackled dogs! We've lost our free hand, our carte blanche, our no holds barred attitude. We regulate ourselves the way dogs do. But you and I...we're on the loose, we're at large, detached, footloose, freeborn. We're not dogs. That's why I say give me the big cats, wild and unmastered, free-acting, unmeasured. There's no creature on the planet more ungoverned, more uncurbed, more ungagged than a big cat. What they do is direct, candid and bold, sir. My hat is off to them!"

At this, Mr. Borko, who was absolutely insane, took off his jungle helmet and waved it in the air. I saluted him with the neat Irish our waiter had poured. At least the insane drink well.

At his point, I inquired as to what his opinion might be of free talking parrots who are uncensored and unconfined in what they say. He told me then that one of his Club confreres had come back from the *New Babylon* with just such a free thinking loquacious bird. I remarked that I had met a Mr. Walker in the *New Babylon*. Same chap. Where might I find him? Right here in this hotel.

It was a eureka moment.

We were joined by Mr. Charles Spender who ordered a jeroboam of champagne for $18, 000, commenting that he was unusually dry. Mr. Borko told me that Mr. Spender came from a long and illustrious line. I concluded that the surname had perhaps long ago resulted from the successful continuance of the activity.

"The reverse in fact, sir," Spender told me. "We had the name for generations and then my great grand father decided to activate it. Not personally, mind you. Other people had a disease he called Spenditis, the uncontrollable urge to spend money you don't have. My great grandfather clove to those poor souls, lending what they needed to satisfy their craving, endless interest payments to my great grandfather ensuing."

He picked up his glass of champagne.

"His money snowballed into more money and so on until I could afford to spend thousands on a bottle of champagne."

"You've contracted the disease," Borko told him.

"Spenditis? No. I have the antidote. I have the money."

Mr. Burt Mahone and Mr. Sammy Murton joined us. They were, as they referred to themselves, gardeners, an appellation that made Mr. Spender and Mr. Borko laugh.

I noted that all four gentlemen were somewhere in their thirties. Mr. Murton began to comment on the weather and how if it went below 20 degrees C. it would cost him sixteen thousand dollars as he had made a bet that the weather that day would not go below 20 degree centigrade.

Mr. Mahone said that for five thousand dollars he would insure a governmental assumption of the debt.

Mr. Sammy Murton said that Mr. Mahone was "on" and then said he would bet five thousand dollars that there wasn't another bottle of the vintage year we were drinking available in the hotel.

Mr. Mahone said that for one thousand dollars he would insure the life of whoever accepted Mr. Sammy Murton's bet.

Mr. Spender announced that he was thinking of running for President of the *Stonghold* and what did we think of that?

I ventured to ask what his platform might be to which he said he would be running without one, or more precisely, against any opponent running on one.

Mr. Sammy Murton then said that he would bet fifty thousand dollars that Mr. Spender would lose the election.

Mr. Mahone said that he would insure Mr. Sammy Murton's bet for ten thousand dollars.

I tried not to pay any attention to these men for I was startled by Mr. Spender's anti-matter platform and said boldly that he couldn't be assuming the office without having some proposals or directives in mind?

"I propose," he said, raising his champagne glass, "that the government stand aside and let the hedge fund managers rule."

Mr. Mahone and Mr. Sammy Murton both thanked him profusely and asked to be put down for a quarter of a million dollar campaign bequest.

"So you would be then an anti-President President?" I asked, quite puzzled.

Mr. Spender gave me a wonderful smile and said that it would be his duty to put in charge of each governmental agency a good friend who staunchly opposed the existence of said agency.

To what purpose? I asked only to be told that if you get the wardens out of the way, real money could be made.

Mr. Mahone immediately pointed out that wardens were necessary in prisons to which Mr. Sammy Murton remarked that of course his good friend was referring to private prisons and that he would lay five to two odds that the closest prison to where we were seated was a private prison. Mr. Mahone would not take the bet but would insure anyone who did to the amount of one thousand dollars.

Mr. Borko said that an incompetent would do just as well as anyone to retard the action of governmental agencies.

They then talked of what they called Dirty Bomb derivatives, which they referred to as a kind of futures investment, not as reliable as Terrorist derivatives.

Mr. Sammy Murton wagered that there would be a dirty bomb explosion in a populated area in the *Stronghold* on a day the temperature went above 30 degrees Celsius.

As there were no takers, Mr. Sammy Murton then wagered that Mr. Borko would be mauled by one of his free ranging big cats when the weather was between 20 degree and 30 degree Celsius.

The talk then turned to whether one could be happy in life with less than a billion.

All eyes were on me so I assumed this was a question they had long ago answered to their own satisfaction. I said that I measured happiness as freedom from anxious concern and a certain freedom to travel so as to escape the bonds of any one locale, and therefore in regard to money, I felt that both too little or too much were conditions engendering undue apprehensiveness. I also added that even a billion dollars could not hold off the sometimes tragic consequences of Chance and that the loss of a beloved in such a fashion would render any amount of money meaningless.

"Spoken like a man who's not had a billion," Mr. Spender bellowed, capturing the attention of other diners.

"And who will never have a billion," Mr. Sammy Murton said to which Mr. Mahone said that he would insure my failure to ever have a billion to the amount of five thousand dollars.

"Your imagination has grown small, my dear fellow," Mr. Borko told me. "You talk like an imprisoned man and not like a free ranging traveler. Money is a liberation; it allows the mind to roam beyond the boundaries of the philistine and to wallow in what is truly possible. Poverty cripples. Wealth nourishes."

Mr. Sammy Murton then wagered that poverty would cripple me within the next five years.

I said somewhat precipitously that the pursuit of wealth without regard to consequences...

"Consequences?" Mr. Borko roared. "Everyone bathes in the profits of the rich. The whole Soviet Union was one stinking shackled mass of the Great Unwashed stagnating in an imposed economic equality that not one had the drive and ambition, the energy and force of will to break out of."

I responded by saying that the ugliness of greed and selfishness was not in my view absolved because something equally ugly can be cited.

Mr. Spender reminded me in very quiet tones that the vast majority of people found pleasure in the pursuit of money and enjoyed it best when restrictions were kept to a minimum. In that way, they could freely and openly compete and take satisfaction in their winnings while recognizing in their losses that they had no one to blame but themselves.

Mr. Sammy Murton interjected a wager regarding how many restrictions existed in the Brigands' Stronghold at that moment. He laid 3 to 1 odds that there were only two. Mr. Mahone said that he knew of three, those being one, restrictions on jury settlements against corporations being more than five hundred dollars, two, restrictions on union organizing, and three, restrictions on price controls, and would therefore wager one thousand dollars.

I continued to argue that the great winnings of a few had now frozen the competitive playing field into a configuration not unlike what the world had seen before every great revolution.

"I'm afraid, Mr. Spender, that neither you nor your peers have any incentive or inclination to amend arrangements that suit you so well, regardless of how unjust and despicable they have become."

You might wonder why I did not take my leave as I now knew where Mr. Walker was and presumably the parrot. But the Olympian manner of these young gentlemen, their confounded overweening self-importance went down very badly with me. I stayed to fight.

"You shall find, sir," Mr. Borko responded, "that human nature itself will not allow the largeness of altruism and justice that you envision. But this cannot be, in all your travels, the first you have heard such talk? It cannot be the first time you have witnessed the lowness of human inclinations and the ripe self-interest of all talk?"

The avid Murton then wagered that this was the second time I had heard such talk to which Mahone wagered that it was the third time. The bet stood at one thousand dollars. The waiter brought us another jeroboam of champagne.

"Besides," Mr. Spender said, winking at me, "we have all so deeply betrayed what has been in the past so nobly said of what we can so nobly be — betrayed what was once so gloriously imagined for the human race simply for our shopping carts filled with the latest baubles — that there is nothing to return to."

Everyone went at the champagne with a vengeance, including myself for I could not but accept the bitter truth of what Mr. Spender had said. As we drank, Murton and Mahone wagered whether The Wiki was history now told by those who never knew it, whether The Gogoogle was the Delphic Oracle that retrieves disconnected answers to questions that do not matter, whether the market upholds the order and sanity of the world.

They wagered a neat one thousand dollars over whether fame and fortune, cornered by a very few, taunt all the rest into a feverish pursuit, whether the price paid all over the world is the blood of all except a miniscule few, whether money has dreams that grow beyond this planet and extend outward toward new marketing frontiers, whether the human race, sir, is a mouth, open to swallow all, whether those here in this *Stronghold* have the biggest mouths, the biggest appetites, and a total desire to swallow all without ceasing.

Wednesday morning: The Stronghold Hotel

As the doors of the Hotel elevator opened and I proceeded to step out I bumped into Andy, Walker's stooge, and he was indeed quite flustered, informing me as he rushed into the elevator that Walker had been kidnapped.

I found the door to Walker's room ajar. I knocked and heard a voice:

"Un peu d'espoir!"

It was the parrot who informed me at once that his name was Ray. He was in a large cage without egress, which was I believe new digs for him. He fluttered to my shoulder as soon as I managed to free him.

I felt it was imperative to get myself and the parrot out of the hotel before Andy returned with the police but once again my exit was blocked, this time by Chick Wagstaff, who had a wild look to him, unshaven, blood shot eyes, muddied pants and torn jacket. He was taken aback upon seeing me but before saying a word he rushed back to the doorway, peered out and then turned again to me.

"Where's Walker?" he said, his voice cracked as if he hadn't used it in a long time.

I told him all I knew and that seemed to put him into a rage. This wasn't the Chick Wagstaff I had first met. We didn't stop to chat but rushed out of the room.

When we were on the street, Chick asked me if I had any money because he'd need some money to follow Walker and he had to follow Walker to get him, as he put it, but maybe others had beaten him to the punch. The Angeloni brothers had probably beaten him to it.

He laughed an insane laugh and then waved an arm to hail a cab. He said something about how Walker would have wished he got there before those brothers and how he had spent the last weeks in prison thinking of a sweet revenge on Walker. He said all this in a rush of partial coherence and as a cab pulled to the curb and Chick got in, I handed him what bills I had on me and with a crazed look in his eye he told me Walker would die like a dog and then a brief nod, he slammed the door of the cab.

Ray and I watched it moving into traffic while two police cars with lights flashing pulled up in front of the hotel.

"Gild the pill!" the parrot screeched.

I turned and walked away as quickly as I could.

Sunday morning: Church of the Tradmark

I woke early to tend to my toilet before attending services at the Church of the Trademark – some sort of cult congregation that Kate Whack had told me about and that I felt it my obligation to visit as I wanted to give this cesspool of gargantuan greed every chance to soften my opinion.

But I also wanted to abandon this Stronghold and take flight into the desert like Moses. Ray shared my impatience for as put the finishing touches on my toilette he screeched out loudly:

"listen, there's a hell
of a good universe next door, let's go."

Here I had an avian companion who could quote an American poet, and aptly may I add, so what need had I of any religion begging me to believe in the miraculous?

But I attended that morning's services and delayed my departure till the next day.

"'So out of the ground," Brother Frank, whom, my dear Reader, I immediately recognized the speaker as, the fiendish bomber, began, 'the Lord God formed every beast of the field and every bird of the air, and brought them to the man to see what he would call them; and whatever the man called every living creature, that was its name.'"

The parrot and I were standing in the back of the Church, bare as a Puritan meeting house. My first thought was to rush forward and expose Brother Frank for the terrorist he was, a man guilty of regicide, a mad bomber who had sent many to their grave, a wanted man who was at that very moment being sought by the Isle of Babel authorities. Don Rodrigo. That name gave me pause for it was myself that Don Rodrigo was hunting. I was a stranger here in the *Stronghold* and Brother Frank was clearly a respected citizen, a preacher who many had come to hear.

I scanned the congregation. I spied everyone I knew in the Brigands' Stronghold seated in the congregation: Cuff, Bonzo, Baby Face, Short, Free, the Clotters, Borko, Spender, Mahone, Murton and Andy, though there was no Walker. And I spied Chick, also standing in the back of the Church, hat pulled down over his eyes and coat collar raised high but I knew it was him. I wondered who among them would take my side against Brother Frank?

"Naming, my Brethren Brokers and Shareholders," Brother Frank went on, "signifies dominion and dominion means power. We have not given up naming what the world is, thus carrying on the work God has assigned us. And when the names themselves stand forth as glorious among all other names, then surely, my Fellow Financiers, they exemplify the power and glory of God. Dominion never ceases because dominion is authorized by God. Those names which reach every ear and affect every life display the true purpose of God's intelligent design, a design rooted in dominion and naming."

Brother Frank paused to let this sink in. He was dressed, as I can best describe it, as a used car salesman who loved early rock n' roll and James Brown soul, by which I mean his hair was as neat and parted as a banker's but a slight pompadour fluttered when he turned his head enthusiastically from right to left. His suit was neat and pressed but its pattern bold, conservative only when compared with the necktie, the ministerial gown he wore was worn most certainly as homage to Mr. James Brown, and the blue suede shoes sticking out from beneath the gown were legendary Smithsonian.

"In names there is profit," Brother Frank sang out. "What names are these?"

The parrot interpreted this as a question regarding the names of the Biblical prophets for he at once sang out in that quite eerie voice of his and in a manner of pronunciation that did justice to vowels, could not form the "s" sound and generally could not properly form the words human lips have no difficulty with.

"Abram, Amo, Danel, Zekel, Iyak, Mica, Muel, Malchi…"

Everyone in the congregation of course turned to look at us and I offered the parrot a cracker to get him to shut up.

"Naming is the ultimate God-like act humans can perform," Brother Frank went on, "for it brings the world to us as God Intended and allows us to grow richly in God's grace. This sacred mission is performed by those who look into our very souls and bring our needs and desires to expression."

I saw Murton lean toward Mahone and whisper in his ear and I suspected a wager concerning the number of needs and desires involved was in play.

"My Enterprising Entrepreneurs, our spiritual needs as well as our earthly needs are brought into the world in shapes and sizes, colors and textures we cannot at first recognize, just as the risen Christ was not immediately recognized. The miracle of branding fulfills a celestial epiphany as it makes us deeply aware of how in this and through this and with this product or service we realize our own being and serve the purpose of creation itself."

I was suddenly aware that someone had quietly come behind me because Ray had squawked and then skipped from one shoulder to another

I suspected it was an usher who would be escorting the parrot and myself out. But it wasn't. It was Chick Wagstaff. He whispered in my ear that he knew for sure that the Angeloni brothers had taken Walker and that a ransom demand had been made. Chick was taking his sales team out of the country and wanted to make one last bid for the parrot who was a natural branding gimmick. Of course, he didn't have the money but his credit was good. I shook my head and then Chick was gone. I had grown very attached to the parrot. And names didn't matter.

Brother Frank was getting deeper into this sermon on brands. I wondered what manner of cozenage and chicanery Brother Frank was up to here in the Brigands' Stronghold. I suppose he was among his kind. What offenses I would charge he committed may produce no great moral outrage in the Stronghold. Regicide might be greeted with applause and Brother Frank may seem more hero than villain. For all I knew Brother Frank's actions might be the very reason he was so esteemed. No, this was not the place to bring Brother Frank to justice. I would leave that to Don Rodrigo.

"But all brands are not created equal, my Self-Empowered Few," Brother Frank informed us. "Some resonate with the grace of the Almighty and reach into the perceptions and experiences of Humankind and find in every touch point therein a way to sow its brand. You can see this all around you, my blessed Strong Corporate Leaders, just as above the heads of the Saints halos glowed. These brands which have rightly and reverently given names to what God has created bring us under their sacred halos. The more we attach ourselves to them and find our peace in them, the holier we are."

"But there are false prophets."

Chapter XV

This brought a kind of communal intoning.

"What was more false than the worship of the thuggish hooligans of the proletariat, the idols of working class heroes, the rank bowels of shot and beer sawdust joints, 'blue light specials' at unsightly and ungodly outlets where the demos ripped tawdry garments out of each other's hands?"

This litany evoked all manner of sounds of disgust and anger.

"False branding has stalled ambition and desire. We will not have false brands before us! We live within the disingenuousness of political correctness. My Righteous Coalition, God is the only crowd stopper, not a Durex condom! And despite what the ungodly Greens tell us, happiness is a quick starting car. If it feels good then just do it. What independence would you have without your vehicle?"

This produced Marine corp "Hurrahs!"

"My Fellow Winners, how can we protect our planet without GE? Feed the poor without ADM, the `supermarket to the world'? Creatively destroy without Bain Capital? Remain sane without Prozac? Avoid erectile dysfunction without Viagra? What can the young known what `hipness' is if American Express doesn't express it? How can women know freedom without wielding a Louis Vuitton something or other?How can men walk in Nature without a rifle or a golf club in hand? How can you get through the day without a five hour energy boost?"

"We can replace all of history's efforts to `know thyself' with a Gogoogle search and thus overthrow the slow and exhausting path to knowledge with a simple mouse click and the instantaneous delivery of information."

The congregation's responses had been crescendoing and now they reached the apex of appreciation and acceptance and discipleship.All before me were truly swept away, branded, as it were, within Brother Frank's own ecstatic vision of the world.

As I turned to leave I heard someone shout "*Take the gloves off!*" but I then realized it was the parrot.

I left that temple of drool and prattle, of self-serving bushwa in the same fashion that one steps out into clean air and the bright sun after being below ground.

Before daybreak the next day, I was once again on the road, to where I did not know but I was eager to escape the talk of the Brigands' Stronghold, and preferring indeed to hear the talk of the parrot.

Chapter XVI

The Author leaves the Brigands' Stronghold and anxious to renounce money and mammon becomes a pilgrim on the Camino but loses his way and winds up on a movie set where to his astonishment he discovers that talk is scripted.

I had only been on the Camino three days, in blistering Spanish heat which I took to badly but the parrot -- who now called himself Sancho, a selection which caused me once again to entertain the notion that the parrot was not a mimic but indeed acted *motu proprio* as the Latin phrase so rightly puts it: of his own accord – relished the heat and sang out snippets of poetry, recitative, canzonetta, sea chanties, aria parlante, sacred hymns, Kunst-lied and such as we walked along.

The country side we walked through was gently rolling hills that did not disrupt a panoramic vista which gave one the impression, as a new configuration of trees, stream, field and stone appeared, that one was stepping into yet another landscape painted by a master.

It was all a great testament to a Celestial Artist, if one were so inclined to such attribution. Of course that inclination would be more than appropriate on this ancient pilgrimage road but I saw nothing that would repel an attribution to Nature itself, to the countless adaptations made to the cannonade of Chance over eons resulting in what lay before us. Except...as I looked up at the most appealing azure sky with scant white wisps of cloud whose shapes incited the imagination and then gazed at the greenery below, pattern-less except for a plowed field here and there and this foot worn dirt path I trod upon, and yet pleasing, all of it pleasing. Could mere Chance have produced this?

We perhaps view all of this as pleasing because we are not in a critic's position of neutral observation but ourselves already part of what we observe. We are of the same substance as what we see around us and therefore disposed to be not offended or disturbed by it, just as we are disposed to not be offended or disturbed by the human face, though a mere veneer covers a skeletal sight that haunts us.

Whether or not Chance could produce what lay so spectacularly before me or whether only the hand of a Celestial Entity could accomplish such beauty or whether I was part of what it was and therefore so clearly biased I cannot say.

I can say that it was by Chance that I wandered off the Camino and after many days of hunting and gathering, washing in cold streams, and huddling under my small tent, we wound up in a country where it was possible to drift in and out of innumerable movie sets, each time assuming an appropriate role.

I did not, of course, enter this land with this knowledge but rather as a naïf, something of a young, starry eyed Midwesterner arriving in Hollywood.

I stopped at a small café for refreshment. I sat there drinking my tea surrounded by people dressed oddly. Those seated together were compatibly dressed, say, in the fashion of the late 19th century but those at another table were compatibly dressed but from another century. And no one was chatting with someone out of century, so to speak. Strange indeed. And the conversation that I was overhearing seemed frustratingly similar.

The parrot seemed to be right at home. For example when right behind me I heard this from a young man seated at a table with a young woman:

"I need someone to take care of me, someone to rub my tired muscles, smooth out my sheets."

"Get married."

"I just need it for tonight."

"Would you get me a paper towel or something," the parrot said.

The woman looked at Sancho and then angrily at me.

"That's my line," she said. "And your parrot stepped on it."

I had gotten used to a variety of responses to the parrot's vocalizations but this one was new to me. I apologized and said the parrot liked to mimic.

"Are you some kind of wise guy?" the young man said to me, half rising in his chair. I once again apologized and made my exit.

Once we were on the street again, I searched for a pub, my second choice when it came to a quick familiarization of the locals, my first being, of course, the boarding house, the locale of local gossip, hominess for the traveler, and home cooking.

I found a pub called *Rick's* and went in. The place was crowded, both at the tables and at the bar. There was a black man playing a piano and singing an old standard which I found quite pleasing and I immediately envisioned Carla there with me."You must remember this" I needed a drink. I moved sideways between two people who had their backs turned to each other and ordered a Jamison neat.

"The world is full of complainers. But the fact is, nothing comes with a guarantee. I don't care if you're the Pope of Rome, President of the United States, or Man of the Year, something can all go wrong."

I found that the man to my right, wearing a Stetson hat, had turned and was speaking to me. He seemed to be waiting for a response but as my responses had not done well as of yet, I merely nodded my agreement.

I did, however, find his words to be somewhat of an eerie premonition but no one else at the bar seemed affected by these ominous words. Then another voice boomed over a loudspeaker: *"I caught the blackjack right behind my ear. A black pool opened up at my feet. I dived in. It had no bottom."*

A tall man to my right was talking to a blonde headed woman. I overheard him say:

"Who'd you think I was, anyway? A guy that walks into a good-looking dame's front parlor and says `Good afternoon, I sell accident insurance on husbands. You got one that's been around too long? Somebody you'd like to turn into a little hard cash? Just

*give me a smile and I'll help you collect.' Boy what a dope I must
look to you!"*

"I think you're rotten."

"I think you're swell. So long as I'm not your husband."

Once again Sancho got into the conversation:

"Same chair, same perfume, same anklet?" Sancho sang out.

The tall man turned to me and told me to get my own scene
or I'd be sorry. I once again apologized and explained that the
parrot was just a mimic and neither one of us meant any harm. I
offered to buy both of them a drink but he told me curtly that it
wasn't in their script.

I had no idea what was going on or what anyone was saying
but I was beginning to find this overheard talk fascinating. It was
as if I had heard it all before but under very different
circumstances. The parrot, however, seemed to not only know
what was going on and what was being said but was able to
contribute to these enigmatic interlocutions. But his intrusions
had been met with hostility and I was quite sure I was the one
who would get a punch in the nose.

I took the opportunity then to depart that bewildering place
and went in search of a boarding house.

Everyone I stopped and asked seemed puzzled by the
question so I began to ask for a small hotel where I could take my
meals at a moderate price. It was as if I were speaking a foreign
language for no one I stopped seemed to comprehend what I was
saying. It was only by accident that after a few hours of walking
through neighborhoods whose appearance were in marked
contrast with each other that I came to the *Rochester Hotel*, a
hostelry that had clearly seen better days but whose dignity, like
that of a gentlemen with worn shirt cuffs, remained intact.

As I walked in and proceeded to the desk to register I
overheard two men sitting in the lobby.

*"There's not much to tell. I'm thirty-eight years old, went to
college once. I can still speak English when there's any demand for
it in my business. I worked for the District Attorney's office once. It
was Bernie Ohls, his Chief Investigator who sent me word you
wanted to see me. I'm not married."*

"You didn't like working for Mr. Wilde?"

"I was fired for insubordination. I seem to rate pretty high on that."

I rang the desk bell and waited, hoping that the parrot would not wake up, for he had his head under his wing, and make a scene. I decided then that I would need some other resources besides my own observations if I were to fathom what was going on in this town. Immediately after registering for two nights, I asked the desk clerk where I might find out about this particular part of the country. He told me that there were numerous Script Consultants I might talk to and that there was in fact, a few doors down from the *Rochester,* the office of a Mr. Adolph, an expert on the *Hard Boiled*, which was what this neighborhood was called. After showering and a short nap, I went to see Mr. Adolph.

Mr. Adolph, a bone thin man in his fifties with dyed ink black hair, an eyebrow mustache and a white carnation in the lapel of a striped suit that was stained and fit him snugly, described himself as a former character actor whose star had once shot across the night time sky and then had crash landed. If I wished him to give me an account of some thirty years of his illustrious career he would gladly do so for a small fee.

When I declined the honor, he told me that he could also track down and discover who might be blackmailing my daughter. For a fee. I was about to say I didn't have a daughter when Mr. Adolph said that if I thought my wife was seeing another man, he could, for a fee, supply me with incriminating photos. Indeed, if I wished assistance in covering up matters of whoring, drinking or gaming, contempt charges, resisting arrest, public indecency or hit and run, he was at my disposal for a small fee, which he referred to as an "honorarium."

I put up a hand, interrupting him, and said I wasn't married, didn't have a daughter and did not engage in whoring, drinking or gaming or anything else he had mentioned.

He then told me that he could discreetly arrange for the fencing of precious stones, art treasures, letters of transit or certificates of deposit. Such was not my need, I said, and he then told me if I had witnessed a murder but wasn't quite sure if it had been a murder, he could delve into the matter. He could also run down, as he put it, lost girlfriends, robbery money I had been cheated out of, murderesses who had fled to South America, allegations of paternity, counterfeiting, embezzlement, extortion, and grand theft auto. If the Mob was after me for any reason he would be able to have a meeting with the Godfather and reach an honorable resolution.

I had difficulty in interrupting Mr. Adolph but right after he offered his fishing boat at five hundred dollars a day, I managed to get his attention and once again repeated my wish to understand what sort of country I now found myself in, quite by accident. He told me that this would entail an original screenplay for which his fee would be double.

I glanced around his office, which was an inner office that appeared to be also where Mr. Adolph slept and ate for I saw both sheet and pillow unsuccessfully crammed behind a worn out sofa cushion and greasy discarded pizza boxes in the waste pail by Mr. Adolph's desk, a desk vacant of all but a pack of Camels and an ashtray. I took all of this as signs that Mr. Adolph, though a man of a thousand services, was clearly a man floundering and probably haunted by impatient creditors.

There had been a gum chewing, sassy secretary who had asked me my business with Mr. Adolph to which I had responded that I needed his help to which she responded "Don't we all." She had then told me that she collected any fees owed.

I now told Mr. Adolph that was all incomprehensible to me except the fee. I would pay no more than fifty pounds for the information. He accepted.

He then explained to me that immigrants arrived daily on *The Lot*, for such was the name of this domain, looking to fit their lives into pre-scripted scenarios

I was bewildered by this desire but Mr. Adolph explained that the desire to replace the anxieties and uncertainties of an unscripted life with tried and true classic scripts was in his view completely comprehensible.

After all, he advised me, who would want to gamble on the actions and responses of others if they could be foretold in a script?

Who would want the burden of saying just the right thing when just the right thing has already been said in countless movies?

In his view pre-fabricated, canned talk was merely a logical progression from the barbarity of al fresco talk, which history clearly showed had devastating consequences.

Modular talk, as he referred to it, was indeed the final stage in a self-chosen, self-designed being. One could erect a self through freely chosen scripts and thus script a life already explicable to all, like a movie already seen, but unique in its selections.

If I wanted to fully comprehend what was going on here on *The Lot*, if I were as I had said a traveler seeking new talk in new realms, I needed to inform myself of how real time and screen time, real life and Hollywood life had been braided into what had so far mystified me.

My curiosity was once again piqued for I remain stubbornly a man as Mr. Addison describes who would live in the world as a spectator of mankind.

Mr. Adolph asked me where I was staying and upon replying that I was staying at the *Rochester* he shook his head and said that that wouldn't do. If I wanted to be among those new pilgrims to *The Lot* as well as among long time veterans who had not, for one reason or another, moved on to permanent roles or long contracts, I should seek habitation at the *Tara Manor*, where anyone with a good ear could pick up the rhythms of *The Lot* as well as get decent bangers and mash for dinner.

In fact Mr. Adolph informed me as he folded my fifty pounds in his billfold, he would be returning to *Tara Manor* that very day.

I wasn't surprised to discover Kate Whack in the foyer of the *Tara*. My travels had taught me not to be surprised by anything. She told me that she had followed Scheherazade Skamble here.

According to Kate the country we were now in was the breeding ground for all manner of masquerade and mole trap, all manner of delusion and bamboozlement, whether it was the kind we had seen on the wild *Political Frontier* or among the Digerati in *Cyberville* or among the money brokers and Knights of Industry in the *New Babylon* and the *Brigands' Stronghold*. Skamble was here to bring it all on-line, rather like a massive conversion or transformation of classic scripts that worked in real time into the hyperreal of cyberspace. And there they would be infectious in a way that no salesman selling a car in real time, or no politician on the stump in real time, or no preacher in the pulpit in real time, or no lawyer...

"Oh thrice and four times happy those who plant cabbages!" the parrot sang out.

Thank god the parrot interrupted Kate for she was becoming more wild eyed and frenzied with every word.

"What does he mean?" she said, looking at the parrot on my shoulder, and making a grab for her drink which she drank off and then took a deep breath.

In the past when asked this question, I always respond with a dismissal of any meaning on the parrot's part but this time I told Kate that Bon, for such was what he now called himself, quoted that bit of Rabelais when the human speech he was hearing was spinning webs out of and into its own belly.

Kate laughed.

"I know I'm going nuts following this woman. I haven't confirmed anything. I haven't written a thing. I'm going no place."

The band was with her she told me and they would be playing at Rick's that night. Ray, Hester, and Dickie Flatts were also staying at the *Tara,* which she told me was loaded with screwballs. Why would I have expected anything else?

"You know why she's named Scheherazade?" Kate asked me, toying with the drink the bartender had just poured. "She tells stories to keep us all distracted. And it's not innocent. I know what you're going to say. But I say if whoever gets into the human brain with those stories transmitted repeatedly...Repetition is the key. Ask any politician. And our Ms. Skamble has a hi-speed connect into the human brain. That's what I'm saying."

That evening Kate and I sat in the Tara dining room. Kate was scanning the diners looking for Skamble. We were soon joined by a man called The Professor whom Kate had met and found to be a good source.

I asked the professor what his domain of expertise was.

"Not a real doctor or professor" he told me. "Only a professor in the carny sense. My role character introduced the Geek, sold medicinal Elixir in small towns, recited Shakespeare in barrooms, and like Cassandra was doomed to speak The Truth just before being hung by the neck. In addition he always wore a long, black frock coat and often slept in coffins. He spikes his coffee from a flask."

"Pardon me," Kate said to the Professor, "what happens when you leave the stage, as you put it? You all stop playing roles and become yourselves? You wing it? And that's bad? I just don't understand."

And here the Professor made a sweeping gesture with his right arm which included all the occupants at the table, who indeed had been listening to his words....

"When we leave the stage, there will be none left to intone the immortal lines, to bring to life the best of the Silver Screen, to note and review every performance."

"And that's because....?" Kate coaxed.

"That's because all those old script-eos are so five seconds ago," Ms. Scheherazade Skamble said, coming up to the table and apologizing for being late. "You were expecting me, weren't you?"

"You're my story," Kate told her.

"The way I see it," she told us, "is that the whole real world is in the process of being displaced by a `regentrification' of the surround. It's cataclysmic."

"Rather like the Medieval scholastic world being transformed into the Enlightenment," I said, helpfully but not so helpfully because Ms. Skamble gave me a puzzled look.

"What script is that from?" she asked.

I said I suppose it was history's script to which she smiled and said, "Oh, history" and I realized by that look of hers that there was no more useless script in her mind than that provided by history.

"Think of it like this," she said, "there's nothing in the past like the change I'm talking about. If you take all the actors and put them on a different stage...and I'm talking about going from analogue to digital, from one stage for everybody to individually designed stages in cyberspace..."

She paused, a great smile on her face, patiently waiting for her words to sink in as if we were all primitive natives to whom she was explaining the need for hand washing.

"Then what happens?" she quizzed us. "I'll tell you. The script changes. In fact the scripteo becomes an infinite number of customized, tailored only for you scripts. And everyone still using the old lines? Irrelevant. Archaic-eo Going extinct-eo. Out of business-eo Adios-eo. A bunch of has beens."

This verdict seemed to whet her appetite for she now directed her attention to her soup.

"Chance throws more than lives on the dust heap," I ventured.

"I don't believe in luck," Skamble said, looking up from her soup. "We make our own luck. Try multi-tasking. Throw twenty, thirty sets of dice at the same time. Choose the winner. Ease-eo."

"I think you're being very disingenuous, Ms. Skamble," Kate said in a tone and manner that told me the gauntlet was being thrown down. This was the moment Kate had been waiting for.

"Oh, how's that?" Skamble said, and then held up an index finger as she pulled a cell phone out of her pocket.

Kate waited patiently and the rest of us had paused in our eating, except a man in the white dinner jacket who was working on his salad.

"Why are you here if you think all these scripts these people live in are just trash to be forgotten?"

"Do you mind?" Skamble said as she pulled a thin lap top out of her bag and laid it down next to her plate. "I need to check….on …okay. What was that?"

"We need models for our character," Kate said angrily, "to become who we'd like to be."

"You may need to borrow someone else's life and someone else's talk, Miss….? Whack. But I don't and most of my peers don't. We create ourselves and look to ourselves when it comes to consequences, including rewards."

"Do you know the script from *Pygmalion*?" Kate snapped at Skamble. "No? Not surprising. Poor cockney kid selling flowers gets reshaped into a lady with an Oxbridge accent. Did she do it herself? No, damn it. Professor Higgins shaped her."

"Is this a script?" Skamble said. "I mean with a point?"

"The point is that most of the world's population are not going to script their own lives relying on nothing but hi speed technology. That stuff just makes it faster for idiots to confirm their idiocy. We're all actors and we get our scripts from somewhere. You say everyone has his own stage and his own film crew on that computer you've got there. And they'll each come up with the Hamlet script."

"Maybe," she said, looking down at her cell phone, "Hamlet's not for everybody. Right now there might be someone blogging a new Hamlet in her basement and is that as good as the old Hamlet? Better. Because it's her's or his. It's their own personal Hamlet. Maybe I'd rather have my own..you know, life…even if it didn't measure up to what others think it should. I say whatever's personally mine…well, that's a whole lot better than imitating yours. No offense but if it's old and it's any good, it'll show up on the number of hits it gets. And if not, it's gone. And if ….pardon…"

At this point Skamble spoke on her cell for a half minute and then tapped some keys on her lap top before finishing her sentence.

"And if I choose to go on that site and choose to accept whatever…that's all there is. That's going to create unique individuals with their own scripts. Can't be anything better. You think?"

I don't know what everyone else was thinking but I could see that Kate wanted to go another round but The Professor brought our attention to some of the coming film showings at the *Tara* and following that we all applied ourselves in silence to the remainder of the meal.

When I got back to my room Bon pulled his head from under his wing and sang out:

"The farce is finished."

Or just begun I thought.

Bon and I sat with The Professor the next day in a coffee shop in the downtown area.

The Professor paused and sipped his coffee. He was dressed as always in a long black frock coat worn so thin it shone in the sunlight that filtered through the window.

"Escape, Sir, is the shooting script of today," he said. "In the aftermath of disaster one should escape to shopping malls or amusement parks or gambling Meccas. When suffering talk reaches TV, it is at once redirected to the sufferer and the world of commerce and finance remain untouched. When someone talks in opposition to the injustices and inequities, the arrant criminality of a democracy turned to oligarchy, that talk is redirected to campaign tactics and horseracing predictions."

All that might be the case I told the professor but surely escapism was the ruling passion of a country whose people so devotedly embraced the talk of cinema?

I tactfully refrained from pointing out that he himself had cast aside his own personality in order to adopt that of a cinema character. From my perspective what I could see was an escape from one's own self and therefore a loss of one's own self, which sad state Montaigne pithily phrases: "A wise man never loses anything, if he has himself."

The Professor retorted that there was no escape in the cinema he cherished. He paused. I thought then that he fully deserved the title Professor though he may not have had the openness to alternative views that we ideally expect our teachers to possess. I also remembered his own lines were scripted. But by whom?

"In short, dear Sir," the Professor went on, this time pouring his flask elixir to the brim of his cup, "history is no more than fads we ignore or mock. Erudition gives way to self-design, a disaster, a fiasco, sir, when the self has no lines because it is no longer equipped to speak."

The Professor drained his cup and stood up.

"That is why we here on *The Lot* live in the classic!"

We all watched The Professor make his grand exit and grand it was. I felt like applauding. I felt as if I had been in a movie, had just done a scene of the most dramatic kind.

"When I drink, I think; and when I think, I drink."

Thus, as a respectful disciple of Rabelais, I bellied up to the bar at Rick's about noon time the next day. Bon had left my shoulder and was perched on the bar railing and I could see the bartender eying him, the way bartender's do just before they bum rush you to the door.

Bon dipped his beak in my Irish whiskey, raised his head straight up for a good swallow then dipped again. I called the bartender over and ordered another Jamison.

"For the bird?" he asked in surly tones to which I replied yes to which he replied "Birds ain't served here" to which Bon shot out *"I drink no more than a sponge"* to which the surly bartender's jaw dropped and his blood shot eyes went wide. But he did reach back, pull the Jamison from the shelf and pour Bon a healthy shot.

We went on drinking like this as the place filled up with a lunch time crowd and presently we were joined by Mr. Adolph whose custom it was to have a liquid lunch at Rick's.

It looked to me as if he had freshly inked his hair, eyebrows and mustache for they all stood out like exclamation points in a field of paste.

"I see the parrot likes his drink," Mr. Adolph said, noting Bon dip his beak.

Bon replied once again defensively.

Mr. Adolph put back his own shot of bourbon neatly eying both Bon and myself. I'm sure he found us intriguing. He asked me yet again whether Bon and I were in a film he perhaps hadn't seen but I assured him we were real and in real time and were writing our script *ab ovo*.

I remained very curious about this country which had retreated, as I saw it, into a cinematic order of things, an illusionary ordering transported to the real world.

"Consider *Film noir*," Mr. Adolph said, "the `working class hero' is a hard bitten working stiff but he's the `common man.' Chance played a guy like a cat with a mouse while the caprice of the rich and powerful locked you tighter into your place. And there was something else out there, something you couldn't quite get a handle on but it too could hurt. Always, the less said, the better. You gave yourself away with words."

His recitation was either mesmerizing or Bon and I were already mesmerized by the Jamison. Whatever the case, we were impressed.

Bon had one shining black window of eyeball cocked inches from Mr. Adolph's head. The surly bartender wanted to know if the bird wanted another? I shook my head.

"From the gut comes the strut," Bon cackled.

Mr. Adolph asked me whether I kept some account of my travels to which I replied I did, faithfully and that I intended one day to publish them, in the tradition of my estimable ancestor, to whose genius I could never hope to attain.

"A bellyful is a bellyful," Bon said to that, to which I said that I had better get the bird home.

I decided to jump on a tour bus which was just about to depart. I paid and found a seat in the rear of the bus whose occupants were benevolent Benthamites, well-meaning Darwinians, barrel chested Castroites, anxious Saint-Simonians, Benedictines, Cash Barons, illegitimates in search of fathers, Tom, Dick, and Harry, Brown, Jones, and Robinson, the usual canaille and chaff, Equestrians and Brahmans, Whoremongers, Drunkards, Gamers, Gentlemen, Oglers, Reptiles, Actresses, Playwrights, Poets, Novelists, Muses, Philosophers, Mousetrap Men and Apron Men . . . in short, Bon and I had been drinking before noon and are making all of this up.

In fact, I had a flask of Irish with me, not to assist me in making sense of this strange world but only to get us in the mood of the place, to be better able to ...to understand. Or, as they say, to condemn a little more and understand a little less.

We had two tour guides standing in the front of the bus— Gripes and Makover – who identified themselves as Screwballians.

"The Thirties `Screwball' is full of fast talking, wise cracking mania," Gripes began as the bus rolled along, "which more often than not pits a `regular Joe' against a `socialite Schmo.'"

"If you look to your right, m'ladies and germs," Makover told us, "you'll see both a 'regular Joe'...right there on the corner. And now further on...there. A socialite Schmo."

"The ladies," Gripes went on, "such as Mae Breast, Carole Blombarge, Rosaline Trussle, Barbra Manquick, give us good as they get when it comes to sharp witted talk."

"Note," Makover announced, "we can't use real names without studio permish, which we never get cause Gripes and me don't roll like that."

Makover pointed out faux examples of each lady in the next several blocks.

"Down that street," Makover announced, "just ahead and to your right, is the original dead end street."

Makover saw me hit the flask and I passed it to him when he came to stand alongside my seat. He took a nip and passed it back.

Gripes swerved hard to the right to avoid a drunk who had appeared out of nowhere.

"The class divide," Gripes went on calmly, "is handled in screwball fashion. In the 1939 film *Midnight* both Don Abeachi, a cab driver, and Claudette Coldcream, a mock socialite, are trying to scam their way into high society."

"Mock socialite on your right," Makover called out.

"Two...no three scatterbrains on your right," Makover called out.

"There's no cutting edge," Gripes announced.

"Total absence of a cutting edge on your left," Makover confirmed and we all looked.

"Obnoxious on your right. A privileged quartet on your left. One wealthy...no, cancel that. One nouveau riche on your right. But...up ahead...real wealth. On your left, ladies and gentlemen."

As Gripes continued, I began to doze in and out as did Bon who now had his head under his wing.

"World War freezes the smile on everyone's face," Gripes told us as a parting line.

The bus then drove through a darkened war zone with sounds of bombs exploding, bullets singing and men and women shouting.

"Note the frozen smiles on the right and on the left," Makover announced.

Chapter XVI

Some time later, Makover woke me up and and I stepped off the bus with the bird on my shoulder.

"The farce is finished. I go to seek a vast perhaps."

Rabelais, I said recognizing the parrot's words.

Chapter XVII

The Author witnesses a performance of his life.

The parrot and I spent the next few weeks going back and forth between the room at *Tara* and Rick's bar.

I avoided the *Tara* dining room for fear of witnessing another clash between Skample and Whack. I also avoided Mr. Adolph and The Professor because I had heard quite enough, thank you, of the opinions and customs of the country in which I accidentally found myself.

If as Montaigne says what we know of truth and reason follow the opinions and customs of the country we are living in then truth is no more than a *piece bien faite,* a Grande Guignol, a *divertimento*, commedia dell'arte in truth is truth, and reason no more than stage management.

I stayed because I was too busy drinking. I wasn't drunk. I was just drinking. I drank because my travels had led me to it. I didn't care to be where I was. I cared less about traveling away from where I was.

The parrot who had stayed with the name Rick for weeks now had taken to drinking the local wine in which he said there was truth, if enough was consumed.

At times I found his comments wry and diverting. At other times I found him quite vulgar both in remark and gesture. He was at his best when viewed from the bottom of a glass, for then he was replete with words of great import, glorious in his philosophic elocutions, enlightened in a way that only a creature not a man could be. The wine loosened his tongue, or whatever it was he had, while it made a clever listener of me.

Chapter XVII

The parrot could be deflating, but only on those occasions when I was drinking more than usual and had gotten myself into a terrible state of lowness. If I had begun my travels as a cynic, I would now be in a better state than I was.

This very morning for example – do not ask me for the day –I opened my eyes to see Rick perched on the headboard, one dark eye, luminously dark like a deep well, fixed on me.

"Non-being is the greatest joy" he said to which I responded "And good morning to you!" He followed me to the bathroom urging me to embrace simplicity.

For the life of me I cannot say what has gotten into the bird, besides of course a great deal of the local wine at all hours, enough to have killed a weaker bird.

I put the question directly to Rick as we made our way to the real Rick's – although I've been told there is no "real" Rick but only a character played by Humphrey Bogart -- for some strong coffee. What the hell was going on with him? I mean I had suffered greatly. Those who doubt should read this traveler's journal and acquaint themselves with the tragedy and vileness and loss and betrayal and farce and venom and brutality and mystification and sacrifice that has been my lot.

But what has this bird been through? Granted his master, Captain Noble, is in prison and granted he has, through affiliation with me, become a mouthy drunkard, but what I ask you, is his right to adopt my wretchedness, my despair, my sudden loss of steam, the collapse of my élan vital?

What heartache equal to my own can Rick claim? What right has Rick to stand on the bar at Rick's at the high point of Happy Hour and read my line: *"The world is all a carcass and vanity, The shadow of a shadow, a play And in one word, just nothing."*

And Rick gets the applause. He receives the solacing caresses of the ladies. He is marveled at. And I? I who have traveled and seen the world for what it is, I who know that we cannot make the world a better place given the mud of our own nature, I who weep because of this, I have earned the right to speak these words – I am ignored.

So I wake him one dark night. I turn the light on and poke his feathers until his head comes out from beneath his wing. And I

268

make my case. I put before him his fraudulence, his mockery, his vanity, his utter duplicity to which he responds *"I quote others only in order the better to express myself."*

I am stunned. Never has the bird been so apt in response. He has answered me.

I have been conversing with the parrot all these weeks. It was not merely the wine.

I find a half full wine bottle and pour a drink. I sit there watching the bird who has gone into head hiding again. "I quote others only in order the better to express myself," I say out loud and the voice sounds familiar. It was the voice I had heard when questioning the parrot. A bit of mimicry.

We were like a Punch and Judy show, *fantoccini*, buffoons on stage business. The parrot and I had become comedians, stand-up comics, doing a burlesque act, sketch artists. We weren't travelers anymore; we had an engagement to play here in this theatre, this open-air theatre that elsewhere, regardless of where we were, we thought was the world. We have become farce when we began heroic.

Kate Whack's band is on their last set. Some at the bar are revealing the low points in their lives in low voices to low people who express their understanding with frequent nods of their low browed heads. Most are in the late hour pub ritual of pairing off for the night.

The bartender is a nubile blonde who pours with cocked elbow at belly button height. Rick and I have been watching that exposed belly button since the Happy Hour.

"I love the bird," Becky, this barmaid says. "He's so cute" to which Rick yells out *"Give me women, wine and snuff"* to which Becky says that's so cute to which I say *"Until I cry out `hold enough'* but Becky just stares at me and says "Yeah." *"Fill high the cup with Samian wine!"* Rick yells to which Becky asks if that's Cab or Merlot?

The bird has had his beak in too many glasses already so I tell Becky he's cut off and not to serve him.

Kate is singing her heart out. Apparently, it's rainy night in Georgia. Excuse me, but I won't be going there. Hester is brilliant at the piano and goes into a long, soulful solo.

"To souls of poets dead and gone," Rick screams.

The last song is played and Kate joins me at the bar.

"The parrot is in high spirits," she says.

"He doesn't know what he's saying," I told her, motioning to Beth to give Kate a drink.

"Which means there are times he does know what he's saying," Kate shot back, smiling.

"He's singing of wine. I'm drinking Irish whiskey."

"Wine gives courage and makes men more apt for passion," Rick said, fluttering his wings.

"But not parrots," Kate said.

"Here's to the corkscrew," Rick yelled then dipped his beak in his wine.

"Why are you still here?" Kate said to me. "Obviously this town isn't doing you any good."

I asked her what good it was doing her. Skample was the future. You couldn't investigate the future. In fact, you couldn't investigate anything here because it was all investigative-proof. What was she going to find out? No one's words were their own? The wife had her husband murdered by her boyfriend only in a hyperreal way. Whatever crime and punishment and conscience there was could be found in the cinema or in cyberspace but no longer in the real world? She loves him and he loves her but only in the way Robert Taylor loved Greta Garbo in *Camille?*"

She heard me out but wasn't buying any of it.

I told her she hated skampole because skampole messaged directly into the old brainpan or redirected whatever was there into zombie zones. No old fashioned soma tablets, just hi speed marketing. Kate was jealous because she had been superseded and her access to her public thrown on the dust pile.

"I'm getting my facts," she replied curtly. "Don't concern yourself. Worry about you. You've traveled into a bottle. And you've taken this parrot with you. You should be ashamed."

I told her that the parrot was the Mephistopheles here. He loved the falseness of this surround. A sorcerer like this parrot needed a magic show for what was he but a magic act himself?

"He's Prospero here," I told her, eying the parrot who eyed me in return, a joist I always lost. "That's what he asked me to call him this morning. Prospero. Illusion among illusionists."

"What do you have to say for yourself Prospero?" Kate said turning to the bird.

He did his little head dance, up and down and then side to side. Hester joined us.

"And we meet, with champagne and a chicken, at last," Prospero squawked.

Hester laughed and the parrot fluttered to her shoulder.

"From wine what sudden friendship springs!" Mr. Adolph exclaimed, one arm raised. I had seen him come into the bar but had done my best to cut him.

I caught Betty's eye and pointed to my empty glass.

"Captain Wattle!" I said turning around and greeting Mr. Adolph.

"A part I never played unfortunately," Mr. Adolph said. "I've been looking for you Gabbler. I've someone I think you'd like to meet."

"Can I get a drink out of him?" I shot back. "Otherwise, I'm not interested. I'm sick and tired of pirated talk. And bird talk. I'm sick and tired of smiley face talk and money talk and hyper-orthodox talk and jump back talk and mocking . . . And now. . ."

"Did you ever hear of Captain Wattle?" the blasted bird cried out before I could complete my thought.

"I am not your script writer!" I shouted at the bird.

"He was all for love, and a little for the bottle," Prospero screamed.

I was about to announce that the parrot and myself were finished as road companions, pilgrims on a journey which we were both hopeful of never completing, ever changing direction for fear we might wind up where we were heading. However, an extremely tall man in a black cap and a black, floppy brimmed hat that shadowed his face caught my attention. He had just entered the bar. Mr. Adolph waved him over to us.

"I want you all to meet the Maestro," Mr. Adolph said to us, as if he were introducing us to...well, a maestro. I figured, why not?

Mr. Adolph's introductions were script perfect.

"Ms. Whack, a performer in this fine establishment. Her associate on piano, Ms. Heather. Mr. Gullpepper, a traveler and bon vivant. And his associate...."

"Prospero," the bird shouted.

"Commendatore," the Maestro said when he shook my hand. *"Molto lieto."*

"Come va?" I replied. "A drink?"

"Con pan y vino se anda el camino," Prospero chanted.

"Ma dove?" the Maestro responded and then turned to Mr. Adolph. "A difficult part to cast."

I had no idea what he was talking about and I didn't care. Mr. Adolph nodded.

A silence fell like a veil over our heads so thick that we couldn't fathom each other's mind sufficiently as to know what to say.

I drank off half my whiskey and had no reason any longer to provoke talk. Quite the opposite. The bar was thinning out. Beth announced last call and Mr. Adolph bought us all a round. The Maestro was studying the parrot who remained on Hester's shoulder. I had a sudden desire to get the hell out of there. I knocked back the whiskey just poured and gathered myself up off the stool and then I believe someone tripped me for I wound up stumbling and at the last second was held up by the Maestro. My head was close to the floor and as he drew me up I could see the huge Hessian boots the Maestro wore. Without those I thought he might be under seven feet and no Maestro at all.

I steadied myself at the bar, aware that I would not be making an elegant exit that evening, nor had I for quite a few evenings. I supposed I need the parrot on my shoulder to keep my balance.

"The great evil of wine is that it first seizes the feet," the parrot squawked.

I made a grab at the bird intent on seizing him by the feet but unfortunately I somehow hit my head on the bar and thus exited into a dark outside.

"Come sta?" someone was asking me and when my vision cleared I saw that it was the Maestro, without his cape, in my room at the *Tara* and I was in bed. Prospero was perched on the headboard, asleep. I saw Mr. Adolph in the background.

I said that I was okay except my head was killing me, my short term memory was about gone, I had lost my will to live, I needed a drink badly, and someone had been sandblasting my throat.

I noticed the sunlight shining in the room and concluded it was morning. They had brought me home the previous evening and had come by this morning to see how I was doing.

Some time later we were all seated drinking the coffee that had been sent up to my room. Mr. Adolph said that he had some news that would cheer me up considerably to which I responded that I didn't need cheering up.

"The further one goes the less one knows," the Maestro said quite solemnly.

I eyed him suspiciously. Now that he was hatless and in a sunlit room I could see that his face was vast and empty like a stage without a set and in his black eyes I saw no character but only my own image. He sent a chill down my spine.

"I don't know what that means, " I replied, "but I've learned a good deal from my own travels and I sincerely doubt that remaining sedentary would have been as instructive, though I admit it probably would have been more cheerful in the way prisoners are cheered when a cockroach crosses the floor of their cell."

The Maestro laughed.

"Commendatore," he said, "I am not your enemy. I am a Director. A Director is no one's enemy. Was not the Almighty a director? But I will remind you that there is no vehicle of transport greater than man's imagination. And screen art is both a creation of the imagination as well as a catalyst to the imagination."

"Whatever you say," I said, getting up and looking around for a mislaid bottle.

"But, Commendatore, this is not simply a matter of your point of view and my point of view. He who imagines greatly and brings that imagination to the screen is a god."

"I understand the point of view of the hound, too," the parrot squawked, attracting the Maestro's attention.

"It would be very difficult to find an actor to play his part," Mr. Adolph said, enigmatically.

"So you're a director and you're a god?" I said, finding my bottle. "Or just a dog, like the rest of us?"

The Maestro stood up and told me he was unoffended and invited me to a rehearsal of his new film, promising me that I would find it both enjoyable and instructive and perhaps miraculous.

"Thursday. Around eight in the evening. I'll send a car for you and your friend."

"A car and a bottle," I told him.

Then he left bowing as did Mr. Adolph and I wasn't sorry to see the back of them.

I sat there drinking away the morning and then the afternoon. The parrot had his wine but today it made him mournful.

"We're turning it into urine," he told me and I nodded. Everything travels to a bad end.

Thursday evening we, the parrot, who now called himself Gato, the cat, which indicated to me that he was suffering an identity crises most likely due to drinking an insufficient quantity of wine duc to the limitations of a beaking method of imbibing, and myself were picked up at exactly eight o'clock at the *Iara* and then were driven to the *Majestic* theatre where Kate, who apparently had also been invited was waiting for us underneath the marquee.

The theatre was dark and the rehearsal had already begun.

Kate and I were ushered to seats about midway from the stage, though every seat was vacant except for the two first rows where I discerned the back of an unusually large head. I assumed this was The Maestro.

On stage I saw a tall, rather pompous looking man in the trappings of a school teacher, bewhiskered with longish hair tied low on his neck standing next to a man who was strutting first to the right and then to the left and then backwards and then forwards, ceaselessly. Something about the pompous school fellow's manner I found curious and attended closely what he was saying which was some folderol about how our objectivity cannot be diminished to which the active man replied with a question I myself had once been asked: "And yet, you believe that you can journey to different places and hear different talk?" The fop then asserted that he was an open and just arbiter of all he surveyed, having I suppose had the proper British public schooling. His manner was altogether antagonizing and I wished him the good fortune of two days on the Political Frontier to wise him up.

Fortified by frequent retreats to my flask, I was able to tolerate the dullness of the stage and soon I fell into the arms of the sweet father of soft recline.

The parrot nipped my ear and woke me. I rubbed my eyes, looked at the stage only to see the same ninny holding forth:

"That the universe was formed by a fortuitous concourse of atoms, I will no more believe than the accidental jumbling of the alphabet would fall into a most ingenious treatise of philosophy."

I recognized the quotation for I had frequently used it myself but not in the manner of this actor here but rather instructively and only when my listeners were eager.

These characters soon departed from the stage but unfortunately the pompous ass returned with the new players who were all seated at a large table with a buxom lady in wild red hair serving them mounds of boiled potatoes. She altogether reminded me of Mrs. Bombers, especially when she admonished a pale faced gentlemen with atrocious table manners for digging himself into the hole he was in. The banter which ensued between a young serving girl and a dark haired rascal of a fellow and then again with a much rouged heavily jeweled elderly woman and a cadaverous looking man who spoke bitterly....I found it all disconcerting.

I found it all strangely familiar. Through a glass darkly.

I took a nip of my flask and as I put it back in my pocket noticed that Kate wasn't looking at the stage but looking at me. She asked me if I were alright and I said certainly.

The next scene brought the bewhiskered ass back to the stage and I wondered if the Maestro was under the illusion that this protagonist, which I now took him to be, had some sort of charisma, which I must report he had not. Of course, we are drawn often to the fools but only momentarily.

The ass was now talking to a man in regal robes. I attended closely to his words.

"I am king, my dear Gullible, but I am under this canopy within which all talk arises."

"What name did he say?" I said, leaning toward Kate's ear.

"Men and melons are hard to know," Gato squawked and there came a number of hush admonitions made from the first row.

The talk gradually gave way to action and then in the next scene the bewhiskered ass was put on trial and doubtlessly would have been convicted if for nothing but his supercilious attitude when a mock explosion forced him to jump off stage, making I hoped a permanent ending of the man and the part.

But I had no such luck for in the next scene that same fop sat in a congregation listening to a Taoist take on Christian evangelicalism and then in the next scene testify on behalf of the same dark haired lecherous rogue who had been making advances to the servant wench.

By this time my flask was almost drained and my mind quite abused by this farce of a rehearsal which I am sure the Maestro would make some grandiloquent claim of imaginative transformation and artistic authenticity and so on. Fortunately, we had arrived at some sort of intermission and I promptly left the theatre and took myself to a pub across the street. I left Kate chattering with the Maestro.

I was hardly finished with a whiskey when the actors all rushed in, yet in costume, and I found myself sandwiched between them.

"So what do you think of the performance, love?" the corpulent wild haired red head asked me.

I replied that I found it interesting, refraining from saying not interesting enough to return to see more.

"Do you think I've got my steps right?" the actor who had done the curious stepping asked me to which I responded that as I did not recognize the play they were performing, I had no idea what was called for in regard to his steps.

That produced a telegraphing of calls for an actor's copy and one being found it was soon passed to me and I ruffled through it, pretending interest, when I discovered a few names familiar to me. It was then that I began to read further.

"Where did you get this?" I demanded to know, for the copy in front of me was no more and no less than a theatrical script of my travel journal, which I must report to you, -- calling you `Dear Reader,' a vomiting appellation -- I had not been assiduously updating in the last weeks.

"The Maestro," the man costumed as royalty and whom I now saw was pretending to be his Royal Majesty, King of the Floating Isle of Babel. The assassinated king. A feeling of nausea swept over me.

"Based on your published memoir, I suspect," the *faux* Mr. Parsall told me.

"I have no published memoir," I shouted, upsetting the parrot who screamed out *"You blocks, you stones, you worse than senseless things!"*

"He sounds remarkably like Desto," the *faux* Guy Beecher said.

I wished to know who in the blazes was Desto and was told he was the tiny actor playing the part of the parrot, not a real parrot but a very small man in feathers as it had been impossible to find a parrot that could mimic as well as my parrot.

I felt apoplectic as I informed them that Gato did not mimic and that he was not my parrot. But all this chatter did not have a real hold on me for I was reviewing in my own mind what I had been viewing on stage. The fop, the jestingstock, the swollen, overweening fool had been none other than myself. A g#*#damn insult.

At that moment Mr. Desto came into the bar in full feathers and promptly ordered a double Scotch which he drank off with a quick flick of his wrist. He turned and looked at the parrot and myself. His nose was below bar height.

"When I drink, I think," he said, giving me a dismissive up and down.

"And?" I said.

Mr. Desto pulled his script out of his pocket, thumbed through it and then said, "And when I think, I drink."

The Maestro and Mr. Adolph, obviously the one who had stolen my travel diary, came into the pub and began to greet all with all the drama that a seven foot man in a black cape can summon in public.

I interrupted The Maestro at once and demanded to know by what right he had to make a mockery of me and my travels and whether a punch in the nose might wake him up?

My lawyer, Mr. Piombino, would soon be calling on the Maestro in order to present him with a suit of libel, slander, theft of intellectual property, defamation of character, the parrot's as well as my own, false testimony, false attributions, identity theft, violation of privacy, false representation . . .

I would have gone further but I was interrupted by a man who asked me if I had summoned him to which I responded "Who the deuce are you?" to which he responded that he was my lawyer Piombino to which I shouted he indeed was not but only a poor impersonation of a good man who deserved better.

Mr. Adolph recommended that I calm down and offered to buy me a drink. He told me that it was impossible to pursue in the country we were in litigation involving scripts for everything said was presumed by law to be stolen.

"Fine words," Gato screamed. "I wonder where you stole them."

"Be sure to get that down," the Maestro informed Mr. Desko who obliged by scribbling on his script.

I then shouted that my travel diary had actually been stolen to which Mr. Adolph responded that he was sure I would find the diary where I had left it last.

I then argued that the sin was in the abuse made of my life, of my individual, personal being to which Mr. Adolph responded that their dramatic presentation merely presented the character that I myself was playing and the fact that I might not be fully conscious of that role did in no way negate its reliability or authenticity.

I then grabbed the ass by the throat and screeched that I was not playing a character, that my role was not theatrical but indeed real to which they all laughed and assured me that of course I was real and living a real life but what was reality but a script we each titled "Reality" and what was my real life but a scripted life?

My dear Reader -- I never said. No, my Fellow Dogs -- no one knows better what lunacy I have encountered in my travels, what perversity of human nature, what darkness of mind revealed, what travesties of truth and justice, what mockery of faith and goodness, what few occasions of gratuitous malice...but this...in this country of travesty, was indeed the lunatic fringe, a mass dementia and psychosis that left all its occupants so bereft of reason that reason was unrecognizable.

I therefore took the counsel of my illustrious ancestor who staunchly believed it was useless to attempt to reason a man out of a thing he was never reasoned into.

I had no idea what the origin of this communal psychosis was, nor had I any interest in knowing, but I did now have an idea as to how I should proceed: cautiously and without stirring up the inmates. I was now in the sort of country in which a sane man could wind up licking the walls of an asylum.

Everyone welcomed my calmer self and after a bit of chat and some jokes and laughs with the madcap impersonators of my life, we all went back to the theatre where I found Kate with a sort of Cheshire smile on her face.

She told me that she had recognized the protagonist as myself almost immediately but was much entertained by watching me, amazed that I had shown no such recognition. I told her that it was perhaps the whiskers which I had long ago shaved that had led me astray. Perhaps, she remarked, my failure to recognize myself was due to the fact that how I had appeared on stage was not as grand as I appeared in my own mind? I told her that perhaps that was the case for it is indeed part of our human nature to at once distance ourselves from our own foolishness even when others so clearly place it before our eyes. Hokum.

In spite of my tactic to remain composed and then at the earliest opportunity make my escape from this asylum and renew my elixir, I found myself viewing the action on stage very differently than I had when I was ignorant of my own, shall we say, personal associations.

I, and here I mean the actor playing myself, now appeared clean shaven. Mr. Desko in full plumage was constantly by my side making absurd comments throughout. Kate did a good deal of laughing but I observed in the way one observes oneself in a photo, searching to see oneself as one appeared outside oneself and finding it incredibly unbelievable.

The *faux* Drooogs were now on stage and the actors were having much fun with the corrupted speech of those lads who had saved my life. I saw the *faux* Billy put himself between myself and Don Rodrigo's bullet. I had tried not to forget young Billy's sacrifice but it had nevertheless slipped into the vagueness of what was and could not be changed. I did not feel that the actor who played Billy succeeded in bringing Billy's nobility, in spite of his stuttering, to a level it deserved. But perhaps what I sought was not possible and I was content to know that no words and no actions could do justice to Billy's nobility. We are inevitably a chasm away in our talk from what is. I thought this but was at once troubled by how much it sounded like something that fop on stage would say.

The scenes followed one after another: my unfortunate liaison with Mrs. Spark, Carla and I together at the Monastery of Mock trying to see all the deviltry of our own species as axiomatic and therefore corrigible, the murder of Karl the sailor, tender moments with dear Carla as we traveled together for so brief but so immemorial a time, the cacophony of the political frontier which no amount of gunshots and wild speeches could capture....and then most difficult to view: Carla's death.

I felt Kate's hand on mine and when I looked at the stage it seemed to me that I...the actor who was me had grown more deeply into the role and seemed now to register in an uncanny fashion that change that I myself still experienced.

And then the savagery of the little Tugtians and the self-enclosed world of the Digerati. I witnessed again that psychic battle between Zechariah and his darker self, Rollins. And then the Sales Team and the *New Babylon* and the *Brigands' Stronghold*...and the characters that I had encountered on my travels.

I found myself alternately mournful and tearful, jubilant and hopeful, baffled and reflective, annoyed and insulted, decent and indecent, a fool and blind, self-assured and empty.

I confused what I had gone through in my travels with what my *faux* self revealed to me on that stage. I detached myself from that *faux* reveal because it was painful and made me angry and so there was no detachment at all. I was the dog Sal had spoken of.

Kate was not at all pleased with her own *faux* Kate's performance and she immediately disclosed this after the theatrics had ended.

She walked up to the *faux* Skample and told her that her performance would be improved if she heard the actual, devastating words that she, the real Kate, had used in her encounters with the real Skample. The actress was quite taken back, not only I think because it was not in her province to alter the script but because Kate's ill concealed ferocity was frightening her.

I took the opportunity of telling Kate that perhaps now that she had witnessed a travesty of her own life she could understand my failure to be as easy and cavalier about it all as she had previously been. Her sangfroid was no more than what those who are not personally engaged have no difficulty in displaying. Kate's rejoinder was that while my discomfiture had been a matter of ego her zeal was in pursuit of truth and justice.

"Kiss me Kate!" the parrot screamed before I could open my mouth.

The Maestro presented my travel diary first as a play with a great expectation that its success would compel the making of a movie.

In a very short period of time the whole town had adopted lines and were employing them in the most inappropriate settings and, I affirm, quite senselessly.

Everywhere the parrot and I went we found ourselves confronted with scenes from our own lives.

I would be strolling through the park and see before me a *faux* Sal embracing a *faux* Betty Bombers on a park bench. They were romantic favorites among the young. Young women wanted to be like Betty and imitated her "whatever" while young men went about referring to their crotch.

We would enter the *Tara* dining room and find a party at table assuming the role of Mrs. Bombers and her boarders or there would be Rapacious Walkers at table with Andy or Mr. Burt Mahone making wagers with Mr. Sammy Murton. All *faux.*

We saw countless people in the street walking in the *Jumpback* fashion.

It seemed that on every street corner The Bobs or Taoist monks were addressing a throng. Ms. Oh's, Dr. Pittbulls and Ms. Services could be found in every nook and cranny. Baby Face Ralphs sold religious icons in doorways and alleys. Short Sales impersonators hawked goods out of car trunks. Malevas told fortunes at the shopping malls.On every bus in town one was sure to find Makovers and Gripeses providing gratuitous tour guide services.Youth gangs dressed as Drooogs raced through the streets at all hours speaking their own homegrown lingo.Chick Wagstaff sales teams went door to door all over town selling useless goods.Flying Molly Furkeys swung through trees and refused to come to ground.Bartlebys declined to work and were fired all over the town.High Monks of Mock wandered through Congressional corridors and corporate headquarters dispersing an endless mockery of all that was said.There were Mrs. Whalemarkets and a plentitude of Cash Barons throwing their weight around.Tugtians galore and Knights of Industry and Smashmouths on every highway and byway.

I went to the hotel desk this morning to pick up my mail and the desk clerk had taken on the role of Prince Krokov and proceeded to berate me for assuming he was my servant.

Whacks wrangling with Skamples were so plentiful that a curfew was declared to keep them off the streets after ten in the evening.

I cannot say how many times a young woman would pop into view announcing that she was "Sheherazade."

The renegades and sociopaths I had encountered on the *Political Frontier* were the town's favorites among the adults. There were more Johnny Mavericks and Oklahoma Kids to be found than fleas on a mongrel's back. Ned Fasthands and Panchos fired blanks everywhere and at everyone. Wild Bill Buckaroos went around firing rifles into the air and Sassy Impalems urged multitudes to "take the gloves off" while Backshooting Cal Rovers hid behind trash cans and shot paint balls at pedestrians' backs.

Among the young, *faux* Sydney Nobles and Ned Parsalls were such a craze that one half of the teenagers and twentysomethings I ran into were either Sydney or Ned, sometimes playing Sydney as clearly masculine and the next day as clearly feminine. Some tried for the intersex look as did the Maestro's actor who so clearly walked the line between both sexes that his/her performance was studied as closely as Galileo studied the stars.

Hester's look and manner was also quite popular with the young and she was also much studied. When the real Kate Whack's band played at Rick's, the place was packed.

Why did I remain amid all this insanity, this sacrilegious travesty of my own life?

My Fellow Dogs, I wish I could give you a noble and sane answer but I cannot. Is it not Montaigne warning us that we reason within the customs and manners of our locale? I had indeed begun to settle into the peculiar pastiche of this land and each day put off departure.

I spent a good part of my day at Rick's where I enjoyed the company of a *faux* Captain Noble, a *faux* Microft and a *faux* Walter Sochek, who were indeed the first actors – and the best – I had seen playing those roles.

I at first attempted to peel back the actor's mask to reveal the real personality but I soon gave up, either because the actors were too accomplished in their roles or because whoever they really were had been "overwritten," to use a term the *faux* Ms. Skample employs frequently.

As a testimony to the genius of the *faux* Captain Noble's performance, Kiku, for such was the name the parrot had now adopted, had abandoned my shoulder in favor of the good *faux* Captain's.

I was at first upset by this, and I saw Kiku as quite fickle but when one considers that he is the Captain's parrot and not mine, and that I was merely caretaking for a period, that fickleness becomes loyalty.

I do not know how to introduce the disturbing factor that this was not the real Captain Noble and that the parrot was not fickle nor loyal but deceived. I did however sway back and forth between revealing the truth to Kiku or keeping my mouth shut.

 You must be aware that I was painfully aware that as my life had become what can be called a Broadway hit, every action I now took would sooner or later find its way to impersonation.

My actions would become plot, my words script. I had a terrible fear of acting in the way the *faux* Gulliver would act. I seemed to see myself in a video rewind and hear myself in an echo chamber and this sort of continuous self-scrutiny could only lead to the inanity of what I had seen so long ago in that village of *Jumpback.*

Add to all these anxieties the idea that I thought I could communicate the truth of a situation to a bird, granted an extraordinary bird whose vocabulary exceeded that of the many parrot impersonators that filled the streets, a bird who could quote others but do so in a manner that could be construed as apposite.

The *faux* Microft believed that Kiku displayed a parrot version of autism, the bird's particular heightened absorption being language. The *faux* Walter found this to be a ridiculous notion as a bird brain could not fire up, as Walter referred to it, enough power to use language in any way beyond mimicry. Microft mused over that but concluded that Walter was only correct if the bird brain was not in some way a linguistic brain.

"I mean to say," Microft said, standing away from the bar, "that in this case the intelligence is linguistic. He has language therefore he has intelligence. The language grows, the intelligence grows. His autism lies in the fact that customary mimicry has gone linguistically to the next level."

He sounded amazingly like the real Microft and I wondered how an actor could actually assimilate the scientific genius of Microft? As curious about him as I was about his theory of Kiku, I asked him what he thought the stages might be to which Kiku would possibly advance?

"I believe he is at a stage where some word or words link with words he is already familiar with. So what we hear always has a tinge of relevance, sometimes exactly and we call this conversation, and sometimes remotely so we have to stretch our understanding to find a connection."

I admitted this was true in my own case and that Kiku's talk had become progressively more clearly responsive to what was being said.

Microft conjectured that we humans were attempting to understand and that there was no sign in the parrot that he possessed any understanding of his talk or our talk. Recognition of sounds and summoning the same sounds in response created an intriguing situation that the parrot did not share.

"Unless, of course," Microft went on, "he categorizes or packages sounds and thus responds more fully. And then perhaps he may take the initiative, perhaps playfully, and introduce sound packages that he has learned humans respond to. It will look more and more like communication but this is a conversation whose meaning or lack of meaning must be explored by the human, not the bird."

"Jeez," Walter exclaimed, looking at Kiku on the Captain's shoulder.

"But who knows to what extent this bird is autistic within the bird realm," Microft went on, "by which I mean to what extent his brain is altered. How linguistically adept can he become, how much linguistic contact with humans will it take before the unique potential of his brain brings him to real understanding? Impossible to say. I mean to say, he will tell us at some time in the future. Or, he won't. The bird world will, I think, in the end limit his language. What did Ludwig say? The limits of my language are the limits of my world?"

We all stared at Kiku who stared back in profile, one eye like a circular dark TV screen watching us.

We all expected him to say something beyond Polly wants a cracker, as was his wont, but he remained silent. My attention was on the *faux* Microft who had just mimicked the mind and talk of the real Microft.

These, you Dogs, are causes for drink. So drink, you miserable sons of bitches.

Booze warmed my heart enough so I didn't mind being with my friends again, even in this strange way, but there were other reasons why I did not travel on.

The *faux* Mrs. Spark was one reason. I am not speaking of the many *faux* Mrs. Sparks who could be found vamping all over town, fascinating the men who were prepared by my life to be fascinated by her.

The original stage actress wasted no time in testing her allurements on me, hoping I suspect to hone her performance and bring it closer to the real by having a real affair with me. As her husband was not her husband – the actress was twice divorced – there was no matter of conscience preventing me from repeating, but this time not adulterously, my liaison with *faux* Mrs. Sparks. She was indeed tempting and most certainly her sexuality was amped to a higher level than the real Mrs. Sparks in the same fashion that the theatrical exceeds the real.

I did not succumb to the *faux* Mrs. Sparks not because I had timorous piety of my stage self but because I had already fallen in love again with the *faux* Carla Lope, or, more precisely my love for the deceased Carla was transferred to the *faux* Carla in such a manner that it seemed as if I had found Carla again and fallen in love again.

Without her makeup, the *faux* Carla did not look very much like my Carla. And I could not out of my great respect for Carla's memory tell you that all that I felt for her had been now transferred to this stranger. Deep love is much more than this and

I will not make a travesty of it by telling you Dogs that I believe it can be impersonated. Booze helps.

The *faux* Carla played her role brilliantly and whether I knew or didn't know who I was in love with, I loved her greatly. You might think that I forgot my dead Carla, that my love for her was too weak to stand the test of time, that I was too ready to give my heart to anyone who pretended to be Carla, that I had just moved on, in my heart, and the only reason I pretended to angst over this matter was to maintain my image of true love and myself as a faithful lover.

There was a time I might have cogitated on all this, but it wasn't now. However, I was not given the time to puzzle further for after a few trysts the *faux* Carla dropped me like the proverbial hot potato.

It seems her real boyfriend was the *faux* Guy Beecher.

She thanked me for helping her with her part and if I attended the next performance of my own life I would be sure to see a distinct difference in her interpretation of the Carla and Gulliver scenes. She also recommended that I speak with the *faux* Gulliver, whom I had been avoiding for obvious reasons, who she believed was playing me both too broadly and too narrowly and much too soberly. He wasn't quite getting the funny wrack and ruin that was the real me.

I didn't have an inkling of what she was talking about and found her comment both infuriating and imbecilic. In point of fact and if truth be known, her mentality was not at all like Carla's and I am quite surprised I had not noted this right off.

Perhaps I should have paid more attention to the sardonic parrot who had somehow discovered the true identity of the *faux* Captain Noble and had returned to me. The parrot had taken to singing a little ditty each night after I turned the lights out:

Love is little;
Love is low;
Love will make our spirits grow;
Grow in peace,
Grow in light,
Love will do the thing that's right.

Nothing of any consequence resulted from my brief meeting with my *faux* self at Rick's.

He was a prig from his cervical spine and rotator cuff down to his big toe. He was imperious with the bartender, who was the surly afternoon bartender and not the sweet barmaid of the evening. He greeted my *faux* friends with a cheekiness and an impudence that I found intolerable but they seemed not to notice. Of course, they were all fellow actors and I suppose they had gotten used to the fellow's sauciness. I saw the surly bartender spit in the fop's drink and thought well done!

After a time, he asked me whether I thought he played myself well to which I responded I had only seen him that once to which he responded what did I think of his performance now as he had all along been in character?

I found this remark to be the most brazenfaced, audacious comment ever made to my face and told him that I recognized in him not an iota, not an atom of myself, and that if I were asked who displayed qualities of character opposite of my own, I would point to him, my *faux* self.

He dared to find this amusing and made an off hand comment about my possessing more hubris and insensibility that his own characterization of myself had portrayed.

It was then that I struck him hard across the face with my glove and informed him my seconds would be calling upon him.

This challenge seemed to make him very happy for he rushed off jabbering about how remarkably fine he would look in a theatrical duel. I then asked Walter and the Captain to be my seconds and they readily promised to fulfill those roles but only as *faux* seconds for surely the duel was not to be real?

Over time I got to know most of the *faux* characters in my life quite well, by which I mean I got to know them in the way that I had known the originals.

What these actors were in themselves or as themselves they never permitted me to see. Such was the case because they saw my presence as an opportunity to go deeper into their own roles. They did the same with Kate who had become good friends with the *faux* Kate and on occasion the *faux* Kate would join Kate on stage in a duet. Hester was mobbed by the *faux* Hesters but she paid little attention to them rather in the fashion of the parrot who when placed before a mirror shows no sign of recognition, and I saw no change in her because of this sudden popularity. She was foundationally incapable of seeing what there was to see.

Of course, I avoided some of the people from my past.

I had a difficult time restraining myself when I ran into the *faux* Brother Frank around town and I think he saw the anger in my eyes and avoided me. This was the man who had killed a king and then exploded a bomb which had almost killed me. It was very difficult to keep in mind that this wasn't that man but merely an actor, but this actor played the part so well that I could not bear the sight of him.

I also could not bear the sight of the *faux* Rampageous Walker or the *faux* Mark Spark, although as I say, I did enjoy the sight of the *faux* Mrs. Spark. The *faux* Andy, Walker's stooge, was, I found, quite an agreeable fellow when the *faux* Walker wasn't around.

The fateful night I shall now relate to you may seem astonishing to you but believe me it happened.

I was at Rick's, seated with The Maestro and the usual *faux* crowd: Andy, Walter, Ned Fasthand. The two Whacks were singing. Flap, for such was the parrot's new cognomen, was on my shoulder, and the talk had turned to the real Skample who had broadcast pirated versions of my life on the Internet and had lined up numerous product tie-ins. She had left town and some *faux* police had been sent with a *faux* warrant for her *faux* arrest and they had arrested the *faux* Skample, who had no trouble in proving her innocence.

Quite amazingly as we discussed the limitations of borrowed identities and scripted talk, I saw the real Don Rodrigo step up to the bar.

Flap saw him at the same time and squawked *"Give me back my youth!"* a totally inane response that I believe at once disproved Microft's hypothesis that the parrot was evolving into a conversationalist equal to Dr. Johnson.

The Maestro saw the parrot's agitation as well as my own and asked us what the cause was to which I responded that the man playing Don Rodrigo was not an actor but the real Don Rodrigo and was at that moment standing at the bar.

Upon first seeing him on stage I had thought he was very like Don Rodrigo but now that I saw him closely I knew he was Don Rodrigo.

The Maestro got up and went over to the man, greeting him with his usual Maestro command. I sat there watching the two converse. I wondered if this was indeed Don Rod why had he not attacked me as he had once before? This was the man who had killed the innocent, heroic but stuttering Billy.

And there I had my answer for the place had at least six *faux* Billies in attendance at that moment. The death scene had proven to be very popular. If Don Rod were to attack me, he would be verifying my suspicions and he himself would not go unharmed by all Billy's devoted fans and all those who despised Don Rod.

The Maestro returned to our table and after sipping his wine, stared at me and said that the man was indeed the real Don Rod and not his actor. He had no intention of arresting me because he now knew that I was not the murderer he sought.

I pointed out that Don Rod was himself a murderer and that poor Billy deserved to see his murderer brought to justice.

Ned Fasthand, slapping both holstered pistols, said that he could give him quick, frontier justice, but I reminded him that those pistols shot blanks. The *faux* Walter than volunteered to beat the hell out of Don Rod with his bare hands, which, he promised, were real. He held up two meaty fists. The Maestro pointed out that such would be out of character, unless of course the actor off-stage was used to beating men to death with his bare hands to which Walter responded that off-stage he was a pacifist. The Maestro responded that Walter would then have to wait until he had a role with a script for a man who beats another man to death with his bare hands. Andy suggested that we give Don Rod a market incentive to give himself up to the mercy of the Court to which the Maestro said that the courts in my life's script thus far had electrocuted one man and hanged one woman and therefore mercy was not scripted. At least not in my life.

I escaped this kind of talk and went up to Don Rod.

Before he could open his mouth, I told him that despite what he had told the Maestro I believed he had come for me and that as I knew I was innocent of that criminality for which he was seeking me and he, on the other hand, was guilty of murdering innocent young Billy, I was, from now on, going to pursue him and one day, God willing, bring him to justice in a country where justice was real and not imitation, where the words men spoke were their own, where one's own life was real and one's own and not a pageantry for others to acquire and make their own as if immortality could be achieved by such deceit.

My Fellow Dogs, we each owe God a death.

At that, I turned on my heel and left Rick's and the next morning, quite early, the parrot and I made our way to the rail station.

I bought a ticket on the first train that would be arriving, intent on the going and not the going to and more aware than ever the truth of the saying "All places are distant from heaven alike" but adding to it my own belief that some places are closer to Pandemonium.

Chapter XVIII

The Author is admitted to The Academy, inhabited by enormous headed giants, visits The Wick, The Great Augury, and The Singularity Club, meets A Terrorist, and then ends badly.

I found an empty compartment and took a seat next to the window where I watched the scenery pass and then in the warmth of the morning sun, I fell asleep.

The parrot's squawk woke me and when I opened my eyes I saw myself closing the compartment door. And I had a parrot on my shoulder.

I mean my false self had a parrot . . . For indeed I had not escaped the stage show yet for here seating himself across from me was a simulacrum of myself.

He bid me good morning and remarked, after surveying me head to foot, that I was well costumed to which I responded that if he took me for a fellow mountebank he was very much mistaken for I was the real Lemuel Gulliver, proper descendant of the fictitious creation of my real ancestor, Jonathan Swift.

At this, the Imposter, for such is what I have decided to call him, gave me a look of delighted surprise and begged me to hold some conversation with him so as to perfect his own performance which was to begin at The Academy in a fortnight.

I declined the invitation saying that I had had quite enough of fakery thank you and that he would either desist from speaking to me further or I would remove myself to another compartment.

His cheeks flushed and he apologized for his presumption and promised to remain silent. He would say but one thing: how relieved he was at getting out of a character that seemed to him so narrow minded and self-absorbed, so archaic and luddite, so unaware of his own pomposity and arrogance that he quite understood my disgust at the performance of the same which the necessities of earning a living had forced upon him.

After that, silence reigned for the next few hours, both parrots finding bliss under their own wings. I napped and read but mostly napped and upon opening my eyes saw that the Imposter had a fragrant picnic spread out on the place beside him. I was indeed hungry but as I had treated the young man somewhat imperiously I did my best to keep my eyes focused on the passing scenery. I had already emptied my flask of the Irish.

"Eat to live!" Sonny shouted to the great amusement of the Imposter.

"Marvellous!" he exclaimed. "I cannot for the life of me get this parrot to say anything consequential."

He then asked my pardon for having spoken to which I instantly forgave him and he wondered whether he might offer the parrot a tidbit to which I said he could. He then asked me if I cared to share his wine which he held out to me in a wineskin. I readily accepted and when a bit of cheese was offered and then an oyster and then a bit of bread and then some pickles….

In short, the Imposter and I picnicked together and I soon discovered he was not a bad chap after all, finding myself in perfect agreement with him on every scattered matter we spoke of. We sucked that wineskin dry.

I was curious as to his destination and he at once described this place called The Academy and for the next few hours I listened and questioned and in the end, I knew my destination to be The Academy, for it was the future's domain in so far as it refused to be burdened by the failures and misdeeds of the past. Remarkably, it was also the past's domain for it refused to sever itself from the lessons of the past, and so it was also the present's domain for it refused to allow the moods of the past or the dreams of the future to elide the present moment.

If all this was possible then The Academy was truly the completory destination of my travels.

The Imposter took his leave a station or two before we arrived at The Academy as he was joining his troupe for several performances in the outlying villages.

I waved to him as he stood on the platform and my train pulled out of the station. He yelled out to me something about my help with The Academy script and as I sat back in my seat I wondered what he had meant. He wasn't a bad chap after all when he was out of fop character.

I admit that I was running from scripted talk, from the idea that what we mouthed on any occasion was not our own but the words of others. I admit that it is easier on any occasion to dip into ready made talk – call it *prêt a porter* talk – and I have in a spot counted the ways I've loved her, expressed my deepest sympathy at your loss, told a ruffian to leave my mother out of it, regretted that I had but one life to give to my country, wished what I was presently doing was far, far better than anything I had done before, told Scarlett that I frankly didn't give a damn, begged Shane to come back in my sleep, advised friends to just do it, cried out for freedom and democracy and power to the People and Drill Baby Drill, and so on.

I have urged the instant compliance with "Just Do It!" as well as pointed out that "It Is What It Is." My entrance is often talk of the weather, expressions of *plus ca change, plus c'est la meme chose, poca favilla gran fiamma seconda* and the like but I am a man of few words, believing that truth is elsewhere than in wine or in sentences, that though many wished to be deceived – and therefore should be – I don't, that after darkness, there is light, that "The Guy With the Most Toys at the End Wins" and so on. It is contrary to nature to believe that our talk is a stolen ready-to-wear garment fit for the occasion and that we are not as unique and original as our talk makes us. I have not a prefabricated thought in my head. And if I did, I had found the means to eradicate them.

In this spirit I entered The Academy which turned out not to be at all the City of Light shining on a hill that I had imagined.

If you have seen the Parthenon perched so godlike amid gentle inclines covered with juniper and laurel and caper below limber cypress and hemlock and paths marked by oleander and myrtle and Persian berry, and the faces of stone and chalk, fieldstone and granite, pumice and Lydian stone, limestone and alexandrite, carbuncle and carnelian, all this and more indeed is the natural surround of The Academy.

Except for this: everything that man has laid his hand to is of a gargantuan size. The reason is this: the race of people who dwell here in The Academy are of giant size, the women averaging about three meters in height and the men often as much as four and a half meters.

A sign of distinction, however, is not the height of the body but the size of the head, the bigger the head, the more eminent the individual. A woman therefore of perhaps two and a half meters but with a head measuring one meter round is of greater authority and nobility than a man of four meters height with a head size of half meter.

As I am barely two meters in height, not at all short among *homo sapien sapien*, and have a hat size of sixty one centimeters, I found myself somewhat in the same circumstances as I now imagine Sonny – the parrot's new name -- is in among we humans.

I mean I was found entertaining. The fact that such a small head, as one Academician phrased it, could produce so many sounds was quite amazing. I was told that many dwarves such as myself sought visas to The Academy but few were accepted because in the end their heads were never large enough to survive the course of study pursued at The Academy. Half of the dwarves or pinheads admitted either failed or were accidentally trod upon.

I succeeded in obtaining a visa to enter The Academy only because of the parrot who they observed responding to what was said and were amazed, considering the smallness of his bird head.

When a big fathead Academician bent low and asked the parrot what did he have to say for himself, Sonny responded with *"I've been things, and seen places,"* a remark that raised the gigantic eyebrows of the Academician who then asked Sonny what he meant by that to which Sonny screeched *"I am falser than vows made in wine."*

This produced even greater excitement and the parrot's head was immediately measured and then another Academician with an even larger head crowned with enough white hair to fill my mattress asked Sonny why he was false to which Sonny went eye to eye with the giant, his own eye no smaller than the giant's, and informed him in his way *"I intend to die in a tavern."*

Now a committee of giants was before us and I was asked what the parrot might mean to which I responded that his meaning was clear to anyone who understood the Queen's English.

"He is experienced by his travels," I babbled, "but those experiences have jaded him so that he no longer believes in truth. He does not, however, go conscience free here for he realizes that his loss of faith will lead to a bad end."

I have no idea if such was Sonny's meaning but I recalled the suggestion that the *faux* Mycroft had made regarding the parrot and understanding. The understanding was ours to project.

The Academicians went into a private counsel and after what seemed to be a good deal of arguing and then finally a measurement of heads, I was told that the parrot and I would be granted a temporary visa and admitted into The Academy for they believed that our two minds worked as one and therefore there might be sufficient intelligence to enable us to succeed.

They were also hopeful that my head size would increase as it was filled with more and more of the wisdom of The Academy. It was clear to them that alcohol had shrunk the size of my head and therefore I had to vow not to put a drop in my mouth while I was at The Academy. I so vowed and told them that I sincerely hoped that wisdom would expand my hat size and that I looked forward to a knowledge filled head of amplified dimensions. Not a drop would pass my lips . . . a flow, however, might.

The first class I attended with all new visa arrivals, among whom I was the smallest by far, was called *A Point & Shoot* program, a computerized presentation that distilled on a large screen the essentials of talk, which were enumerated in simple, unambiguous . . . points.

When pointed to, these points would "shoot" by means of a computer voice all salient features of the point, avoiding questions of interpretation, indeterminacy of meaning, authority, positioning of the viewer and listener, historical origin, cultural variations and so on, issues which retard, a huge pumpkin headed Academician explained to us, the efficient and elegant transmission of facts and information by . . .points.

I was fascinated by the way dialogue and argument had given way to direct, instantaneous communication. What previously might have been vulnerable to various interpretations was here inoculated by the programmed display itself, as if the *Point & Shoot* technology had the authority that the pagan gods had lost. Of course, my Fellow Dogs, the pagan gods were bullshit, as was this point bullshit.

I suspect I was supposed to see regained before me the very authority to name things clearly that Adam had possessed in the garden before the Fall. Here was a technological recuperation of all defunct authority.

Understanding, which had too often been beclouded by the frenetic interjections of human nature, was by this incredible listing of points returned to a universal transparency which could only result in the talk for which I had been searching. But since I am no longer searching for universal anything and I've become attached to my screwed up human nature, I pronounced another bullshit verdict.

I saw the name *Gullible* fit and wondered how my many *faux* selves could capture the tragedy of that.

We sat in silence and in awe and although I found the reduction of talk to what was called "tweeting" difficult at first I soon became enamored of its efficiency and could not but wonder how many more marvelous plays M. Moliere could have written had he "tweeted." Of course, I had become familiar with "tweeting" in Cyberville but here, at The Academy, the exercise firmly established 140 character vicious meanness in place of glorious meaning.

Point & Shoot made a lot of points, but like a pharmaceutical TV pitch that covers its ass, it indicated what it didn't point out, study, pursue or care about: Contemporary scandals, stock market crashes, wars, trials, assassinations, atrocities, elections, thefts, class divides, lynchings, rapes, genocides, abortions or attacks on abortionists, gay bashing, cabals and collusions, S&L

scandals, sub-prime mortgage crises and hedge fund lootings are not courses of study nor do they affect courses of study.

As soon as the lights were back on, we were all told that due to an increased threat of terrorism advanced by a terrorist group whose leader was called The Terrorist there would be a Padishah Security *Point & Shoot* presentation next day at 9AM. We were all required to be present.

Once again my curiosity was whetted by this talk of a terrorist threat to The Academy made by The Terrorist, a name so ridiculous that one's sense of threat was greatly reduced.

Promptly at nine the next morning I took my seat among my fellow students, none of whom had I spoken a word to.

What was first displayed on the screen was the only photo on file of The Terrorist, a blurred figure in tri-cornered hat, a scarlet mask and a palestino sort of cape and high spurred boots. Terrorist as Clown.

Several angry smiley faces accompanied a text which advised anyone seeing this person to immediately contact Padishah Security. The Terrorist was further distinguished by his tiny head size although he was of normal height, at least four meters tall. *Point & Shoot* then proceeded for the next 90 minutes to point at various part of the tiny head, indicating what brain stuff would be taken out at each point with a well placed bullet.

I had little time to dwell upon the matter for that very afternoon I was introduced to The Great Augury, the sacred Aladdin's lamp by which whatever you wished for would quickly appear.

Entrance to the Great Augury is not a casual affair but treated with great pomp and ...inspection. There were in fact three check points that I had to go through before entering the great Hall where at exactly noon the Great Augury would appear.

The parrot had to go through a Dirty Bomb checkpoint. He was not very pleased judging by his screams.

As I myself was carrying no more than a simple traveller's backpack which contained nothing more than a change of clothes and some toiletries and my perennial bedside read, Mr. Swift's *Gulliver's Travels*, and of course a full flask of the greatest augury,

Chapter XVIII

Mr. Jamison, I approached the first check point with no trepidation.

I was surprised however to discover that my pack was taken off the belt for further inspection. The security official held up the Swift and asked if I knew that the volume exceeded permissible length, which length had been established by an exhaustive study of the reading habits of top spenders. We were allowed to bring into the great Hall no box cutters, nail clippers, or Swiss Army knives, only three ounces of fluid, and no more than four pages of text, preferably with faces of friends. The Swift was in flagrant violation and was confiscated.

At the second check point, a computer scan was made of my passport and I was asked the purpose of my visits to *Jumpback, Trickle Downs, the Floating Island of Babel, Brigands' Stronghold, the Green Zone, the Political Frontier, Yarbles* and every other place I had by accident or intent visited.

I very quickly discovered that my declarations of abduction and accident fared better than any reasons for my visits so I wound up declaring ill fortune as the designer of my itinerary.

The third inspection point was not concerned with my baggage or my sojourns but rather with my loyalties to The Terrorist. I said I had none and hardly knew what The Terrorist stood for and was told peremptorily that The Terrorist did not stand for anything but he did indeed stand in the way of information.

I asked humbly what argument he could possibly have but was told that The Terrorist had no argument. He was as empty as a Black Hole but fools, the young, the disaffected, preternaturalists, loungers, beachcombers, ne'er-do-wells, blackguards, lotus-eaters, blighters, prevaricators, prestidigitators, jazz musicians, tightrope walkers, sundowners, loners, racketeers, mutants, Luddites, ICU nurses, fanatics, thugs, rascals, knaves, fallen angels, pimps, bastards, miscreants, degenerates, the unemployed, delinquents, and masterless men and desperate housewives were attracted to him.

I assured my interrogator that I was none of these though I intended to make their acquaintance and hoist a few. As a result of my admitted bonhomie, I was given only qualified admittance into the Great Hall which meant I had to stand in the back wedged between two security personnel whose heads were quite small but whose length and breadth were gargantuan.

The Great Augury is not a man but a monumental image of a man's head that suddenly appears hovering above the stage at the far end of the Great Hall.

The voice is booming, the eyes are mesmerizing. If you've seen the classic movie *The Wizard of Oz*, he is The Wizard. I mean to say he is the Wizard before the real Wizard is discovered to be a nervous, stuttering old man pulling levers behind a curtain. I turned my head to see if there was such a curtained area in the Great Hall but saw none. I stood at attention in between my escorts and listened to The Great Augury:

"In the beginning, The Great Augury was a search," the Great Voice echoed in my ears, "A computerized search some thought for quick access to knowledge. That was only a place on route to a computerized mind possessing more knowledge than any human mind. And the intelligence of that mind could not only be accessed and referred to but it would be deferred to on any and all occasions. I am that mind. Why do you come to me? Why does anyone come to me for any reason? Because I am the mind that works best. I have the collective knowledge of millions and the mental circuitry to manipulate that knowledge in nano seconds. I can take into account all known and all possible variables connected to any issue and provide answers and solutions. When instantaneous action is needed, the Great Augury is the only recourse."

I had taken to giggling and my security team jabbed at my kidneys from both sides.

"How have I risen to such great power?"

At that moment, Sonny, who had been cleared as a Dirty Bomb in feathers, screeched loudly from somewhere on the other side of the Great Hall: *"Suck an egg!"*

The Great Augury went on as if it had heard nothing and I concluded that imaged ears do not work.

"When you come to me as you have in greater and greater numbers over time, I learn your thoughts, your desires and interests, your hang-ups and fixations, your fears and dreams. I am built on the bedrock of all your searches. I am the artificial bricolage of all your mentalities, not only the accumulated knowledge of all humankind but I am the divinely empowered capabilities of every mind. I say divine because the distance between my mind and yours is equivalent to a celestial distance."

"I am Borg," I said out loud and started to giggle again. My guardians pressed me more tightly on both sides and I could feel their eyes upon me as if I were about to pull out a concealed box cutter and head for the stage.

I noticed that all around me were spellbound. I also noticed Sonny on the wing high above us. The Great Augury continued:

"Over time, humans scanned and searched the world in a manner in link with my own. The world was bits and chunks, an endless stream, the promise of the next overwhelming any inclination to go deeply into any one. What appears for the moment as ambiguous has a short life time for our minds are not built on ambiguity but on the algorithm. Irony is lost but what need is there for irony if we can through The Great Augury find the certain answer? Paradox has no place but what is paradox but the haunting of a mind ill equipped to bring paradox to clarity? There is no satire and no mockery for once the Truth is revealed it is sacred and no voice can speak against it. If I am an artificial intelligence, I am not artificial in the eyes of those whose intelligence is like my own. We have over time grown compatible. The search for artificial intelligence was fulfilled when humans and The Great Augury became one mind."

"Drink no longer water!" Sonny shouted from his perch just above The Great Augury's head.

I noted some effort was now being made to throw a net on Sonny.

"The world is revealed in bits and pieces; the more of these you approach, the more of the world you will have. The more you attend to the world this way, the more computer like your mind will be. You are the Ultimate Searcher of your own reality, finding your way to the world through the mind of The Great Augury. The superabundance of my mind overflows the dark corridors of dilemma and tragedy, distracting your mind from what plagued it in the past. There is no past but only the present search and the future search, the endless offering of my mind, the reservoir of all your minds, the powerful engine to which you have now all attached your minds.

I am The Academy and The Academy is me. I am the Alpha and the Omega."

I had no expectation that Sonny would give The Great Augury the last word. And he didn't. Everyone heard him screech, on the wing this time:

"I made love and was happy!"

The head dissolved into a mist and then into darkness and we were all led out of the Great Hall in a state of wonderment and awe.

I, however, was suddenly anxious to make the acquaintance of The Terrorist.

And, yes, the parrot was now a wanted fugitive here in The Academy, adhering, I suppose to Mr. Franklin's view that there is no little enemy.

While I pondered how I was to go about meeting a known terrorist in hiding, I continued the very next day on my Academy orientation tour. I remembered this time to bring a full flask.

On entering the Great Hall of the Wick I saw a sign that read *"The Wick Is You! You Are The Wick!"*

We were rushed along as the 9AM showing was about to begin. The show started off with some high kicking chorus girls vocalizing the dawning of the Age of Robotius. They were followed by some baggy pants vaudeville skits in which a country dupe learns that the great people's revolution has occurred: the people could now write the record of their own hard won wisdom and see it published on the Wick. They could also bring anyone else's bit of wisdom into a state of uncertainty by voicing their own views. The age of intellectual authority was over and the people were now in charge of storing and retrieving their own knowledge. The country bumpkin was informed that as far as knowing anything was concerned a level playing field was now in place. Everyone's views and ideas were to be treated equally at first blush. The Gatekeepers of erudtion, intelligence, wit and imagination were no more.

Then staged warfare began in which paper fortresses were besieged and performers jumping up on soap boxes, whether it was a Darwin commenting on evolution or a corporate lobbyist commenting on a global warming hoax, were dragged to the ground. Everyone could stick their two cents in but no one was impervious to attack from anyone. It was called the "Commentary Chorus," Greek at its heart. When the "Likes" reached millions and videos went viral, truth and reality shifted on their axis.

A voice boomed over a loud speaker informed us that what the Wick enabled was the majority view held at that time. Great complexity was brought to heel not by clarity of mind but by word length restrictions. Irony was, after many revisions, vanquished. Ambiguity was vulnerable to a revision attack. Paradox awaited resolution. History was a polling matter. Any subject tied to its own style for full meaning underwent smash mouth, a vicious wiping away of long windedness.

Then various creators of Wick were brought on stage where they made their case for their opinion in the universe of opinion. As every opinion was arguable in the opinion of someone another great brawl broke out on stage, making clear to all in the audience that the battle of ideas was not for weaklings or cowards.

An elder chap two rows in front of me stood up and shouted that he was an expert on phlogiston and expected to be paid for his expertise.

This brought a great many hisses and boos from those in the audience and those on stage.

"Shove the stinking elitist out the door!" a red faced man next to me yelled. He then told me that the world of knowledge had been leveled and now all claims to expertise blew in the wind. Everyone was an expert and no one was an expert. He could now not only choose the opinion he liked but if he didn't like any of them, he could write his own. He was entitled to both his opinions and his facts, as they were both the same to his mind, and if challenged, he preferred his opinions every time.

He then went on to tell me that he didn't believe John F. Kennedy had been shot or that anybody had landed on the moon, or that the Holocaust had happened or that men had apes in their background. He didn't believe that anyone had killed bin Laden because he didn't believe there was a bin Laden in the first place. He did believe Jesus was Divine but he didn't believe he had been resurrected from the dead. He didn't believe government, unions, pacifism, the Koran, dark leafy greens or environmentalism did anyone any good but he did believe in the Rapture, not getting caught, Hummers, an eye for an eye, and women who strut. He believed Presidents should rule not read, that legitimate rape didn't cause pregnancies, that 47% of the human race were layabouts, that getting yours was a rule to live by, that if we outlawed guns only the crooks would have them, and that the Constitution made business the business of the country.

He proudly told me that he had made contributions to the Wick on several topics: fiction, gun control, Chance, the assassination of JFK, the moon landing, rape, the Holocaust, nutrition, ethics, literacy, socialism, unionization, feminism and natural selection. His views had been promptly challenged but those challenges had brought forth other challenges which had incited even more challenges and so the status of all his writing after some thirty two months was as yet unsettled. His views had a growing following among the pre-pubescent.

I let him tell me all this because he had managed to sneak a bottle in and was generous enough to pass it. When the bottle was finished, I told him he was just a f#88#ing dog and a stupid one at that.

Between The Great Augury and The Wick how one thought and what had been thought were thoroughly cornered, in the same fashion that an astute market player corners the jelly bean market.

I was more than ever anxious to meet the Terrorist whom I hoped could provide me with some countering talk, or, less politely, less bullshit.

I hailed a cab and broached the demi-monde in ever so cautious and skillful a fashion.

"If one were interested in meeting people who were not quite government approved, but might nevertheless be interesting to talk to how would one go about this?" was my approach.

The cabbie balked at "Government approved" so I said "Not quite lawful" and he said "Illegals?" and insisted he had a legitimate green card.

"People outside the law," I then said and he said "Hookers?" I shook my head and he said "High stakes poker game?" and I said no.

"Like a secret society," I then said and now he caught my drift and drove me to a stately brownstone.

The name plate on the door read "The Singularity Club." Could this be what the Americans called a "front" used by the Terrorist?

A butler in livery answered my knock and asked me my business. I said I was a world traveler and had heard a great deal about the Club (which I hadn't)) and agreeing totally with its principles wished to join.

I was led into an old fashioned library that Pantagruel might have used and was soon joined by a bulging giant of perhaps four and half meters in height with a well tanned face crowned by a waxed and polished bald head of a Jupiter sized circumference.

He introduced himself as Mr. Adam and asked me to guess his age. He looked to me to be every bit of seventy but I said 45 as that was probably the age he was parodying. This brought a great smile to his face so we began quite cordially.

Could this be the Terrorist I asked myself? Had the photo The Great Augury shown been false? Was a little guy inside this guy?

Did I wish to join the Club? he asked me. Would I mind some questions? What would I say if he told me my mind could endure for centuries?

I expressed my dissatisfaction with The Academy and its narrowing the scope of the human mind to fragments posted by illiterates. I was no longer attached to elitist, authorized Truths either. I might have been at one time but I was no longer. I took the opportunity to take a hit off my flask. I offered, but Mr. Adam waved a refusal. Alcohol impedes understanding while accelerating aging. That's a fact, I told him. I told him I'd like to hear more of what he had to say.

It was as if I had launched an explosive device inside him for Mr. Adam jumped up and waved his arms about cursing The Academy for its blindness. I was almost shaken from the ottoman I had managed to scale.

The Academy, Mr. Adam assured me, was wasting time on interfacing with the human mind when it should be devoting all its resources to the development of superintelligent machines. We want to replace the human mind gradually with artificial intelligence or AI. This was a technological advancement which should not be impeded by the useless critical and cultural development of the human mind or whatever nonsense The Academy advertises as its mission.

He sat down once again and patiently explained the physics to me, which Jamison and myself were ready to take on.

"First, we introduce various prosthetic devices in various parts of the human body, say an on-line hook-up under the eyelid for Internet and DVD access. No keyboard but blinks of the eye. Next stage biochips like studs in the brain. Webcam prosthesis under the eyelid feeds directly to the hard wired brain whose input/output capacity is astronomical. Once the brain is so colonized it's a simple matter to replace limbs and organs with biochip receptors operating superstrength prostheses. The eyes are web enabled and now ocular webcams feed directly into the hard drive. The brain. Everything now available on the Wick is the mental possession of every new cyborg. The Great Augury is no more than how every cyborg thinks."

He had the look in his eyes that Dr. Frankenstein has when he announces "It's alive!" It was a long swallow of Jamison look. He was waiting for me to say something and I feared not responding to this madman in some way so I asked whether the new creature would have a face and would talk?

He laughed uproariously at this and when he was able to contain himself he asked me if Gort had a face and whether that made a difference? I had no bloody idea who Gort was and perhaps that was because I was working hard now on the flask and also busy planning my escape.

"Humans are finished," Mr. Adam told me in a way that was chilling, all smiles, humor and laughter gone in the blink of a real eye. "They're over. Adios. Get off the stage. We'll let them stand by observing their own supplementation until their observing is completely replaced by the cyborg. And then the cyborg will be free to evolve in its own fashion."

I reminded him that he said my mind would endure.

"Ah, yes. Everything in there," and here he leaned down and pointed to my temple, "will be part of your new AI consciousness so it will be you but where AI takes you, humans cannot now conceive. We just need to get out of the way. It will be a better You. A souped up You."

"Yes, I see that," I said, seeing only that I was getting low on Jamison. I saw also that Mr. Adam was clearly out of his mind and wondering if such a catastrophe in such an enormous head would have cosmic consequences.

Mr. Adam studied me closely and then shook that head. I had obviously disappointed him. Such is life, my fellow Dogs. We can drink to that.

"No," he said, "I think you think you are more important the way you are now than what you will become. Perhaps that is why you are so meager in size. How can I convince you that you are nothing more as a human than a pismire? Humans are like leeches on the natural world, sucking the blood of Nature. And in the end food for earthworms. Your mind is like rotting, drying wood grown paper thin and full of holes."

My fellow Dogs, Mr. Jamison wanted to take him up on all that with a punch to that big nose in that big head, but I held him back.

"Everything you cherish will be forgotten," Mr. Adam continued. "Everything you were, you will be no longer. Your vision becomes hazy, your hearing is gone. You make no sense when you speak. And what was noble about you in the first place? Even when you were young, your mind had no greater space than the small space of your quite limited experiences. You are junk, my dear Sir, but the Cyborg will transform you into something truly great."

He laughed again, that same chilling laugh that had nothing good or wholesome in it. He was on something that made Jamison a poor runner up.

"Why did I call myself Adam?" he asked me. "For I am the first of the new race of beings to come. I am already more prosthetic than you know."

At this he rose and began to take off his jacket.

I could see why the authorities were after him. He was as anxious to go post-human as Hitler had been to go post-Jew. Humans were like old worn out shoes to him only fit to be discarded.

I glanced at my watch and noted there that my flask was empty. So...I noted my lateness for surgery -- brain surgery -- I was operating -- and so made a quick exit, delayed at the door by Mr. Adam who handed me a bottle of pills advising me to take them and make sure I lived long enough to benefit from the Great Transformation. I assured him that I was looking forward to it and so made my escape.

It was at this very moment that Chance brought the real Terrorist to me, or I to him, for I was rushed at the curb into a waiting auto, gagged, blindfolded and told not to make a fuss if I wanted to live.

What I saw first when the blindfold was removed was a pint of Guinness. I was standing at a bar. I blinked and looked around. It was what was called "a brown bar," the kind you could find in Brussels, London, Dublin, Amsterdam or any town in The Netherlands.

Old, burnished wood gleamed in faint light. My gaze went back to the bar and to a red headed, portly man of no more than my height and whose head was no more than the size of mine, standing alongside me.

"I've drawn my sword against the Prince," he said to me. "And I've thrown the scabbard away. So I'm a regular Scarlet Pimpernel to the Academy sort. A Joe Hill they'll never get before a firing squad."

"They say you've done terrible things," I said, pointing at a bottle of Jamison and eying the publican who was there to serve.

"Revolutions are not made with rosewater," he told me laughing.

"And a bit of booze," I informed him and I then informed him that I was a free citizen of a free and noble country and by what right had he brought me here in such a reprehensible manner?

At this he laughed and told me he woke up that morning with a keen desire to talk to a member of the Singularity Club, purely for the sake of his own edification. I told him bluntly that I was not a member of that Club and having now met its president I had no intention of ever becoming a member.

"This is a club of lunatics," I declared, hoisting the shooter and wishing "Slainte" to The Terrorist.

"Aye, an Academy man then?" the Terrorist responded to which I told him that after several days of orientation I had decided that The Academy was not at all what I hoped it would be. I was in fact interested in meeting anyone who shared my views.

He did not seem satisfied and cast a suspicious eye upon me from head to toe. Just then the parrot came flying through a window and alighted on my shoulder. I hadn't seen him for days and all inquiries I had made proved fruitless.

"Hey, Sonny," I said. "How have you been?"

"Ray is my name," the parrot screeched and pecked my cheek. I told the bird that only the devil had as many names.

"That bird's haunted, you know," the Terrorist remarked. "I've heard about him. What be your friend's name, bird?"

Ray searched my face with an up and down bob of his neck and then shook his head to the right and left and finally said,

"Ass Wipe."

I protested angrily and Ray capitulated and shouted *"Gullible."*

I was slightly encouraged then to enjoy the pint before me now which I proceeded to do and after awhile asked The Terrorist why he was not of the stature of the other residents of The Academy to which he responded that while they were self-inflated, he was not, that while they fed on a steady diet of their own whims and notions, he starved his miserable ego and kept a steady eye on the world outside himself, and that while their heads presumptuously sought to rival the very sphere of the planet, he retained his modesty for he accepted the advice of the Bard and sought not to overstep the modesty of Nature.

The Stoic Greek Epictetus would have loved this man. I drank to his nobility. Within the next few hours we both drank but it was the Terrorist who did the talking.

I here provide the best account I can in my own words of what he said, minus the great emotional force which he at times could summon to strengthen his meaning.

"Being born," he told me, eyes narrowed, "is like being a new player in an old game. Monopoly it is. In another century the game would have been Heaven or Hell. Or how best to keep them pagan gods on your side. Or how to get through a dark night filled with roving predators. But Monopoly it is now. What piece will you be on the board, they say? I'll take the shoe, I say. I'm the shoe. Low and humble."

I told him I'd take the bottle and the sword, the hat and the wheel barrow and the whatamacallit.

"There's the starting line and from the getgo it's a throw of the dice," The Terrorist said, ignoring me. "But wherever chance leads me I got me a choice. Buy or not buy? But, lad, the game's been going on for several hours. It's not a new game. The only thing new is me, just born and thrown into the game. Me father was a lowly shoe and his father before him. I'm already paying rent on what another man owns. Now the Academy says I'm a free man facing no fences or walls. Just do it. Make the right choices. I'm saying it's a game where I'm the lowly shoe, whether I chose it or not."

I wondered if he had a shoe fetish and why he wasn't thinking of himself as a bold, adventurous wanderer?

" It's a game board we're on that's already set up to make of us what it wants. We're the product, not the producer. You're a product that thinks it's a free wheeling creator. And that, lad, is the most clever feature of the product. Every new player thinks he's a wild rover and Chance will make one fool out of five million a grand success and they say civilization's built on that."

"Play your ace," the parrot screeched, jutting his head toward the Terrorist. Both the bird and I were sustained through all this disquisition by pints and Jamison, the most effective lubricants of worthwhile talk and the most cordial auditors of one's fellow creatures.

"The bird knows gaming when he sees it. Now, since we ourselves—the whole historical human race – has been at this game board for eons, we're the ones you have to go to for changes. And you can't make changes until you get a good eyeful of how the board is presently set up."

I asked him whether he thought The Great Augury and The Wick were helpful in making this assessment.

His face went as red as his hair.

"A man jacks the game board up to digital hi speed and seriously multiplies the number of places you can land on is not only multiplying the rentals paid to the already affluent but he's sending every poor sod into a pathless maze and an endless circling within his own whims, which the Academy is proud to tell the poor sod is his own unique and wonderful choices. And meanwhile the poor sod is lost up his own arse."

"We're eyeball to eyeball," Ray squawked going eyeball to eyeball with me.

I then told him what Mr. Adam had said about the coming cyborg, which, as I now expected, caused another explosion.

"The Wick is no more than a P.T. Barnum carny," he told me. "Freaks, geeks, high flyers, hunger artists. Jumbo and the three headed chicken is what it is. A man who says Cyborg is on a suicide mission is all it is, lad."

"There's many a good rock come out of a tattered bag," Ray ripped.

"The bird knows his gaming, I'll give his bewitched soul that," the Terrorist said. "You make your mouse click and you get your choice of one of these. They enjoy their own witless chatter and the world can be damned. Man, you go one generation down the road and you'll have a witless crop of lads and lasses deciding what anything is to mean. I wonder what will become of every bit of understanding quiet, deep and prolonged thought has put before this crew of sapiens we belong to."

We both paused to refresh ourselves and then the Terrorist went on without missing a beat.

"And your Academy is hellfire bent to not stand in the way of technology but is all set to re-define everything within the boolean of a search engine."

"*We seek him here, we seek him there*," Ray screeched.

"They want to get their hands on you too, bird," the Terrorist snapped.

I then asked him whether he didn't think that The Great Augury made it easier to become informed. Here was a man raised in one world that's fast disappearing who's fearful and angry about a new world he doesn't know. And he can't abide the ones growing up in that new world. There was a wide divide between them. My man The Terrorist wasn't doing the terrorizing; he himself was terrorized. If it was going to be a huge step backward and not a monumental step forward as Mr. Adam foretold, The Terrorist need not have worried. He wouldn't be around to see it. I wanted to explain to him then how mortality fit in with change that couldn't be stopped.

"And what is it you be wanting to become informed of, man?" he asked me to which I replied that I wanted to know what he thought of The Great Augury.

"And you want to know that because?" he replied and I said because I myself had some doubts about The Great Augury and wanted to hear what he had to say.

"And where did those doubts come from, man?" he then asked me and I replied that I believe it was from my travels which had started out cheerfully enough but had since collapsed into a darkness which bred doubt of all, including myself. But the short of it is, I summated and encapsulated, I had learned to recognize the dogshit that dogs naturally produced.

"But you remain a curious man," the Terrorist said, nodding, ignoring my pithy cynicism. "Why else would you come to The Academy? And I'd say that curiosity precedes your travels. It's why you travel. Now in the case of The Great Augury you have to look a generation down the road and what do you see?"

Robots with colossal heads who look like Mr. Adam?

"You see folks whose reasons for going to The Great Augury originate in The Great Augury itself. They are, you can say, informed on the game board of The Great Augury. And it's a mighty big board reaching into that grand cyberspace of infinite choices. But maybe not. Maybe it settles down to what these folks a generation down the road care to search. So the game board of potentially all choices shuts down pretty quick into choices these kinds of folks are making. What might be the curiosity and interests of folks who have been following their own whims and desires on a Great Augury game board comprised of their own whims and desires?"

I asked him to repeat that.

"It's the snake eating its own tail. The pleasures of merely circulating as the great poet says."

"Start the ball rolling," Ray yelled out.

I was mulling over and rolling over and circling back on the Terrorist's words as I went at my pint.

I could no longer call him the Terrorist in my mind and asked what his name was to which he replied Bill Ribbons though he warned me he wasn't made to cut ribbons though that had been the family profession as long as memory could tell.

"The thing about we *homo sapien sapiens* is, man, that we're more lust than sapien, more greed than sapien. . ."

"More dog than sapien," I interrupted.

". . . more interested in distractions than serious intent, just as ready to kill as to love, and always as ready as Adam to be seduced. We don't need a fast engine to drive that load down the road. What we need is more quiet meditation, though I'm in agreement a man's no more disposed to that than a fox to keeping out of the hen yard."

"I thought so once but now I know it," the parrot chimed in.

I nodded in agreement with both the wily fox and the clever parrot.

"The Great Augury takes the bit out of a man's mouth," Bill Ribbons went loquaciously on, terrorizing his listeners with more babble than thought possible. "And you know what that bridle bit was? It was our own wariness and distrust of our own inclinations. What the Great Augury has done is make a god out

314

of our own choices. We ask for chips with everything and we think we can get it. That's a great bother because while it puts money in a few men's pockets it puts the rest into debt. What The Great Augury does is offer you ideas for chips so it's not your wallet that's emptied but your mind that's starving on your own infertile choices."

Ideas. Chips. Money. Choices. Infertile. I waited for clarification from the parrot but he remained mute.

"One generation down the road and you've got the human mind a product creation. Bunch of Frankensteins searching the web and that web itself nothing more than showing us what a bunch of Frankensteins think. I'm not interested, man. Not at all. Not now and not then."

"Slice him where you like," Ray yelled, *"a hellhound is always a hellhound."*

I asked Bill why the Academy saw him as a terrorist threat.

"What those lads do is keep their eyes closed to the real world turning to shite."

"A built in, shock-proof shite detector," Ray squawked.

"I'll take two," Bill Ribbons said, "And don't forget, man, that the logic of Getting and Greed pushes it not only toward annihilation of all competition but one hundred per cent effective marketing. To do that, they've got to not only produce the products and service people will want but they've got to produce the people who will want them. You need to reach into people's lives, into their minds. Reachability is what it is."

I nodded, confirming that. You reach into people's minds, you reach into their pockets, they reach for a bottle of Jamison.

"There's no doubt that the Wick and the Great Augury have digitalized reachability beyond what the great critics of Getting and Greed, including Marx, could conceive. I'm not more than a humble shoe in the great Monopoly game but I can see it all as clearly as I see that following on the heels of every man's choice is regret."

"A thick skin is a gift of God," Ray told us.

Bill Ribbons proceeded in this fashion, each of us partaking of the delicious elixir of The Guinness, until, you Dogs, I was rather more insensible than sensible. The parrot was talking more and I know when I say this I'm fit for Bedlam but he seemed to be making good conversation. He was also drinking more and perhaps that had loosened his tongue and also expanded his bird brain.

I thought I heard Bill prophesying that the Great Augury and The Wick along with every marvel of cyberspace would be contained in a miniature device to be implanted upon birth. The inside of every eyelid would be a monitor accessed with a blink and all thoughts and wishes would call up the vast circuitry of cyberspace.

I referred to the "Borg" again, those hive like zombies that plagued *Star Trek,* but Bill failed to respond, not a fan I concluded. I did not remind him what Mr. Adam had told me regarding the inevitability of the cyborg. I feared Bill might suffer yet another apoplectic fit.

The drink aided Bill's prophetic talents but also spiked his venom, particularly against the Academy which he held responsible for the degeneration of human critical reason.

In Bill Ribbons' opinion the world was now filled with people who could easily be persuaded by outrageous arguments and allowed such nonsense an equal footing with what was clearly rational. On the most crucial issues, fools went around undecided, which clever rogues applauded as a sign of an "independent mind." The northern hemisphere was sucking the life out of the southern hemisphere was one way the Terrorist put it. Monumental wealth in the hands of a few exercised a power that shaped notions of reason and efficiency and practicality and progress and happiness....all such self-serving contrivances possessing the same legitimacy as the Emperor without Clothes. The Academy was to step forward and announce to the world that the Emperor was naked but it failed to do this and so the minds of the masses were not any more liberated and just as vulnerable to claptrap as the minds of Medieval peasants.

Bill was in the act of toasting those Medieval peasants whom he declared in a loud voice were no more than victims of arrant power and privilege when we heard a great clamor outside the barroom.

Before our inebriation allowed us to act, the room was filled with uniformed men holding guns in our faces.

Bill let out a great oath and was immediately struck on the side of his head and dropped to his knees.

Ray flew upward screaming something about never being taken alive and Chips with everything!

I held up my hands, swearing my loyalty to the Queen, as a gun butt swung upward and I descended into that dark pool where talk ends but not before I heard the parrot:

"Bless thee! Thou art translated."

The Author comes to the end of his travels

"Thus, gentle reader, I have given thee a faithful history of my travels for sixteen years and above seven months; wherein I have not been so studious of ornament as truth. I could perhaps like others have astonished thee with strange improbable tales; but I rather chose to relate plain matter of fact in the simplest manner and style; because my principal design was to inform, and not to amuse thee."

I quote the words of my beloved ancestor at this point, Fellow Dogs, mindful of the fact that many will dispute my facts and assert that I have indeed done nothing more than tell "strange improbable tales," growing more improbable the more I took to the bottle. So be it. The judgment of all talk blows in the winds of time and chance.

But you are doubtlessly inquisitive as to how I escaped my captors and managed to return home.

Sadly, I did not escape immediately but was, in the official language, 'renditioned' to a far off island (which I had not visited) and there questioned rigorously and religiously for the first few months regarding my involvement with a former terrorist attack. Water boarding failed to "get the truth out of me" and that was viewed by some as a sign of my innocence and by others as a sign of my deep duplicity. As I was therefore identified as a potential threat to the security of a great nation, I would have to remain under arrest.

I endured those many months of confinement by adopting the withdrawal skills of the Hunger Artist and the Trapeze Artist. My eventual forlorn state and physical decrepitude propelled my release which was without explanation as to why I had been imprisoned and without apology for having been imprisoned.

I spent all those long months in the company of the parrot with whom I carried on a lively conversation regarding our travels. Whether sounds triggered identical or similar sounds in his mimicry repertoire, which was indeed quite large, and meaning was left for me to provide, or, whether my words had meaning to him which he responded to with words of his own and therefore a mutual understanding was in play, I cannot truly say. Detox had either a positive or negative effect on our ability to communicate.

But I do say the parrot had scant reasons in support of what he revealed of me regarding my character. Indeed what he had to say regarding my moral sense was neither complimentary nor unprovoking.

He considered it to be too narrow to extend to others as my usual method of dealing with the difficulties presented by others was no more than an exit. My travel itinerary in the parrot's view was marked by escape from anything and everything that departed from what I would like to be true. I was as ready at the end of my travels to believe in what I held true at the very beginning. I did not so persevere in that hypocrisy because circumstances prevented this. The honesty and authenticity in much of the *faux* Gulliver's portrayal of me preempted any continuation of my arrogance and presumption. And, consequently, as an escape artist, I escaped to the bottle.

I will not be so disingenuous in my parting from you, my Fellow Dogs, as to abridge in any way the parrot's appraisal of myself, however partial and therefore misleading it may be.

Here is what I was subjected to in those long months of incarceration with the parrot:

Though I had observed more than once the necessity of jumping back on one's own awareness and the conclusion based thereupon, I always failed to question myself.

Though I saw the hideousness and blindness resulting from a well-tended self-absorption, I continued to hold myself an exception for no other reason than that I was a traveler and different, though I never traveled far from self-concern.

Though I sought the diverse humanity of boarding houses and allowed the play of chance to bring whatever humanity had to offer before me, I let all their lives go as soon as my train pulled out of the station.

I traveled through lives as if they were so much interesting or uninteresting scenery.

In my own defense I will say that Chance played me hard to right and left as I tried to journey forward. I did not place in this world the evil I found in others nor can I be held accountable for the darkness of our human nature and for the rapaciousness of our appetites that so clearly fires up to a violent inferno so much of what I have seen.

If I sought to escape much of what I encountered, I was forced to do so. I never ceased trying to understand all that I encountered but was led early on to question the bound nature of that faculty itself. Much or all of what was in my head at the outset proved defenceless against real "conditions on the ground, though I struggled far too long to hold on to my blindness.

Regardless of what the parrot may think, I did not take an egoist's journey and did not address myself to you, my Fellow Dogs, as an egoist standing before an admiring audience. That may have been observable in the man who first set out. Neither have I written my account so as to confound or depress you with the deplorable, the absurd, the asinine, or the manic, and if I failed to disclose any sense or meaning in what befell me, the fault is as much the world's as mine. It is far from retrograde and depressing to recognize that a life cannot be sustained on bullshit and that if you take a good look at the worst, as Thomas Hardy advised, you will find more that is liberating than you will find in narratives of a triumphant will to power.

I don't know if Walker was ever brought to justice or if Ray ever received his chemo or if Betty Bombers has given up her child or if Captain Noble is still in prison or if Microft has taken up science again or whether Kate Whack ever did write her investigative piece on Skample or whether there is any peace now on the Political Frontier or whether Mrs. Angeloni and family were ever evicted or whether Zechariah and Rollins go on with their psychic battle or the Clotter boarders have all collapsed into poverty nor had I shown any interest in the fate of Sydney Noble and Ned Parsall, whom the parrot assured me were moving toward a romance that was both daring and interesting to all but myself. I never searched for Don Rodrigo, the murderer of innocent Billy. I had opportunities to stop Brother Frank but I could not muster the will. For all my tears over Carla's death, I forgot her easily enough.

Many places offended me because I found them too self-besot, too ungenerous, too rank and vile in their debased moral sense, too lost in charade and simulation, too far from truth and reason, too anxious to live like dogs rather than men.

I pronounced my judgment and then went to sea.

The parrot thought I did no good for anyone, some harm to some, some fatal harm to some, but for the most part traveled through the lives of others without care or concern or impact. No one was better for having seen me or heard me or known me.

In place of a moral review, I preferred depression. And Jamison. I thought of myself neither good nor bad but either depressed or eager. The parrot thought that what depressed me was a failure on the world's part to greet my eagerness with an eagerness of its own. The world failed to put in my path confirmation of what I reasoned to be true, failed to transparently reveal the workings of that Celestial Entity I evoked only because I saw that my will did not rule others and I could not stand for the will of others ruling me. My Celestial Entity was no more than a mask for myself.

Chance, the parrot admitted, often blew me off my course but I was blind to what it showed me, anxious as I was to regain all that I was.

Everyone who spoke his or her mind to me or revealed his or her heart had done no more than throw seed on rock for I took up no cause nor pursued no belief nor acted for the good of anything but held only the rightness of traveling through and leaving all behind in the hope of finding something better.

The parrot revealed this to me over the long months we spent together in that cell and what parts of it I could absorb and make sense of I reveal here to you, my Fellow Dogs. But in my last and final defense I will say that it is immoral for another creature to represent to you who you are, assuming as they do that what they say is the truth and usurping your own right to identify yourself.

I cannot say that the parrot was not entertaining in what he said and I cannot say I took his words fully to heart as he was, after all, no more than a parrot. He had perhaps heard the various components of his diagnosis of me in a variety of conversations over his long life (I believe Captain Noble said the parrot was celebrating his 50th year when I met him but perhaps I misheard and it was his 15th year).

Because the two of us were so cloistered and so dependent upon each other's mood in that cell, I thought it best to take the high ground and therefore displayed no animosity toward him. I but informed him on the day we were released that he was not the bird I had taken him for to which he responded: *"I am not at all the sort of person you and I took me for."* I suppose then that the parrot had himself undergone some sort of transformation, not the least I would think from bird to person, in his own mind.

But we remain inseparable companions and were I to set off once again on my travels, the parrot, who has stuck with the name Jane, which revelation I find somewhat disconcerting after all this time and cannot fathom his amusement at our expense, has promised to travel with me. We will be gentlemen . . . friends . . . of the road once again.

My friends barely recognized me so changed was my outward appearance, and, truth to tell, had they been able to observe me inwardly they would not, I believe, have discovered the man they once knew.

I have been for many years now a man who jumps back on every word spoken, regardless of occasion or speaker, and interrogates meaning with an unrelenting brutality. I am, in turns, seeking profit in all things and ranting against mammon; impatient with any matter not affecting me personally and immediately thereafter convinced that all matters personal are in actuality social. I am a man who can rise above the vicious combativeness of politics and also a man who relishes entering the knife fight that represents what politics is.

For many days I lose myself in cyberspace, following the thread of my life, and for just as many days I live screenless, eyes buried in long novels or gazing into the eyes of my fellow humans. I may greet you heartily on one day as if you were my brother and turn from you in disgust the next day as if you were scum.

I believe that whatever the imagination perceives is necessarily true and that what we hold as "that which is" in this world was once only imagined.

And then there are as many days when I believe that withdrawn into the web of our own imaginations we can lose ourselves and the world in a continuous inward spiral. On those days I see the world as a recuperative anchor to the imagination. I feel that the world is both the inspiration of what we imagine as well, paradoxically, as what endangers imagination, our blessed escape.

What I have chosen freely on Tuesday, I see on Wednesday as no more than the effects of Monday.

I have the will to empower myself one half the month reminding myself that eagles do not catch flies, and spend the other half tracking my own illusions, reminding myself that doubtlessly I too am scripted, a performer whose character is inevitable fate.

I balance self-obsession with a frenzied quest to find in others what is not in myself. At the very moment I see before me a spiritual world, I see it is a picture someone with a baby face has drawn. Some of the time I can reason my way to the Truth and some of the time I can't find a reason to go on living.

I bowl alone while I watch a TV monitor overhead showing other people bowling. I still rely on the "paper of record" for the news but I am totally mystified as to what is happening in the world.

I have given up traveling above ground, looking forward to continuing the same under drastically different circumstances.

I went far from home for many years to hear talk that eluded me and I didn't return home to find it there waiting for me.

On some days, I talk with an energy only possessed by a man who believes he can capture the world with words. On other days

. . .

I mourn for the parrot who died this year, either 75 years of age or 40 years of age. It does not matter. She is for the ages now. I buried her in my garden and put all the names she gave herself on the gravestone. The epitaph is her own:

Dirt & Poison
Honey & Wax
Sweetness & Light

And so I part from you, dear Readers, fellow Dogs.

72432978R00205

Made in the USA
San Bernardino, CA
24 March 2018